Wings of the
Morning

Wings of the Morning

FREDERIC F. VAN DE WATER

Ives Washburn, Inc.

New York

MANUFACTURED IN THE UNITED STATES OF AMERICA
VAN REES PRESS • NEW YORK

To B. O. McAnney

In the forty-fourth year
of our friendship

*Wings of the
Morning*

I

THE FOREST had run unbroken from the river to the lake; from the frontier forts of Massachusetts to the first habitant settlement, far in the north. The serial wars of French and British, thundering to east and west, had left this lovely wilderness unmarred, but now, during an uneasy interval of peace while the pattern of new conflict assembled, men were invading the empty country that armies had bypassed.

Axes shattered the ancient stillness, heretofore disturbed only by the voices of wind and water. Log houses rose beside the Connecticut, and beyond the dividing mountains, villages were born in a fair, broad, western valley. Tidings of land, rich past belief, lured further dissidents from the lower provinces.

The pioneers, drawn from among the reckless and the restless, the dissatisfied and the venturesome, brought little with them into this reputed Eden save ambition and a craving for liberty, and straightway found these endangered. New Hampshire claimed the territory and lavishly granted charters that New York disregarded. Massachusetts reached for a portion of the area on the pretext of earliest settlement.

Singular, largely vocal warfare raged in the west, where a chronic disturber of the peace, one Ethan Allen, trumpeted of flaying and disembowelment for all his adversaries. In the east, the ancient enmity of Whig and Tory was complicated by hatred, borne by the many, for law courts and officials maintained by New York for the benefit of the few.

Here, in the nascent "New Hampshire Grants," settlers struggled with a still more tangled version of the extremities that were thrusting their kindred in the rest of New England toward war.

Twenty years earlier, abiding peace had lain upon this austerely lovely land. Men had come north in search of its benison. Though they had failed to find it, the legend had endured through the later, increasingly distressful years.

There was grave trouble in the older settlements now; critical trouble in blockaded, prostrate Boston; trouble, even more confused, in the raw, young villages of the Grants; yet the ancient tale of peace and plenty continued to lure the aspiring.

One of the credulous, a travel-worn young man, woke on a late October morning in the hollow he had found beneath a roadside hemlock, rolled out of his blanket, ate the cold remnant of the mush he had boiled for supper, and with all his worldly goods upon his back, set forth elatedly on the last stage of his journey.

A wretched track, misnamed "the Great Road," ran north from Brattleboro's moldering fort and scatter of mean houses to climb through the gloom of pines toward a dazzle of red and yellow maples. Beyond their still fire, the rutted way pitched downhill, and Job Aldrich saw, halted at the foot of the slope, the very chaise that lately had overtaken and spattered him. It stood now with one wheel deep in mire while its driver, green cloak thrown back and laced hat awry, tugged at the bridle of the bogged horse and swore proficiently.

The plight of the lofty person who had whirled by a weary traveler pleased Job. He was minded for an instant to plod indifferently past the vehicle and its bedizened owner. Instead, he halted and asked needlessly:

"In trouble, sir?"

The other let go of the bridle. Rage could not thin the full-lipped mouth, and the greenish eyes in the crimson face still were canny. Their close regard made Job uneasily aware of the grime upon his homespun frock that hung unbelted over breeches of blue and white fulcher cloth; of the stubble on his jowls and the mud that daubed bare feet and legs. There was no call to

[4]

feel ashamed. He had proper shoes in his pack, but a man would be spendthrift to wear them out, a-journeying.

If Lord High and Mighty had walked clear from Stockbridge, Bay Province, in this autumn of 1774, and had slept out every night but two, he would look quite as unsightly. Job was tempted to tell him so, but the other's shrill speech thwarted him.

" 'Trouble,' d'ye ask? Man, dear, ye need only look. If there be, in all of Cumberland County, one road overseer worth his weight in sawdust, I've yet to hear of him, so I have. 'Tis still only October, yet I'm trapped in the King's highway, thanks to knaves and shirkers. And what's to be done about it? Answer me that."

The appeal softened Job. He stepped to the drier side of the road and twisted himself free of his pack with the ax bound along it. His unladen body felt light and competent. He told the man who had resumed his aimless tugging at the bridle:

"Coil up the reins and stand clear. Whale him when I bid you."

He squatted behind the chaise while groping hands found purchase on the axle. Job balanced himself, caught breath, and heaved. His legs drove mid-shin deep into chill mud, but the half-buried wheel came out with a kissing sound.

"Now," he grunted and thrust the chaise forward. The horse floundered, lurched, and, enlivened by lashings and curses, dragged the vehicle onto firmer ground.

Sparks, kindled by his efforts, swam across Job's sight as he returned to his pack. While he resumed it, his beneficiary babbled:

"Man, dear! Ye have power in ye. Ye must permit me to reward ye. Brush is me name, sir; Crean Brush, no less. Representative in New York's Honorable General Assembly from Cumberland County. Permit me."

He fumbled in a red, brocaded waistcoat.

"Thankee, no."

Job felt awkward in the man's florid presence. Nothing Amos had related of the Grants had prepared his brother for Mr. Brush with his lordly clothes and airs. The man was urging:

"Come, now; I insist." Coins chinked in his plump hand.

[5]

"No," Job said again. The other hesitated, looking doubtfully from the chaise to his companion's soiled person.

"At least, me dear man," he begged, postponing decision, "ye'll tell me to whom I'm indebted," and when Job dryly gave his name, persisted:

"And from where, if I may be so bold? Stockbridge, indeed? A long jaunt, and not for pleasure, I'll be bound."

"No," Job repeated wearily. Amos, in extolling the excellences of the Grants—the plain men who lived there, the land's beauty, the soil's surpassing fertility—had omitted to mention the inhabitants' appalling curiosity. Since Job had crossed the Massachusetts line, successive questioners had pumped him dry, turned him inside out, and searched his seams. For all his brave raiment and his graces, Mr. Brush was no better than the rest of them. He was asking more carefully now:

"And of which party, pray?"

Earlier responses to the inevitable question let Job answer it now with practiced ease.

"I'm a newcomer, sir, who aims to live at peace with his neighbors. I have no other politics."

"No politics!" Brush repeated without belief. "But still a King's man, I trust."

"Surely; no other's."

The inquisitor's face relaxed, and he struck soft hands together.

"Now, flay me, sir; I was sure of it. I had ye well surveyed before ye spoke, Mr. Aldrich; I did indeed. Welcome to Cumberland County, sir, where loyal men are sorely needed."

He looked again from Job to the chaise, then blurted:

"I'm for Westminster, and it would please me to set you on your way."

They crammed themselves and Job's pack into the narrow seat. The chaise began a jolting progress.

"Now, d'ye know," its driver exclaimed, "I've failed to ask whither ye are bound."

"To Fulham," Job replied, "though now, I hear, it mostly is called Dummerston."

[6]

"Dummerston?" Brush found evil taste in the word. "Why Dummerston?"

It was better, Job had learned, to give down all at once than to have information milked out of him, a squirt at a time.

"Amos, my brother, commenced a betterment in Dummerston before he died. I bought his right from Hannah—his widow. Lot Ninety-four is my pitch, now."

He could not quite keep pride from his voice.

"Amos," Brush repeated. "Amos Aldrich. Now, I recall him. Killed by a fall at his own house-raising. My sympathy, sir. I wish I might compliment you as sincerely upon your purchase."

He shook his head and pursed his mouth, plainly waiting further inquiry. Job did not speak. Hope should not be exposed to disfigurement by every chance acquaintance.

"Now, I, meself," Brush pursued, "have better land to sell among law-abiding folk. If ye'll be guided by me—"

Job carefully hid his distrust and said:

"Amos held that Ninety-four was prime land."

"And so it is," his companion returned heartily. "Or it would be, if 'twere bettered. For your lot in Dummerston and—say five pound, Bay tender, I can let ye have an intervale hundred in Westminster, cleared and fertile.

"Ye'll do well," Brush pursued, watching slantwise the impassive, dark face at his shoulder, "to let me advise ye. Not Dummerston; not for the loyal settler."

"Ehyah?" Job asked woodenly. No one in the Grants was going to hoodwink a Stockbridge man.

" 'Tis a nest of rebellion," Brush went on with righteous disapproval. "A few sound men, I'll grant ye, yet the town is riddled with pestilential rascals, little better than Ethan Allen and his Bennington bandits, of whom ye may have heard."

"Ehyah," Job repeated. "News gets far as Stockbridge, now and then," but the irony failed to reach his seatmate.

" 'Twas me privilege and pride, sir," Brush orated, "at the Honorable Assembly's last sitting, to assist in framing the measure that outlawed Allen and his imps of darkness and set a price upon their wicked heads. York's present governor, I assure

[7]

ye, is a man of resolution, as certain scoundrels shortly will learn. I have their names, sir; I know 'em all, from Ethan Allen to the so-called Doctor Solomon Harvey."

He mistook Job's stifled sound for approval.

"Doctor Harvey of Dummerston?"

"The very same, me dear man. A brand ready for the burning."

The letter that, after passage though many hands, had brought to Stockbridge news of Amos Aldrich's demise and burial had been signed "Solomon Harvey, Town Clerk and Practitioner of Physick." It had been an elegant letter that had greatly comforted the dead man's widow and brother. Job swallowed what he had been half minded to say.

The Great Road crept out of the lofty forest and skirted a clearing where sunshine blazed and men piled logs for burning. They paused to stare after the travelers, and one worker saluted them—thumb to nose and fingers spread.

"Friend of yours?" Job asked without expression.

"Joe Temple," Brush answered bitterly. "A freeholder in Dummerston. Ye see what I mean?"

They entered further woodland. Gloom that immersed the chaise seemed heavier for its brief passage through brilliance. The Grants, whatever else they lacked, were royally timbered. Job had never seen the like of these great-girthed, towering trees.

"For good or ill," he said slowly, "I'll view my pitch first. Amos held—"

He forebore to repeat his late brother's praise of Lot Ninety-four, lest it quicken more disparagement by Mr. Brush, who surprisingly smiled and nodded agreement.

"And who would blame ye for that? Man, dear, view it by all means. Then, if ye're minded to sell, I can show ye many ways to better yerself. If 'tis employment ye wish, 'twill be forthcoming. Sheriff Paterson, in these times, can use more deputies. Loyal men are not so plentiful here that we undervalue them."

The chaise ground uphill over rain-scoured gravel and jolting water bars and emerged again into sunlight. The forest had been felled on either hand and, to the left, a track more meager than

[8]

the Great Road skirted a field where pale cornstalks stood among rotting stumps. Brush drew rein.

"Yonder, me dear man, is the Dummerston road, though I'd leave ye more willingly elsewhere."

"Thankee," Job said as he slid from the chaise.

"Now, me dear man," Brush urged, "command me if I can aid ye. Ye'll be welcome at me home, Brush Hall, in Putney. To our next meeting, then."

The chaise rattled away. Job settled his shoulders in the pack harness and turned his face toward Dummerston. He marveled at the cornstalks' height. Beyond the rough clearing, he came upon a proper field, fenced by overturned stumps. He leaned against their interlaced roots and looked across a glistening pelt of wheat stubble. Twelve bushel of grain to the acre, he judged, maybe more. Whoever had harvested it was a good man with a scythe.

From the wheat field's far boundary, the forest climbed a hill. The crowns of lordly pines ran jaggedly across the brilliant sky, and maples shone below them like kindling fire. The vast wealth of the Grants' timber promised a good livelihood to anyone as handy in the woods as Job—granting that men here were not as ill disposed as Mr. Brush had said.

According to his telling, folks in the Grants were no more peaceful than in the lower settlements, where neighbors increasingly defamed the King, his ministers, the Continental Congress, and each other. If Dummerston people, too, wasted working time in quarrels over the Intolerable Acts, Non-importation Agreements, and other matters that talk never could change, then Amos had praised this land falsely, and his brother had been gulled.

It was foolish to take to heart the babble of a slick stranger. Job was, by grace of the deed he cherished, a freeholder with property to use as it pleased him best. The thought, as always, cheered him and brought a smile to his square, swarthy face. Since the distant time when he had begun to work the Stockbridge farm for a younger brother's share, he had longed with a still, deep passion for land of his own.

While his widowed mother had lived, he had curbed that intense desire, for they had valued each other greatly. Her death, and then Amos's, had made Job a landed man. He, who hitherto had owned no more property than his pack now contained, had become the still only half-believing proprietor of a hundred acres and an unfinished house. After twenty-two years, his proper life was beginning.

The sky was intensely blue above the fiery hills. Somewhere beyond his sight, surrounded by the splendor of trees like these, the clearing and the dwelling Amos had begun awaited their new owner. Job, angry doubt forgotten, moved away from the stump fence. The lines, he told himself, ignoring Brush's warning and borrowing from Scripture, were fallen to him in pleasant places. He turned and, with a bridal feeling, followed the road farther.

He could hear in the valley that fell away to his right a brook's gay voice. Another sound thrust itself through the water's laughter, and he recognized the soft thunder of a corn mill's stones. Before him, the trees stood back from the road again. He came out of shadow into the noontide's glare and, from the crest of a bared hillside, looked down upon small houses and a bridge. Below a dam stood the mill, its wet wheel ponderously turning.

Midway on the descending road two men stood in front of a clapboard dwelling and argued so heatedly that they did not heed the stranger's approach. Job paused beside them.

"By your leave," he ventured.

The elder disputant, who leaned on a pitchfork, was spare and brown. A fan of hair above frontal baldness flared, gray and stiff as hedgehog quills, and his narrow eyes seemed of the same substance as the fork's bright tines. His adversary was shorter, wider, with a scratch wig and three-cornered hat perched above a pear-shaped face.

"By your leave," Job repeated, more loudly but as vainly. While he drew breath for a third appeal, the mill shut down and the lean man's speech tore through the sudden silence.

"Wal, s'pose you go back, Bildad, an' tell Jedge Chandler,

Billy Paterson, an' t'other blood-suckin' varmints I ain't a-comin'."

"Len," the other replied with an offensive show of patience, "if I do, you'll set out the hull court term, an' more, to Westminster jail. I ain't here to argue, Len. I'm a-summonin' you to jine the fall panel of jurors for the honorable court."

"By your leave," Job repeated desperately and so loudly that the late speaker, aware for the first time of his presence, half turned, then nervously faced his adversary again.

"Honorable court!" Len snorted. "Now, ain't that comic? Lemme tell you something, Bildad Easton."

His voice became a caterwaul, and he pounded the fork's butt on the ground to stress each word.

"The 'honorable court' is naught but a deevice got up by York gentry to milk honest folks dry. Jedges, clerk, sheriff, an' the hull kittle-billin' are thieves—no more, no less."

"Now, Len," Easton deplored piously, "that ain't no way to talk. Know as well as me courts are commissioned by His Excellency, Governor Tryon, an'—"

"Hell's fire roast Butcherin' Billy Tryon. If—"

"That's real close to sedition, Len. Don't go rammin' into trouble. Governor Tryon is loyal agent of King George the Third, God bless him."

This was like the strife that lately had upset Stockbridge but more full-throated and vicious. Job was minded to go his way and had started on when Len's squall checked him.

"Bless who? Bless His Holiness, the Pope of Canady an' pimp for the Great Whore of Babylon? God damn him, s'I, an' all his pocky ministers who framed the Quebec Act!"

Breath whistled through his nose. Easton looked pleased, yet he deplored:

"Now you done it, Len. Before a witness, too. Hollerin' treason on a public highway is punishable by—"

"Bildad," the other bade, "you git."

"I'm your friend an' neighbor," Easton mourned, "but I'm dep'ty sheriff fust. Best come along peaceful, Len."

"You git, Bildad, or by God I'll skewer your guts."

[11]

The poised fork shook. Easton took a backward step. He glanced prudently behind him and then recited shrilly:

"Leonard Spaulding, in the King's name I arrest you for—"

Spaulding gave a coughing sound and drove his weapon forward. Easton clapped plump hands to his plumper middle, squealed, and turned to run. His assailant, leaping after him, bumped against Job. Both men staggered, and the fork clattered into the road.

From a distance, Easton shouted a blurred threat and then resumed his flight. Job set a foot firmly on the fork handle.

"I'd leave it where it is," he counseled, "for a spell, anyway."

For an instant, they faced each other in silence. Hinges squealed, and Spaulding whirled about.

"No," he yelped. "Git back into the house, ye dinged fool."

A tall young man stood beside the dwelling's open door with his hand still on its latch and grinned. He was so deeply tanned that Job thought him an Indian until he saw that the amused eyes were gray.

"No more sense—" Spaulding began and hastily swallowed the rest. The young man grinned more widely:

"It seemed to me," he replied with mock solemnity, "that you were outnumbered a mite. My mistake."

He backed into the house while he spoke. His eyes, as he closed the door, met Job's and invited him to share some hidden jest.

2

$\mathcal{S}$PAULDING MUMBLED ABOUT the folly of invalids who refused to stay a-bed and, bending to hide embarrassment, retrieved the pitchfork. The tall young man had looked entirely hale to Job, but he kept his counsel and endured in silence his companion's scrutiny. This first encounter with Dummerston folks was justifying Mr. Brush's darkest utterance.

"Who be you?" Spaulding demanded suddenly. "Whar from?"

Here it came again—the tedious, delaying round of questions —but when Job patiently had recited his name and mission, his companion cast aside uneasiness and exclaimed:

"Wal, now! Do tell!"

He hurried on, voice twanging like a plucked fiddle string. Spaulding, it appeared, had been of the congregation at Amos's house-raising and consequent funeral. Each had been the best a new town could afford and closely related.

"Five gallons of Medford rum an' five of Billy Negus's cider brandy, Amos provided. Enough for the raisin' an' his funeral, too."

Everything would have gone along agreeable, Spaulding confided, if Job's brother hadn't got a mite cocked before, in accordance with tradition, he, as house owner, had essayed to dance the length of the newly seated rooftree and, falling, had perished.

"Lamentable accident, I don't deny, but died happy, wouldn't wonder. Laid him away in the new graveyard, below the meetinghouse we're a-buildin'. Still lack a ordained minister, but Elder Hooker, who's a man of larnin', preached a sight better'n most reverends. Did all we could for Amos."

"Beholden to you," Job said gruffly. The other darted an anxious glance toward the house.

"Wal," he said in furtive dismissal, "won't be keepin' you, longer. Mistrust you'll want to get over to your pitch. Prosper there well as anywheres—'cept mebby if this was Canady an' you a Goddam Frenchman."

His face contorted, and his voice took sharper edge.

"Fit 'em, last war. Leftenant in Butterfield's company, Ruggles' regiment. Whopped 'em good, but now the King gives 'em back their Popery while he starves Boston town."

He spat. Job hesitated, then asked for direction. He wondered whether Spaulding's quick compliance was due to the young man he had sent back into the house. There had been a warming quality about the stranger. It would be pleasant to meet him again.

Beyond the bridge, Job took the road's left fork. The way clung to a hillside above a full-running brook. Neither its cheerful sound nor glimpses of darkling pools, linked by the lace of rapids, entirely soothed him. He was still trying to fit together the assault he had witnessed, the intrusion of the reputed invalid, and Spaulding's anxiety, when another clearing shone ahead.

The reek of pickling hides puckered his nostrils, and he came out into sunlight to plod past a neat house with a tannery behind it. Before the steaming doorway a knot of men disputed. Their gestures were violent; their voices loud. One of them picked up a length of wood and shook it to stress his argument. Job quickened his pace, looked away, and was deaf to the hail shouted after him. He had had enough of quarreling for one day.

The road curved, bearing him from the men's sight and down to a ford. Its steppingstones were slippery with fallen leaves. The weight of his pack hampered Job, and the dusky depth of a pool, below the shallows, made him more careful still. He had barely crossed the stream when, behind him, a voice bawled, "Hey, there!" so loudly that he stumbled and almost fell.

He recovered and turned about, irked by his momentary fright, to face, across the brook, one of the group that had stood before the tannery. Homespun breeches and shirt seemed over-

[14]

tight for the stranger's thick body. His heavy face, reddened by haste, was pulled into a scowl. He held, clubwise, the stick Job had seen him flourish, and panted:

"Hailed you. Why'n't you halt?"

The arrogant question, the insolence in the narrowed eyes galled Job. He asked slowly:

"Why should I?"

The inquiry tripped the other.

"Why?" he blustered at length. "No—vagabond comes skulking into this town without he gives account of himself. That's why."

He waved his bludgeon. Job knew it would serve him best to hold his temper, yet it struggled to get free. He had already met with more trouble this day than a man should be expected to bear meekly. Anger, mounting, impelled him to grin at his adversary.

"Happens, youngster," he said, purposely ignoring the fact that the man was at least his own age, "I'm a freeholder in Dummerston."

"Vagabond and liar as well," the young man crowed. "Think I don't know my own neighbors? Your name and your errand, sir. Speak up."

"Wal," he demanded when Job shrugged, "will you answer, willing, or must I teach you manners?"

He stepped down as he spoke, to stand at the brook's crossing, face creased by wrath, club tight in his fist. His threat deafened Job to prudence. Blood pounded in his ears and sudden heat abolished weariness.

"Now, it's in my mind," he said, almost blithely, "that already I've answered more than enough questions. Take your stick elsewhere and find someone that scares easier."

He did not heed the pious inner voice that deplored this furthering of a quarrel, and was grimly pleased to see that his counsel had stupefied his adversary. He stood with mouth open while his face grew dark. Job waited for an expectant instant, then laughed and deliberately turned away.

He wheeled about more quickly, for the other man had uttered a bleating sound and was coming toward him through the shallows with long, splashing strides. Job got a blurred glimpse of teeth that gleamed in a twisted face and a club, swung high. He ducked the blow that whistled past his ear and, meeting the charge with the weight of his pack behind him, drove a shoulder into the attacker's midriff.

Breath belched from the man. Job, struggling for balance, saw him go backward into the pool below the ford.

Water rose in a ragged sheet and fell apart in spray. The forsaken club pitched among the clashing ripples. Its owner, reappearing, sought for footing, went under again, and then, standing shoulder deep in the pool, uttered gargling coughs. Strands of hair streamed like paint across his dripping face.

Anger faded and left hollowness behind it while Job watched his victim flounder to the stream's far bank and haul himself ashore. Water poured from him as he got to hands and knees and then, still jerked about by violent coughing, caught hold of an alder and finally regained his feet. Job hesitated, then turned again to the uphill track. From a distance, he looked back. The sodden young man still clung to the alder.

The pack had doubled in weight. Rage had fled, leaving Job chill and penitent. He withstood the impulse to return and try to make peace with his late opponent, yet a sense of guilt oppressed him as he toiled onward.

Anger was of the devil, and violence a crime. He still could hear his mother solemnly intoning that doctrine. She had been raised a Quakeress, and her inherited loathing of strife had been fortified by the death of her husband in the last of the French wars. She had inspired her younger son with her longing for peace. He had hoped to find it in the Grants, yet already he had been false to his mother and himself.

He paused, breathlessly wondering how much farther he must climb. Before him, the thin road still led upward, and on either hand trees pressed close. Before he went on, Job lifted his eyes toward the fragments of sky that shone among interlacing branches, and asked for wisdom to profit from the errors of this day and for strength hereafter to do justice, love mercy, and walk more humbly with God and his neighbors-to-be.

He had clambered only a little farther when he saw roofs jutting through the trees above and, as he pulled himself up the final, still steeper pitch, heard laughter and children's voices.

Job paused panting, at the edge of the village. Small houses, a few log-walled, others clothed in weather-darkened clapboards, and two painted a seemly red, bordered a single wide street, presided over by the gaunt bulk of an unfinished meetinghouse. The track he had followed crossed the broader way and led downward again into forest. He tried to remember Spaulding's instructions, and failed.

On the raw common, barelegged youngsters who had been piling leaves stared at the stranger and then retreated slowly toward the dwellings, save for one who stood his ground and scowled. Doors were opening along the street; heads were peering from windows. Job quailed at the prospect of further cross-questioning and approached the glowering boy.

The child's dirty face was pinched, and his fustian frock fell straight to his knees, as though it enclosed no substance. Voices were calling from house to house. A woman came out of the nearest to stand, shielding her eyes with a hand. Job asked abruptly:

"What's your name, bub?"

Cords stirred in the boy's thin neck. He swallowed with a clicking sound and then said, hoarsely:

"Whatever 'tis, 'tain't 'bub.' "

The surly voice slid up into a squeak. He was older than Job had thought, though undersized, and his eyes were defiant.

"This is Dummerston village, isn't it?"

" 'Tain't Albany."

Others were deserting their dooryards to join the staring woman. Job checked the impulse to shake information from the undeservedly hostile youngster, fumbled in a breeches pocket, and held up a copper penny before the suspicious eyes.

"Yours," he promised, "if you'll tell the way to the Aldrich pitch."

[17]

The boy gaped, hesitated, then jerked his head toward the road that vanished into the woods.

"Yonder 'tis," he gulped. "Keep bearin' right," and, as Job dropped the coin into the outstretched palm, blurted, "Aldrich—he's, he's dead."

"Ehyah," Job answered over a shoulder. "I know."

He strode away, careless of upraised voices behind him. At the edge of the forest, he turned for an instant. Adults, crowding about the boy, had hidden him.

An hour later, a rutted, uphill track led Job into a clearing where the skeleton of a house loomed, gray and disconsolate. Too spent to feel elation, he got out of his pack harness and let himself down on the nearest stump. The sun was warm on his shoulders, and the silence was broken only by his own rough breathing.

Long before he trusted himself to stand again, he had begun to estimate his possession. It belonged to him, he thought, eyes darting to and fro, like nothing else on earth. This opening in the forest, ringed about by tall, painted trees, the unproven promise of the land beyond them, were more completely his own than parent, child, or wife could be; his to use well or ill, to divide or keep entire, to sell or rent or give away, with none to gainsay him.

Amos always had been a good hand with salts and pearlash. Ninety-four stood above the reach of valley fogs that bred fever and ague. Job's brother had wasted no time in idleness. Better than two acres had been cleared, and from more than half of the opened land, stumps had been grubbed and stones removed. They had been used, no doubt, for the foundations of the half-finished dwelling and the still-unbuilt barn. Others had gone into the walls of the square ash house.

Amos always had been a good hand with salts and pearlash. He had been a provident man, as well. While bettering his pitch, he had planned to make it yield a cash crop.

Suddenly, Job's throat ached, and his eyelids smarted. These forsaken enterprises, for an intense instant, brought his dead brother into the clearing's bright stillness where leaves dropped from the encircling trees like unwilling tears. The land and the work of Amos's hands were waiting in mournful expectancy.

Job would do right by them. Together, they would fulfill their late owner's intentions and—his heart leaped at the thought— carry them further. This was the beginning, he told himself and furtively wiped his eyes; this was the commencement of a shining project that would continue while Job Aldrich endured.

He got up stiffly, but slack knees and swimming head opposed further investigation until he had eaten. Job rummaged in his pack for his tinderbox, piled dried twigs on birch bark, and got a fire going. The chunk of salt pork he had skewered on a green stick scarcely had begun to broil when hunger overcame him and he wolfed it, half raw.

When he rose again, he dug deeper into his pack and brought forth the deed that would guide him along the lot's boundaries, but before he ventured farther, he more closely inspected the clearing, testing the soil between his fingers, approving the line of apple seedlings that stood a handbreadth high. Job didn't see how any man could have accomplished more than Amos in less than three summers' labor.

Cellar walls had been well laid; sills, studding, plates, and rafters of the house had been firmly mortised or pegged. With luck, a kitchen could be made weather-tight before snowfall.

Beyond the dwelling, Amos had stoned up a spring. Its over-flow sparkled through frost-blackened mint and still-green cresses. Job knelt and drank. The icy water stung his throat. On impulse, he soused his head, withdrew it, gasping, and began to pull off his frock. He would be better for a bath. He still was blindfolded when someone hallooed from the clearing's edge.

Job gave muffled answer, got back into the garment, and peered through the studding at the approaching stranger—a thin man, breathless from haste, who carried a firelock. He stared for a long instant at the other's dripping face and matted dark hair.

"Seen your smoke," the intruder said at last.

His mild gray eyes were sunken, and there were lines of weariness about his mouth.

"This," he pursued, "is the Aldrich pitch—or was. Yours now, mebby?"

"Ehyah. Job Aldrich."

"Wal, now! I'm Nat French." Rigidity left him, and he grinned wanly. "Your near neighbors: Betty 'n' the boy 'n' me."

He held out a clammy hand. He wasn't too spry, the husky voice confessed. He had had the shakes all summer, but they were easing off, like always, with the coming of frost. French had been troubled by the smoke on the hill. No Indian danger, these days, but there were all sorts of folks abroad.

"New come from Bay Province, ain't you? What news from there?"

"Little that's good," Job replied and, seating himself, submitted to the inevitable cross-questioning. His patience had worn thin when French paused and considered the sun.

"Best be gettin' back," he said and added firmly, "You'll bide with us, for now. Live a mite easier than you would here—and Betty'll send me back again if I come home without you."

"I was minded," Job hesitated, "to walk the boundaries."

"Ehyah," French nodded understandingly. "Wouldn't wonder. I'll tell Betty you're comin'. Meanwhile, I'll take this for surety."

He picked up the pack before its owner could interfere and slung it, staggering slightly.

"Follow the road further an' you'll find us. You'll be real welcome."

The clearing was filling with shadow when Job re-entered it, but sunlight still gilded the rafters of the unfinished house. He wished, though the frosty air prickled in his nose, that he were to spend the night alone here. It would be pleasant, to review, undistracted, all he had found.

He had tramped from one blazed tree to the next about the oblong of "one hundred acres more or less" that comprised his property while pride and satisfaction well nigh had overwhelmed him. Never had he seen soil so rich as this dark leaf mold. The timber was lordly: maples, gnarled and immense; hemlock in abundance; enough tall pines to mast all the King's ships; and mighty stands of ash and elm that would make the best of salts when felled, burned, and leached.

The land reached easily upward, promising tillage too nearly level for rain to gully, and in the lot's northeast corner, rose more steeply into a rounded hilltop, where a swath of trees had been overthrown by ancient tempest. Job, skirting the tangle of gray trunks, clambered to the summit and, through the opening left by the blowdown, looked into the west.

A length of river shone in the valley, and beyond it, hills rose, each duskier than the last, until the farthest blue range met the sky. Beyond this barrier lay still more empty land, unimaginably vast. In a thousand years men could not settle it all. The strength of the hills was His, also. Moses, on Pisgah's height, might have known like awe.

Job turned away from the humbling prospect. His own property was spread below him. The scar among crowding treetops that was his clearing would spread into broad fields of wheat and corn. His breath came quickly, and his heart swelled. Here was fulfillment of the longing born in him. He closed his eyes and, before he followed farther the boundaries of Lot Ninety-four, prayed that he might deal wisely and well with this dear land of his.

On the southern edge of his pitch, Job came upon a full-flowing brook. Leaves sailed on the brown current, which he followed upstream until forest ridges, closing in, offered the site for a future milldam. He bore this knowledge, with the rest of his trove, back to the clearing, and his hands shook as he stripped himself beside the spring.

The cold water Job splashed over his grimed person seemed to abolish the last vestige of doubt. He could not in a single viewing uncover all of his land's virtues or list at once what he had found, yet chief of the treasures he had brought back from his survey was an uplifting sense of freedom and of peace and of good, everlasting labor awaiting him. He would hold fast to these, asking no more, offending no man, he and his possession prospering together.

[21]

When he had pulled breeches and frock over his damp body, Job considered his reflection in the spring's dim mirror. He was bearded like a lynx, but he could not mend that, since French had taken his pack. He went down through the darkening forest and followed the road farther. Windows were bright in the house that stood in a far larger clearing than his. He shouted when he reached its edge, and from the barn his neighbor answered him.

3

NATHANIEL FRENCH appeared, lugging a milk pail, and hailed his guest.

"Wal, now! Feared mebby I'd have to go fetch you."

Job peered through the dusk at a smoking stone oven in the dooryard and the oblong house beyond it, then considered the log barn that propped a monstrous manure pile. A field ran dimly to the forest's blackness, and he heard in the distance a river's endless sigh. He told his host:

"You've a good pitch."

Nat deplored: "Have to move the barn, else dung'll be over the eaves. Aimed to do it this summer, but I ain't been too hearty, and Will—he's my brother an' bides with us—has been away quite a lot."

"A good pitch," Job insisted.

"View yours?"

"Some."

"Favor it?"

"Not too bad."

"Better'n that." Nat bent and resumed the pail. "No call to tarry here till we're frostbit."

He drew on the latchstring with his free hand, thrust open the door, and stepping out of the released shaft of light, waved his guest forward. Job moved into the warmth of a low-ceiled kitchen. The unsteady glow cast across it by logs, ablaze in a vast fireplace, weakened the flame of a tallow dip upon the table. He sniffed pleasant smells of wood smoke, soap, and something savory a-cooking. The Frenches kept a good house.

"Wife," Nat called, " 'tis our new neighbor."

He pushed his guest toward the hearthside settle and bade: "Set you there an' thaw a mite."

A woman came from an inner chamber as Job turned. She glanced at him shyly and bobbed a curtsy. Betty French was awkward in the russet homespun that plainly was her appearing-out gown, but her smile of welcome made her pocked face almost comely.

She faltered response to her guest's greeting, accepted the pail from her husband, and withdrew. The settle creaked as Job and Nat sat down together. In the adjoining room, a small voice gurgled and then lifted into lusty wailing.

"Hosea," the father explained with pride. "Four weeks old today. Third we've had," he went on more ruefully. "Lost a boy an' a girl from lung fever."

"Nothing ails this one's lungs," Job chuckled. He felt light and easy. Firelight shook across the wide floor boards and reached aloft to the herb bundles and festoons of leathery dried apples along the ceiling's beams. This was a snug house. Job thought of his own and asked:

"Sawmill handy?"

Nat grinned at the question's explosive sound. There were always sawmills a-plenty in new country, he explained, but Job had best visit Alex Kathan's on the other side of town. He had drawn a mort of lumber to the Aldrich pitch and had hauled the unused back again after Amos had been killed. Alex was a neighborly man and honest.

" 'Cordin' to his lights, that is," Nat amended in haste. "Favors York more'n I like."

Betty ventured, "Supper's laid."

At the oaken table in the kitchen's center, host and guest sat before a pumpkin, scalped, scraped free of seed, then filled with milk and baked. Talk was scant while they dug wooden spoons into the porridgelike interior of the orange globe. Betty French, as became a housewife, was deferring her own meal until menfolks had eaten their fill. She moved quietly between the kitchen and the bedchamber where the baby still fretted and, when her husband and guest had wearied of pumpkin, set a bowl of hasty pudding before them.

"Wal, now!" Nat sat in mock surprise. "This ain't a holiday."

She blushed and turned away without reply, but Job knew the luxury was her welcome to him.

He leaned back from the table, at last, and considered with lofty amusement the doubts that earlier had beset him. A man was likely to run into trouble when entering new country. Maybe he had met with more than his share, but that was behind him now.

Thought of the endless wilderness he had viewed from his hilltop soothed and fortified him. No one who lived close to such majesty need share in the piddling squabbles of mankind.

Nat dipped water into a chipped blue bowl from the steaming kettle on the crane. The draft he was preparing had a lordly smell. He raised the bowl briefly to his lips.

"Health," he said and, offering it to his guest: "Blackstrap ain't too bad, if you get used to it."

The brew scorched Job's throat. Rum, molasses, and hot water, his host explained, were recommended by Dr. Harvey as a cure for fever and ague. They were easier to stomach than most of his remedies or any that the herb woman, Zurvilla Alvord, concocted. Nat drank again and smiled at his guest.

"We'll be good neighbors, you and me, and you'll do well here, if only—"

"If only?" Job prompted.

"Wal," Nat confided, trying to express all his doubt in a single rush of speech, "folks is—uneasy, seems. Most settled under Hampshire titles, but now York claims clear to the Great River an' sets its own courts and officers over us. A many don't like that. Some are still for Hampshire. There's others that follow Solomon Harvey an' favor jinin' Cumberland County to Bay Province. Quite a pother, these days."

"Rest easy," Job assured him with confidence. "I aim to keep clear of politics. I—"

"Hold on," Nat bade and then, as someone called again from the clearing's edge, opened the door and shouted, "Who's thar?"

He said over his shoulder to his wife, "It's Two-pound-ten."

The uneven beat of approaching footsteps seemed to catch up and repeat the phrase: "Two pound ten; two pound ten." A voice cried shrilly, "Greetings, all!"

Nat, closing the door behind a bent elder, demanded, wavering between welcome and worry:

"Now what? Trouble, I'll be bound."

The intruder's fur cap was pulled down to meet unshaven jowls. Above beard stubble a sharp nose twitched, and the eyes that straddled it skipped about the room to fix themselves on Job. He looked down from the close scrutiny and flinched. The stranger's feet, planted on either side of the cane that helped support him, were bare, dirt-blackened, and toeless.

"Neighbor Alvord," Nat was reciting as he proffered the bowl, "this here is Job Aldrich, brother to Amos."

"Do tell!" Despite the long draft Alvord had taken, something still rattled dryly in his voice, like a pea in a willow whistle. He scanned the room, stared at Job again, and demanded:

"Whar's your woman?"

"Woman? I'm unwed."

"Thunderation!" Alvord piped. "Then I've misled the hull settlement. Told 'em you'd brought a fam'ly. Wal, I'll set it right on the morrow. Moses Alvord is trustworthy. Frenches'll bear me out."

"Two-pound-ten," Nat demanded while the visitor drank

[25]

again, "what's gone ill, now? You'd not be abroad so late, with Zurvilla home alone, else."

"Ill or well, who can tell?" Alvord shrilled while cane and stubbed feet beat out the cadence. "News I have, indeed; though mebby," he added with artful hesitation, "you've heered it a'ready. No? Wal, folks, Leftenant Spaulding, this very day, went into Bildad Easton with a pitchfork. Wounded him, sore —or so I'm told."

He rattled through the tale of the assault while Nat shook his head and Job resolutely held his tongue.

"An' then," this peculiar towncrier concluded elatedly, "Leftenant stuck him, an' Bildad, he run, lamentin' dreadful."

"Wal," French said, half unwillingly, "try to bully Len, an' you've picked the wrong man."

"Indeed and indeed!" Alvord cried, feet and cane pounding. "Wal, neighbors, I still got many to tell an' far to go. What else I hear I'll bring you. Reliable—that's Moses Alvord."

They heard him thump away into silence. Betty tiptoed into the bedchamber. Nat stood and looked disconsolately at Job, who remained mute. It would do no good to reveal his small part in the recent quarrel.

His host was not as reticent. His hands twisted as he said aggrievedly:

"Things keep a-pilin' top of each other, seems. Be as wild here as 'tis Bennington-way, pretty quick. S'pose, now, York'll arrest Len."

"Well," Job said slowly, "sticking pitchforks into your neighbors isn't exactly legal, where I come from. Law's law, way I see it. Aim to keep clear of it."

"Do you, now?" Nat's voice was bitter. "When you're made to serve on a jury panel for a hull month, while your hay goes to ruin or your winter's wood lays where 'twas felled, mebby you'll be a mite less legal."

"Well, maybe," Job granted and, to avert further dispute, asked, "This Alvord: he—all right?" He tapped his forehead.

Nat thankfully veered away from argument. Two-pound-ten,

he reported, had had his toes froze off in the last war and was a mite tetched, too, most likely.

"Sister's crazier, though. Captivated by Injuns and never got over it, seems. Some hold she's a witch, but I don't believe in such."

Job yawned widely in spite of himself. His host moved quickly to the table and took up the tallow dip.

"Past bedtime," he apologized, "an' I've kept you up, spent though you be."

He led his guest up a steep stair to one of the two small rooms crammed beneath the roof's slant, and there bade him good night. Job knelt and prayed, long and thankfully, before he got himself to bed.

Sunlight in his eyes brought him fully awake. The guilty belief that he had overslept was fortified by movement and voices below. A door slammed, and feet went across the yard.

Job hurriedly drew from his pack his appearing-out clothes: linen shirt, woolen hose, brass-buckled shoes, and a worn suit of brown broadcloth.

At length, he stole downstairs, shaving gear in hand. Betty stammered reply to his greeting, and at his request, ladled water from the fireplace kettle into a basin. Nat, she faltered, had gone out with Will to milk, and breakfast was nigh ready. Job found her shyness contagious and went outside.

He had settled himself on the steps and was rubbing yellow soap into his bristled face when men came toward him from the barn. One was his host. The other, who bore the milk pail, Job had last seen hanging like wet wash on a streamside alder.

4

NAT CALLED CHEERILY, "Wal, slugabed!"
Job lifted a dripping hand and, too dismayed for
further response, silently watched the others advance. He had not been mistaken. This was indeed his late
adversary. His shirt and breeches seemed to fit him still more
snugly. Maybe, Job thought with nervous amusement, they had
shrunk.

The hulking young man halted for an instant, as though
recognition were an obstacle, and then came on while his heavy
face grew darker.

"Aldrich," Nat said, unheeding, "this is m'brother, Will."

Job ended the taut silence:

"We've met, already."

He admired his own composure, particularly since it confused
Will French, who scowled and breathed loudly.

" 'Met a'ready'!" Nat fumbled. "Why'n't you tell us?"

"Didn't know 'twas your brother," Job explained.

Will's attempt to speak ended in a growling sound, and he
shifted the pail from one big hand to the other. He was sullenly
wrathful; that was certain. Equally clearly, he was afraid that
an abasing story was about to be told. Job smiled up at him and
said easily to Nat:

"We met for only a moment, t'other side of the settlement.
Clean forgot to mention it."

Will French's windy sigh seemed to ease interior pressure.
His brother, still unaware of tension, took the pail and bade his
guest:

"Get on with your shavin'; past time for breakfast."

He went on into the house. Job dipped his hands in the basin

[28]

and scrubbed his jowls. Will's feet shuffled in the frost-bleached grass. Speech at last burst from him.

"Beholden to you; in a measure, anyway, for holdin' your tongue."

The admission half-strangled him. Job answered quietly:

" 'Twasn't anything worth bragging about."

A softer answer might have been better, but he found himself unwilling to soothe a person who stood above him, stiff-legged and threatening.

"Brag or not as it suits you," Will said in a hushed blare. "Won't ever best me again."

Job ignored the barbed replies Satan offered him. He put the basin aside and balanced a chipped fragment of looking glass on his knees. His bland disregard became more than his opponent could stand in silence.

"Pride yourself on not tattlin', no doubt," Will jeered. "Wager you ain't told Nat 'twas you prevented Len Spaulding from givin' Bildad his just deserts."

"Hold that against me?" Job asked, so politely that the thick face above him took on a purplish hue.

"Not only me, but all right-thinkin' folks. No place here for Yorkers. You'll find that out."

The meek were to inherit the earth. That did not keep Job from saying precisely:

"Not a Yorker and I'm a settling."

"Be you, now? Mebby you think I can't run you out of town."

Job unfolded his razor before he looked up again at Will.

"Well," he drawled, "that'll depend on how many you bring along to help you, next time."

He stropped the blade gently on the heel of his palm while he spoke. Will hesitated for an instant, then snorted and plunged into the house. Job checked his impulse to follow. It would be sorry repayment for Nat's and Betty's kindnesses, and further betrayal of his mother's cherished creed, to press a foolish quarrel. This time, at least, he had kept his temper, yet he found his hand so unsteady that he waited a long moment before attempting to shave.

[29]

Voices were clashing in the kitchen, but he could not make out what they said. Maybe that was as well, he thought wryly, and tried to divert his mind with the prospect before him, considering the neat dooryard and, beyond a stone wall, cornstalks stacked in precise rows. Shakes or no shakes, Nat was a prime farmer.

Job still could hear an invisible river's windy voice. Past the cornfield, forest began again, and above its tarnished foliage, a hill, dark with pines, humped itself against a cloudless sky. Black Mountain, most likely. He drew a long breath and plied his razor. It was a fair land, and his stake in it was too large to risk by further bickering.

Washed, shaven, and with his dark hair clubbed and neatly tied, he turned half-unwillingly to the house. Betty, standing on the hearth when he entered, exchanged her exasperated look for a forced smile. She glanced toward the table where the brothers sat, so stiff and mute that Job knew he had interrupted further wrangling. Will roused, glared at the intruder, and then addressed Nat loudly:

"Tories, Yorkers, trimmers, and neuters: high time town was rid of—"

"That's a plenty," his brother broke in sharply. "Fill that loud mouth of yourn with something it can swallow."

Will obeyed momentarily, but as Job bore his shaving things upstairs, he heard the dispute break out again. Only fragments reached him. While he thrust belongings into his pack, he heard chairs pushed back. Feet pounded across the floor, and a door slammed. Job drew on his coat, wondering drearily whether strife must follow him wherever he ventured in Dummerston, and forced himself to go downstairs again.

Betty French's round face was so severe when she set a filled bowl before her guest that unreasonable guilt stirred within him and he said awkwardly:

"Sorry to have caused you trouble; my fault, I guess."

The woman had started to turn away as he spoke. Now, she wheeled about and, shyness forgotten, said with hushed violence:

[30]

"No sech thing! 'Twas all Will's doin'; forever bawlin' like a bull calf of tyranny an' the like. Sometimes, wish he'd—"

Vehemence choked her. Her mouth trembled, though her eyes still were parched by anger.

"Him and Nat," she said more quietly, "has gone out to the barn. You can breakfast in peace—or what's left of it."

Her evident distress impelled Job to say:

"I've been a troublesome guest, but I'll leave beholden to you both."

"Leave?" she repeated. "Leave after you've just come, an' besmirch Nat an' me? Anyone leaves, 'twill be Will with his brag and bluster. Could spare him. Why on earth can't folks live pleasant and peaceful?"

"Been wondering about that for quite a spell," Job admitted.

In the bedchamber, the baby gurgled and began to wail.

" 'Twould hurt us if you left," Betty said hastily, "an' shame us 'fore the neighbors. Why, you're the nearest one we've got."

She hurried away to tend her wailing child.

Job bent over the bowl before him, resolved to gulp down only enough to stay him and then to hurry away before Nat and Will returned and the quarrel revived. He altered his intention with the first spoonful of the hot pease porridge. By its smoothness and savor, he judged it had been in the pot at least five days, maybe more. He finished it hastily, with further gratitude to his hostess, and stole from the house.

He had gone a furlong through the morning's cold brightness when he remembered he had no knowledge of where Solomon Harvey, town clerk and practitioner of physick, lived or how to reach the sawyer, Kathan. He would not go back, but would seek for guidance, elsewhere.

Job hesitated an instant where a lesser track forked uphill from the main road, and was half-minded to follow it for no better purpose than to view his property in this clear morning light. He thrust the impulse away. He would have all the rest of his life to spend in his land's company.

The road, spattered with the red and gold of fallen leaves, crossed a brook that, by the lay of the land, might be Job's own, and then began a long, crooked ascent. On either hand, great trees walled the way, soaring like the pillars of a giant's palace. Massive trunks formed haphazard colonnades where blue dusk lurked, and made still more dazzling the sunlight that shafted down through the dwindling roof of foliage.

Job was sweating and breathless when he reached the end of his climb, and before him, the road slanted downward. He paused. He must be standing on a shoulder of Black Mountain, with the French pitch below to the west and his own further to the north. It was good to feel the beginning of acquaintance with this lordly, lovely land. Amos, in praising it, had not stretched the truth. Job, despite his late difficulties and Will French's windy threats, had done well to settle in the Grants.

He stepped out again, almost gaily, and beyond the next turning, came face to face with a smaller traveler.

"Well, now!" Job said, halting.

The scrawny youngster who had confronted him yesterday on the settlement's Common squinted and said uncordially:

"Seekin' you."

He was not visibly pleased by the meeting but hitched up his frock, dug into a pocket of his frayed breeches, then held out his hand.

"Yours."

Job looked from the penny to the sharp, unchildish face.

"No, yours; paid you for service."

The boy shook his head as though his neck were stiff.

"Pa says—I didn't earn it."

"Ehyah? An' who's your Pa?"

"Jacob Laughton; that's who. Hold's it ain't—seemly to take pay for nothin'. Bade me give it back."

He thrust the coin at Job.

"Now hold on," the man urged. "If you didn't earn a penny yesterday, you could earn it now. Will you guide me to Town Clerk Harvey's house?"

"That ain't worth a penny, either. Besides, he's gone to tend Tamar Knight. She's a-bearin' again."

"Well, could you show me the way to Alexander Kathan's?"

"Further," the boy granted. "Clear over to Canoe Brook, but maybe it ain't worth—"

"'Tis to me. Call it a bargain. What's your name?"

"It's Jake, after Pa."

"All right, Jake. Step out."

"Needn't walk slow, either. I ain't a child; fourteen—almost."

He was a dwarfish almost-fourteen, but he had gravity beyond his years. Job was amused, yet embarrassed, by the dignity with which Jake paraded his patron the length of the settlement street, gravely hailing adults who appeared in the doorways but ignoring the lengthening train of childen who followed the travelers.

"Where Doctor Harvey lives," the boy said, nodding to a small, red dwelling. "That is, when he's to home—which he often ain't."

He wheeled upon their attendants and shouted:

"You brats go home; else, you'll git lost."

They hooted, but as he led Job down a road that was little more than twin ruts on a hillside, the children fell behind and, at the forest's edge, turned back.

Guide and guided had marched far into the woods' dim stillness before curiosity overcame Jake. He asked at last:

"Settlin'?"

"Wouldn't wonder."

"Whig?"

"Not certain."

"Wal," Jake warned, "you best be. Time's a-comin' when there'll be none but Whigs in all Cumberland County. Pa says so. Hope it don't come too soon."

"Meaning you're not a Whig?"

"Think I'm a Tory bastard or a Yorker pimp?" Color fired the narrow face. "Meanin', when we whop 'em, hope I'm old enough to jine in."

He had a monstrous animosity for so slight a being. Apparently, even the children of Dummerston were spoiling for a fight. Job sighed. He followed the boy past a clearing with a

[33]

house and barn in its center and presently out upon a broader way.

"The Great Road," Jake proclaimed and, pointing to a track beyond it: "Yonder's the way to Kathan's."

Job was willing to be rid of his guide before conferring with the sawyer.

"You've earned your penny," he said briskly. "No need to come further."

The boy did not seem to hear but was staring intently down the highway.

"Goddlemighty!" he breathed at last. "Look!"

Job could see nothing in the aspect of the four men who tramped toward him to warrant excitement. They were commonplace enough—or were they? They moved in an unusually tight group: three of them abreast and another, closely following.

"Leftenant!" Jake announced in a hushed squeal. "They've took him! Quick!"

The roadside brush rattled as he scuttled into hiding. The compact group drew closer, and Job recognized two of the three who marched abreast. Leonard Spaulding lurched along with wrists lashed behind him. When he lagged, the men on either side pulled him forward, while the fourth kneed him from the rear.

Spaulding was bareheaded. There was a wet, red blotch on his bald scalp. Clearly, he had not submitted meekly to capture, for the lank man on his right had a darkening, half-closed eye, and Bildad Easton, on his other side, limped heavily.

The pounding of Job's heart seemed louder than the approaching footsteps. He must not let pity for the prisoner's stumbling gait and slack, gray face curdle into resentment. He would keep clear of trouble henceforth; on this he was solemnly resolved.

Job had witnessed the assault that had brought deserved punishment down upon the assailant. Violence—he could hear his mother warn him—only bred more violence. He turned toward the hoof-churned way that led to Kathan's mill.

He did not see Easton's sloe eyes glance at him indifferently

[34]

and then widen, or hear him speak hurriedly to the man who trod at the captive's heels.

"Is he, indeed?" a tight voice cried and, lifting higher, called: "You, sir; you, I say; come here!"

Job went on, wondering whether his pace too closely resembled flight. He was deaf to a second hail, and curses that were squealed after him. He heard the party move on. When he looked back at last, the Great Road had been hidden by crowding trees, and Jake was bearing down on him, headlong.

The boy stumbled, reeled against Job, and caught his arm to keep from falling. For an instant, he clung there, gasping. The thin hands clawed at the man's sleeve. Jake shuddered, choked, and then crowed thinly:

"Not—this way. They've—taken Leftenant; damned—Sheriff Paterson 'n' his dep'ties. Gotta—warn folks. Come on."

Job caught the scrabbling fingers and looked down at the frantic small face.

"I've business," he said, "with Kathan. Already told you."

It was right and proper to keep away from strife, yet he was shamed by Jake's look of disbelief.

"Mean," the still breathless voice asked, "you'll let 'em captivate Leftenant an'—"

His throat closed upon the enormity.

"I mean," Job answered, more loudly than he had intended, "that law is law, and I won't meddle with sheriff's business."

Jake choked again and stepped back. He fumbled beneath his frock, jerked forth the exploring hand, and cast a small missile at Job. It struck his chest and dropped before him.

"Thar!" the boy sobbed and, additionally outraged by his own tears, screeched: "Take your dirty penny, you hell-deservin' Tory."

5

OB WENT DOWN through woodland toward Kathan's. It was ridiculous to let a scrawny child's rage trouble him, yet it was still another evidence of the enmity that had poisoned this outwardly serene new country. The sheriff's posse and their captive, Will French's animosity, young Jake's fury were the evil made manifest. Job had expected to find in the Grants refuge from the quarreling that beset Stockbridge. He could not have been more mistaken, he thought grimly.

Tall trees that hid the sky were like the pines on Lot Ninety-four. Canoe Brook fell over its ledges with a companionable sound. There was more than enough empty land in this half wilderness to guarantee peace to all men who truly sought it. Job tried to cast off depression and stepped out more briskly. With his pitch to better and the Frenches his near neighbors, he had no cause to despair.

Nevertheless, when the road ran out of the forest, he halted, wondering uneasily what greeting he would get at the square house with a single great chimney that stood back from a pond in the broad clearing. A gaunt building at the water's far end sat amid piles of lumber and mounds of edgings like an old hen among her chicks.

A half-grown youngster hurried from the mill. He pried up a gate beside the dam, and Job heard a vertical saw rouse and begin to grunt like a rooting hog. The boy stared at the stranger, then ran back to the building. After a moment, a man came out and approached Job, who asked:

"Kathan?"

The other nodded, though his round, freckled face did not

stir. He waited woodenly until Job had told him name and mission. Then, the sawyer's grin, as he held out a thick hand, reached toward his flaring ears.

"Wal, now!" Kathan marveled. "Amos's brother! You're real welcome."

Business could wait, he pursued firmly, while he and Job wet their gullets. He had cider down-cellar that, with a tetch of spirits, would liven a gravestone.

Kathan led his guest into a kitchen, rich with the smell of frying doughnuts. A little girl stared at the stranger, and a woman, so angular that the sawmill might have fashioned her, lifted her scarlet face from a seething kettle when her husband had named his visitor. She bobbed a curtsy, then turned upon Kathan, who had taken a wide-mouthed jug from the cupboard.

"Alex, not early as this!"

"Cider, Mother. Cider's wholesome."

"'Tain't, when laced with rum."

"No more'n enough for flavorin', Mother."

Margaret Kathan sighed, but when her spouse had returned and had led Job out to the doorstep, she brought a bowl of doughnuts and set it beside them.

One pull at the jug made Job feel that sunlight had been let into his darkened being. He spoke of the unfinished house and of his need for sheathing, shingles, clapboards, and flooring.

"Yonder 'tis," Kathan nodded toward the mill where the saw still throbbed. "Johnny 'n' me'll draw you a load, this afternoon."

"There's the matter of price."

The other stared.

"Amos paid for it all; sash to boot. You didn't know?"

Job had not known; or Hannah, either. He had made a better bargain than he had thought. He drank again and felt uncommonly well.

"Hauled it all back," Kathan was saying, "after Amos's ending. Ain't safe, these days—"

He broke off to look for a minute into the distance.

"Come here," he began again, more carefully, "twenty-one

year ago, with Pa an' Ma. First settlers—first that stayed, anyway. Bettered m'self. Always figgered our get would have it better still. Now—I ain't sure."

He lifted the jug, drank, and went on dolefully:

"Thought we was shet of war for everlastin', but there's another comin' if folks have their wicked way."

The deploring voice could not lessen the ease that the sunlight without and a kindred warmth within were spreading through Job. The singular relaxing warmth let him view the Laughton boy's late fury as comic and Spaulding's capture as trivial. He found himself telling Kathan of both, almost gaily.

"Wal," the other offered, when Job had ended, "don't surprise me. Boy needs birchin'. Len's a good neighbor—in a way, that is. Lawless though, like a many. Folks come into the Grants seekin' something. They ain't quite certain what 'tis, but most of 'em hold it ain't what they've got."

In the old days, Kathan confided, when settlers were almighty humped-up to keep from starving and freezing, there was no loose talk about liberty and such.

He looked at Job sharply and demanded: "You for the King?" and, when the other nodded readily, went on with more vigor:

"Wal, then! Grants belong to York, King says. So York sets up courts to serve us. Won't have 'em, folks say. Want to be free, rule themselves, an' have no law but their own—meanin' no law at all, way I see it."

He cleared his throat with a scornful sound.

"York taxes us a mite more'n Hampshire did, I don't deny, but damn' rascals spend more time squealin' about quitrent than 'twould take 'em to earn it, thrice over. Some seeks to jine with Hampshire. Solomon Harvey, Charley Davenport, and other loud-mouths hold Cumberland County belongs by rights to Massachusetts. Most folks don't know what they do want, but they're willin' to fight for it. God's sakes! Ain't we had enough war?"

"Killed Pa to Quebec," Job offered. The thought filled him with agreeable melancholy.

"Uncle Phineas died of the pox to Ti. Held he was fightin'
to end all war. How'd he feel now?"

"Grieved," Job supplied, after reflection.

"To your pa," Kathan proposed, gulped, and passed the jug.

"To your Uncle Phineas," his guest returned politely. He
drank to the departed with an unseemly chuckle.

Kathan's face was glowing, but his resentment was unabated.

"Come ten days earlier," he told Job, "you'd have seen, clear
enough, what's goin' on. We held a county convention, to Westminster."

He momentarily seemed unable to stop shaking his head in
disapproval. Most folks, he went on, when he had succeeded,
figured the meeting would be another protest against York
courts, their cost, their officials, jury duty, and the like. But no!

"No?" Job echoed.

"No, no, no! Honorable delegates," loading the words with
irony, "spent most of their time cussin' their law-abidin' neighbors."

"Ehyah?" Job held out the jug.

"Lemme see, now," Kathan resumed, wiping his mouth with
the back of his hand, "if I can mind jest what they did resolve.
Convention voted that all who favored livin' by the King's own
statutes should be considered"—he sank his voice into hoarse
solemnity—"should be considered 'as loathsome animals, not to
be touched or to have any society or connection with.'"

He drank again, as though to wash away the quotation, hic-
cupped and looked reproachfully at Job.

"'Loathsome animal' is what I am for living lawful and tryin'
to keep the peace. That's what you'll be too, if you ain't set on
treason and rebellion. Oh-oh!"

Kathan peered into the emptied jug with a bereaved air. He
picked up the remaining doughnut and, when his guest refused
it, carefully broke it into equal parts.

"Share an' share alike. Friends in peace an' war."

"No more war," Job objected. "Wars ain't—sensible."

"Neither," his host assured him earnestly, "is folks."

Margaret Kathan came to the door and looked down at them.

[39]

"Like I feared," she said. "Dinner's most ready, Alexander, and not a mite too soon. You'll bide," she informed Job.

"Deed he will," Kathan answered. "Haulin' lumber to his place afterward—him an' Johnny an' me."

Though it was close to sunrise, Job still lay abed at the Frenches while his mind circled like a fallen leaf in a brook's eddy. From below, came the stir of a waking household: soft scuff of feet, low speech, and crackle of reviving fire.

The listener scowled, wondering whether Will had returned. Nat, shamed and distressed by his brother's late violence, had begged his guest to stay. Betty had added a quiet appeal. Will, they had explained, was squiring his fancy to a quilting bee and likely would bed at the Houghtons', on the other side of town. In any event, they had promised, there would be no more trouble; they would see to that, and Job had remained, though not so sure.

Brief experience had persuaded him that trouble was as natural to Dummerston as the air its people breathed. The best, perhaps the only, way to keep free of it was to get up to his pitch and stay there.

He sat up and rubbed his head, as though friction might set his thoughts in order and, matching his present confusion against the hopeful beliefs he had brought from Stockbridge, grinned ruefully. Yesterday had not been a good beginning, nor yet an entirely bad.

Job swung himself from bed and sat on its edge while he reviewed his, the Kathans', and the laden sled's passage through the settlement last afternoon. Something had changed the bright October day since he had traversed that very street a few hours earlier.

There were more persons abroad, and their aspect, too, had altered. Men stood at the wayside, women on doorsteps, and watched with an unlikely air of indifference as the small red oxen drew the load past. Even the children were muted and wary.

A few of the stiffly loitering spoke dryly to the Kathans. The remainder furtively peered at them and their companion. Job had the impression that excitement had been hurriedly clapped into hiding, lest a suspected stranger view it. He felt ill at ease and lonely.

A tight group of men, gathered before the unfinished meetinghouse, abruptly hushed their argument as the Kathans and Job approached. He wondered whether they had been discussing Spaulding's capture and his own refusal to interfere. The boy, Jake, doubtless had carried that tale far and wide. Job was grateful when the shielding forest rid him of the uneasy belief that scornful eyes were following him.

Folks, Kathan had ventured with the pose of a justified prophet, were all haired-up again. Trouble was a-brewing. He could feel it in the air, see it on the neighbors' faces.

Job had remembered then that his deed still rested in his pocket, unrecorded. He had had no inclination to turn back.

Kathan, whatever his politics, had proved a neighborly and generous man. When the sheathing had been unloaded before the unfinished house, he and his gangling son had stayed for a spell, working so deftly with Job that, before they had left, one outside wall of the kitchen-to-be had been covered.

While they were still occupied, Nat French, roused by the sound of hammering, came up the hill. Two-pound-ten, he reported, was spreading the call for a meeting, next morning, at Charley Davenport's house to consider Spaulding's plight.

"Ehyah?" Alexander Kathan asked, through a mouthful of nails. "Wal, comes natural, I guess. Once folks start lawbreakin', they can't quit."

"Mebby," Nat granted. "Still an' all, 'tain't our law we're resistin'; 'tis York's."

"Is they," Alex inquired, "statutes to your law, wheresoever you got it, permittin' folks to pitchfork each other an' curse the King?"

French did not answer and presently went away. When the Kathans, too, had left, Job had tarried in the clearing to consider the work accomplished and draw fortitude from the companionship of his pitch. The sheathed wall pleased him anew, yet he had been unable to regain the clean, uplifting satisfaction he had found in his property when first he had seen it. Now, perched on the bed's edge, he still could not feel it. That sober rapture might be recovered during the day of undistracted work that lay before him.

Job rose and reached for his clothes. From the foot of the stair, Nat called:

"Hello, there! It's been a nice day."

A bowl of mush and maple molasses remained on the table when Job hurriedly entered the kitchen. Betty smiled at his apology, but Nat, standing before the hearth, waited impatiently while his guest breakfasted.

Will, Job saw with relief that immediately irked him, still was absent. This day was beginning well, if tardily, and it was full of promise. If nothing new interfered, he surely could get the kitchen entirely walled by nightfall. He rose briskly from the table. Nat said:

"Past time we was gettin' over to town meetin'."

He turned toward the door. Job swallowed loudly.

"Town meeting? No call for me to go, being still no more than a stranger here."

"Freeholder, ain't you?" Nat inquired. "Been summoned with the rest of us."

"Guess," Job demurred, "meeting'll get along well enough without me."

His host stood silent an instant and twisted his locked hands.

"Best come along," he said at last. "Ain't fair to yourself, else. Folks'll be more neighborly, likely, if they come to know you. And if you've got a grievance, it's your place to speak it. That's what town meetin's for; know that as well as me."

"No grievance, special. It's just that—" Job began and stuck.

Maybe it was cowardice that hindered him. Maybe Nat was right, and if he hid away on his pitch, folks would be still more prone to suspect him. Already Job was aware that it would be harder than he had expected to live inoffensively here.

"Aimed," he said obstinately, "to get on with my house. Not too much time to get a room tight before snow."

"Lose you little if you 'tend meetin'," Nat protested. "Deed still ain't recorded, an' Solomon Harvey's sure to be there. Wish that you'd come."

"Then I will," Job told him.

6

THE AILING NAT on his rawboned, white horse and Job, walking beside it, came down out of the forest and into the settlement. Its street was half blocked by men who stood, dark and ungainly as drowned trees in a beaver pond, before a weather-stained dwelling that plainly had been too small to hold them all.

Nat rode across the common to tether his horse, leaving his companion to join the meeting, unsponsored. Faces, turned toward Job, were so barren of interest or welcome that he wondered wildly whether he were entirely visible. He stumbled and halted on the rim of the gathering.

A table had been brought to the shallow porch, and a lean man in snuff-colored coat and smallclothes sat beside it. He stroked his hooked nose with a pen's feather and talked to a porky person whose bulk filled the doorway. Job looked about him with a pretense of unconcern. Alexander Kathan caught his eye and smiled. The comfort of this silent greeting was lessened by sight of young Jacob Laughton. He stood beside a wizened man who was an enlargement of himself, and stared back venomously.

On Job's other hand, a person decently arrayed in worn, black broadcloth considered him for an instant, then ventured:

"Aldrich's brother, wouldn't wonder."

"I be."

The man held out his hand. The dark eyes in the ruddy face were friendly.

"John Hooker, sir, your servant and unworthy elder of this flock. I knew your brother, Mr. Aldrich. A sad loss."

He enclosed Job's hand in a warm clasp and launched further speech through his nose in a ministerial chant.

"It was my melancholy privilege, friend, to commit the mortal dust of Amos Aldrich to its final resting place. Your brother was a true man and a patriot. Providence, I am certain, has raised up another in his place."

His look was searching. Job was spared reply by a shrill voice crying:

"Meetin'll be to order."

The stout man had stepped forward to the edge of the porch. His companion, still seated at the table, was glaring through spectacles he had set astride his beaky nose and uncommonly resembling an ill-tempered owl.

"First step," he hooted, "is to choose a moderator."

"Dr. Harvey, town clerk," Hooker muttered.

Someone nominated Charles Davenport; another voice cried, "Second!" and a grumbling endorsement followed Harvey's call for a vote. The fat man bowed and cleared his throat.

Job could hear only fragments of the moderator's halting address, and by the crowd's mounting restlessness, his loss was slight. Davenport ended at last and wiped his face. Harvey rose and spoke again.

All present knew the reason for this meeting. Leftenant Leonard Spaulding had been spirited away by agents of infamy and thrust into jail.

He had stressed his announcement by thrusts of his masterful nose and now jabbed it promptly toward Davenport, who, rousing, hastily asked the will of the meeting.

"Free Len and burn down the damned jail."

Job recognized the blustering voice. Will French stood close to the steps, and the nape of his neck was red. About him, men stirred and mumbled to each other.

[44]

"My feelin', too," Davenport agreed. "Still an' all, there's ways and means to consider."

He waited expectantly. Kathan offered at last:

"Might be—useful was all here told why Len's been jailed. God-damned His Majesty an' assailed Dep'ty Easton, didn't he?"

"Not enough," Will bawled, and Harvey smiled at the meeting's lowing agreement. Color, flowing into Kathan's round face, blurred his freckles.

"Do the folks here hold," he asked tightly, "that Len Spaulding's doin's was lawful?"

"Not accordin' to the damned York law, mebby," a long man crowed, his leather jerkin flapping like featherless wings. He quickened again the wordless sound of approval. Something, Job felt uneasily, smoldered beneath the crowd's surface like coals in a banked fire. He knew that Hooker was watching him. Another voice throbbed like a hard-plied saw:

"Got courts, ain't we? Let 'em jedge Len."

"Mister Mawderator!" The man in the jerkin waved his arms wildly.

"Joel Temple," Davenport nodded.

"Mister Mawderator, does Enoch Cook hold they're our courts, for God's sake? No such thing; they're York's. We goin' to leave Leftenant Spaulding to the damned York gentry?"

Will raised a sharp yelp. Others hesitantly echoed it. In the restored silence, Cook's voice whipsawed:

"Let's find out what's the meetin's pleasure. Aimin' to fight the hull of York Province?"

Nat, who had returned to stand near Job, looked toward him and grinned dubiously. A solid man in fustian began to jump up and down.

"Fight 'em all," he shouted, "if need be, 'fore we leave Len to the hands of the oppressors—Easton an' Paterson an' that hog's bladder, Crean Brush, with his lordly air and his fancy woman."

The men about him nodded and muttered approval. He drove on:

[45]

"Hell's fire take 'em, an' Jedge Chandler, too, an' butcherin' Billy Tryon an'—an' the tyrant who hires Tryon."

He ran out of breath. Kathan's voice was dry:

"Want to point out to the meetin' that what we've jest heard Billy Negus holler is what Len Spaulding's in jail for speakin'. Treason, that's what 'tis, and no loyal man'll bide an' listen to more of it."

Will hooted and others followed his lead, crying derision after Kathan, who had turned from the crowd and was walking away, a mutely accusing figure. Job was half inclined to follow him, but he met Hooker's estimating eyes and remained. Dr. Harvey spoke hastily to the moderator, then lifted his own voice to break the irresolute silence.

"Now," he cried, "haste will benefit no one. This is a question that demands judgmatical consideration."

His spectacles flashed, his hooked nose hacked the air as he went on, stretching each word into a hollow sound: No treason had been spoken and none intended. The quarrel was with York; not with His Majesty, who nevertheless was served by rascals. All who loved freedom, whether or not they honored the King, soon would have the opportunity to uphold a new instrument of liberty.

"I mean," he proclaimed, with another thrust of his nose, "the Provincial Congress of Massachusetts, soon to assemble in Cambridge town, a body of true patriots with whom Cumberland County's freemen would do well to ally themselves."

He smiled at the stir of interest and held up an admonishing finger.

"Now, then! Rash action will not serve our imperiled neighbor. We must consider; we must consult. Wherefore, Mr. Moderator, I do move that you be empowered to select a committee who will meet with the true men of Brattleboro and Putney; aye, and those of Guilford and Westminster, as well—and to adopt such measures as may—befit the emergency."

Men snickered. Dr. Harvey allowed himself the trace of a grin when a dozen voices seconded his motion and the meeting bawled assent. A few week noes roused laughter. Behind Job, Hooker said quietly:

"You didn't vote."

There was nothing more than inquiry on the ruddy face.

"I'm new here," Job explained, "and no friend of politicking."

"Neuter?" Hooker pressed. His mildness might have been a snare.

"If it's only neuters who want to hold their land and work it in peace."

"No," the other said slowly, "that's what most of us want. Only—"

He paused. The meeting's dangerous entity was dissolving. Lately baleful, now shabby, men talked in low voices as they trudged away. Hooker laid a hand on Job's arm, guided him to the steps of the unfinished meetinghouse, and urged:

"Visit with me for a spell."

They sat together in silence that had grown awkward before at last the elder broke it.

"I presumed," he ventured, "that Amos's brother would be of his mind."

"I know," Job answered. "Mistake, though. Didn't see eye to eye, Amos and me."

He could find only friendliness on the other's face and went on more confidently:

"My mother, she came of Quaker folks. Favor her, I guess."

"And you disapprove of the meeting and what it has done?"

Job hesitated. It might be wiser to hold his tongue, but his companion's warm interest was persuasive.

"Don't aim to praise or blame. Came here to live peaceful and as I please."

Hooker rubbed his knees thoughtfully.

"Most of us here," he said at length, "came out of bondage of one sort or another to find the same peace and freedom you desire. We're plain people who hold all men should be equal under law that they, themselves, establish. So far, you agree?"

"Maybe," Job offered warily, lest the man's companionable manner sway him.

[47]

"Well, then," the elder pursued, "we haven't found here what we came a-seeking—yet. York gentry impose York's law on us. Many hold that this is tyranny and not to be endured."

He looked hopefully at his companion and then intoned:

" 'The Prince that wanteth understanding is also a great oppressor.' Proverbs, twenty-eight, sixteen. Wherefore, friend, we hold it right and just to oppose York rule."

The dark eyes were expectant. Job grinned.

"If we've come to matching texts, I'm minded of another that bids us render unto Caesar the things that are his."

"Well, now!" Hooker exclaimed with pleasure. "A reading man!"

"Quite a lot of Stockbridge folks," Job replied dryly, "can read." He regretted his sarcasm when his companion flushed.

Nat approached, leading his horse, and paused beside them. Hooker hailed him pleasantly, but Job shook his head in response to his host's look of inquiry and watched him mount and ride away.

"I hear," the elder resumed, "you've had a—well, troublesome time since you came into town."

"You could call it that," Job conceded.

"And you're still resolved to take no part in the present quarrel?"

"Harming no one," the other persisted, "meddling with nothing, working my pitch."

"You're overhopeful, my friend."

"And maybe obstinate," Job added, smiling. "If I can't live to my taste here, there's empty land a-plenty, north or west."

"You think you can find peace there?" Hooker inquired. "Don't deceive yourself, friend."

He cast his speech again into the nasal singsong.

"For I say unto you that you can take the wings of the morning and dwell in the uttermost parts of this land, yet still you will not find peace while plain men strive for freedom that the lordly deny them."

He laid his hand on Job's shoulder, shook it gently, and resuming his natural voice, pursued:

[48]

"That I do truly believe, friend. In time, it will be made clear to you. Bide here and work your pitch and learn. You cannot escape God's purpose."

"I still hold that God's purpose—" Job began stubbornly. He checked himself and recognizing the vanity of further argument, grinned into Hooker's concerned face.

"Elder," he amended, "I'll follow your counsel one step, at least. I'll go to the town clerk and record my deed."

Dr. Solomon Harvey sat down behind his office table, pushed aside books, a mortar and pestle, a stained alembic, and a box that leaked gray powder. Then, setting his spectacles more firmly, he examined the deed to Lot Ninety-four.

The paper crackled as the physician–town clerk turned it over. He scowled, as if he wished it were the applicant's neck he held between his stained hands. The scents of drugs and dust weighted the air of this untidy chamber. A human skull, perched on a shelf beside slanting volumes, grinned at Job. It was not a cheerful room, but it failed to depress the visitor. Dr. Harvey might become less wary when he found that the deed was in order. He might even welcome the new freeholder to Dummerston and permit him to ask an urgent question.

No young woman so fair could live, or even visit, in any town without all being aware of her name and whose dwelling she graced. It had been scarce ten minutes since he had met her in Harvey's dooryard. She had come out of the house with a lardy matron and a sunburned man who had been at town meeting. Never before, Job reflected with awe, had so much of importance happened to him in so scant a time. The ambitions that had brought him to Dummerston and all his future intentions had been shaken out and redirected. God, surely, had had a hand in opening a new prospect, more spacious and uplifting than the view from Job's hilltop.

Dr. Harvey laid down the paper and leaned back in his chair. His spectacles magnified the accusing eyes he turned upon his caller.

"A legal deed," the physician was admitting grudgingly. "You wish me to record it?"

Job nodded. It was best to wait. Harvey, if questioned in his present ill temper, likely enough would withhold the name of the beguiling vision. The waist bound by the brown shortgown had been incredibly slender; the bodice had been molded with throat-closing loveliness.

"The fee," the owl-like voice announced, "will be one shilling," but when Job had produced it, the doctor let the coin lie upon the table while his bitter eyes raked the visitor up and down.

"'Tis my duty," Harvey said as though the words hurt him, "as clerk of this town to record your deed."

"Ehyah," Job agreed vaguely.

Below the red petticoat's hem, wool hose and square-toed shoes had only stressed the entrancing slenderness of her feet and ankles. Her nose had been short and straight; her hair, honey-colored; her mouth, cherry-bright, and her wide, gray eyes, meeting Job's for an instant, had uprooted his heart. Dr. Harvey drew a hissing breath.

"It is also my duty as a patriot," he pursued in a hooting tone, "to warn you that this town will welcome no Tory."

Job stared at the creased forbidding face.

"Happens," he retorted, finding his voice at last, "I'm not a Tory. I—"

Harvey slammed a palm down upon the tabletop as though flattening falsehood.

"Oh, no!" he cried and rocked in his chair. "Who brought you into Dummerston, sir? Who but the Yorkish, Toretical, cutthroat, high-church, tea-swilling minion of tyranny—Crean Brush, no less?"

The hooked nose lunged.

"Don't try to deny it. You were seen, sir."

"Now, hold on," Job begged. "I was seen helping Mr. Brush draw his shay from a mudhole; I was seen taking a lift from him by way of thanks. Nothing more."

[50]

His temples were throbbing; his throat grew tight. Harvey ignored the explanation. His lens-enlarged eyes glittered.

"I knew your brother, sir. His death I do deplore. He was welcome in Dummerston."

"And I am not, because I helped a stranger?"

The doctor dismissed the inquiry with a wave of a snuff-stained handkerchief.

"D'ye stand there and claim that was all? You did not prevent Leonard Spaulding from giving Bildad Easton what he well deserves? You did not see the Leftenant led away into captivity yet raise neither hand nor voice? You have not consorted with Alexander Kathan, who, through mischance, is still an assessor of this town, yet suspect? Don't lie to me, sir. We have watched you well—and liked little we have seen."

"I have told you no lie."

If the young woman were to return, she would see the new-comer standing, browbeaten like a school dunce. The thought seemed to bring her into the stuffy room and discredit further meekness. Job heard himself saying:

"Furthermore, it is possible, sir, that I don't care a stiver for your likes or dislikes. Have you considered that?"

"What is this?" Harvey shrilled, only half believing.

Job tingled as though he had swallowed another long draft of Kathan's brew.

"And hereafter," he went on, "you may speak more softly. I am not hard of hearing."

He thought the tall girl would have admired the edge to his voice, though a remote portion of his own mind decried it.

"I came to Dummerston," Job told the speechless town clerk, "to find a peaceful living and to your house, expecting common politeness. Wrong, both times, seems."

Harvey, recovering, drew breath with a whooping sound and looked about him, as though for assistance. He considered the muscular person who loomed above the table, and said in a strangled tone:

"I can promise you, sir, this will not end here. You will be—unwise to settle in Dummerston."

"I already have settled," Job pointed out and added as the physician inflated himself for further speech, "My fee lies there. Be pleased to enter my deed."

Harvey's head jerked so viciously that Job could almost hear a great beak snap. The doctor trimmed a quill with trembling fingers, pulled a folio toward him from the table's end, and fell to writing. The pen scratched and sputtered. Its wielder finished the transcription, sprinkled sand upon it, and held out the deed to its owner.

"Little good will it do you," Harvey promised and swallowed thickly before he added, "I do not think you will bide long on Lot Ninety-four."

"That is as may be," Job retorted. He pocketed the paper and turned to leave.

"You shall hear more of this," the doctor cried after him.

7

JOB STRODE from the house, looked about him, and forgot the physician's warning.

The settlement's street lay empty in midday's sunlight, but a handful of persons lingered on the common. He squinted, hopeful that he might see a comely young woman in red petticoat and brown shortgown among them.

It was as well that she was not there, since the thin possibility had left him breathless. He shrugged and stepped out briskly. There was work crying to be done and half the day already spent.

He turned by the meetinghouse into the road over the hill. Cold air, smarting on his face, urged him to walk still faster. The sky was fiery blue, and wayside maples were paying out gold leaves from their dwindling store. He could not recall another day so fine.

It had been providential, he reflected with awe and satisfaction, that Amos had framed so ample a house. Job, until now, had thought it overlarge for a solitary man. Its size had become a happy portent.

Nat and his wife were still at the table when their guest entered the kitchen. Betty rose and bore away the baby. Her husband explained that they had not expected Job back so soon, else they would have waited dinner for him. Will had not returned. Likely, he had gone to ready the folks in the nearby settlement for the conference today's meeting had voted.

"Look," Nat went on, scanning the other more closely, "well pleased with yourself. Deed recorded?"

"Wal, then!" he exclaimed when Job had nodded. "Now you're a proper freeholder. Calls for a tot of rum, I'd say."

He hurried to the cupboard. Betty, returning, brought a wooden spoon, gave it to her guest, and thrust the stewpot toward him. Nat brought two full horn cups, handed one to Job, and raised its mate.

"Health! Neighbor, you're real welcome."

His companion drank, blinked, and offered at length:

"Doesn't seem so, exactly."

"Eh?"

Wily purpose had begun to form in Job's mind. He hid it by rueful confession:

"Town clerk wasn't—well, real friendly. Recorded my deed but advised me not to settle."

"That," Betty burst out, "is Solomon Harvey all over. Can't abide anyone thinks a smitch different from him."

She shrank under her husband's astonished stare, then blushed with pleasure when he nodded.

"Ehyah. Better if he politicked less an' physicked more. Wouldn't worry over what Solomon says."

"It's not just him," Job pursued craftily. "Other folks, too, don't seem—friendly."

[53]

"Takes time," Nat assured. "Find 'em neighborly enough when they come to know you."

"Now," the other pursued as indifferently as possible, "there was a man, red and rugged, with two women. They met me in Harvey's dooryard yet never passed the time of day."

He bent over the stew. Betty reflected:

" 'Red an' rugged'? Dan'l Houghton, most likely. One woman real portly? Then 'twas Dan'l an' his wife, Beulah."

"T'other one," Job said carelessly, yet did not look up, "was younger and—better favored."

"Melissa Sprague, Beulah's sister, most likely," Nat hazarded and his wife added dryly:

"Will's betrothed, one of these days, wouldn't wonder. Courtin' her steady, anyway."

"Do tell!" their guest said and went on eating. He had learned the young woman's name and with whom she lived, and was not greatly dismayed to hear that Will would be his rival.

Will did not own a hundred acres, free and clear, or a house already framed—possessions that must recommend their owner to any prudent maid. Job thrust himself back from the table.

"Past time," he said, "I got up to my pitch."

Nat, standing with head slanted, did not seem to have heard.

"Someone comin' a-horse," he said and opened the door.

Job heard the rhythm of hoofs break and end. Nat stood aside for the visitor to enter.

"Wal, Dan'l," he hailed. "Just talkin' of you, in a way."

The face of the intruder was redder than when Job last had seen him in Dr. Harvey's dooryard. He nodded to Betty and, breathing loudly, fumbled in his frock's bosom.

"This here's the new neighbor—" Nat began, but Houghton had drawn out a paper and hastily had unfolded it.

"Solomon," he interrupted with anguished haste, "wants I should read him this here. It says—"

He bent over the document and recited in a tight voice:

"Province of New York, Cumberland County, Town of Dummerston, October 29th, 1774: To either of the constables in the town of Dummerston, Greeting. In the name and behalf of the freeholders of the above town and by the authority of the same, we command you forthwith to warn all persons who have not been in this town one year and are liable to be a public charge to depart out of this town with their families, if any they have, and particularly one Job Aldrich, late of Stockbridge in the Province of Massachusetts Bay. By the hand of Solomon Harvey, town clerk."

Houghton looked up with face scarlet and eyes so deeply meshed in wrinkles that it seemed he was about to cry.

"Wal—there 'tis," he blurted, wheeled about, and clumped toward the door. Nat's strained voice checked him.

"Dan'l, hold on. What's all this? Job ain't a—a pauper."

Houghton stood with his hand on the latch.

"Dunno 'bout that," he faltered. "Done like Solomon said I should. Constable, ain't I?"

He fled. They heard the hoofbeats fade away. Nat said stupidly to Job:

"Solomon's warned you out of town."

"Why? For what?" the other asked so blankly that his host assumed an ill-fitting confidence.

It was Grants' custom, he informed Job, thus to deal with strangers if they were likely to become public charges. Men, so warned, were not obliged to leave but, having been notified, could not thereafter ask the town for aid.

"Still don't see," he pursued, scowling, "why Solomon picked you out. Highhanded, I'd call it."

"Not real heartening," Job agreed grimly. "Just as well to know, though, that the town wishes me elsewhere."

Betty muttered beneath her breath, and Nat twisted his hands. He said wretchedly, as his guest rose:

"That ain't so. Find most folks'll be neighborly; that is, if you're minded to stay."

"Aim to," the other answered curtly and stepped toward the door.

Job had driven himself uphill so ruthlessly that now his lungs rebelled and forced him to halt beside a blazed beech on his property's boundary. The rich, dark soil beneath his feet, the great trees about him, the brook that wove a silvery thread of sound through the autumnal silence soothed and sustained him, but only for a moment. Dismay overtook him.

Before Job had even spoken to her, Melissa Sprague would learn from her sister's husband that the newcomer had been warned away from Dummerston like a stray dog. He shrugged, and resumed his climb more slowly and paused again at his clearing's edge while he rid his mind of soreness by picturing his house as it would look, completed.

It would stand, foursquare and sound, with a newly included second chimney and hearth to make the bedchamber extra snug. It would be a sightly dwelling. He thought of Melissa again and resolved, for her approval, to adorn his home with coatings of red ocher and skim milk.

The day was wasting while he stood idle. The angle of the sunlight reproached him. Job roused and went briskly toward the sheathing he and Kathan had piled. He heard brush rattle behind him and a thick voice crying:

"You, there; halt, sir."

The command snatched away Job's breath. He jerked about and waited, half-defiantly, while three men pushed from the forest and hurried toward him. The foremost called again:

"I am the law, sir. Don't stir."

Job knew them now. He had seen the doughy Easton, Benjamin Gorton, whose smitten eye had blackened further, and the sheriff, Paterson, marching Leonard Spaulding away to jail. Here came more trouble, a panicky inner voice whispered. Job strove to ignore the warning. He had done nothing to offend Yorkers.

The sheriff's face seemed swollen by internal pressure that had bulged his eyes and squeezed his voice into a throaty squeal. He halted before Job, surveyed him wrathfully, and then demanded of Easton:

"This the rascal?"

"Him," the deputy confirmed emphatically. "Ain't a bit of doubt."

Paterson coughed and spat largely. In the boding pause, Gorton waved a club and sidled closer to Job.

"We're here," the sheriff began balefully, "to have a word with ye, me man. I hailed ye yesterday. Why did ye not halt?"

It was wise to go carefully; it was best to make no further enemies, however arrogant their manner. Job answered:

"You didn't say you were the sheriff. Besides, I had an errand to do."

Paterson took another forward step. His deputies were edging in on the suspect's either hand.

"Hereafter, ye yokel," the sheriff counseled in a pent voice, "when I command ye to halt, ye are to do so immejitly. D'ye understand?"

Mr. Brush had spoken with the same odd accent. Job found it affronting, but he held his peace and nodded.

"Now then, Aldrich," Paterson demanded, "where are ye from? Bay Province, eh? 'Tis maggoty with rebels, and no doubt ye are one of 'em."

"Peculiar, if I'm a rebel, that Dummerston folks should warn me out of town."

"Warned ye, indeed?" For an instant, surprise made Paterson waver. "And who was it that 'warned' ye, eh? Solomon Harvey? A contumacious scoundrel that it'll be me pleasure, one day, to hang."

The deputies stirred and muttered. The scowl still lingered on the sheriff's face. He rubbed thick palms together and said at length:

" 'Tis possible we've misjudged ye. That, we'll determine. Now, Job Aldrich, you witnessed on the morning of October 28th, at or about nine o'clock, the unprovoked and murderous assault on me deputy, here, by Leonard Spaulding of Dummerston. Eh?"

It was plain enough now. Job was expected to betray a neighbor.

"Perhaps," Paterson was saying with mocking courtesy, "I don't make myself clear."

"Clear enough," Job answered with more confidence than he felt, "but I cannot answer."

"And why not, sir? Ye have eyes; ye have ears."

The sheriff's face was acquiring a purplish hue. His arrogance already had set pulses to pounding in Job's ears. They quickened as he answered:

" 'Murderous' I would not call it, since he was scarce pricked by the fork. Whether 'twas 'unprovoked,' I do not know."

He expected explosion, but the sheriff smiled broadly.

"Do ye not? Ye'll come with us to Brattleboro and there post bond to appear as a witness, or away ye go to Westminster jail as accessory to Spaulding's felonies."

"Accessory?" Job objected.

"Accessory," Paterson insisted. "At need, me deputy will charge you with being Spaulding's accomplice. Eh, Bildad?"

"Indeed and indeed," Easton recited glibly, "he aided Spaulding in assaulting me and urged him to further violence."

Gorton chuckled. Job, gasped, then faced his accuser:

"Well you know," he retorted, no longer trying to keep heat from his voice, "that 'twas I who kept him from pricking you behind, as well as before."

The flabby deputy looked inquiringly toward Paterson then turned and struck Job across the mouth.

"Don't give me the lie, you bastard," he cried.

Job looked stupidly for an instant at the red fingers he had pressed to his lips. He gave a hoarse sound and lunged at Easton.

"Resists arrest!" Paterson cried. "Take him, boys."

Gorton caught the raging man by the shoulder and swung him about. As he twisted free, the deputy brought down his club. . . .

Job drew himself up to hands and knees. The darkness and the roaring faded. Pain fed a starkly simple intention.

"Take care!" Paterson shouted.

Job came up like a released spring. Gorton, bleakly grinning, lifted his club high. Job made no attempt to avoid the blow. Instead, he stepped in and drove his fist against the deputy's uninjured eye. . . .

Beyond the anguish that enclosed him, he heard dim voices speak inconsequences.

"Ye hit too hard," one complained.

"Wish it had been harder," another wheezed.

Hands found Job's armpits, lifted and held him erect until the world ceased whirling and the blur before him solidified into the sheriff's congested face. Easton was clinging tightly to the prisoner's right arm. Gorton clutched the left with one hand. He had clapped the other to his eye and was swearing steadily.

Paterson said with relish:

"Ask and ye shall receive, eh, Aldrich? Witness or jailbird: which will it be?"

"I'll not testify," Job said through locked teeth.

"Jail it is, then," the sheriff told him with ghastly cheer. "Bring him along, boys."

He waved them forward, but Easton hung back. He offered uneasily:

"Trouble, like as not, if we take him through Dummerston settlement."

Paterson scowled, then nodded agreement.

"Better," he confirmed, "if we cut across the hills."

8

THE SUN WAS low when the crooked trail that posse and captive had followed through the forest brought them out upon the Great Road near Westminster. It was dusk when they climbed the last long slope into the village.

The highway ran broad and straight between opposing rows of lighted houses to a church, looming tall in the twilight, and dividing there, skirted the structure's either flank, to unite again beyond it. Pain, like a loose weight, rolled about in Job's skull. His escort, he considered with dreary satisfaction, was scarcely less exhausted than he. Easton and Gorton lurched along at either shoulder, and Paterson, trudging in the rear, was too spent to taunt his prisoner.

Beyond the meetinghouse, a square mansion, lofty and arrogant among its humbler neighbors, was ablaze with lights. A still larger, darkened building lifted its black hipped roof and cupola against a paler sky.

The posse turned Job out of the highway, stumbled across an area still littered with chips and shavings, and halted before Cumberland County's new courthouse and jail. It boomed like a drum while the sheriff hammered on its door. This opened cautiously, flatly outlining a man's figure against dim, interior glow. A cylindrical lantern of perforated metal, hanging from a beam, cast freckles of light along a hall that ended at a staircase.

The deputies dragged Job down the passage, which was filled with the scents of fresh lumber, stale liquor, and a foul privy, to a cell door. The jailer opened it. Paterson's hand between the captive's shoulders pushed him toward a tallow dip that, set on a stool, feebly illumined a narrow room with a single barred window.

The door closed. The key ground in the lock. While Job stood, vainly striving to muster strength enough to bear him to the nearer of twin cots against the far wall, the man who lay upon the other, rolled over and sat up.

"Now what?" he snarled.

Job leaned against the door and wondered how much longer, even with this support, he could stand.

Shadows, as he rose and lifted the dip, flowed down over Leonard Spaulding's face. The wavering flame struck sparkles from his stiff gray hair.

He demanded, "Who be you an' why—?" advanced a step, and then exclaimed, "B'God, 'tis the newcomer—Amos's brother."

Job could only nod. Above the bristling beard stubble, Spaulding's eyes were narrow.

"What on earth—?" he began, then moved forward quickly and got an arm about the other's body.

"Best," the words buzzed in Job's ear, "that you lay down for a spell."

Spaulding stepped back after a moment and considered the still form, spread upon the cot.

"Tetch of somethin'd do you no real harm. Jailer keeps a dram shop t'other side of the hall for the pleasure of the God-damn' Honorable Court."

He went to the wicket and shouted:

"Whipple, Pollard Whipple! Horn of rum here, an' lively."

He returned at last, treading carefully, cup in hand. Job choked over the harsh fluid.

"Dretful stuff," Spaulding acknowledged, "but 'twill serve, mebby."

The other drank and lay back again. Darkness flowed over him. . . .

A hand, fastened upon his shoulder, shook Job, reviving the pain in his battered head. He blinked up into Spaulding's concerned face.

"Wal!" the man said with extravagant relief. "Been comfortin' myself with the thought that corpses seldom snore. Breakfast's so long past, must be nigh dinnertime. Wouldn't want you to miss that treat."

He peered more closely at his cellmate and asked in an altered voice:

"How be you, Aldrich?"

Job was slowly tying one fact to another. This dirty chamber was a cell. He was in jail, Westminster jail. The sheriff and his deputies had marched him here.

"Could be worse," he answered and sat up, carefully, for the movement refilled his head with anguish.

"Beholden to you," he added at length.

Spaulding hesitated.

"Obleeged to you, seems," he corrected. "That is, less'n Whipple's been lyin' even more than commonly. Says you're here because you wouldn't be Crown's witness against me. Eh?"

Job nodded dully.

"That commenced it, I guess. Then a deputy, Gorton by name, clubbed me."

"Did he, now? Bastard clubbed me, too."

Spaulding ran a finger over the crusted wound above his forehead and added with satisfaction:

"Nigh ruined his eye for him, though."

"Guess," Job admitted ruefully, "I blacked t'other. I—I lost my temper. Regret it, now."

Spaulding ignored the contrite admission. He slapped his knee and acclaimed:

"You punched Benjy, too? Now praise God for his mercies."

He peered more closely at his cellmate and demanded:

"What ails you? Cause for pride, ain't it?"

"Not to me." Conscience demanded that Job explain himself, though he felt the seed would be cast on barren ground. "Came here seeking peace. Footed it clear from Stockbridge to be shut of quarreling and fighting."

He compared his earlier hopes with his present plight and found he could go no further. Spaulding's sharp eyes were raking him.

"Wal," he offered at length, "if that's why you come, you was—misdirected. Fightin', Aldrich, scarce has commenced in Cumberland County. Wait an' see."

Job looked about him.

"Seems," he offered with a forced smile, "as if I might be obliged to wait."

He swallowed with a clicking sound. Spaulding hesitated, then offered briskly:

"Get out today, if you've a mind to. Mean it," he insisted, meeting Job's disbelieving stare. "Send for Paterson, tell him you'll be witness against me, put up bond to appear, and you'll go free, quicker'n scat."

"No."

"Why not? Save yourself at small cost to me. Once Bully Paterson an' Fancy-nancy Jedge Chandler gets me into court, I'll be pork, anyways."

[62]

"No."

Spaulding nodded, as though he had added a sum correctly.
"What I figgered," he said. "You're a bullheaded fool,
though."

Again he scanned his companion closely and asked at length:
"What else be ye: Whig? Tory? Yorker? Neuter?"

"None of them, I guess," Job replied with care. "I want to live
my way and let my neighbors live theirs. I don't hold with striving and fighting. It's my belief that one violence leads to a worse
and folks should be friendly with each other."

"Quaker talk," Spaulding scoffed.

"Maybe," Job granted. "My mother was of Quaker stock."

"Did she teach you to assail dep'ty sheriffs?" the other inquired with a grin.

Job was thankful that the jailer, a grimed and toothless person, entered at this moment with the prisoners' dinner of dubious
stew and tasteless rye-and-Injun bread. He lingered to swap in-
sults with Spaulding, who relished the exchange. When, at last,
Whipple withdrew, Job fell into easier talk with his cellmate,
who got small comfort from the tale of Dummerston's late town
meeting. Resolutions and conferences, in his opinion, were a
poor way to rescue anyone.

"Wal," Spaulding said resignedly, "there'll be better times
comin'. We can always think of them."

"Right now," his companion retorted, "wouldn't say they'd
got far forward."

He thought that Spaulding had not heard for he sat, staring
at nothing with narrowed eyes. At length he nodded as though
he had reached some obscure decision and offered in a wary voice:

"Forrader than many think. Someday, the Grants'll be free,
Aldrich, free an' united, east an' west, spite of Cumberland
County dolts who still uphold York or Hampshire or Massachusetts. Time'll come when we'll belong to nobody but ourselves. That's what the strife you decry is furtherin'."

"Further it much," Job asked maliciously, "by pitchforkin'
Easton?"

"Hah!" Spaulding retorted. "Furthered it some."

He bent forward and went on in a husky half-whisper: Men who already were ridding the western Grants of York authority were helping their brethren here in the east toward similar revolt. Emissaries from Bennington frequently came by stealth into Cumberland County. On the day of his assault upon the deputy sheriff, Spaulding had had one of these agents hidden in his house.

"You seen the damned reckless rascal," he reminded Job, who nodded, vividly recalling the brown stranger with the merry eyes. "York's outlawed him, along with Ethan Allen, Seth Warner, an' the rest of 'em. Bildad missed a prize, that day. Twenty pound, on the barrelhead, to whomsoever takes Alvah Reynolds—dead or alive."

One day's imprisonment had ended and another crept after it. The idleness they had imposed was waxing torment to Job. He paced the strait limits of the cell until his feet ached, then sat and looked out from the single barred window.

A dingy building, with a sign in faded lettering that proclaimed it "The Royal Inn," stood at the foot of the long slope that the courthouse crowned. Firewood had been heaped untidily beside it, and across the way, a log schoolhouse and a small dwelling faced the tavern. Beyond them, the Great Road ran north through lately cleared flatland into autumnal haze.

While Job watched the occasional traveler out of sight or peered down upon children at play about the school, his mind plodded a dreary circle. If he had done this, he might still be free. If he had not done that, he would not now be caught in this stinking trap, with his possessions and hopes imperiled.

Recoiling from further profitless thought, Job sprang up and resumed his pacing until his overtried cellmate implored him in the Deity's name to light somewhere and perch for a spell.

"Might try a mite of patience under affliction," Spaulding prescribed toward the end of their second day together. "Court sets, a week hence. If you'll be Crown's witness—"

"I've told you no."

"Great day, Aldrich! Jest butcher yourself."

Long after his companion had gone to sleep, that night, Job lay tautly wakeful, futilely reviewing his plight and finding no solution. He had got himself into trouble beyond redemption. In truth, he had taken his first step toward disaster when he had turned his back on Stockbridge and had set out for the Grants with what seemed now a piteous trust.

The husk mattress crackled as Job turned over. He had expected to find, here at the edge of wilderness, peace and security on his own land. It appeared that he had bought, instead of a haven, a hundred acres of battlefield.

He heard a late-faring horseman ride down the hill and, halting, halloo before the tavern. Job thought resignedly of his land and a tall young woman, both lost to him now. He thrust them out of mind and, in fancy, followed the Great Road north to the farthest settlement and beyond, where the highway dwindled to a fading trail and this, in turn, became no more than a line of blazed trees, leading deeper still into unpeopled forest. In that empty land, he might have found the tranquillity he sought.

He fell asleep and woke to find sunlight in his eyes and Whipple bawling curses in his ear.

If his lordship would deign to rouse, the jailer derided, there was a gentleman to see him, though perhaps Baron Aldrich was not in the mood to grant audience to one so humble as the Honorable Crean Brush.

Beneath his sarcasm, Whipple was impressed. He spared Job no time to order himself but hustled him, pursued by Spaulding's scandalous comments, across the hall and into a rum-scented chamber. The visitor, cloak thrown back and flowered waistcoat shining, leaned against the counter and sipped a morning draft. He set down the pewter tankard and stepped forward.

"Me dear man!" Brush exclaimed, his voice as warm as his handclasp, and turned to the jailer. "Inquire Mr. Aldrich's pleasure. Nothing to drink? Then, ye may leave, Pollard."

Whipple unwillingly retired. Brush enveloped Job with concern. He had returned from business elsewhere only last night and, learning belatedly of his friend's plight, had come at once to offer his services.

"A lamentable mistake, so it is. Sheriff Paterson is a sound man but sometimes overzealous. Now, how can I serve ye? I'm not without influence. If 'tis a bondsman ye need, command me."

He smoothed his waistcoat with small, self-approving pats. His voice and smile were so hearty that Job found himself blurting the whole sorry tale. When he had ended, the other shook his head and clucked deploringly.

"Man, dear, I warned ye against Dummerston folks."

"'Twas none of them brought me here."

Brush ignored the retort. He pursued:

"A tempest in a teapot, nothing more. Ye testify against the rascally Spaulding and 'tis done with."

"I have said," Job returned heavily, "that I would not."

"Ye're obstinate," Brush sighed, "and difficult to aid, yet Alexander Kathan speaks well of ye, and he's a loyal man. There are too few such in Dummerston to keep a single one imprisoned. Ye said on our first acquaintance that ye were a true subject of His Majesty, God bless him. And ye're still so, I judge."

"Ehyah," Job granted, with the uneasy feeling that he was being worked into a corner.

"Suppose," said Brush with an absent look in his greenish eyes, "that ye're arraigned before Judge Chandler, charged with no more than, say, resisting arrest. Suppose ye receive only a light sentence. 'Tis essential," he went on with bitterness, "that ye be punished, for that will recommend ye to the Dummerston rascality and, after your release, ye'll be welcomed by all the chief villains in that seditious settlement."

He hesitated a moment, pursing his lips, and then asked quickly:

"In return for such clemency, would you pretend to be a rebel, like the rest of 'em, yet keep me informed of the scoundrels' intentions? Eh, sir?"

"Now, wait," Job begged, but the other seemed not to hear him and continued with an oratorical roll in his voice.

"I submit to you that it is better to aid in restoring peace to

Cumberland County than to stand aside while the wicked tear it further asunder. Me dear man, consider the reward: Ye'll be secure in possession of your property, with more to accrue, if ye desire it; ye'll be well paid for information ye bring us; lastly, but by no means least, ye'll be supporting the rule of His Majesty, who does not forget loyal servants.

"I beg ye," the sleek man urged, preening himself, "not to answer me now and hastily. I urge you to reflect upon me offer and accept it for your country's and, particularly, for your own welfare.

"Ye'll have ample time," Brush hurried on, "before court sits, for judicious thought. When ye are ready to agree, as I pray ye will be, word to your jailer will bring me here again, instanter."

Against his will, the eloquent persuasion momentarily swayed Job. While he wavered, his companion drew his cloak about him and, stepping quickly to the door, shouted for Whipple.

"I shall await your decision," Brush assured the prisoner as the jailer led him away, "with confidence."

The cell door slammed behind Job. Spaulding, looking up, said nothing until Whipple's retreating footsteps had faded, then offered acidly:

"Begun to suspicion the Honorable Mr. Brush had spirited you away."

"No," Job returned and sat down heavily on his cot. For a moment, he evaded his cellmate's questing eyes, while an unwelcome inner voice persuasively recited the advantages that had been offered him. He could return to the land he had believed lost; court Melissa with new confidence; live at surface peace with his neighbors.

Job twisted about and desperately laid hold upon confession as the best means of hushing the seductive voice. He told Spaulding hoarsely:

"He promised to let me off easy, if I'd spy on Dummerston folks."

He leaned back and, having destroyed temptation, wondered how, even for a moment, he could have entertained it. Relief impelled him to tell his scowling companion the entire substance of Brush's proposal.

"Said no?" Spaulding inquired when Job had ended.

"I promised nothing. He bade me wait and consider."

"Hm! Better that way, I guess. Let the bastard stew. 'Bastard' is too flatterin' a pet name for the Honorable Crean Brush; him an' his scarlet woman."

Brush, Spaulding pursued with malevolent righteousness, had taken to himself a British officer's widow, who would have forfeited her pension had she married again.

"So Crean, he's wed her with the left hand and lives with her in the great house, nigh here. Built it with money he's wrung, York fashion, out of us folks. . . . Now what?"

Whipple had returned. He jerked a thumb toward Job.

"Movin' you," he announced. "Mr. Brush's orders. Step out."

"Fearful," Spaulding demanded, "he'll ketch somethin' if he bides here?"

"Treason's ketchin' an' you stink of it. Lively, Aldrich."

The jailer led his prisoner along the hall and, near the foot of the stair, locked him into the companion of his earlier cell. Job sat on a cot's edge and rested his head on his hands.

Days as identical as drops of water went by with only a waxing despair to distinguish one from another. Spaulding tried to engage his fellow captive in shouted discussions of Yorker iniquities, since these gratifyingly enraged Whipple, but Job was too despondent to encourage them. The new courthouse-jail already was verminous. He was becoming appallingly dirty and bearded. There was a sullen ache in his head, and new, inner heat kept him continually thirsty. Likely, he thought with faint concern, he had caught prison fever in this foul place.

He woke one morning to find the courthouse briskly astir. New voices spoke loudly in its hall; feet sounded on the stair, and there was movement in the chamber overhead.

The flustered jailer, appearing with the prisoner's breakfast, informed him spitefully that court was organizing and would begin its sessions on the morrow, but that Job's time was shorter still. Judge Chandler would examine him later today.

"Mr. Brush," Whipple said unwillingly, "bade me inquire if you had word for him."

"None," Job said at last.

9

*I*T WAS PAST noon when Whipple led the prisoner up the stair and into the uncompleted courtroom with its still-bare beams and studding. Three men were seated on the judges' bench, and Paterson, standing before it, broke off talk with them to jerk his head toward Job.

"Yonder he is, Your Worships."

He spoke as though the captive's appearance were sufficient evidence against him. The throned judges, the clerk at his desk below their bench, the men who had ceased their talk in the rear of the courtroom—all had turned to stare at the soiled and bearded figure. Their amused disdain ignited a small coal of anger in Job. Whatever the outcome, he would yield nothing to these well-clothed, well-fed, washed, and shaven folks.

The central figure of the lofty three whispered to his associates, and when they had nodded agreement, spoke. His manner was easy, yet Job sullenly resented the neat, gray wig and the black broadcloth habit, with falls of lace at its throat and wrists.

It was the court's wish, the fine gentleman was saying, that this hearing be informal. He clasped white hands before him and looked down with a tolerant smile.

"Now," he said, as though addressing an erring child, "I am Thomas Chandler, principal judge of Cumberland County's Inferior Court of Common Pleas. These"—he bowed in turn to the fat elder on his one hand and the small, foxy man on the other —"are my assistants: Judge Wells and Judge Sabin. We represent His Majesty's justice, which all men must obey. Do you understand?"

"I do," said Job. It was going to be easier than he had feared to resist this schoolmasterly person. Chandler's light voice chimed on:

"The court has been informed that the prisoner has refused to appear as a witness in the case of the Crown versus Leonard Spaulding. Furthermore, he has resisted arrest and has maintained a defiant attitude while in jail.

"Now, you know," Chandler protested, "it is your bounden duty to testify; it really is. Continued refusal will bring you into contempt of court and that would mean a prison sentence and, quite possibly, the confiscation of whatever property you may possess."

He paused to smile expectantly.

"Now that I have explained to you what penalties your wicked conduct will bring down upon you and have pointed out your duty, may I presume that you will be guided by me?"

"No."

Job's mentor gasped and had trouble regaining his superior pose. His face was almost as red as Paterson's.

"Is it possible," Chandler demanded of the culprit, "that you purposely are defying this honorable court?" and waited, eyebrows raised.

"I will not testify against Leftenant Spaulding," Job said clearly.

He got grim satisfaction out of Chandler's blank astonishment and the look of outrage that quickly replaced it.

"Now, by God," the judge began in a new, raw voice, "if a filthy hobbledehoy fancies for an instant that he can flout me—"

His fat associate muttered to him from behind a cushion of a hand and after an instant Chandler nodded reluctantly.

"Take the prisoner back," he bade Whipple, "and lock him up again."

[70]

He turned to the lowering sheriff and his words had new edge. "Spaulding's case is first on the docket. See to it that this man also is in court tomorrow morning. If he persists in his insolence—"

He left the threat hanging.

The cell door closed behind Job with a final sound. He went to the window. The afternoon was ending, too. There was an odd peacefulness in complete disaster. From his own cell, Spaulding lifted a raucous voice:

"Ain't freed you yet, Aldrich?"

"Not yet." The jauntiness sounded hollow.

"Come to terms with His High Mightiness?"

"No."

"Might better, m'lad." The speaker intended that his words should reach the courtroom. "All twelve apostles could appear for me tomorrow and 'twould help me none—not with Chandler on the bench. He don't like me, nor I him, though I've the better reasons. Tom Chandler, Sam Wells, and Noah Sabin are the rascals who—"

Whipple pounded along the hall. His outraged speech blurred Spaulding's tirade. While they yelped at each other, Job turned again to the window. Horses were tethered before The Royal Inn, and from an ox-drawn sled men were adding more wood to the nearby pile. Job pictured his clearing, half blue, half gold, in the sunset hour.

Down the hall, the quarrel had ended. Spaulding raised a more temperate voice:

"Still hold you're a knothead, Job, yet I'm beholden to you. Prove it when I get out of here—if ever. Sight better friend you've been than some I've trusted more."

"Well—" Job began and could go no further.

"Hope," his fellow prisoner pursued bitterly, "the neighbors and other folks had a real edifying time to their conference over me. Mourned, no doubt. Ain't done nothin' else."

Job left the window and lay upon his cot. He heard the company come downstairs with loud speech and laughter, clatter

[71]

along the hall, and depart. He did not stir or speak when Whipple brought a bowl and tallow dip and set them on the stool. Job's head was throbbing more painfully. He turned away from the light and fell asleep.

The dip had burned out when he woke. The courthouse was so still that he could hear the thudding of his own heart and a faint stirring in the outer darkness. It might be wind, yet it sounded more like the halting progress of a stray cow.

Spaulding began to snore. The bold trumpeting derided the punishment morning would bring him. Job recalled with sympathy the man's recent comment on his neighbor's enterprise. Few in Dummerston, it was plain, were of his friend's tough fiber.

The blast of sound seemed to throw Job from his cot. It came again as he got to his feet—a splintering crash that rocked the building. Whipple yelped and fled, pattering through the darkness to some indefinite refuge aloft. Spaulding's shout was lost in the muffled roar of voices. The courthouse door burst inward, and tumult poured along the hall like an undammed stream.

"Len!" someone cried. "Len, where be ye?"

"Who be you?"

"Jonathan Knight," the other returned with a nervous cackle. "Me an' the neighbors has come a-visitin'."

The passage filled with trampling and a tremulous, ruddy light. Job, pressing his face against the wicket's grille, saw men massing before Spaulding's cell. A grizzled elder held a torch aloft. Someone cried:

"Whipple's gone an' tuck the keys."

"Wal, chop the door apart," another called.

A burly figure, ax in hand, shouldered through the crowd. Will French looked about him in silent warning. The clamor dwindled as men gave way. Will balanced and struck. The blade flashed and bit deep. The axman wrenched it free. He struck again and again while bellowing hailed each blow.

The cell door swung back with its lock cut away. The crowd surged forward. There was shouting and pounding within the cell and then the flow reversed. Job saw Spaulding's gray crest

[72]

bob and vanish and reappear while madmen pulled him about, beat his shoulders, and yelled in his ear.

Knight's voice rose above the jubilation:

"All right, neighbors. Now we'll take Len home."

Others bawled endorsement. Some already were shuffling toward the shattered outer door. Spaulding's speech sawed through the uproar:

"Hold on, now. Aldrich's in t'other jail room. Ain't leavin' him?"

After an uncertain instant, a hollow voice demanded:

"And why not, pray?"

Job could picture the thrust of Dr. Solomon Harvey's beaked nose.

"Why not?" Spaulding echoed wrathfully. "Neighbor an' freeholder, ain't he?"

"A Tory dog," Harvey retorted, "and well kenneled here. Already has been warned out of town, and now we're rid of him."

Knight's dry voice supported the physician:

"Come to free you, Len, and none else. We're wastin' time."

"Be we?" Spaulding shrilled. "Squander a sight more 'fore I'll leave Job Aldrich prisoned. Got himself jailed 'cause he wouldn't appear against me."

Dispute boiled up. Knight shouted angrily at last:

"Well, for God's sake, free him then an' have done with it. Whar's French?"

The wicket in the door of Job's cell was a dark crisscrossing against the unstable torchlight. Will's head swung in and out of view as he hacked at the lock.

The broken portal slammed inward against the wall. For an instant Job wavered. He stifled senseless pride that inclined him to refuse release, and stepped forward, shamed and smarting, into the glow of the torch.

"Wal," its holder marveled. "So you're Aldrich? Never would have knowed you."

"Whew!"

It was Will's sole comment. He held his nose ostentatiously

[73]

as he strode down the hall to join those who crowded out through the doorway. Job followed. The shallow heartiness of the few who hailed him only made him feel more alien.

The night's still cold set him to shaking. Men were stumbling down the courthouse steps, and above the torch's guttering fire the sky was sown with stars. Spaulding called from the darkness: "Whar's Aldrich?"

Job answered, yet waited until the last straggler had moved off. He could hear, as he passed through the village where lights were rekindling, the feet of the marchers on the frozen road, far ahead. Beyond the settlement, he was compelled to halt and cling, gasping and quaking, to a tree until the violent chill had spent itself. When he recovered, no sound reached back from the darkness before him. It would properly requite the callous men who had freed and then deserted him, if he were to perish here, alone and unbefriended.

The maudlin self-pity grimly amused Job. In truth, none of his rescuers, save Spaulding, would care a stiver whether he lived or died. He best could requite their indifference by getting back to the Frenches without their aid. He moved on, closing his mind to thought of the miles before him.

Activity and the sullen, inner smoldering could not entirely repel the cold. It crept up his sleeves, leaked down his neck, and numbed his feet. The road was an endless gray smear upon the gloom. He tried to ignore the effort each step required.

By the angle of Charles's Wain, it was past midnight when Job limped by Putney's black huddle of houses. The worst, he assured himself, was over, but after he had turned into the way that angled off from the Great Road toward Dummerston settlement, another chill laid hold upon him. When the seizure diminished, he knew with a pang of fright how nearly he was finished.

Job looked about him and belatedly recognized that he was gaping at possible salvation. Nearby, there was a break in the trees' dark circle and the aperture was half filled by an obstacle that he finally identified as a chimney and roof, outlined against the sky. He staggered toward them, felt a rutted way beneath

[74]

his feet, stumbled, and paused. The shout he attempted was little more than a croak.

Deeper gloom before him resolved itself into a building. Job could smell the sweetish scent of kine. He crept along the barn, supporting himself against its wall. At length he found and clung to the latch of a heavy door. Warm air poured over him as he pulled upon it. He heard a horse snort and the loud breathing of cattle. He got the door closed behind him, advanced blindly, tangled his legs in loose hay, and pitched forward. . . .

It seemed to Job that he scarcely had slept, yet, rousing against his will, he saw that darkness had faded and the sky was golden beyond the open door. Again, he felt the pain that had waked him: a bruising pressure upon his ribs. He looked down stupidly at a firelock's muzzle and listened without immediate comprehension to a cold, clear voice.

"I shall not bid you again," Melissa Sprague warned. "Stand up at once."

IO

JOB'S EYES traveled without belief along the leveled musket. Its hammer was at full cock; its flint looked no harder than the girl's narrowed gray eyes. Her finger stirred within the trigger guard, and Job, still embedded in hay that had been pitched from the mow, moaned in alarm and tried to rise.

His knees gave way and threw him against a manger. A red cow stared up at him with more sympathy than he found in Melissa's face. She had stepped back while he reeled, but she still held the musket ready and, when at last he stood erect, demanded:

"Why were you skulking here?"

She was as bright and chill as the dawn and must lately have risen. Below her homespun gown, slim ankles were bare and her feet had been thrust into oversize slippers.

"I was not skulking," Job objected and tried to rid his person of clinging hay.

"What else? Thieving?"

He answered with what scant dignity he could assemble:

"I'm Aldrich. I'm a Dummerston freeholder."

Melissa's eyes widened. Could this—this scarecrow indeed be the well-favored young man she had seen for an instant, weeks ago, in Dr. Harvey's dooryard? She asked coldly:

"Should that recommend you?"

Nevertheless, she lowered her firelock, hesitated, and then inquired:

"Is it your custom to lodge in other folks' barns? I heard you were to Westminster and—"

He completed for her:

"And in jail? That is true."

By her doubtful look, he knew she had not heard of last night's rescue.

"A runaway," Melissa said slowly. "My sister's husband is constable. He is still abed, but I easily can summon him. If I let you go—"

The new sun was reaching inward to kindle glory in her hair. Her loveliness made Job angrily conscious of his own squalor. He said bitterly:

"I am prison-foul, but I beg you to search me if you think me a thief."

She shook her head and weighed the musket as though she had forgotten its purpose.

"If I have misjudged you—" she began and turned as a shadow slid into the barn. The portly woman who cast it halted at the doorway.

"'Lissa," she rattled, "ain't you done milkin'? What's—?"

She rocked and caught the doorjamb with a mottled hand.

"Now, Beulah!" Melissa began, but her sister whooped for breath and squandered it in a screech.

"Beulah!" the girl cried vainly. Mrs. Houghton looked away from Job and again assailed the morning's stillness:

"Dan'l, Dan'l! Cap'n Wright!"

A door opened. A male voice bawled inquiry.

"In the barn!" the woman cried. "Hurry!"

"Sister," Melissa begged. "It's—"

"Shoot if he as much as stirs," Beulah urged, staring at the culprit with eyes like raisins in a suet pudding. "Why don't they hasten? Dan'l! Cap'n!"

Clattering feet approached. Two men in disarray completed the elder woman's effort to block the doorway.

"Great day!" Daniel Houghton panted. " 'Tis Aldrich!"

His grizzled companion nodded agreement. Nothing, Job felt numbly, was lacking to this abasement. His responses to the men's questions were surly and brief. The constable heard them with no more sympathy than, earlier, Job's rescuers had shown. Houghton had been among them and had returned, bringing Azariah Wright with him, only to be wakened betimes by this tarnal tumult. What call had Job to be lurking here to frighten womenfolks?

"Walked back, alone," the suspect mumbled, "till I could go no farther."

Melissa spoke quickly. Likely enough the trespasser had meant no harm, though when she had found him in the hay he had frightened her enough to send her back into the house for the firelock.

There was silence when she finished. At last, Houghton said grimly:

"Wal, Aldrich, if you're all through with m'barn, mebby you'll leave me have it, now."

By extreme effort, Job got his feet started. Beulah stood aside while he walked unsteadily through the doorway. He feared he might fall with hostile eyes still upon him and staggered on until he was beyond their view.

In the barn, Houghton turned to Wright and offered:

"Saved all this fuss if, last night, we'd left the cuss where we found him."

He spoke loudly to rid himself of unwilling distress, born of Job's meek departure. Melissa, too, was troubled. She ventured:

"Mebby we should have fed him, 'fore he left."

"Fed him!" her sister repeated indignantly. "Wouldn't have that filthy critter on my doorstep, let alone in my kitchen. He's a runagate and a Yorker. Will says so."

"Mite peculiar, ain't it, then," Wright asked of no one in particular, his eyes puckered by thought, "that 'twas York's sheriff jailed him?"

Houghton grunted, finding censure in the question, and fell to milking.

Melissa went slowly toward the house. They could have dealt more kindly with the trespasser. Rid of beard stubble and grime, he had been a pleasing young man, spite of all Will said against him.

Melissa was a little out of patience with Will. He had become too sure of late that she already was his possession. She wished, now, that Beulah had not come out to the barn so inopportunely. Aldrich, folks said, had a real good pitch.

Job had halted to recover his breath. The night's cold had whitened the roadside brush, and the upper branches of trees were streaks of fire in the young sunlight. Smoke was rising from the chimney of the house where succor had been denied a desperately weary man.

He looked about him. The frost-cracked road led off through forest toward the settlement. A reviving remnant of pride cried out against further exposure to Dummerston's scathing belittlement. He could not, would not, limp through the village under the silent scrutiny of its residents.

Job tried to recall the lay of the land. He decided to circle wide of the settlement and come into the Black Mountain road beyond it. It would be a longer journey, yet two hours' walking should bring him to Nat French's pitch.

When the sun's height told him that at least three hours had passed, Job admitted he was lost. He found a moldering log, sat down heavily, and rested his aching head upon his knees.

He never should have ventured into this unfamiliar wilderness where cold lay like still water beneath the tall, contemptuous trees. Job pressed his hands against his throbbing temples. A blowdown's tangle first had turned him from his chosen course. He recalled, too, skirting a swamp at weary length. More recently, he had been forced aside by a lichened cliff, too steep to climb. He had kept telling himself that Black Mountain's ridge must be just ahead. The most valiant pretext no longer could encourage him.

Job let himself go for a moment and bent forward, head on knees again and arms dangling. He was alarmed to find how willingly his senses slipped away and, forcing himself to stand, resisted their mute yet eloquent persuasion. Moss was deep beneath his feet. Here was a restful place where he might lie for a little while—only a few moments—then rise, refreshed.

He stiffened, breathing warily through open mouth. He heard only his heart's uneven thudding and had begun to believe that his ears had tricked him, when the sound came again. No owl or catamount uttered that cry. Beyond the screening trees, a woman was calling.

Job's attempted reply was only a croak, but the thin voice responded and, while he lurched forward, guided him. Each stride was a heavier task, but dark boles, moving aside as he advanced, disclosed at last the sun's unhampered brilliance, and he saw, black against the glare, an approaching figure.

All at once, the last of his strength left him. He leaned against a tree and vacantly watched the creature's advance. She was barefoot, bareheaded, and her gray hair had been woven into many small braids that formed a spiky coronet above a grimed and toothlessly beaming face. Beneath the tattered brown gown that seemed her only covering, her shapeless person billowed at every stride.

The apparition halted close to Job and surveyed him archly.

"Lost in the woods, wa'n't ye?" she chanted. "Felt ye, seen ye, by the power that's in me this day."

She caught his shoulders and, standing on tiptoe, brought her face close. For an instant, their eyes engaged, and the glint in hers sent a prickling along his spine.

"Ailing an' spent," the woman crooned. "A distressful time ye've had, but Zurvilla'll mend ye, dearie. Trust Zurvilla."

She slipped a fat arm about him and guided him out of the forest, across a clearing where brambles arched over ancient stumps, through a littered dooryard, and, at last, to a sway-backed log house.

Job sat on the dwelling's threshold and stared at the horn cup Zurvilla Alvord offered.

"Drink," she bade. " 'Tis herbs and simples, dearie, brewed with the right words said. Ye need have no fear."

The draft puckered his throat. The woman brought out a deerskin and spread it on the ground.

"Lay here," she urged, "while I ready a bed for ye. Not that way, sweet lad; east to west as the sun goes."

Job obeyed and dissolved in a warm, black tide.

A hand upon his shoulder woke him, and he looked up without recognition at two blurred faces.

"Still a-fevered," a voice crooned, "but 'twill pass, dear lad. Let Zurvilla and Brother Moses get ye to bed, now."

Hands, firm on either arm, raised Job, guided him into the house, and lowered him at last upon yielding substance. They turned him gently about as they stripped away his clothing. He swallowed a pungent fluid and lay back beneath a weight of coverlids. Long afterward, he was roused and blinked at a dip's small flame.

"Drink once more, sweet lad," the woman wheedled. " 'Twill sweat the pizen out of ye. There! Sleep now, dearie, sleep."

Job woke, wet and weak. He lay on a pallet before a hearth where embers glowed, and heard, beyond his sight, the pad of bare feet on the puncheon floor. Ancient cobweb, with husks of insects entangled, dimmed the single visible window. At another time, the sour reek of the house would have revolted him.

It was a pleasure, now, to find that he could breathe deeply again.

The still-unseen woman was humming in tuneless rhythm as she moved about. Job said faintly:

"I'm awake and whole—I think."

She came quickly, knelt beside him, and laying a grimed palm on either side of his face, considered it carefully.

"Aye," she granted at length. "Feeble ye still be, yet healed, like Zurvilla promised. D'ye still have pain, darlin'?"

Job managed to grin.

"Of starvation."

"She'll bring ye tea," the woman tittered delightedly, "a tea of cherry bark and rhubarb root that only Zurvilla can brew proper. Later, ye can eat, dear man, but not yet. Zurvilla knows; ye can trust Zurvilla."

"Why should I not trust you," Job asked gravely, "when I owe you my life?"

I I

AN ENTICING smell roused Job from slumber. The woman, squatting on her heels beside the pallet, beamed on him.

"Be ye so minded," she told him with ponderous archness, "Zurvilla'll let ye eat a mite now."

She gave her patient a steaming bowl and a wooden spoon, then lifted and supported him against a fat shoulder. Hunger seized Job as he dipped into the savory mess. Zurvilla tittered and laid a delaying hand on his.

"Slowly," she crooned. "A bit at a time, darlin' man. Ye shall have it all, dearie."

He tried to obey and fancied he could feel vigor spread with each swallow.

" 'Tis succotash," the woman said proudly, "cooked, like the Abenakis taught Zurvilla, in a bake hole. Ye'll not find its like in all Cumberland County, though 'twould be tastier," she conceded wistfully, "if dog, 'stead of pork, was the meat to it."

Presently, she took back the emptied bowl, overcame Job's protests, and made him lie back again.

"Rest now for a spell," she prescribed, "an' ye'll be whole on the morrow. Trust Zurvilla, sweet lad."

Job stretched himself and yawned. In the far distance, he could hear faint rattling that he identified, at last, as the sound of hammers, briskly plied. This evidence of activity, elsewhere, increased his own comfort. He must have slept, for suddenly he became aware that hushed voices were disputing outside the house.

Job got himself up on one elbow and twisted about. Zurvilla and her shaggy brother stood beyond the open door. Two-pound-ten said huskily:

"Warned me he wa'n't to be told an' I'm warnin' you."

His sister nodded. Alvord pursued:

"Some hold 'twould be better if Harvey tended him."

Job saw the woman flinch and, with pity and sympathy, heard her protest:

" 'Tain't noways needful. Brother, tell him not to come here. He—he skeers Zurvilla. He—"

The man's cane pounded.

"Can't do that—exactly," he confessed. "Ye know how Solomon is."

"He's a wicked man," she wailed. "If he comes, he—"

Fright throttled her. Job called loudly:

"I'll have no dealings with Dr. Harvey. If he's minded to interfere, I won't see him. You may tell him so."

He hastily covered his nakedness as Zurvilla bustled into the house with her brother stumping behind her.

"That I truly mean," Job insisted, pleased by the strength of his voice. "I will not see him."

Zurvilla blinked and rubbed her nose on her forearm.

"Sweet lad!" she whispered. Her brother shuffled his stubbed feet.

"Wal," he conceded, "whatever ye say. Sister," he jerked his head toward her, "wants I should tell Nat he can't come for ye till late tomorrow. Folks—"

He checked himself with a thump of his cane. The woman drew the covers more snugly about Job.

"Then tell Nat that I say so, too," he bade Alvord. "I'm beholden to your sister for more than likely I can ever repay."

The hand Zurvilla pressed fleetingly against his cheek still was clammy from recent terror.

"Repaid entire, a'ready," she mumbled and hurriedly followed her brother from the house, closing its door behind her. Job could not hear what else the striving voices said, and presently forgot them in grim contemplation of his own lot. He found himself willing to meet and measure it now.

He had come a long, downhill way since first he had entered Dummerston. He had been warned from town, reluctantly freed from jail, driven without mercy from the Houghtons' barn. Anger, as he recalled that eviction, tightened a knot in his belly. For all Melissa's alluring fairness, she could not have treated him worse had he been a thieving Indian.

Had it not been for a demented old woman and the skill she had acquired from God knew where, he might now be lying dead and already half forgotten in the forest. Though he was mending, his plight had not lessened. He still was a fugitive from justice, if any authority remained in this lawless land.

The far-off hammering continued. Job included in his helpless enmity the men who were building something, somewhere, with no thought of their neighbor's desperate straits. He must not brood childishly upon possible reprisal, but consider what his course should be after Nat had come for him tomorrow. Job could feel decision slowly taking shape, like hot iron under a smith's sledge.

He woke in the night. Snoring resounded from the nearby bed where Alvord slumbered, and in the loft above, Zurvilla

[83]

stirred. Job stared at the banked fire's dull glow. He found his intention cold and hard.

He had planned to ask Zurvilla in the morning for hot water and the opportunity to use it. Lying taut and wide-eyed in the darkness, he withdrew that intention. Job would not stretch the woman's hospitality by further demand upon it. He was more than willing that Nat should see how Dummerston had misused a newcomer.

He held to his determination in the morning when Two-pound-ten brought dirt-stiffened clothing and helped the convalescent dress. While they breakfasted on lumpy gruel, the distant hammers resumed their industrious pattering. When Alvord had left on some obscure errand, Zurvilla spread the deerskin in the dooryard and Job, at her direction, lay upon it in the tepid sunlight. He had found his legs too weak to carry him down to the French pitch and composed himself to wait, with what patience he could muster, for Nat.

The woman brought him, at noon, another bowl of succotash. It seemed insipid now, yet he ate it to please her. At length when the shadow of the house reached out to cover and chill him, Job rose and re-entered the malodorous dwelling.

Zurvilla looked up from herb bundles, spread on the table, and the humble anxiety in her eyes moved him to ask gruffly:

"What can I do in return for all you have done for me?"

She simpered and looked hastily away.

"Naught," she confessed at last, "save to tell Dummerston folks Zurvilla ain't—what they hold she is."

"Little," he shrugged, "will they heed what I tell 'em, or don't. I have few friends among Dummerston folks."

"Aye," she agreed, as though she already had known, hesitated an instant, and pursued in a strained voice. "Abused ye like they do Zurvilla. They say wicked things of her; set their brats against her."

Her shoulders drew together and she whispered:

"Dretful times is a-comin': black times, bloody times. Zurvilla knows; she larned a deal from the Injuns while she was captivated. Sometimes—"

She drew breath with a whistling sound. Job pitied the frantic creature whose fingers were fumbling with her mouth. He told her gravely:

"I have cause to be grateful for what they taught you."

This pleased her. She tittered and ogled him.

"Sweet man," she bridled, "Zurvilla can do more'n heal sufferin' flesh."

She hesitated; then, reaching obscure decision, went on in singsong rhythm, pale eyes holding Job's:

" 'Twas the Abenaki wisewomen taught her herb medicine an' the words to sing when it's a-brewin'. Larned her, too, the secrets of the Above and the Below; to view the past an' tell the future. Oh, 'tis strange things she's seen, dearie."

She looked about the chamber, as though eavesdroppers might be lurking, then brought her face close to Job's and chanted softly:

"Shall Zurvilla guide ye, darlin'? Shall she show ye what's before ye?"

The rapt scrutiny again sent a tingling along Job's backbone. He said evasively:

"I have no silver to cross your palm."

She did not seem to have heard him. She had assumed, for all her flabby bulk, the air of an intentionally naughty child. Leaning still closer, she whispered:

"Ye'll not tell Brother Moses, dearie? When the power seizes Zurvilla, it maddens him. D'ye promise not to tell him?"

"I promise," Job said indulgently.

"Then," the woman chanted, "give Zurvilla your hands, sweet lad; lay them on hers."

In idleness, he had gone too far to refuse. Compliance might comfort her and could do no harm. She was holding grimed palms toward him. Job placed his own upon them.

Zurvilla's hands were strong. Her eyes had closed; her face had grown slack, and her body had begun a slow, rocking motion. She said suddenly from deep in her throat:

"Poor lad, poor, misfortunate lad. Far are ye from your heart's desire, this day; further still will ye go."

[85]

"That," Job answered, trying to dispel unwilling awe, "would scarce be possible."

He failed to divert her. The thick voice went on:

"Much will ye suffer, darlin'. Oh, death will stand nigh ye an' blood be spilt and there'll be sore pain for ye. Dretful things will ye look upon, yet remember then, sweet man, what Zurvilla tells ye now: When it seems blackest, then will ye find what all men seek and few gain. Zurvilla—"

From the dooryard, Nat French loudly called Job's name. The woman caught the table's edge and clung to it, gasping and gray as a stranded fish. Obedient to wordless appeal in the white-ringed eyes, Job rose and went out into the cold glow that sunset was spreading across the hills.

Nat, standing beside his horse, bade curtly:

"Tell Aldrich I've come to— Goddlemighty! 'Tis Job!"

"Ehyah," the other agreed. "Or the leavings of him."

His friend's face puckered as though he were about to weep. He never had thought, he babbled, to see a neighbor in such a plight. He had not come sooner because Two-pound-ten had bidden him stay away until Job was healed.

"Knowed," he pursued, scarcely lowering his voice, "that Zurvilla is wilder'n a hare in March yet if I'd mistrusted a mad old harridan would serve you so—"

"If it weren't for her great kindliness and skill," Job broke in harshly, "I'd likely be not only unwashed and unshaven but dead and unburied."

Nat flinched as though the bitter voice were a lash. He made no attempt to resist the accusation but only said that the night would be chill and a still-puny man had best get home. Job went back to the house.

"I'm going now," he said loudly, but there was no reply, though he thought he heard faint movement in the loft. If terror had driven Zurvilla to hide there, it would be better not to disturb her further. He closed the door again, with his gratitude unuttered.

At Job's insistence, his host brought water and fresh clothing to the barn and stood by with a lantern while his guest scrubbed and shaved. At length, Nat gingerly gathered up the discarded garments, promised that his wife would wash them, and led the way into the house. The kitchen was filled with soft light and the smell of food. Job was relieved to find Will absent. Betty looked up from the hearth with a smile:

"You're real welcome," she told Job and added shyly, "We was—worrited."

Her husband, opening a cupboard, announced overloudly:

"Dram of cider brandy'll do him no real harm. Bill Negus fetched it. He—"

Nat hastily swallowed the rest of the sentence, lodged the jug in a crooked elbow, and filled two horn cups. They supped luxuriously on corn bread, fried pork, and milk gravy. The men had moved to the settle beside the hearth, and Betty was clearing away. Nat rubbed his knees and said with large indifference:

"Bed whenever you've a mind to. Want to view your pitch as soon as may be, wouldn't wonder."

Job cast off hesitation. He said bluntly:

"If you'll lend a hand, I'll bring down my belongings. I'm leaving."

He wished a whole town, instead of his friends, could hear the announcement. Nat's mild face was blank. He echoed:

"Leaving?"

"Ehyah," Job said crisply. "Whenever my legs will bear me."

A spoon fell from Betty's hand and clattered on the table.

"Mean," Nat groped, still without belief, "you're—quittin' Dummerston?"

"Aim to," Job confirmed and added bitterly, "Always providing the sheriff don't get me first. Forget I'm a jail-breaker?"

Relief ironed the scowl from French's forehead.

"Oh, that?" he scoffed. "Rest easy, Job. Paterson'll make you no more trouble. Folks has taught him a real useful lesson."

"Taught me, too," Job returned implacably. "I've had a belly full of Grants' teachings."

"But," Betty began insurgently, "you ain't heered—"

Her husband's stern regard silenced her, but she continued to lean on the table and look toward Job. The distress on her pocked face touched him, but before he could speak further, Nat protested:

"If 'tis Will who's troublin' you, no cause to go. We won't see much of Will, hereafter. Engaged himself to ride express into Bay Province for the committee Harvey's gettin' up."

"It isn't Will," Job answered doggedly. "It's Dummerston. Came here to better my pitch and live neighborly. Since then, I've been suspected, threatened, beaten, jailed and—and worse. I've learned from A to Zed about Dummerston."

He discovered that he was half-shouting into his host's unhappy face. Job checked himself, shrugged, and repeated more quietly:

"So I'm going to leave."

Nat's eyes slipped away. He stared at the fire so dismally that the other said with a trace of contrition:

"You've befriended me, you and Betty. If I were your blood kin, you couldn't have done more."

"Will you listen?" Nat begged. "You've had a bad time— that I don't deny. You didn't come here—wal, real opportune. Grants' settlers has got so haired up, they suspicion all strangers. Mebby—" His voice caught for an instant. "Mebby, they think a sight better of you than you figger. There's Len Spaulding, now. Can't say he ain't grateful."

"Mebby," Job shrugged. "He did get me out of jail, spite of the rest of 'em who were willing to leave me there."

"Takes Grants folks," Nat ventured, "quite a spell to change their minds."

"Can't wait for that," Job replied, "with winter nigh."

Anger's rasp left his voice, and he leaned toward the anxious Nat with sober earnestness. Even if Dummerston's people were, by miracle, to become well disposed, November was half spent, the snows were drawing near, and Job was not yet entirely well again. It would be impossible for him to weatherproof a single room in the unfinished house before snowfall.

"Don't go off at half cock," Nat urged. "Sleep on it, anyways."

"I've slept on it, in jail and out," the other said firmly, "for most a fortnight."

12

JOB AWOKE, momentarily lost, and then, reassured, lay drowsily at ease. He had come back from deep slumber and could accept, at once, only the simple knowledge that the bed was soft and he, himself, was cleansed and, for the moment, secure.

He heard Betty moving about the kitchen. She spoke, apparently to her child, for there was no reply. Nat already must have breakfasted and was doing chores. His own tardiness quickened no guilt in Job.

He reviewed his last night's argument with his host, his sojourn with the Alvords, and, beyond that fantastic interlude, earlier travail and torment and humiliation.

"Sleep on it," Nat had urged. Job was grimly satisfied to find that nothing had been changed by slumber. He was Stockbridge-bound; he would not turn back. Not, he thought sourly as he rose and reached for his clothes, that anyone but the Frenches would try to dissuade him.

He looked for a long moment from the window, before he went downstairs. Among the bared trees, leafy oaks still were bronze. The frosted dooryard was pewter-bright. He had intended, if his legs would carry him, to visit his pitch this day. It might be better to wait until he was stronger. He would be unwise to expose himself, in his weakness, to the voiceless appeals of his land and his house. Job's throat ached as he turned from the window.

Betty looked up from the unbaked loaves she had ranged at one end of the table like so many small, white pigs. She smiled hesitantly, asked how he had slept, then placed porridge kettle and spoon at the board's empty end.

Nat, his wife explained, had gone abroad on an errand but had saddled Cephas, if Job were minded to ride up to his property.

"Later," he told her, adding with incomplete truth, "I'm not too hearty, yet."

Betty lingered, rubbing floury hands together.

"Wish," she said in an unwonted rush of speech, "you wa'n't set on leavin'. Nat and me, we hoped you'd maybe—reconsider."

Job swallowed bitter response and, in its stead, said slowly: "Anything else you asked, I'd try my utmost to do."

Betty blushed and hurried from the kitchen. Presently, Job followed, to sit on the doorstep and absently watch the woman's preparations for baking. Wood that had filled the stone oven in the yard had burned to embers, and Betty was raking out the last of these with a fireslice. She smiled as she went past him into the house, to return with a laden tray.

Job wondered drearily, while his hostess transferred the oblong mounds of risen dough to the shovel-like breadpeel and thrust them into the oven, where he would be when the last of this week's baking had been eaten. It might be better not to return to his land, at all, but let Nat bring down whatever had been left there.

He lifted his head abruptly. Hammers that faintly had troubled the silence while he had lain, stricken, in the Alvords' house, had begun to speak again. Their loud and imminent clamor roused the echoes.

Job looked wildly about him, heedless of Betty's expectant regard. The sharp reports came from uphill; from his pitch, or nearby. He stood up so quickly that his head swam. He could hear, through continued banging, the gasping of a saw. Surely, unless he again were a-fevered, men were working close to Job's own house.

The suspicion that neighbors, who had rejected him, now were tearing down his half-built dwelling fell more swiftly than it had risen. The tumult was too orderly for destruction. Job found his voice.

"Who is it?" he faltered. "What are they about?"

Betty, daring greatly, laughed at his bewilderment.

"Cephas stands saddled," she told him almost gaily. "Was I you, I'd find out for myself."

Job did not curb his mount's jolting trot, though it jarred breath from him and left him conscious of little more than the extreme need for haste. He turned from the road into the freshly rutted, uphill track, and when the pace slackened, kicked the horse onward. There was neither time nor necessity for reflection. He was nearing the source of the disturbing noise. In another minute, its authors and their purpose would be revealed, if a reeling body could hold to the saddle.

Cephas groaned and stumbled. Job kicked him again, bent to dodge low-hanging branches, and rode into the clearing. For a moment he sat, exhausted and unbelieving.

His house stood before him, no longer skeletal but a substantial oblong, wholly sheathed and more than half-shingled. The kitchen end was clapboarded; a chimney, within a scaffolding, almost finished.

Job could neither speak nor stir. The oxen were Kathan's. He and Nat were unloading lumber from the sled. Spaulding, aloft, was capstoning the chimney, and Hooker, below, was plying a hoe in a mortar trough. About them, and as intently engaged, were men whom Job had believed his enemies.

The grizzled torchbearer in the raid on Westminster's jail was the first to discover the intruder. Jonathan Knight, kneeling on the roof, had paused with hammer upraised. He twisted about, spoke to the burly Negus and to Enoch Cook, who shared his perch, then called down to Wyman, the tanner, who plied a saw, and to Houghton and Wright, Job's late captors, who were nailing clapboards.

The industrious clamor dwindled as, one by one, faces turned toward the horseman. For an instant no one spoke.

It was Hooker who first shook off the spell. He laid down his hoe and stalked across the clearing.

"Wal, neighbor," the elder smiled. "Welcome home."

Job wrung the extended hand.

"I—" he began, "I—"

He turned away. When he could trust himself to look again, Spaulding stood at Hooker's side and trumpeted greeting:

"Wal, fellow jailbird! 'Twas this way: So laggard in finishin' your home, some of the folks figgered 'twould be best to pitch in an' do it for you, else you might go back to Westminster an' beg Pollard Whipple to winter you."

His stiff hair sparkled in the sunlight, and in his solemn face the little gray eyes were merry. Job faltered:

"Don't know what to say."

As though his distress were indecent, the others had resumed their tasks. Hooker lifted his voice above the hammers' fusillade:

"No need to say anything, friend. When good men come to Dummerston, we aim to keep them, however much they try to get away."

His smile made it plain that Nat had told of Job's late intention. It was gone now. Bitter certainties of an hour before had been swept away; hopes, recently abandoned, were returning.

"Beholden," Job said loudly and, when he struggled vainly to go further, the elder dealt him an understanding slap on the knee and Spaulding's wiry voice again broke a difficult stillness.

"Wal, aim to set a-horse, all day? Light, for God's sake, an' —an' level yourself with the neighbors."

Job grinned, shook his head, and lifted his voice.

"I'm minded," he said more clearly, "that it's custom at house-raisings and the like for the owner to set out a mite of strong drink. There's none here, but if Nat'll lend me some, I'll—"

"No need," Negus bawled from the roof. "Fetched a jug yesterday an' left it with French. If he ain't swilled it all a'ready—"

"Hush your hollerin'," Nat called over his shoulder, " 'tis here. Fetched it up this mornin', but kept it hid till now."

It befitted a day of miracles, Job thought solemnly, that before it had ended he should feel whole again. He had been faintly shamed, earlier, by weakness that had forbidden him to share in work his neighbors were doing for him.

Job had strayed in uneasy exile about the edge of the manifold activity. His uncertain legs had borne him in to view the snugly enclosed kitchen with its still-damp hearth, but his knees had buckled and almost had thrown him when he had attempted to lift a stone for the chimney. Spaulding, from the scaffolding, had bidden him to sit down somewhere and stay there.

Job had chosen as back rest a stump near the clearing's edge. Propped against it, he had tried to consider the still-disordered future and, straightway, had fallen asleep. He had been aroused at noon, had wolfed the snack of cold pork and fresh bread Nat had provided, and then had slumbered again.

He marveled now at his recent weakness. Shadow was creeping across the clearing toward him and his companions. They sat together on unused lumber in sunlight already chilled by the approach of frost.

A half hour earlier, when work had ceased, Spaulding had laid an ear against Negus's jug and had shaken it gently. It would be unthrifty, he had proclaimed, to leave while so much cider brandy remained. Job chuckled, recalling that pronouncement. He felt gay and warm and amazingly well. Knight, squatting beside him, received the jug from Nat.

Hooker and Negus had left together in midafternoon, and now Kathan's ox sled was moving off with Cook as passenger. Job looked from them to his house. Its roof was entirely shingled; the chimney completed and the near wall clapboarded with all the sash in place. In a month, he thought gratefully, he alone could not have accomplished so much.

"Wal!" Knight prompted.

He was holding out the jug. Job took it eagerly. If cider brandy could lessen the stubborn tightness in his throat, he might be able to explain to his neighbors the depth of his gratitude. It was not entirely liquor that set his eyelids to smarting. He passed the jug to the tanner, Wyman, an appropriately leathery little man.

Kathan's sled had vanished into the woods. Spaulding turned from watching its departure and said dryly:

"Jedgment Day must be nigh when Alex mingles willing with rascals like us."

Houghton drank, passed the jug to Wright, and said:

"Harvey's watchin' him close; Cook, too."

"Solomon," Wyman scowled, "suspicions everyone these days —'cept Solomon."

"Wal, Kathan's for the King, ain't he?" Knight demanded. "For York, too. As for Enoch, he's too tarnal mild. No time now for trimmin' and wabblin'."

Job took another pull at the circling jug. He couldn't recall when he had felt so fine. The twanging voices, his easy inclusion in their talk, had swept away loneliness and filled him with affection for these, his neighbors. He was tempted, in his elation, to tell them so, but words still eluded him.

"Harvey holds," Knight was saying, "we'll be free of York, come spring." He glanced at Wyman in surly challenge. "An' Harvey's right, oftener than some folks."

The tanner drank and asked a trifle thickly:

"Warned Aldrich, here, out of town, didn't he?"

"All of us makes mistakes," Houghton said and added tightly, "Regret 'em, too."

"I'd go a long ways," Wyman snorted, "to see Solomon regret anything he'd done."

"Now, John," Spaulding asked in mock surprise, "you ain't turned coat and gone over to York?"

"No, b'God, I ain't, but long as Alex Kathan an' Enoch Cook

[94]

act neighborly an' orderly, no one has a right to browbeat 'em for what they believe."

"Damme," Spaulding told the company with elaborate amazement, "if I don't think he's a trimmer, himself."

"All right," Wyman grinned. "If, otherwise, I can't think different from Solomon Harvey, then I'm a trimmer, along with Aldrich."

Job heard himself say loudly and without intention:

"There's some that Harvey scares a sight more than he does me. Why does he hound Zurvilla Alvord?"

"'Hounds her' nothin'," Houghton scoffed. "Raddled old witch is skeered of her shadow—with reason, wouldn't wonder."

"What reason?" Job persisted. "She succored me, when—others had cast me out."

It pleased him to see Houghton wince.

"Wal, now, there's one reason, anyway," Spaulding said. "Alvords has Gorton kin to Brattleboro an' Dep'ty Sheriff Benjy's one of 'em. You remember Benjy?"

"I remember, too," Job retorted, his voice sounding odd through the humming in his ears, "that Zurvilla's done me much good."

Spaulding grinned widely.

"Billy's cider brandy," he said, accepting the jug from Wright, "ain't done you no real harm, either. Wal, here's to you. Peace an' prosperity on your own pitch, boy; a deal more than your brother Amos ever had."

He drank deeply, glanced at the westering sun, and shook his head.

"Most time we was a-goin', neighbors."

What Job wished to say was clear in his mind, yet he could not get it into speech.

"Won't forget what you've done," he blundered. "Minded this morning to quit Dummerston; maybe sell my pitch. I'm biding here, thanks to you. Won't forget what you've done, I promise you."

"Thar, by God!" Spaulding cried. "We'll make a Grants' man of him yet."

He and the others rose. Their sudden movement made Job dizzy. He was surprised to find himself arguing hotly with Nat as to who would ride Cephas down the hill, and at last accepted a compromise proposal that the horse carry both.

Job turned to find that Houghton lingered, scowling, beside him. The man spoke hurriedly:

"Regret—what happened in the barn. M' woman, she's regretful, too. So'll 'Lissa be, when she gets back and learns how mistook we were. She's gone over to Keene in Hampshire for a spell," he ran on, as though unable to stop. "Her an' Beulah's pa's innholder there, and he's ailin'."

"Oh?" Job asked blankly. Houghton dropped his voice:

"Obleeged to you for not tellin' how we—we served you."

"Oh, no," Job corrected. "Obleeged to you."

Houghton wheeled and fled. Job had trouble getting upon the horse. Nat mounted behind him. They rode downward through low, rich light, streaked by the far-reaching shadows of trees.

The motion churned Job's mind. He dredged one thought from the confusion and held it tightly.

"Tomorrow," he marveled to Nat, "I'll sleep in my own house."

"Come tomorrow," his friend said wryly, "you'll reconsider, wouldn't wonder. Whew! Guess I'm a mite cocked myself."

Job did not reply. He still was too dazzled to view entire the changes a single day had wrought. All that he had thought lost had been restored. Even Melissa was not forever beyond his reach. Houghton had said she would return.

13

ACH MORNING, the Indian Summer's fragile brilliance promised to break, yet the pale sun continued daily to burn away the night's light frost. The soft enchantment laid upon the land let men discount fell tidings that drifted into the frontier settlements like smoke from distant fires.

In prostrate Boston town, so one tale ran, smallpox burned among the starving citizenry while, on the commons of surrounding villages, militia companies drilled, hay-foot, straw-foot, to the drums' dry rattling.

Ethan Allen's guerrillas had driven York authority from the western Grants, and a vision of new freedom was forming there. East of the dividing mountains, another convention had assembled in discord and had adjourned with nothing accomplished save a further sharpening of enmities. None nurtured these more zealously than the embittered Dr. Harvey, who, with his adherents, was planning a still-indefinite day of wrath.

Candles burned late in the physician's home while he pored over dispatches Will French brought from Cambridge and Boston. Harvey penned fulminating replies and then sat, brown, spare, and still, viewing the future with vindictive eyes.

The duty of a true patriot, who adhered to the revolutionary doctrine expounded by Samuel Adams, was severely plain. Massachusetts would be in the forefront of the inevitable war, and when it came, the eastern Grants must stand beside the parent province. Meanwhile all Cumberland County, and particularly the doctor's own town, should be purged and girded for battle.

The laggards would be roused; dissenters, driven out. Ruthless amputation alone could save an ailing community. Brooding like a gigantic owl, Harvey planned his surgery. A sparsely attended town meeting, held at his instance and under his direction, voted that the assessors, Alexander Kathan and Enoch Cook, levy upon the freeholders for funds to purchase ammunition for the defense of Dummerston against unspecified enemies.

Other men were swayed by imperative new forces that ranged the frontier. The carefee outlaw, Alvah Reynolds, brought Spaulding further letters from leaders in the west and left as jauntily as he had come.

In Westminster, York officials tried by prying and spying to uncover the design of impending revolt, which they were too confused by many counsels to challenge openly.

Meanwhile, autumnal sunlight continued to cast its spell; blue haze defined every separate ridge in the distant ranges, and luminous silence that had set each small sound apart now was more roughly broken by axes, ringing in the forest.

Settlers who had readied their pitches for winter turned, in this miraculous continuation of autumn, to enlarging their clearings. Few tried to peer past a shining present that screened a darkening future. In the serene interlude, one man, alone on his remote pitch, felt that his cup of contentment ran over.

It was only dawn's beginning when Job Aldrich awoke. He rolled from bed, raked away the covering ashes, and laid fresh wood upon the bared coals. He turned, then, from the fuming hearth and opened the kitchen door.

The stars were melting in a watery sky; treetops beyond the clearing were washed by colorless light, and the frosted ground shone. Job was careless of the intruding chill. Each morning he performed this ritual of reunion, and once more, as he viewed his property, grave exaltation possessed him.

This was a deeper, more tranquil happiness than he hitherto had known. A wedded man might look with the same awed sense of possession at the woman who still slept beside him while a new day quickened.

Trees were more sharply outlined against the bleaching west.

Gloom that had lain stagnant in the clearing imperceptibly was flowing away. The small wind that ran before the sunrise had a cutting edge. Job shivered, yet lingered in the doorway, soberly numbering his blessings.

He had come at last to his own, ordained place after great and, doubtless, merited travail imposed by Providence that now was visiting immoderate favor upon him.

The weather remained unseasonably fair. Men who once had seemed hostile had become his friendly neighbors. By their labor and Job's own, his house stood externally whole: solid and seemly beneath the steep roof, with a stone chimney at either end. When the interior had been finished off, there would be no sightlier dwelling in all Dummerston.

Before spring, if the snows did not lie too deep, a proper barn would stand beside the house. Its walls' first tiers already had been laid, and Nat's horse had drawn further logs to be notched and fitted.

Nat likewise had supplied a wooden plow with an iron shoe, devised by the lanky smith, Ebenezer Haven, who also was fashioning latches and hinges for the dwelling's inside doors. Job had turned over the better part of an acre of the cleared, dark, forest mold, had leveled the furrows with a treetop harrow, and had sown wheat that should yield sufficient grain for the planting of a cash crop next year.

It had been a good beginning, and the best still lay before him. As far into the future as he could see, he and his land would work together until, at the end, they were joined in still more intimate union.

Job closed the door. While he warmed himself before the reviving fire, he picked up his tally stick of yellow birch and counted the notches it already bore. By his calculation, this was the first Friday of December: the calendar day. The morning's clarity promised that the rest of the month would be equally fair.

He pulled on his frock and then, before he breakfasted, knelt beside his bed. "Bless the Lord, O my soul, and forget not all His benefits."

He sliced salt pork and fried it, crumbling the remnant of last night's journeycake into the spider, and wondered soberly while he breakfasted whether the lot of any man could be more enviable. Here, on his remote pitch, he would work from Can to Can't, from daybreak until dark, undisturbed by fermenting enmities, unobserved by the inquisitive.

Attendance at Sabbath Meeting supplied him with a measure of human companionship and if, during the week, he desired more, the Frenches were handy-by. Nat and Betty always welcomed him, and even Will, on the rare occasions when he and Job met, abstained from further offense, whatever the repression cost him. There was small likelihood of further trouble with Will while Melissa remained away. Job wondered whether memory of her ever would fail to bring a tightness to his chest and throat.

He laid the spider upside down upon the fire and, squatting, while the flames licked it clean, thought gravely of this fair, tall girl. There was little that he did without asking himself sooner or later, whether it would please her.

Job pulled back the blankets to air and, ax in hand, hurried out into the clearing. Chickadees rose from the doorstep where daily he scattered crumbs and he watched them fly away like bits of wind-blown ash. The sky had turned a misty blue, and the tips of the tallest trees had been dipped in gold. He could find no sounds in the silence but the distant river's voice and his own heart's beating.

For a long monent, Job lingered, steeping himself in solitude that was twin brother to peace. He had had few visitors, other than Nat, since he had settled on his pitch, and was thankful.

The most recent callers had been Daniel and Beulah Houghton, who had been visiting the Frenches and had been led by them to the clearing. Job had requited the stiffly apprehensive woman for her earlier heartlessness by a truly Christian display of cordiality that had confused and then had thawed her. She had made amends for her hostility by praising everything visible, and both she and her husband, when leaving, had urged Job to visit them. Beulah had confided that she expected her sister back within the month.

That had been, Job reckoned as he strode toward the barn's beginning, four days ago. If the weather held, there would be additional achievement for Melissa to admire when she returned.

By midmorning, he had notched enough logs for another tier and had begun to work them into place. Uneasiness, returning, crept upon him so stealthily that he was not conscious immediately of its presence. At length, he paused and looked sharply about him. Once more, he could find nothing in the sunny clearing or among the bordering trees to warrant distress, could see no movement more sinister than the scuffle of small birds about his doorstep.

Job bent again to his work, yet, as on yesterday and the day before, he was unable to shake off the nervous belief that somewhere, hidden but near, hostile eyes watched him. The conviction, however senseless, again was blighting the grave joy he had taken in his work.

This no longer was Indian country, where death might lurk in the shadows. If he were not ridiculously alarming himself and someone indeed was peering at him from hiding, the skulker could discover nothing more noteworthy than a man, building a barn.

Job tried to shake off the obsession by activity so violent and reckless that a log, slipping from his grasp, barely missed maiming him. Fright and his loud denunciation of his clumsiness seemed to rout the sourceless affliction, and he forgot it until, late in the afternoon, thirst drove him to the spring.

He bent to drink and remained, rigidly on all fours, to stare at a footprint stamped into the damp earth before his hands. After an instant, his mind, reviving, brought him relief so intense that it shamed him. The haunting presence that had made this small, square-toed track, could have been no one more deadly than a youngster who, imagining himself a ranger or Indian, had been playing a solitary game.

He wavered between amusement and anger and resolved, if

the spy returned, to stalk and dress him down, but he worked, thereafter, without the wretched sense of surveillance.

Job sat with the Frenches and their child on the steps of Dummerston's meetinghouse and shared the basket lunch Betty had brought to stay them between morning and afternoon services. Others whose homes were as distant ate nearby. As appetites were appeased and the solemnity imposed by a two-hour sermon faded, voices were growing brisker, and now and then laughter rose, though it was quickly hushed.

Sabbath meetings had been held, of late, in the spacious kitchen of Charles Davenport's house. Services, this day, were being conducted by the Reverend Elihu Chapin, a parson from Springfield, in Bay Province. He was making a missionary tour of the frontier, and attendance had been too large for any dwelling to hold.

More than a year had passed since a minister had tarried in Dummerston, wherefore mothers had brought their infant children to receive the baptism that Elder Hooker was forbidden by church law to administer.

The Reverend Mr. Chapin, a lean and somber figure in Geneva gown and bands, had chosen for his text: "Bind their kings in chains and their nobles in fetters of iron," and his sermon had been savagely political. He had inveighed against those in authority who persecuted their subjects and had detailed the torments awaiting all tyrants, while the wails of restless babies had pointed his predictions.

Hosea was growing fretful again. He had yelled like an Abenaki when baptized—a favorable portent. Now, Betty gathered him up and bore him into the meetinghouse, and Nat followed her. Job rose, brushed crumbs from his breeches, and nodded to Kathan, who stood nearby. Alex moved closer, hesitated, then lifted his shoulders and said with resignation:

"Treason's got into pulpits, well as everywhere else, seems."

Job answered with more confidence than he felt:

"Massachusetts folks have been hollering such things, far back as I can remember. 'Twas one of the reasons I came north."

"And treason came after you," Kathan commented with a sour grin. "Wal, we can't outdistance it, I guess."

Long ago, Hooker had said some such thing. Job thought of how much more he stood to lose, now, and insisted:

"Trouble'll boil away; always has."

"Mebby," Kathan granted, but his troubled frown remained. "Saul Ellis, the cordwainer, he's come from below. Bidin' with us while he makes shoes for the family. Says"—he swallowed dryly—"says there'll be war in Bay Province, come spring. That's what the Reverend Chapin's furtherin'. He—"

He stopped and inspected the sky with an intensity that puzzled Job until he saw Spaulding approaching, brave in butternut coat and smallclothes.

"Job, Alex!" he hailed. "How be you? Wal, the reverend sir gave us a prime discourse, eh?"

He paused expectantly. Kathan mumbled and walked away. Spaulding looked after him for a moment.

"Now," he deplored at last, "I've got Alex haired up again, though all I aimed to do was bid him an' his folks to the dance we're holdin'—you, too, if it ain't against your principles."

"Dance?" It was hard for Job to picture his hard-bitten neighbors stooping to frivolity. Spaulding nodded.

"Ehyah, to my house, last Friday in February."

Job was pleased by the invitation. He was light-footed, and it was long since he had danced. He answered warmly:

"I'm obleeged, Len. I'd like to come."

"Wal, now!" Spaulding marveled. "Feared you'd be set against sech folly."

"Because," Job inquired, "I find the reverend's discourse hard to swallow? There's worse follies than dancing, way I see it."

"Ehyah," Spaulding said. "Keep forgettin' you're a peaceful man, though I've heered it often enough."

"I try to be," Job returned, smarting under the mockery, "and with small encouragement from some of my neighbors."

Spaulding's face assumed a wooden look.

"Seems," he mused, "I have a neighbor who talked early an'

late of meekness under affliction—and then got himself jailed for assaulting a dep'ty sheriff."

He chuckled. Job stammered sheepishly:

"A man learns by his mistakes. All that's over and done with —I hope."

"Ehyah," the other agreed grimly. "Over an' done with, long as the court don't take notice we're fugitives from justice, you an' me. Neither of us'll be safe, till there ain't no more court."

Job searched the impassive face and asked at last:

"That's what folks are planning, isn't it: to rid themselves of the court?"

"Wal?"

"Seems a peculiar way to keep the peace."

"Job," Spaulding began and then, sensing that someone stood behind him, faced about.

"Hey there, John," he said to Wyman and added with more vigor, "Great day! What's that you're eatin'?"

"Tater," the hard-bitten little man mumbled around a mouthful. "M' woman, she's to Guilford. Taters don't make a bad 'tween-meetin's snack."

"They're next thing to pizen," Spaulding warned. "Everyone knows that. Least they do is cool a man off."

"Wal," Wyman maintained, calmly, "proper eatin' for the Lord's Day, then, I'd say."

"Mebby," Spaulding conceded, "providin' you take enough sweet flagroot, Monday, to get back what taters have lost you. I'm too old for sech triflin'."

He looked from Wyman to Job and grinned.

"Seems neighbor Aldrich is a-fixin' to jine the court party."

Wyman grunted. Under his close regard, Job said defensively:

"No such thing. Just held—and still hold—that a good way to start trouble is to keep the court from meeting."

"Worse trouble, if it does set," Spaulding promised darkly. "Might consider that folks is real tired of bein' robbed."

"Robbed!" Job scoffed.

"Robbed," Wyman stressed, quietly. "Court took Uriah Stark's yoke of oxen from him, last session."

He laid a firm hand on Job's arm and pursued in a level voice:

"Uriah, he owed John Norton, innholder to Westminster, six shilling, an' money bein' so tarnal scarce, Uriah couldn't pay. Had no more cash, hard or soft, than a woodchuck—or me, far's that goes. So Norton sues, and what does the damned court do? Issues a jedgment against Uriah, an' Billy Paterson takes his oxen to satisfy it."

Spaulding spat, as though ridding his mouth of an evil taste. Wyman droned on:

"Wal, Billy put the oxen up for sale an' Lord God Almighty Crean Brush, he bid 'em in for six shilling an' costs—mebby a tenth of what they're wuth. Real profitable for Crean. He has money an' Uriah has none—nor his oxen neither."

He squinted at Job.

"Was you Uriah, would you still favor York's courts?"

"Likely," Job admitted, "I wouldn't." He rallied and added sullenly:

"It was lawful, though. If a law's bad, the people can change it."

"Jest what we aim to do," Spaulding said quickly. "Rid ourselves of York law courts and set up our own; drive York officers out and put freeholders in their places."

He looked with covert inquiry toward Wyman and, finding agreement in the man's slight nod, went on in a lower voice:

"Time's a-comin' when we won't no longer be bled by York. Time's nigh when the Grants, east an' west—"

"Careful," Wyman warned.

The feet of the three approaching men rattled on the frozen ground. The Reverend Mr. Chapin, black cloak billowing, was returning with Hooker and Harvey from the town clerk's dwelling. They passed into the meetinghouse, and Wyman looked after them. It was a long moment before he turned and then his voice and face were grave.

"Ain't real sure," he confessed, "that Solomon ain't goin' to be a problem, himself."

Before Spaulding could protest, he went on deliberately: He had heard that Harvey was organizing a committee to examine his neighbors' conduct and pass judgment upon it. Furthermore, it was said that the physician planned to use the town's ammunition, when purchased, to cow dissenters.

"Where d'you get such talk?" Spaulding snorted. "Solomon's for liberty, well as you or me."

"Massachusetts liberty," Wyman returned, "mebby ain't the kind we want. Whether or no, I'm against Solomon or anyone else decidin' what sort of freedom'd be good for me."

"He can't," Spaulding pointed out, "set up his committee less'n a freeholders' meetin' empowers him. Might 'mind him of that if you suspicion him."

"Wal, mebby I will," Wyman reflected, "but not right now, I guess. Lord's Day is scarce a fittin' time for Solomon an' me to be reasonin' together. What's so amusin'?"

He had marked Job's broadening grin.

"Just wondering," he replied blandly, "whether Dummerston folks ever agree for long about anything. Glad my pitch is far off. It's peacefuler that way."

"Now heed me," Wyman bade, ignoring the jibe. "If so be a town meetin's called, you be there—less'n 'twould suit you better than 'twould me to be ruled by Solomon."

"It wouldn't," Job admitted. "If there's a meeting, I'll attend."

The Reverend Mr. Chapin preached that afternoon from the text: "He shall save the children of the needy and shall break in pieces the oppressor."

He had turned the makeshift pulpit's hourglass twice before he ended his discourse.

14

AYBREAK'S GRAY cold had promised snow, but the storm began with a hissing shower of hail that turned quickly into freezing rain. When logs grew too slippery for safe handling, Job broke off work and returned to his house.

There was no cause for him to remain idle when outdoor labor was impossible. He had enough lumber on hand to begin finishing the further rooms of his dwelling. While the empty building threw back the clamor of hammer and saw, he thought with glee how secure he was here in his own place, shut off by the storm from the striving outer world.

He still lacked sufficient wood to wall in all the rooms and build a staircase to the attic space above, but when this had been obtained, he would be well prepared to meet the winter, however long and severe. He found himself grinning at the prospect.

Two casks of prime salt pork, a crock of maple molasses, a jar of vinegar, and a sack of salt, all bought from Nat, stood in the cellar. Above them hung portly sacks of blended rye flour and corn meal that Josiah Baldwin, the miller, had supplied. There was plenty in store, except possibly spirits, yet by self-denial the three gallons of cider brandy, purchased from Negus, might suffice. Scarcely two shillings of the money Job had brought with him into the Grants remained, yet he felt rich beyond estimate.

In foul weather, he would continue his present task; in fair, Nat and he would complete the barn and, still working together, fell more trees on the French and Aldrich pitches for the spring burning. Ash salts would supply sufficient money for all Job's worldly needs. It promised to be the best winter he had ever known.

When the skies cleared, he would order more lumber from Kathan. If another town meeting were summoned, Job would keep his promise to Wyman and attend. Thereafter, he would stay close to his home all winter long—or until Melissa Sprague returned to Dummerston.

The storm had ended before he went to bed. When he looked out from his doorway into flat blackness, he felt that the cold had lessened and a wet wind blew from the south. Job fell asleep to the light sound of newly formed ice, dripping from the eaves. He had hoped that the weather would keep him immune to intrusion for many days, but next afternoon Moses Alvord hobbled uphill, bearing notice of a town meeting to be held at Charles Davenport's house, three days thence.

Alvord had little further news to provide while he sipped cider brandy before Job's fire. The storm must have been heavier to the south, for no travelers had come through with fresh tidings. Zurvilla was visiting her Gorton kin in Brattleboro and Two-pound-ten seemed reconciled to her absence. Nat French was suffering from a chest cold and had doubted whether he would attend the meeting.

Job's visitor peered wistfully into his empty cup, sighed, and picked up his cane. The ache in his maimed feet, he confided as he left, was sure sign that a warm, wet spell was coming.

Job recalled the prediction, three mornings later, while he greased his boots before the fire and looked out at the billowing mist a south wind blew across the clearing. Nat's cold still kept him indoors. It would be a wet and lonely journey to the settlement, yet Job would keep his promise to John Wyman and attend the town meeting, at whatever discomfort.

His resolution and his person had been thoroughly dampened when he slopped through fog and clinging mire into the village. Steamy warmth, rich with the smells of barnyards and wet wool, immersed him as he tiptoed into Davenport's kitchen. Its proprietor's bulk overfilled a chair set behind a table, and Harvey, standing beside him, book in hand, was reading the minutes of the last town meeting to seven solemn men who sat facing him.

Job crept to an empty chair beside Wyman. The tanner's nod of greeting did not soothe the newcomer, who wondered sullenly why, since most of Dummerston's freeholders had stayed at home, he himself had not had equal sense. Kathan was among the absent, which meant that later Job must undertake another and longer journey to order the necessary lumber.

The owlish town clerk closed the minute book sharply and turned to Davenport, who hauled himself up and cleared his throat.

"Wal now," he announced, "as moderator, I have to read you the warrant for the meetin'."

He bent over the paper Harvey had handed him and, while the physician listened with an author's satisfaction, intoned:

" 'To see whether the freeholders will empower the town clerk to set up a committee to insure the welfare and protect the liberties of the town of Dummerston against all who are judged to threaten them.' "

Davenport paused, surveyed the small company, and then asked:

"Wal, what's the meetin's pleasure?"

The lank Joel Temple who had perched tautly on the edge of his stool leaped up and cried:

"Mister Mawderator, move the measure be 'dopted," and, beyond him, Negus half-lifted his solid person to grunt: "Second."

Davenport began, "All in favor—" but Wyman had raised himself.

"Now jest a minute," he drawled, narrowed eyes moving from person to person to rest at last upon the town clerk. "Time for discussion, ain't there? No need to ask whose idee this is; that's reasonable plain. Like to call the meetin's attention to one fact: This motion aims to give a few folks power over the hull settlement. I'm against it an' so'll all be who aim to live free."

Davenport's face was a brighter red. He glanced appealingly at Harvey, who was settling his spectacles more firmly on his beaked nose. Wyman still was standing. Before he could speak further, the elder Jacob Laughton leaned forward and asked him shrilly:

"Want to set on the bosom of your breeches while Tories, Yorkers, an' sech varmints do as it pleases 'em?"

He looked about him, confident of approval. Spaulding and Enoch Cook, his pale face twitching and straw-colored hair a-bristle, had leaped up and were yelping for recognition. Wyman stood, sucking his cheeks into hollows, until the clamor had abated.

"Still got the floor," he pointed out then, and went on, deliberately drawing out each word:

"Jake wants to know whether I favor lettin' folks with views different from mine hold fast to 'em. Long as they behave themselves lawful, I do. That plain enough?"

"Trimmer talk," Laughton muttered, as Wyman sat down. Jonathan Knight unfolded himself to stand, ungainly and sad as an old horse. He offered:

"Sech a committee's needed, neighbors, I do believe. If we organize we can better resist tyranny."

"What d'ye call it," Cook demanded shrilly, "when you set part of the neighbors to spyin' on the rest. Ain't that tyranny?"

Harvey's hooting voice hushed the dispute. His spectacles flashed as he stressed his words by pecking thrusts of his head.

"I would remind the meeting that the proposal under debate was first recommended by patriots of Massachusetts. Lately the honorable Continental Congress has urged that all communities establish committees of safety, forthwith."

"Wal, now, Solomon," Spaulding twanged, "wouldn't wonder if quite a few of us came into the Grants to get away from Bay Province an' all its works." Harvey flushed and tried to speak, but the other's voice cut him off. "Might remind the meetin', too, that the county convention, last November, considered Congress's request—an' voted it down."

"That," Negus leaned across Temple to retort, "wa'n't a rep'sentative gatherin'. No more'n a score of delegates present."

"Can't," Job was startled to hear himself say loudly, "call

this meeting representative, either, with only ten men attending out of all in Dummerston."

No one replied, yet he knew by Harvey's grim regard and tightened mouth that the comment had pricked him and had been stored away in a vindictive memory. After momentary silence, Davenport called for a standing vote. Negus, Temple, Laughton, and Knight rose in favor of the motion and, an instant later, Job, Spaulding, Wyman, and Cook stood to oppose it. Harvey muttered to Davenport who announced glibly:

"Meetin' approves, five to four, with the moderator castin' the decidin' vote."

Job did not linger when adjournment came. The day was smothering in fog, and he would be wetter still when he got home. As he made for the door, Harvey addressed him in a quietly baleful voice:

"You, sir, are a reckless young man."

Job met the threatening eyes boldly.

"If I were not," he retorted, "I'd have stayed home, like most of the freeholders."

15

BY JOB'S TALLY, it was January 8, when the first snow fell, which, according to weather lore, promised that the winter would be open with only seven more storms.

Gray weeks of thaw and drizzle were succeeded by further of dazzling brilliance and sharp blue shadows, when each indrawn breath stung the nostrils. Then in mid-February, another, wilder storm rode in upon a shrill north wind. It piled a barrier before

Job's door, rolled drifts across the downhill track, and sealed him away from the world.

While the tempest endured, he finished walling one room that, someday, would be his bedchamber, and roughed in the attic stair. During the subsequent dazzling weather, when the drip from icicles along the eaves at noon stressed a vast silence, Job resumed work upon the unfinished barn.

Each morning, he told himself that he must break a path to the road and determine how the Frenches fared. Each afternoon he assigned the task to the morrow.

He did not lack more vital companionship than his inanimate land could offer. The small people of the wilderness cautiously were accepting him as a neighbor. Bluejays yelled at Job from the forest's edge and raided his doorstep to gobble scraps. Chickadees were becoming his familiars, and the boldest now took crumbs from his hand. A gray squirrel who, ignoring his fluffy tail, bore a startling resemblance to Deacon Ziba Potter of Stockbridge, came rippling daily across the clearing to dine.

Adam must have found kindred satisfaction in a less austere Eden, though he, too, had yearned for a woman's assuaging presence. Nevertheless, Job had settled so serenely into solitude that it seemed an intrusion when, at length, Nat waddled on snowshoes into the clearing.

The visitor was relieved and reproachful. It had been days, he wheezed, since he and Betty had seen hide or hair of their neighbor. If he were setting up to be a hermit, he might at least warn his friends.

"Been busy," Job apologized. "Besides, thought it best not to venture far until roads were broken out."

The roads, Nat replied acidly, had been open for the last three days. His irritation was melted by cider brandy. Folks, he reported, settling himself before Job's fire, had been too busy digging themselves out to supply much news, but Will had returned from Bay Province and had brought disturbing tidings. Massachusetts had called a convention to meet at Cambridge. Its purpose, Will had said, was to prepare the colony for war.

"Will—" Job began, swallowed, and ended lamely, "I keep forgetting he's your brother."

"Ehyah," Nat agreed, as though acknowledging a fault. "Reckless talker, I know. Still an' all..."

His voice ran down, and he shrugged. Job had the angry feeling that the peace that dwelt here had been marred. He demanded of Nat:

"Got grievances you need a war to remedy?"

"None," the other confessed half guiltily. "Reasonably content with things as they be, Betty an' me. Guess though," he rallied, "when so many are itchin' to fight, there must be good reason for it."

"Folks always find good reasons for fighting," Job returned with bitterness. "If they don't, Solomon Harvey and his crew'll supply 'em."

Nat sighed and drained his horn cup, but shook his head when his host would have refilled it.

"Thankee, no. Best be gettin' back to tell Betty you're still alive. If the weather holds, I can help tomorrow with your barn. Aimed to see Dan'l Houghton 'bout tradin' me a load of hay, but he's gone to Northampton, now that Melissa's back to keep Beulah company."

Job's heart checked. He was a long time replacing the jug, but his face and voice were composed when he asked:

"When did she return?"

"Dunno," Nat answered, rising. "Recent, I guess. See you early in the mornin'."

"Well, now," Job returned, "next day might be better. Need more lumber from Alex 'fore the snow gets deeper."

The excuse, he assured himself, was not entirely false. The same road led to Kathan's and to the Houghton pitch.

Job was forced to pause and recover breath when, next afternoon, he viewed from the distance the dwelling he had not seen since a long-ago, ignominious morning. Comparing his condition then and now, he took heart and went forward.

A woman was picking her way over the rutted track from

the house to the road as Job approached. Though she was muffled in a rust-red cloak and hood, he recognized Beulah before she halted, clasped mittened hands, and cried in shrill disbelief:

"Land o' goodness! It can't be Mr. Aldrich."

"And your servant," Job supplied.

"But not, I vow," Beulah insisted, as though it were beyond expectation, "comin' to visit with us."

"I'm going," Job explained, his ease increasing as the woman's left her, "to the sawyer's. If I'd not be unwelcome—"

He paused, awaiting invitation. Beulah's eyes shuttled from him to the house and back again.

" 'Lissa," she confided explosively, "ain't to home, right now, but I expect her most any minute. 'Twould pleasure us both," she pursued to drive disappointment from young Mr. Aldrich's face, "if you'd tarry for a spell when you come back from Kathan's."

"Fear I'd be trouble for you," Job demurred, conforming to custom, but Beulah's denial was vehement, and he ended it by agreement, adding politely:

"If so be you're going my way, I'd be pleased to squire you."

"No," Beulah faltered, "no. Jest—takin' the air. Expect you later."

She scuttled back to the house. Her headlong entrance startled Melissa, who, bare armed and girt by a bespattered apron, looked up from the wooden tub set on a bench and demanded:

"Now what? Surely you ain't been to Haven's and back already?"

" 'Lissa," her sister panted, "get into your blue lustring. Job Aldrich is comin' a-visitin'."

She babbled the tale of her encounter. Melissa's face was bright, but her voice had edge.

"Thought, by your haste, 'twas the King at least."

Her sister stifled the impulse to compare a prospering, well-spoken young man with Will French, to the latter's detriment. She turned instead and peered through a window.

[114]

"Goin' to Kathan's," she announced ominously, "an' still in sight. Want I should call him back, now?"

"No," the girl admitted, and wiped sudsy hands upon her apron. "Still and all . . ."

She left the disparagement unuttered. Beulah did not press her advantage. 'Lissa always had been hard to command, and she had been increasingly willful since Will French had taken to courting her. Her sister heard her moving quickly about her bedroom and turned to the tub with a gratified smile.

Haste had taken Job's breath again when the trail led him into the snowy glare of Kathan's clearing. He found Alex in the mill and secretly fretted at the delay while the sawyer laboriously wrote down each item of the order.

"Tomorrow," Kathan promised, "if the weather holds—and Solomon Harvey don't object."

"Harvey?" Job repeated without thinking, and his friend nodded.

"Him," he confirmed grimly. "To town meetin', wa'nt you?"

Job rebelled at the prospect of endlessly discussing politics while Melissa waited to receive him.

"Heered," Kathan was inquiring, "what Solomon calls the crew meetin' voted him? 'Committee for Detectin' Conspiracies,' no less. Enoch Cook an' me, we're a conspiracy, wouldn't wonder."

"What are you talking about?"

"Enoch an' me." Kathan's voice was surly; his freckled face wooden. "As assessors, we've been bid to buy ammunition for Dummerston. Ain't goin' to do it. Harvey's committee can punish me everlastin', but I still won't provide powder an' ball so neighbors can murder each other."

"Alex," Job begged desperately. "I'm in haste. I'll visit with you tomorrow. Harvey and his crew aren't all of Dummerston."

It was weak assurance, he thought as he hurried away, but, hard-pressed, he could devise no better. Not until Beulah greeted him at the Houghtons' door and he saw Melissa standing behind her, could he rid himself of the memory of Kathan's dull wretchedness.

Job, seated on one of the twin settles that flanked the Houghtons' hearth, belatedly decided that he was grateful to his hostess. Beulah's intemperate welcome had flustered him and had made Melissa's greeting, by contrast, dauntingly cool. The older woman had embarrassed the visitor by her attentions, had plied him with mulled cider and seedcake, deploring meanwhile the deficiencies of each, but now she had compensated for earlier offenses by her withdrawal on the arch plea that she had work to do elsewhere.

Melissa was perched on the opposite settle, with small buckled shoes set precisely side by side. Job dared not look overlong at her demurely inclined face or the distracting outlines of the young body enclosed in the blue gown, lest inner burning parch his throat entirely.

He feared, when the girl looked up, that she had read his mind, but she smiled and said with enviable calm:

"I scarce would have known you."

Melissa, though immune to Beulah's enthusiasm, conceded that this swain, though thrust upon her, was personable. Certainly, she thought a little wildly, his appearance had vastly improved since their last meeting. Her face grew brighter when Job answered huskily:

"And you are fairer than I remembered—even."

The girl pressed her lips together and said reprovingly: "You are bold."

Will, she thought, with oddly mingled satisfaction and irritation, was bolder still. She glanced again at her companion. This grave young man, with the steady eyes and the firm mouth, now softened by a trace of mirth, might serve as a scourge to discipline Will. Job was saying:

"I need to be bold, since I have commenced so late."

Melissa assumed a puzzled frown.

"I don't—understand."

"Commenced late," he interpreted promptly, "though

[116]

through no fault of my own, to prove how greatly I—esteem you."

It might be pleasant and profitable to encourage this reverent young man, particularly since favor she showed him would punish Will, who had ridden away in a cavalier fashion on some stupid political errand this very day. Melissa felt anger stir again as she recalled how he had laughed at her protests and had refused to tell her when he would be back or even whether he would reappear before the Spauldings' dance. She looked at Job, again, still with an air of guileless bewilderment:

"And if I forbid you?"

"Why then," he told her, "I must be bolder still and disobey you."

His smile made her wonder with a twinge of alarm whether he could have learned of her quarrel with Will.

"I don't think," she told him uncertainly, "that I should listen to you."

Job looked toward Houghton's musket, resting on pegs above the fireplace.

"If you wish to drive me forth again," he grinned, "the firelock's still handy."

His unabashed comment reminded Melissa of the sorry part she had played at their last meeting. She tried to recover balance by saying contritely:

"I was frightened and—and foolish. I wish you might forget it."

"There is a way to make me forget all else," he assured her. "Let me squire you to the dance to Spauldings'."

Melissa looked at Job so intently that, for an instant, he wondered if he had reached too far. Her gray eyes were wide, her lips parted in apparent alarm, yet actually she was surveying the double opportunity he had offered her. By accepting his invitation, she would acquire a reliable escort and at the same time fittingly humble Will.

"Dan'l and Beulah," she said to gain time, "they'll be going, too."

"Meaning," he asked, hoarsely, "that I'd be—unwelcome?"

"Not to them," she corrected, still wavering on the brink of decision.

"Then, to you?"

Already, Job could imagine her hand, lying warmly within his clasp, his arm encircling her pliant waist. Melissa saw ardor in his eyes and made up her mind.

"Nor to me," she murmured.

"Must I use the firelock to persuade you?"

"No need." She pictured Will's rage under merited chastisement, and her smile took away Job's breath. "I'll be real pleased to go with you."

He felt his face heat and his heart pound wildly. Already, he had gone unexpectedly far toward winning this radiant being with gentle, half-affrighted eyes and firelight gilding her hair. He had greatly overestimated Will as a rival. Job told Melissa in a tight voice:

"I'll wait on you, a week come Friday."

Again the girl smiled at him.

"Best come early," she bade, "and sup with us, first."

There was to be no end to Job's good fortune.

"If," he returned unsteadily, "your sister has no objection."

"Beulah?" Melissa said with an artless air. "Guess Beulah won't mind."

16

JOB AND NAT, working together, had finished the barn and had begun to cut more trees for later burning. Kathan had sledded in lumber, but it had lain untouched in the empty bedchamber. Snows that had followed the great storm had been too light to hamper outdoor toil.

The advancing year had quickened its pace, as though hurrying toward spring. Twigs of the osiers beside Job's spring had a brighter hue, and a lilac mist lay on the hills. Occasional days that seemed to have strayed out of April turned the drifts to pudding and filled the clearing at noontide with the blithe sound of running water.

Job could not recall an equally mild winter and rejoiced, though Nat spoke darkly of foul weather still to come. He had volunteered, when the barn had been completed, to spend another week in his neighbor's service if Job thereafter would give equivalent aid.

Axes spoke curtly from daylight to dusk on the edge of the Aldrich clearing, and the French horse snaked lengths of felled trees to the mounting heap of logs and branches. Nat was a handy woodsman and an easy associate, yet often, while sitting before the fire in the brief interval between supper and slumber, Job wondered wistfully whether he would know again the tranquil security that had enveloped him while he had been snowbound and solitary in his own house. It might be that he would never recover that singular serenity until he had won and wed Melissa and had brought her here.

He had resolved not to see her again until the day of the Spaulding dance, but to spend the interval in unremitting toil that would improve further the property he soon would bring her to view. He found that, though they were physically apart, she was continually in his thoughts. All his hopes and fears revolved about her shining presence.

When Nat predicted further foul weather, Job was immediately worried, lest another storm blight his tryst. If the day was clear, he prayed fervently that the dedicated Friday would be even fairer. One earlier dread had vanished. Melissa, by choosing Job as her escort, had shown him that she was pledged to no one else. Job felt no trace of an old anxiety when Nat announced that his brother had returned to Dummerston.

There had been a carefully calculated purpose in Melissa's refusal to accompany the Houghtons to Sabbath Meeting. She had used this ruse before to win a few uninterrupted hours with Will and was certain he would read invitation into her absence from morning service. Nevertheless, she was startled when he burst without warning into the kitchen.

She rallied and tried with small success to greet him primly. Will laughed, drew her close, and ignoring her protest, raised her head roughly and kissed her on the mouth.

"Don't try to pretend," he said, releasing her, rumpled and breathless, "you ain't glad to see me."

He laughed again. It was an irksomely confident sound. Melissa, reordering herself, did not reply at once. She had sought this opportunity to punish her suitor, but now she was not entirely sure she welcomed it. Will had heat that melted resolution.

He stood, hands on hips, and grinned at her, so sure of himself, so arrogantly male, that for an instant she was inclined to yield. Recognition of the weakness impelled her to say, even more sharply than she had intended:

"Did you leave all your manners at the lower settlements?"

Will chuckled, admiring her brilliant face and disdainful pose.

"Why," he marveled, "what a spitfire it is!"

"If so," Melissa pursued, ignoring the jeer, "you'd best go back and get them, before—"

"All in good time," he interrupted, still ignoring her disapproval. "I ride south again, day after tomorrow. That soon enough?"

His crass assurance stung her. Melissa said deliberately:

"Sooner the better, far's I'm concerned."

He looked at her more closely.

"Wal, now!" he mused aloud. "Changed our tune, haven't we?"

Melissa knew this air of tolerant amusement was designed to plague her and vindictively waited the time when her new weapon might strike him deepest.

"For all of me," she answered coldly, "you may come or go as it pleases you."

Will chuckled, though a trace of doubt had narrowed his insolent eyes.

"Fine words!" he acclaimed with heavy raillery and then, moved by her bright loveliness, altered his tone: "'Lissa, if you're still annoyed because I'll not be here to take you to Spauldings', I've already told you—"

"Oh, that!"

Melissa dismissed the subject with a light wave of her hand.

"Small difference to me," she went on deliberately, "whether you're here next Friday."

"No?" Will derided.

This was the designed, anticipated opportunity. Melissa seized it with malicious deftness.

"No, indeed; not in the least. I'm already bespoken."

He stood so still that, for a thwarted instant, she thought he had not heard her.

Will licked his lips and repeated, as though the word had no meaning:

"Bespoken?"

"Ehyah; bespoken."

She had braced herself for explosion; not for this small, dull voice that demanded:

"Bespoken by whom?"

Melissa did not spare the rod.

"Job Aldrich," she answered precisely, yet she felt uneasy under Will's unwavering stare and went on, more weakly than she had intended. "Since you wouldn't squire me—"

"Couldn't," he corrected. It pleased her to find him even momentarily on the defensive. "Express rider's time ain't his own."

"So you say," she returned, enjoying his distress. "Well, Mr. Aldrich, he asked to escort me and—"

Will had inflated himself by a hoarsely indrawn breath. Now, he blared:

"You ain't goin'; not with any man; special, not with Aldrich."

He shook his head like an angry bull. Melissa inquired:

"Meaning you'll be back for the dance?"

"Meanin'," he told her in a hushed bellow, "I ain't goin' to allow it."

"But you won't be here," she pointed out and smiled.

He swallowed loudly. His grimace bared strong teeth and almost closed his eyes.

"Neither," he promised, "will Aldrich be to the dance."

"No?" Melissa inquired, stirred by the prospect of rivals dueling for her favor. "Like to know how you can stop him."

"Wait an' see," he told her ominously. "'Fore I'll leave him tend my maid, I'll—"

He gulped and turned as the kitchen door opened and the Houghtons entered. Daniel hailed Will cordially, but Beulah's greeting was moderate. She looked sharply from her flushed sister to the smoldering young man and added:

"Could see by the tracks someone had come visitin'. Thought maybe 'twas Mr. Aldrich."

Dr. Solomon Harvey drew snuff into either nostril, dusted his nose with a soiled handkerchief, and looked from his rebellious express rider to the dispatches, folded, sealed, and stacked on the table. Each letter had been designed by the physician's own pen to strengthen resistance to a mounting tyranny. Each, according to its contents, would add substance to the edifice he and dedicated men in Massachusetts secretly were building.

The doctor matched scowls with Will French and asked in a grimly quiet voice:

"Need I ask you, sir, to repeat your oath to the Sons of Liberty?"

Will shuffled his feet and breathed loudly. Harvey made further acid inquiry:

"Or recite the penalties dissenters may suffer?"

The hulking young man found no mercy in the owl-like face and hurriedly looked elsewhere.

"Still hold," Will's surly voice insisted, "it's cruel hard for a man to ride his behind black an' blue for his country while a scurvy trimmer—worse'n that maybe—goes his way without let or hindrance."

"Now, there's no cause," Harvey reproved, "to be so—circumspect. Who d'ye mean?"

"Job Aldrich." Will launched the name like a missile and the physician lunged forward in his chair.

"Job Aldrich, eh?" he demanded. "And pray what's he done?"

His eagerness drove the accuser into fumbling explanation.

"Ain't sure. Suspicion him, though, more an' more."

Harvey jerked his head so sharply that his wig slipped.

"A devious, slippery rascal," he agreed, resettling it. "Dummerston would be well rid of him. That I have held since first I saw him."

"Way I feel," Will confirmed warmly. "Needs a close watch over him, I'd say."

He swallowed thickly and stumbled on.

"If someone else rides express this week, mebby I could uncover what he's up to. Something," he added, hopefully watching the doctor, "seditious, I'll be bound."

Harvey shook his head.

"No," he said flatly. "You serve the cause best as my express. Aldrich has been watched before to no effect. However," he went on thoughtfully, "I promise you he shall be observed while you are away, and if what you suspect proves true, you need have no fear that he'll be dealt with lightly."

He sat more stiffly erect, and his bitter eyes seemed to dwell upon a fair and distant prospect.

"You know as well as I," Harvey said at last, "that the day when we shall strike a blow for liberty is nigh. We shall purge Cumberland County of its oppressors and the trimmers, trucklers, and neuters who consort with them."

He thrust his head forward.

"Men like Aldrich," the doctor tolled, "who condone the evil done by Yorkers and British will learn to their sorrow that they who touch pitch are themselves defiled."

He relaxed and went on more soberly:

[123]

"He will be watched as closely in your absence as though you were here. That I promise you. And now, sir, it is time you were up and away."

He picked up the dispatches. Will accepted them sulkily yet with a certain satisfaction. Though he must ride, instead of biding here and, in some still undetermined fashion, bringing Job to book, Solomon's promise had made the journey considerably less of a trial.

17

THE KNOWLEDGE that this was the long-awaited Friday lifted Job from slumber. He groped to the door. By the stars, it still was an hour to daybreak, but he bared and replenished the fire, knowing he could not sleep again.

Before dawn washed the windows, he had blacked his shoes with pork fat and soot, after polishing their brass buckles with ashes and salt, again had inspected his appearing-out clothes, and had got himself into his workaday frock, breeches, and boots.

Job gulped his breakfast, as though his own haste might hurry along the intervening hours, and went downhill to help Nat pile wood for the burning. Young sunlight stretched across Black Mountain to color the western ridges. It would be a fine day. He chuckled and walked faster.

Nat looked up from his milking.

"Wal!" he marveled. "Mite betimes, ain't you?"

"Quitting early," Job explained. "Dance to Spauldings' to-night."

"You don't say!" his friend returned with mild irony.
"You and Betty going, too?"

Nat finished stripping the cow.

"No, we ain't," he confided at length. "Truth is, when a man has a woman that suits him real good, him an' her get more enjyment to their own home than they're likely to find traipsin' to the far end of town an' back again."

"Ehyah," the other said thoughtfully. "Wouldn't wonder."

A scant half hour of sunlight remained when Job, booted and carrying his shoes in the pockets of his coat, set out from his pitch.

The slippery road across the mountain delayed him. The sun was setting when he paused for breath at the end of his climb. Twilight was thickening as he came into Dummerston village. Lights shone in the houses, and across the wide valley, stars were kindling above the sooty New Hampshire hills.

The settlement's street was empty, though beyond Job's view on the hill below the common, children were playing or quarreling shrilly. The worst of his journey was over. In the gathering darkness ahead, warmth and light and Melissa's greeting awaited him. The invisible tumult grew louder. Youngsters, likely, were snowballing each other.

Job stepped out briskly, thankful that his route led him away from the conflict. It could not be entirely playful for, through the screeching, a thin wail of anguish reached and halted him. It rose again; a sound so plainly despairing that he turned and ran toward its source.

He paused beyond the common and looked down upon shadowy confusion on the hillside road. A dozen yelling boys retreated and, scooping up snow, darted forward to fling it, not at each other, but toward something, or someone, they had penned against the bank.

This was not pastime; it was savage attack, and a single word the avid young voices had begun to yelp in unison sent Job charging downhill.

"Witch!" the youngsters chanted. "Witch-witch-witch!"

They whooped with glee and gave way before their victim's blind rush. A fresh storm of snowballs exploded palely upon the dark figure. Once more, it uttered the tormented wailing, and Job recognized that desolate voice.

Zurvilla Alvord slipped and pitched forward. While she tried to rise, an assailant leaped in and kicked her.

"Witch! That's for you, witch!"

The woman lay prostrate. The juvenile mob closed in upon her. Young Jake Laughton had drawn back to kick again when a palm smote his cheek and overthrew him. Job, shoulder-deep among the ravening youngsters, struck out with either hand, relishing each smarting impact, rejoicing as the strident uproar collapsed into squeals of pain.

Many of the late assailants were weeping as they fled uphill, but from a safe distance Jake paused to squall defiance. He ran when Job lunged toward him. The scurrying sounds of flight died away. The woman, prone in the road, whimpered and stirred.

Zurvilla sat up, snatching at breath. Job raised her. She clung to him, her wet, upturned face glimmering in the dusk.

"Oh dear!" she moaned. "Oh deary-deary me!"

"Hurt bad?" he demanded.

She shook him with her struggle for breath.

" 'Twill be even worse for me," she sniveled, "if Brother Moses larns what's befallen. Warned me special not to come home through the settlement, but 'twas late and 'tis the shortest way."

Zurvilla shuddered, let go of Job with one hand, and wiped her eyes. She had been returning, the quavering voice ran on, from a stay with her Gorton kin in Brattleboro. She had thought she could get through the village unseen, but the boys had ambushed her.

"Misused her dretful," she wailed, "her that never harmed no one. Kilt her, mebby, but for you. Lost her basket, too, with all her belongin's an' the 'baccy Myra sent Brother. Cussed rapscallions—"

She fell to mumbling in a strange tongue. Job released himself and, searching the roadside, found the trampled basket. Zurvilla scarcely heeded when he returned it to her. She was looking about her like a hunted creature.

"Soon," she muttered, " 'twill be dark. An' them—them Mohawks likely is still a-lurkin'."

She turned and caught Job's arm.

"Sweet man," she wheedled, "come with Zurvilla through the settlement—just through the settlement, darlin'. She's still —still afeared."

Even now, the Houghtons might be waiting supper, while Melissa grew more and more impatient.

"Be easy," he told the quaking woman. "Take you all the way home, if you wish."

The common was deserted and the village street empty. Frost was stiffening the snow. It crunched beneath their feet as they moved on to the forest's edge. Here, Job's companion halted.

"Taken ye far enough from your way," she told him. "Zurvilla can get home safe now, sweet lad. An' ye'll not tell Brother Moses? Bless ye, darlin', for a merciful man." The windy voice grew shrill. "As for them young devils an' them what seeded an' bore 'em, she'll larn 'em all what it means to abuse Zurvilla."

Job hesitated, though fretting to be on his way.

"I could set you further—" he had begun when the woman cut him off.

"No," she crooned, "ye'll do as Zurvilla bids ye," and in the gloom he felt her eyes meet his. "Haste to your lady bird an' squire her to the dance, dearie. Pleasure yourself while ye kin, sweet man. Black times are a-comin' for you an' her an' all. Zurvilla knows; Zurvilla sees."

Job left her and strode back toward the village. It could not be as late as he had feared, for the afterglow still bleached the west. Bewilderment was succeeding his anger over the attack upon a moonstruck old woman. How, he wondered, had she divined his purpose?

He hurried through the settlement. Air blew against his

cheek, and a flying fragment of ice splintered on the street before him. Someone stirred in the shadow between two houses, and a thin voice cried:

"Stinkin' damn' Tory! Serve you worse 'fore I'm through."

The threat was followed by sounds of flight. Job grinned as he went on. Zurvilla's second sight had not discerned young Jake's ambush.

The Houghtons' horse puffed gusts of steam as he hauled the sled uphill to the Spaulding house. Its windows blazed, dimmed, and blazed again as figures moved behind them. Job, sitting alone and unhappy on a plank laid across the sled body behind the driver's seat, listened intently and was mildly relieved. Since he could hear no music through the muffled throbbing of many voices, it was likely the dance had not commenced, and Melissa had been deprived of another reason to be offended.

The sled had halted. Job scrambled out to hand down the women folks, perched beside Daniel. Beulah's clasp was warm, and she smiled encouragement. Her sister, alighting, ignored the outstretched palm. Job tried to catch her eye, but she kept her hooded head averted. Melissa still was unwilling to forgive the agitation he had caused her.

She had been worried, as suppertime had drawn near, by her escort's continued absence. Then, the possibility that he had forgotten his obligation had transformed concern into indignation. Finally, she had recalled Will's threat and had wondered, wavering between excitement and dismay, whether he had fulfilled it and forcibly had restrained his rival.

Melissa had been both dashed and angry when, after supper had been set out, Job had appeared, stammering apologies but offering no excuse for his tardiness. She had greeted him coldly, had let him sit alone during the ride to Spauldings', and was planning further punishment as she and Beulah breasted the freshet of sound, released by the opened front door.

Daniel drove toward the rear of the house, and Job walked after the sled. It was difficult to resent mistreatment by a creature as lovely as Melissa in her green shortgown and a petticoat the very color of her hair. He wished now that he had explained at once to her and the Houghtons the reason he had been delayed. He had feared that the tale of Zurvilla Alvord's plight and rescue would have sounded overboastful and the disaster that then had befallen him had driven everything else from his stricken mind.

Job shuddered, recalling Melissa's brittle mirth when, as he had bowed to her, one of the shoes he had carried in the pockets of his coat had fallen out with hideous clatter. He had bent to recover it and had dropped its mate. Thereafter he had stood, hot and helpless with a shoe in either hand, until Beulah mercifully had relieved him.

The runners squeaked through the dry snow. Job had followed the sled past the main house, with its kitchen door invitingly ajar, and now was skirting the long ell. This was dark, save for a single, faintly lighted window in its far end, above a flat-roofed shed.

Houghton found vacant space among the horses and oxen tied to the barnyard fence. "Wal, now!" Daniel suggested, "Len told me there'd be a bowl of his own contrivin' in the kitchen. Draft of flip might ile our jints for dancin', hey?"

"Might," Job granted, but he scarcely had fallen into step with his companion when Houghton halted abruptly:

"Now, surely," he asked, "you ain't a-fixin' to dance in them boots?"

For a stunned instant, Job stared downward. He had forgotten to change his footwear at the Houghtons'. He could not even recall what had become of his brightly buckled shoes. Daniel's chuckle broke the silence.

"In the sled, under the seat," he directed. "Beulah, she spied 'em and fetched 'em along. Forgot to tell you, I mistrust."

Job hurried back, found his shoes, and sitting in the tail of the sled body, drew off his boots. He had changed and was about to rise when a scraping sound drew his mind away from his grievances. He stiffened and peered toward the ell, a darker bulk against a starless sky, save for the dimly glowing window beneath its gable.

It was strange that anyone of Spaulding's household should have chosen to remain aloof tonight. Perhaps one of the family was ailing. If so, he was not bedridden, for Job saw a shadow move across the panes. He gathered himself to go, then again sat motionless.

The stealthy noise had resumed. He heard the faint creak of straining wood and watched, without belief, a dark object loom above the window sill so slowly that it scarcely seemed to move, yet it became, at last, the head and shoulders of a man who stood upon the shed and looked into the lighted chamber.

Job slid from his perch and stole forward. His heart was pounding so loudly that he wondered that the crouching figure above him—thief, spy, or eavesdropper—failed to hear it. The shed was close when the man on the roof turned his head. The glow from the window fell upon a swarthy, scowling face. Job said quietly:

"Well, Gorton?"

18

THE MAN DREW breath with a tearing sound, wheeled, and dropped from the roof's far edge. Job skirted the shed, heard the panicky clatter of flight die away in the darkness, and pursued no further. It was as well, he assured himself, that Gorton had escaped. His capture and the subsequent confusion, likely enough, would have completed the ruination of an already blighted evening.

If Job hoped to salvage any enjoyment, he would be wise to stay away from Cumberland County's complex plots and counterplots. He suppressed the impulse to haul himself up to the shed roof and determine whom, or what, Gorton had seen.

He had groped along the ell's wall to its junction with the main house when an unwelcome thought halted him and shook his resolution. Spaulding, like Job, was a fugitive from York's enfeebled justice. In little more than a fortnight, the court at Westminster would commence its spring term. Perhaps the sheriff was planning to recapture Spaulding. Possibly, Gorton had had an accomplice in the ell chamber. In any event Job must find and warn his host.

Chill particles pricked his face and whispered against his clothing. Before him, snowflakes were sifting down through the shafted light from the kitchen where, even now, Spaulding might be serving flip. Job advanced, halted before the nearer window, and peered into the bright room.

A steaming bowl was on the table, but the men who sat together at one end of the board in no wise resembled revelers. Houghton, Azariah Wright from Westminster, Davenport, and Temple were listening intently to Solomon Harvey, who leaned forward in his chair and was shaken by the hushed vigor of his speech. He paused, looked warily about the room, then started as, through a window pane, his eyes met Job's.

The doctor kicked back his chair, strode to the door, and flung it open.

"And what, sir," he hooted, "are you doing there?"

"I'm looking for Leftenant Spaulding."

"Are you, indeed?" Harvey jeered. "Will you accept my assurance that he is not here?"

"No need. I've already seen for myself."

"Then I recommend, sir," the doctor retorted, "that you do your eavesdropping elsewhere."

The other hesitated, then shrugged and walked away. At the corner of the house, he looked back. Harvey still was watching him.

Job stood before Spaulding's front doorstep and shook, less from cold than recent undeserved humiliation and belated anger. He could not go home, however fervently he wished he were there. Retreat would confirm Melissa in her already low opinion of him. Besides, he must tell his host of Gorton's prowling. Job sighed, brushed snow from his shoulders, and entered the house.

The din that filled the narrow hall enlivened him against his will. Overhead, excited voices rose, fell, and were lifted still higher by shrill bursts of laughter. The whine of a fiddle being bowed into tune wound through the tumult, and a flute warbled fragmentary replies.

Job climbed the stair with unexpected eagerness and paused in surprise. Rows of candles, sparkling on each window sill, and more in a wooden rack, suspended from a beam, lit the upper floor of the Spaulding dwelling that had been transformed into a single, long chamber.

Twin walls, hinged to beams, had separated this space into three rooms. The partitions had been swung aloft and secured by hooks. The floor had been cleared of furniture, save for chairs along the wall and two more at the hall's far end where Knight sat, with sorrowful face bent over his fiddle, and Wyman blew tentatively on his flute.

Women and girls sat along the walls, elaborately ignoring the men who had massed near the stairhead and now, after publishing their indifference by muttered converse and bursts of strained mirth, had begun to disperse in search of partners.

The bolder ones were stalking along the lines of chairs to bend at last over the women of their choice and overcome polite demurral by husky insistence. Job, abandoning search for his host, marked where Beulah Houghton was seated on the far side of the hall. He was still looking for Melissa when, turning, he found her close beside him.

Her gay costume, contrasting with butternut-brown or sumac-red gowns, gave her a blossomlike quality that let Job forget her earlier slights. He asked awkwardly:

"Will you grant me the first dance?"

Melissa shook her head with a trite smile, and his sense of ill usage returned when she told him crisply:

"Reuben Spaulding asked me, long since."

[132]

Job said, "Oh?" and, recovering, protested:

"Where I come from, a maid keeps the first dance for the man who's squired her."

"Where I come from," Melissa returned in spiteful mimicry, "a man who squires a maid don't make it his habit to be late for everything."

He swallowed the reproof meekly.

"Second dance, then, maybe?"

Will never had shown like contrition. Melissa found it agreeable, for variety's sake at least, to have a suitor ready to be ruled. The girl nodded but, when Job grinned, added loftily:

"Providing you're certain sure you'll be on time."

Job, lingering by the stair, watched the dancers move through the figures of "Soldier's Joy." Melissa excelled them all in grace and skill. It pleased him to see that her partner was less expert than she.

"Not dancin'?" a dry voice inquired. Azariah Wright grinned in friendly fashion.

"Not this one," Job returned,

Wright considered him blandly and, at length, offered:

"Hear you're sellin' your pitch." His parched face did not stir under the other's astonished scrutiny.

"Who told you that?"

"Wal, now," Wright returned, "I disremember. Heered it somewheres. Ain't true, hey?"

"Not a word of it."

"Misled, seems," the other conceded woodenly and plodded through explanation. He had a son, about to be wed, who was seeking better land than Westminster now afforded. Azariah had seen for himself that Job had a prime pitch.

"Change your mind, let me know; might make a deal."

He nodded and moved away, leaving the other to wonder whether Wright's proposal had been related to the hushed conference in Spaulding's kitchen.

Job and Melissa danced a quadrille, borne on a wavering melody, guided from figure to figure by Knight's singsong calling. The girl's face had unsettling loveliness.

[133]

At the outset, he had found his throat too full for speech. To touch Melissa was to be acutely aware of all the lithe beauty of her body, so sweetly differing from his own, so exquisitely designed to be its counterpart.

The quadrille's current separated and at last reunited them. Job stepped more surely. Melissa smiled at him and said:

"You dance real well."

"Dozey-doh!" Knight chanted. Job said over his shoulder:

"Scarce fail to, with you as a partner." He added recklessly as they joined hands: "Maybe it's a foretelling."

"Grand right an' left," the caller sang and parted them again. Melissa's eyes were puzzled when she rejoined Job.

" 'Foretelling'?" she repeated. "Foretelling of what?"

"All hands round," Knight called.

Job explained hoarsely as they circled:

"Foretelling of all the years I'll strive to please you as a partner."

"It's time you stopped talking nonsense," Melissa warned, but her face was brighter still.

"It's not nonsense," Job insisted, "and I've just commenced."

He led her back to her seat beside her sister and in new, warm confidence, pledged Beulah for the next dance and Melissa for the one thereafter. As he turned away, he saw Spaulding coming up the stair. Sight of him cooled Job's elation and revived the wretched sense of trouble secretly brewing.

"Wal!" his host asked heartily. "Enjying yourself?"

"Greatly," Job looked about him with assumed carelessness, then asked:

"Someone sick to your family?"

"Sick? Where?"

"In the ell chamber above the shed."

Spaulding cleared his throat with a rasping sound.

"There's no one in the ell," he returned carefully, "no one at all."

"Well," Job shrugged, "I just wondered. So did Gorton, seems."

"What, on earth," the other demanded, "you talkin' 'bout?"

"About Benjy Gorton," Job persisted, "on the shed roof, peering in the window."

"Where'd you hear sech nonsense?"

"Saw him skulking there. Since nobody's in the chamber, he went to a deal of trouble for nothing, seems."

Spaulding slowly extended an arm and braced himself against the wall.

"So did I," Job pursued. "Tried to catch the rascal but he outran me."

"Damn' reckless fool," Spaulding began explosively, then pulled his voice lower before he went on. "Bade him keep the shutters closed."

He muttered profanely and then inquired:

"Who else you told?"

"No one," Job answered. "As for me, wouldn't even try to guess who 'tis you've got hid."

"Hah!" Spaulding rumpled his gray crest with desperate vigor. "Mistrust you don't need to. Harebrained rascal arrives when the hull settlement's to be here. An' now—"

He stood for a moment with eyes squeezed into slits and at length said with resignation:

"Since Gorton seen him, best to get Reynolds away 'fore daybreak, snow or no snow."

He swallowed loudly, peered at Job, and finally acknowledged:

"Beholden to you."

"Well," his guest said, "I thought you ought to know."

This, too, Job thought solemnly, might be a foretelling. He sat with Melissa before the revived fire in the Houghton kitchen while snow sighed against the window. In time ahead, if Providence were kind beyond his deserts, this moment might enlarge itself into unnumbered intimate hours.

The evening that had begun ill was ending better than he had dared hope. Job had danced thrice more with Melissa and had acquitted himself well. When, at nine o'clock, he and her kin had driven away from Spauldings' through the quickening storm, the Houghtons had insisted that their guest spend the night with them. Melissa, now perched beside Job on the make-shift seat, had added her persuasion and he, after a genteel show of reluctance, had consented.

The girl's new favor had seemed close relative to miracle. She still had been lingering in the kitchen when Job and Daniel had entered, after caring for the horse. Beulah, that excellent woman, already had gone to bed and, when her husband had seemed inclined to linger and discuss the dance, had summoned him so severely that he had gone upstairs at once.

Melissa sat with the firelight shaking over her and spoke of the clumsiness of some of her partners with bitterness that seemed to Job, since she did not include him, infinitely amusing. He watched her raptly, scarcely able to believe that, for a suffocating moment on the journey home, he had held her hands to warm them. A time would come—he was certain of it now —when they would sit thus before their own hearth and, rising at length, go arm in arm—

The clock on the kitchen shelf whirred and struck ten. Melissa exclaimed:

"Glory be! It's late."

"Spare me," Job begged, "a few minutes more. I'll be up and away tomorrow before you're about."

"Are you," she smiled, "always prompter to leave than arrive?"

He was tempted to tell her of his rescue of Zurvilla but refrained, lest the tale be tainted with boastfulness like Will's. Instead, he begged:

"Set a time when I can see you again, and you'll marvel how prompt I'll be."

Melissa hesitated and then inquired with startling bluntness: "Do you aim to sell your pitch?"

He stared and at length met question with question: "What makes you ask?"

She seemed conscious of trespass and answered hastily: "'Twas what Cap'n Wright said, I guess."

While Job had handed the women into the sled, Wright had

reappeared, had caught his sleeve, and had muttered urgently:

"If so be you ever want to sell your lot, obleeged if you lemme know."

Job had been irked by his persistence then. He was warmed now by Melissa's concern and told her hoarsely:

"Never let it go while there's a chance that someday you might fancy it."

The girl's eyes dropped, and she fell to pleating her petticoat with uncertain fingers. Job persisted:

"When can I wait on you again?"

Melissa was finding it agreeable, for the moment at least, to have a swain respectful of her wishes. This grave young man who was almost handsome in his earnestness furthermore had property to recommend him. Will, she figured swiftly, would be back early next week and gone again before its end. Her soft speech thrust Job's heart into his throat.

"A week, come Sunday, I might stay home from morning meeting."

It was possible, Melissa thought without regret, that Will would still be here and might intrude upon the tryst. If so, it would be stirring to observe rivals, striving for her favor.

"Nothing," Job was saying with hushed ardor, "can keep me away."

Melissa rose. Her smile dazzled him.

"A week, come Sunday," she repeated and added archly, "providing you ain't an hour late again."

"More likely," Job returned, "I'll be an hour early."

"Past time I was abed," Melissa said. She gave him her hand and at length withdrew it.

"You go on," he told her unsteadily. "I'll cover the fire."

Job, waking abruptly, could not recall for an empty instant where he lay. It was not in his own house, for a window, dimly outlined by the dawn, was in the wrong place. A steady snoring close to his ear enlightened him. He had slept beside Daniel Houghton while, across the upper hall, Beulah, far more enviably, had shared Melissa's bed.

[137]

Hope that had sent Job on tiptoe over the cold floor died a-borning. He chiseled frost from a windowpane with a thumbnail and, peering through the cleared spot, saw snow-laden branches crisscrossing the bright east. The storm had ended in the night and had deprived him of excuse to linger here until he had seen Melissa again.

He had her promise, he reminded himself sternly, as he pulled on his clothing. It was a fair morning, and Nat would be expecting him. There was no valid reason for playing the sluggard.

Job pocketed his shoes and, boots in hand, stole down the stair. Beulah had insisted last night, he recalled with amusement, that she would be up and about by the time he rose, but the kitchen was empty and the house, silent. His hostess would be desolate when she found him gone, but it would be easier and quicker for him to breakfast after he got home.

The new snow, he was relieved to find, was scarcely ankle deep and in the early cold as dry as sand. The east had turned a paler hue than Melissa's hair. The world, Job reflected and lengthened his stride, had vastly improved since yesterday. Never had his heart been lighter or he more blithely confident.

Smoke from Dummerston's distant houses rose straight across the sky, and the risen sun was shingling roofs with gold. Two men were plodding toward him down the hill from the settlement. Joel Temple and Jacob Laughton, it seemed, were early risers, too. Job hailed them cheerfully as they drew near:

"Morning. Up betimes or not yet abed?"

The jest misfired. Laughton and Temple glanced at each other then, silent and angular as scarecrows, barred the way. Job stared at them.

"Now what?" he challenged.

The rawboned Temple cleared his throat with a rattling sound and demanded:

"Whar ye been?"

"Speak up," Laughton added.

Their hostility was contagious. Pulses began to throb in Job's throat.

"If it's any of your concern, and I hold it ain't," he replied, "I spent the night to Houghtons'. What right have you to halt and question me?"

His vehemence abashed them for an instant. Temple, rallying, said darkly:

"We're members of the committee town meetin' voted."

"The Committee for Detecting Conspiracies!" Job mouthed the title so derisively that Temple flushed. "And with whom am I supposed to be conspiring?"

He waited, tardily deploring his anger.

"Times like these," Temple said sulkily at length, "it's needful to protect the town's welfare."

"If you've done with protecting it," Job requested, "will you stand aside?"

Temple complied, scowling irresolutely, but Laughton, holding his ground, yapped:

"Warn you of one thing: You keep your hands offen my Jake, hereafter."

"Well, now," Job answered with heavy gravity, "might do that if your committee'll take him in hand and birch him thrice daily. Can't think of anything that'll better protect the town's welfare."

Job reviewed penitently how often of late he had let himself be party to the strife that simmered in this endlessly quarrelsome town. Since yesterday, he had pursued the sheriff's deputy, defied Solomon Harvey, embroiled himself in Spaulding's intrigue, and bickered with the newly formed safety committee. His own pitch was the sole place in all Cumberland County where he could still be safe from provocation to wrath.

He paused, spent by groundless haste, at his clearing's edge, and his house with young sunlight across its shoulders gave him voiceless welcome. Footprints in the new snow led to his door. Nat, evidently, had come on some errand and was waiting for him.

The latch clicked, the portal swung inward, but Job stood, still and staring, on his doorstep.

The young man on the bed's edge, lifted a sweating gray face. He tried to smile, whispered, "Welcome home, friend!" and quite slowly toppled backward.

19

JOB HAD BEEN shut away from the calm world where bluejays were calling and a breeze went loudly through the treetops. He still stood on his doorstep, still tried to deny the evident. The easy young man he had seen once long ago, lay half on, half off the bed like an overthrown effigy.

Alvah Reynolds's upturned face was slack and glistening, and he breathed in shallow spurts. Job, stealing forward, wondered what circumstance had brought the man here.

He closed the door, lifted the outthrust legs onto the bed, then stood, stupidly staring at his own scarlet palm. Reynolds moaned. The piteous sound roused Job.

He wheeled, raked apart the fireplace ashes, and whittled shavings upon the surviving coals. The kindling was ablaze when he returned from the spring with a dripping kettle. Logs were beginning to burn by the time he had torn his only other linen shirt into strips and, knife in hand, had knelt by the bed.

He had thought he would have to cut away the sodden boots but he managed to pull them off, unslashed. Water dribbled from one but the other spilled red fluid on the floor and the disclosed stocking was blood-soaked. Scarlet tricklings ran down the bared leg from raw holes on either side of the knotted calf. Job pressed wet pads against them and bound them tightly. He hurried to the cupboard and returning, cup in hand, raised

Reynolds's head. The man swallowed, gagged, and swallowed again. His eyelids twitched, then opened wide.

"Be easy," Job said. "You're quite safe."

He did not entirely believe his own assurance. A musket or pistol ball had made the opposing wounds. Reynolds nodded feebly toward the cup, drank once more, and tried to smile. Vitality was returning to the lax face. His eyes strayed and came to rest at last upon his bandaged leg.

Job had risen, had barred the door, and was hanging the kettle on the crane when the other asked in feeble self-mockery:

"Swooned like a green-sick maid! For how long?"

"A few minutes," Job said, turning, "no more."

"Then," the other said gravely, "you have done more for me in a very short space than I can requite in a lifetime."

He flexed his wounded leg, winced, but pressing his lips together, managed to sit up. For an instant, he rocked but shook his head as Job stepped forward.

"It'll pass," Reynolds insisted. "One more touch of those spirits that truly would raise the dead, and I'll be on my way."

Perched on the bed's edge, he drained the replenished cup.

"Praise God—and you—for your mercies," he wheezed, thrust himself upward, stood erect for a reeling instant, and would have fallen if Job had not caught and lowered him to the bench beside the fireplace.

"A little at a time," Reynolds said through locked teeth. "You'll be rid of me soon, I promise."

Job replied, careless for the moment whither the assurance might bear him:

"You are not able to leave, nor would I let you go."

The other looked up with a trace of derision in his pale eyes. He warned:

"I'm Reynolds, from Bennington way."

"Ehyah, I know. I'm Aldrich."

"That I suspected. My friend, you are harboring an outlaw with a price on his unworthy head."

"You're still welcome."

"Will you persist," Reynolds asked with a forced smile,

"when I tell you that the high sheriff and one of his minions came within an ace of taking me and, for all I know, may still be hunting me?"

He shook his head, opposing interruption, and went on with the rueful air of one who had been bested in a game. He had ridden away from Spauldings' while it still had been night. It had been barely daybreak when, as he had crossed Black Mountain, two men had leaped from hiding, seized his bridle rein, and bidden him stand in the name of the law.

"Spurred forward," Reynolds went on with a lopsided grin, "but my horse stumbled, and he and I and one rogue went down together. I ran for it into the forest, yielding my mount and pistols in exchange for a ball through my leg."

He laughed grimly before he continued: He had wandered through the woodland, wading up or down the brooks he had encountered, to confuse his trail and ease the pain in his calf, and had stumbled at last on Job's clearing.

"Quite possible," he submitted, "I'm still being followed, though, by his lamentation, I hurt the man my horse knocked over. Still, twenty pounds, head money, is no trifle and Paterson is—mercenary. It'll do you, or me, small good if he were to find me here, so—"

Job asked, holding Reynolds's shoulder as he tried to rise: "Where will you go?"

"As far as possible," the man answered promptly, "from one who has befriended me. Will you do me one more favor?"

He reached within his cloak and brought out a sealed packet.

"No one else," he warned, "must see this. If you cannot return it to Spaulding, burn it."

Job looked from the drawn face to the package and shook his head.

"Keep it," he bade gruffly, "for you're staying here. You couldn't walk a furlong, hurt as you be. This is my house, and you're my guest, and no one enters here against my will."

"Now, my dear sir," Reynolds asked with forced lightness, "have you considered that to many, including the high sheriff, I am brother to Ishmael and own cousin to Iscariot?"

"If so be," Job returned, striving to match the other's valiant humor, "we're kin, after a fashion. You'll bide here until—"

He paused. He was thrusting himself into peril for the sake of an outlawed stranger.

"Yes?" Reynolds inquired. "Until?"

"Until," Job said levelly, "I am sure it's safe for you to leave."

The other spread his hands in a gesture of surrender.

"Faith," he grinned. "They do not stretch the truth who call you a contrary man."

He sat for a moment, watching the fire with calculating eyes, and then proposed quietly:

"Strike a bargain with you! I'll remain wherever you choose to hide me, if then you'll straightway go and tell Spaulding."

Job stifled impulsive assent, scowled, and objected:

"I've friends closer to hand than Spaulding. French, my near neighbor, is a good man and—"

Reynolds shook his head decidedly.

"No one must learn that I'm here. I've botched my task," he added with faint bitterness, "more than enough already."

"The attic," Job hesitated, "likely would be the safest place, but you'll be left alone and—"

"Let it be the attic, then," the other said briskly.

Job stripped blankets from the bed. When he turned again, Reynolds stood erect and determinedly smiling. His weight bore ever more heavily upon his guide, and when they had toiled up to the slant-walled space beneath the roof his sweating face shone in the gloom. A small sound escaped him as he lowered himself to the blankets Job spread.

"Luxury, no less," Reynolds said loudly. "Now, leave me, I beg you. Time is of the essence."

Job took a single step toward the stair but went no further. He was leaving a helpless man to the dubious mercies of Paterson, who might still be trailing him. He said in a sullen revolt:

"I can't do it. If the sheriff—"

His throat closed. He endured the reproachful stare of Reynolds, who said at length:

[143]

"It's necessary that you go at once. As for Paterson, he would have appeared before this, if—"

The sound hushed the confident voice and beat upon Job's heart. For an instant, the two men gaped witlessly at each other. Someone knocked more loudly, then raised an anxious voice. Job released breath and smiled wanly.

"Nat French," he muttered. "My neighbor," and, turning again toward the stair, shouted: "Coming."

By the time he reached the door, his palsied mind had revived.

"Sorry," he said, as lightly as he could, "I was—above."

Nat blinked and, still breathless from haste, complained:

"Betty and me, we got worried. Mornin's half spent an'—"

He stopped, looked at his friend more closely, and added in another tone:

"What's wrong?"

"Enough," Job returned, still feeling his way and, when Nat asked promptly: "Aught I can do?" cast away hesitation.

"Will you," he asked quickly, "ride to Spaulding's fast as you're able? I'm in sore trouble," he went on, to drive uncertainty from the mild face. "Tell Spaulding"—he hesitated, then pressed on more surely—"that what we spoke of last night has gone askew and he's to come, at once. Will you, Nat?"

French nodded.

"Why not?" he asked. "Neighbors, ain't we? Get to Spaulding fast as Cephas'll let me."

Nat nodded and left. Job, watching his friend hurry across the clearing, found his own eyes blurred.

Reynolds, long body outstretched and head pillowed on his arms, said impulsively when his host had finished speaking:

"I wish—"

He went no further and Job did not heed the suppression. He had seen that a dark stain had spread upon the bandage, and now he offered, in distress:

"You need a doctor's care. I should have told Nat to fetch Harvey."

"No!" Reynolds exclaimed. "By no means."

"No?" Job asked, abashed.

His companion looked at him quizzically and, after a moment, inquired:

"Are you familiar with Grants' politics?"

"Familiar enough," Job returned with bitterness, "to find that, wherever I go, I step crotch-deep into trouble."

"And it sickens you?" Reynolds asked acutely. "Well, you're a settler with land to have and to hold, while I, being trained to the law, relish dissension, of which the Grants, east and west, have abundance.

"And yet," he went on with sudden gravity, "I truly do believe that out of chaos peace and liberty may come."

He atoned for his earnestness with a wide smile.

"Now Harvey," he went on, "distrusts the Allens, Seth Warner, Spaulding, and the rest of us. The learned doctor is zealous for liberty provided it binds us to Massachusetts and he may judge who is worthy to receive it. He wishes to measure it out personally to the deserving, as though it were his damned purges, pills, or powders."

Reynolds looked up thoughtfully.

"Sometimes I wonder whether Harvey would not rid Cumberland County of King George, only to raise up King Solomon in his stead. The less the doctor knows of me, the better."

He yawned convulsively, then grinned.

"I have stupefied myself with my own sermonizing," Reynolds deplored. "There is no need for you to wait on me, for I am comfortable here, and I know you have work to do."

He nodded dismissal yet spoke again as Job turned toward the stair:

"If you are leaving the house, I might be less—lonely with your firelock for company."

After an instant, Job confessed:

"I don't have a firelock."

He felt his face heat under the other's disbelieving stare and stumbled on:

"Left it to Stockbridge. Seemed that in the Grants I wouldn't need it."

[145]

He could not tell whether Reynolds were shocked or amused, and added in awkward self-justification:

"Weapons lead to violence, way I see it, so—"

"So," his companion completed gravely for him, "abhorring violence, you made your pitch in the Grants."

"You find that comical?"

"Less comical than amazingly hopeful."

He laughed. Job grinned and retorted:

"Certainly, there are few places more sorely in need of peaceful men."

"Sometime," Reynolds said, nodding recognition of the challenge, "I'll be glad to examine that contention with you, but I'm too greatly at ease to argue now."

He pulled a blanket up about his shoulders and closed his eyes. Job went downstairs softly. He hoped his profession had not lessened him in Reynolds's estimation, yet he was glad that he had spoken truthfully to one who already seemed his cherished friend. Jonathan might have felt a kindred fondness for the young and outlawed David.

Job looked irresolutely about the kitchen and picked up his ax, half-minded to speed the time of waiting by limbing trees already felled at his clearing's edge. He discarded this intention when he saw how close the sun stood to noon, and went down cellar, where he fished from its keg a pork chunk sufficient for dinner.

He bore his trove up to the kitchen, closed the door behind him, then stood motionless and inanely gaping.

"Don't," Sheriff Paterson warned, "as much as stir until I bid ye."

Flames muttered in the fireplace, and a log crumbled with a soft sound. Paterson stood with his back to the door, swollen body filling the space from jamb to jamb. Snow flaked from his boots, and his hands were thrust into the pockets of a torn and stained blue coat.

The sheriff leered, with eyes red-rimmed and wicked as an angry boar's, at Job who still held the oblong of pork with both hands. In a moment, his reviving mind assured him

[146]

inanely, sanity would return, and this baleful presence would vanish. The wild hope collapsed as Paterson gloated:

"A brace of ye, by all that's holy! Jail-breaker and traitor in one haul! Where is he? Speak up."

"Who?"

The intruder chuckled and replied with heavy playfulness:

"Now, who indeed? The outlaw, Reynolds, ye damned seditious yokel, who I meself trailed hither and ye have in hiding."

A darker hue suffused the beefy face, and the thick voice surged into a hoarse squeal:

"No time nor wish have I to bicker with ye. The man is here. Will ye yield him immejitly or must I—"

His furred paw dwarfed the short-barreled pistol he had drawn from his coat.

"A ball in the guts," he grinned, slitted eyes scanning the kitchen, "might loosen your tongue. Where—"

Paterson broke off again to stare at the stained floor beside the bed. The clogging stupor, the unmanning fright were leaving Job. His obligation was growing clear. He had promised Reynolds that he would be safe here; had said, exactly, that none should enter this house against its owner's will and now—

"Blood!" the sheriff grunted. "Blood! By God, I did wing him, then."

He looked again at Job and bellowed:

"Where is he hid, eh? Answer me, ye rascal, or—"

His crooked thumb drew back the pistol hammer with a small, dire sound.

Job scarcely heeded the question or his belly muscles' contraction as the sheriff thrust his weapon forward. Upstairs a friend lay, wounded and helpless, and whatever might save him would be well spent. He furtively shifted the clammy weight of the pork to his right hand and begged, "Now, hold on!" so abjectly that Paterson grinned and stepped forward.

"Now, hold on!" Job repeated. "Maybe he's here; maybe he isn't. What I want to know is whether if I lead you to him, I'd go free?"

"That's better," Paterson acclaimed, his grin spreading.

"Ye're in no place to bargain, me buck, but if ye produce Alvah Reynolds I'll—"

"Will you?" Job asked through his teeth and flung the block of pork.

He did not see the sheriff dodge or hear the missle thud against the door. A thunderclap had deafened him as he had dived for Paterson's knees. His arms had locked about them. He twisted viciously.

The floor shook as his enemy fell backward. Job threw himself forward and got astride the heaving body. Powder smoke puckered his nostrils, and his ringing ears discerned, as from a great distance, hoarse and broken roaring. Thick fingers pried against his chin; the clubbed pistol grazed his ear.

Job pressed his face against the bull neck and, heedless of the fist that beat upon his skull, clasped both hands around Paterson's right wrist and pounded it against the floor until the dislodged weapon skittered away.

Close to Job's cheek a voice bubbled obscenity. A thumb jabbed at his eye. He got his forearm across the other's throat, drove it inward with harsh delight, while the corpulent flesh beneath him surged and quaked and a mouth, idiotically a-gape, uttered gargling sounds.

The purpose that had entirely possessed him was simple and sharp as a well-whetted knife. The red haze that had confused Job had vanished. He could see clearly and with pitiless glee the bulged and frantic eyes, could trace each crease and welt, each gorged vein in a face so purplish and contorted that it must belong to an inhuman creature, deserving of slaughter. Job bore down more heavily on the throttling arm, and dodged the sheriff's clawing, free hand.

Paterson shuddered, crowed, drove his fist into Job's face and, twisting frantically, unseated him. He fell, rolled over, and leaped again at his still prostrate enemy. A boot, blindly outthrust, cast him backward upon the fire.

Smoke filled Job's eyes. There were ashes in his mouth, and sparks clung like wasps to his neck and hands. He flung himself out across the hearth. Paterson, windily sobbing, had got to

[148]

his feet. He kicked again. Job caught the boot with both hands and twisted.

The sheriff's bellow burst apart as he went down. Job rose, reeled, and fell against the wall. An aimlessly reaching hand closed about the helve of his ax.

Far away, a voice was calling to him, but he did not heed. He stood with the weapon no longer a support but purposefully uplifted. Paterson, dizzily pulling himself up, saw the slow advance, cried out, and lunged toward the door. He had lost both hat and wig. The bared pate, furred by lately cropped hair, was a mark a lesser axman could not miss.

The sheriff scrabbled frantically with the latch. A voice close to Job's ear called: "No!" The sudden weight upon the upraised ax was Reynolds's delaying hand. He shouted "No!" again, and unwillingly Job forbore. Paterson tore open the door, rushed out, vanished.

Reynolds limped across the kitchen and set the ax in the farthermost corner. Job sat down decrepitly on the bed's edge. There was chill emptiness within him. He managed to say breathlessly: "He came to take you," but could go no further.

"Yes," Reynolds acknowledged, "I judged as much. Don't think," he added dryly, "that he'll be back."

He considered his companion solemnly, yet there was sparkle in his eyes. Job swallowed thickly against gathering nausea. He rested his head on his hands and looked up only when Reynolds again paused before him. The man held out a hat with tarnished gilt binding and a trampled wig.

"Yours," he said. "The spoils of war."

Job looked hastily away. Reynolds's shoulders were shaking, and twice he tried to speak before he managed to say in an uncertain voice:

"The pistol, with your permission, I shall keep. I understand now why so peaceful a man left his firearms in Stockbridge."

"I think," Job said, wavering toward the door, "I am going to be sick."

Cold air settled his queasy stomach but did not retard the

dreadful sense of guilt. In madness, he had betrayed his deep
beliefs and, except for Reynolds's intervention, would stand, not
only a hypocrite, but a murderer as well.

He postponed return to the house by tracking Paterson across
the clearing and into the forest. The sheriff had fled with long,
unsteady strides and had not paused to look behind. Job's
marred and blackened face was so dismal, when he re-entered
the kitchen, that Reynolds, seated on the bed with his wounded
leg outstretched, hesitated before he said with quiet earnestness:

"It ill became me to make game of the man who saved me
from jail or worse."

Job swept the dislodged ashes back into the fireplace and said
at length without turning:

"I beg you to tell Spaulding nothing of—what happened,
until after you and he have left. I would rather not—talk of it."

"Then," Reynolds told him cheerfully, "you had best cleanse
and repair yourself, for you look as though you had been pulled
down a chimney, feet first. I cannot," he went on in a more
sober voice, "deplore what you did, since it is due to you, and
you alone, that I am still free."

"I should," Job muttered, "have dealt with Paterson in
some defter fashion. It was," he went on with difficulty, "truly
as though Satan had entered into me."

"Now, if that be so," Reynolds grinned, striving to lighten
his host's distress, "never did Satan more vigorously reprove
sin."

He paused an instant and, moved by the other's desolate
look, went on:

"My dear friend, for so I shall ever deem you, all men must
fight, at need, for what they cherish most."

"That," Job returned woodenly, "I will not believe."

"Faith," Reynold shrugged, "unless Judgment Day is at
hand, you will discover soon enough how right I am and wrong
you are."

Spaulding rode into the clearing, at last, leading a second
horse and so oppressed by anxiety and haste that he ignored

Job's bruises and blisters and centered his attention upon Reynolds.

Was he badly hurt? Could he make shift to ride? Then they had best leave at once before worse befell. Gorton lately had passed through the settlement on a limping nag, but no one knew where the sheriff was or what he was planning.

Reynolds smiled but held his peace while Spaulding rattled on: He would ride as far as Draper with the wounded man, who, if he did not wish to hang, should mount at once. Job helped his guest into the saddle where, sitting sidewise, he looked down and held out his hand.

"Good-by, my friend," he said huskily, "until a more fortunate meeting."

Spaulding, gathering up his rein, addressed Job directly for the first time.

"Beholden to you," he rasped. "Once we are clear of Dummerston, tell Nat French as little as you can manage and all others, nothing whatever."

He turned his horse but halted him again to demand:

"Why was that Laughton brat here?"

"Laughton brat?"

"Young Jake," Spaulding insisted, "pelting downhill as if the devil was after him. What was he up to?"

"I don't know," Job said slowly, "I haven't seen him."

20

*I*T WAS FITTING that dawn, on the day of Job's tryst with Melissa, should be filled with the sounds and scents of spring. All week, the soft, bright weather had held, as though preparing the way for this morning.

Each day's sun had lifted stumps a handbreadth higher above sodden drifts, had strengthened the brooks' voices, had hung a veil of brighter purple across the hills. Yesterday, Cephas, drawing the last of the French logs, had splashed, fetlock-deep, through slush. Job, as he rose, recalled tolerantly his neighbor's dark prediction that further storm must balance this unseasonable warmth before winter truly ended. It would be easy to forgive Nat graver offense than resolutely gloomy prophecy.

Job sat for a long moment, razor in hand, while he thought of his friend's forbearance that had spared a contrite man galling confession. Memory of his struggle with Paterson lay, even now, like a weight beneath his ribs.

When Spaulding and Reynolds had ridden away, Job had girded himself for further ordeal. He had gone downhill to find his neighbor working alone at the task they had agreed to share. Nat had looked sharply at his friend but had said nothing until a log had been unchained and then had limited himself to asking:

"Wal, get everything settled?"

"Seems so," Job had answered gruffly and had forced himself to add, "I was in sore trouble. Mind if I tell you no more than that?"

Nat had surveyed him again, wavered, and finally had blurted:

"This trouble—was it of Will's making?"

"Will?" Job had echoed loudly. "In no way whatever."

His neighbor had grinned with relief.

"Wal," he had said, "there's plenty to do if you've a mind to help."

He had not mentioned the crisis again during the days of uninterrupted work that had followed. Job, plying his razor, reviewed them and was ashamed of his earlier dread. He no longer expected reprisal by a vengeful sheriff, yet the onerous sense of self-betrayal still clung, and he continued to quail at thought of what he might have done, if Reynolds had not halted his fury.

Job opened the door and stood for a long moment, watching the new sunlight climb, bough by bough, down the trees across the clearing toward shadow that still lurked beneath them. He breathed the cold smells of melting snow and thawing earth, sought again for the sustaining assurance that he and his land were in harmony, and once more failed to regain it.

He sighed and shook his head. He had been weighed in the balance and found wanting. It was not a new conviction, and it stung him less than heretofore. The morning was unfolding in splendor, and each brilliant moment brought nearer the time when he would wait again on Melissa. Job could not feel entirely downcast with that fair prospect before him.

The breeze, this Sabbath morning, was as fragrantly soft against Job's face as Melissa's throat might be. Bright rivulets tumbled down at either side of the muddy road. On hillsides where the sun had dwelt longest, boulders and tips of juniper bushes had thrust through the dwindling snow, and once he halted, almost sure that through the voices of freed water he had heard a sparrow's song. As he crossed Black Mountain's shoulder, he looked ahead and, with dismay, saw Spaulding riding toward him.

The morning suddenly grew chill, but there was no lack of warmth in the rider's greeting:

"Wal, now, claw me!" he hailed, halting his flea-bitten nag. "If it ain't the very scoundrel I was thinkin' of! Job, how be ye?"

He scanned the other's face with exaggerated care and asked:

"No honorable scars?"

"None."

The brevity did not lessen Spaulding's amusement. He pursued, keen little eyes glittering:

"Alvah told me all 'bout it on our way to Draper. Sent you his compliments and thanks, and here's mine for good measure."

Job asked bleakly:

"Thanks because I tried to kill Sheriff Paterson?"

"Wal, now!" Spaulding chuckled, letting his feet dangle free on the stirrups. "Half a loaf's better'n none."

It was going to be hard for Job to maintain his penitence among people who held felony a virtue. Before he could protest, the other, abandoning mockery, was explaining that he had ridden with Reynolds all the way to Bennington and, after long conference with leaders there, had returned to Dummerston only yesterday.

"You valuin' peace so high," he chuckled, "likely'll be pleased that folks to Bennington want we should try to keep the goddamn court from settin', a week come Tuesday, without startin' a fight."

He dropped his voice. As many freeholders as he and others could enlist would ride to Chester the next Thursday and there urge Judge Chandler to avoid rebellion by canceling the court's spring session.

"May work," Spaulding shrugged. "Wuth a try, mebby. Otherwise, we'll—wal, there'll be trouble. Like for you to go to Chester with us."

"No," Job returned bitterly. "Haven't I done more than enough already?"

His companion squinted.

"Scalds you, don't it?" he asked shrewdly.

"I'm not—proud of it."

"Goddlemighty, Job! Would you ruther Paterson had taken Alvah!"

"Not that, either. It's just—"

Job subsided with a helpless gesture. If he still was so readily

[154]

confused, how could he hope that a weathered insurgent ever could understand the galling shame and contrition? Spaulding removing his hat, rubbed his stiff hair with a despairing air.

"Damme," he complained, "if I can fathom you. Ain't there nothing you do that you don't later regret?"

Job answered wryly:

"Aim to take satisfaction henceforth in what I don't do."

"Ain't my day for guessin' riddles," Spaulding surrendered. "Hope t'other folks I gotta see talk sense."

He clucked to his horse and rode on. Job went glumly down the crooked road to the village. It had been alarming to find how facilely resolutions he had undertaken in privacy changed shape at the least contact with his neighbors.

It was still early when he entered the settlement. Melissa and the hours she had promised him were almost within reach, yet the shining prospect did not dispel the gloom that had overtaken him. He considered angrily, as he turned into the village street, the failures, compromises, and open iniquities that had been the tale of his existence in Dummerston.

He would lose all he had hoped to gain in the Grants unless, at once and forever, he faced about, kept himself more straitly aloof hereafter from the eternal quarreling, and single-mindedly held fast to the prime purpose that had brought him here. He had his pitch to better and there, henceforth, he would abide.

A sharp voice called, "Hey, you, Aldrich!"

He halted and looked in momentary bewilderment from Harvey's nearby house to the small, dry man who had hailed him. The elder Jacob Laughton stood in the dwelling's dooryard and, grinning like a fox, proclaimed:

"The very man I wanted to see. Come here."

There was affront in the yapping summons. Job, swallowing more heated retort, asked:

"What for?"

Laughton spoke over his shoulder to someone invisible and then replied glibly:

"Jest something want to ask you 'bout."

[155]

He advanced while he spoke, and the rawboned Joel Temple, appearing from behind the house, followed him. They halted in the road on Job's either hand. Laughton said with thin heartiness:

"Saved us quite a journey. Joel an' me, we was jest settin' out to fetch you."

"Fetch me? Why?"

Temple shrugged. His companion said quickly:

"Don't rightly know. Committee's orders. Come along an' we'll find out."

Again, Job choked back refusal. The summons might mean trouble, yet it might have been contrived by Providence to test the sincerity of his latest repentance. He said at length:

"I've an errand to do and little time to spare," and tried to ignore the objection's bleating sound.

"Take scarce a minute," Laughton assured him and Temple, drawing a half step closer, advised dryly:

"Best come in."

They watched him closely. After an instant's hesitation, Job allowed the two men to guide him toward Harvey's dwelling.

They entered the narrow hall. Laughton nodded to a chair, bade Job, "Set thar," and, tiptoeing down the passage, opened the door at its far end and proclaimed:

"Got Aldrich here."

The announcement silenced the conflict of voices within. Chair legs scraped, feet hurried across the floor, and Harvey appeared, framed by the doorway. He held papers in one hand, and there was a smear of ink on his nose. He announced, as though addressing a patient:

"We will see you presently, sir."

"I am pressed for time," Job told him and instantly regretted the protest, since it visibly pleased the doctor.

"Now are you indeed, sir?" he asked with soft malice. "And so is the Committee for Detecting Conspiracies, I assure you; most sorely pressed for time to deal fittingly with all the renegades and worse who have been brought to its attention."

"Am I to understand, " Job inquired, curbing his voice, "that you are holding me prisoner?"

Harvey raised a chiding forefinger.

"Prisoner, forsooth! Your word, sir, not mine. Prisoner or no," he added with a flash of enmity, "you will wait the committee's pleasure."

He went back into the room. After a moment, Will French came out, closed the door behind him, paused for an instant to stare silently at Job, then strode the length of the hall. He spoke in a low voice to Temple and Laughton, who nodded and stood aside for him to leave.

Will paused in Harvey's dooryard, looked about him and laughed. It would have been a pleasure to witness his rival's trial by the committee and to join in questioning him but before him shone a more alluring opportunity. Will would find Melissa before meeting and tell her what had befallen the priggish dissembler she had favored. Later in the day, if he could manage to see her privately, he would deal more vigorously with a contrary wench who had presumed to defy him. It was past time she was mastered.

Families of the village were moving toward the meeting-house, and earlier arrivals already had assembled on its steps. Melissa and her kin might be among them. As Will left the dooryard, a familiar voice hailed him. He halted and watched the Houghtons come toiling up the hill. Daniel greeted him heartily and Beulah with moderation. Melissa, she panted, in response to the question, wasn't feeling too good and was staying to home.

"Oh?" Will said and after a blank instant, mumbled: "Forgot something."

He turned back toward Harvey's house, lingered beside it until the Houghtons had gone on, then hurried down the road to seize this heaven-sent advantage. The false baggage had begged off from meeting before this to receive Will. Today, he thought, jealousy quickening his pace, she expected Aldrich.

A bridegroom, Will thought and laughed harshly, could not feel more eagerly confident than he, as he turned from the road

[157]

and hastened toward the Houghton house. He pushed open the door and entered unbidden. Melissa rose from the fireside settle. Her startled look, her blue lustring gown, were wordless confession that hardened his purpose.

"You?" she said and immediately was angered by her own alarm. Will had no right to come bursting in upon her like a thunderstorm.

"Me," he agreed and laid aside hat and horseman's cloak before he asked, "Expectin' someone else?"

Melissa wondered again, but now with no pleasurable excitement, what would happen if Job should encounter his rival here. There was a wicked glint in Will's eyes, and he was smiling widely, though she could find no cause for mirth. She replied as haughtily as she could:

"I don't know what you mean."

"Don't you, now?" he jeered. "Wal, m'lady, Mr. Aldrich," maliciously piping the name, "won't come a-courtin', this mornin'. Committee for Detectin' Conspiracies has caught up with Mr. Aldrich at last. You'll have to content yourself with me."

She had never seen Will so boldly confident, and unreasonably it thrilled her. Melissa had seated herself again. He came to stand, scowling, above her. His rough, male scent set her heart to pounding; his nearness spread an unsettling heat. Melissa said tartly, resisting his spell:

"No concern of mine what happens to Job Aldrich—or you."

"Don't lie to me," Will warned her. "I'm nigh out of patience with you as 'tis."

"Indeed?" she asked, with feeble mockery. "Should that—trouble me?"

He did not seem to have heard her.

"When you're mine," he said slowly, his eyes holding hers, "skin me if I don't beat you daily."

"Be pleased to remember," Melissa shrilled furiously, "that I'm not yours, nor ever likely to be."

He bent and, catching her wrists, pulled her to her feet. His brutality outraged her, yet quickened perverse pleasure that was linked to pain.

[158]

"You're my maid," Will was saying huskily, his mouth close to her ear, "for better or worse."

"Let go," she demanded. "You're hurting me."

He laughed and, holding her closer still, kissed her mouth long and thirstily. He was drawing her down into strange darkness that filled her ears with tumult and drained away her strength. She slapped him with all her failing power.

For an instant she stared at the red blotch on his cheek. Will grunted, gripped her shoulders, and shook her savagely.

Melissa's mobcap flew away; her hair cascaded over her shoulders and the ruthless hands. She cried out faintly, in mingled outrage and delight.

The violence ended. Will panted:

"Now, will you listen to me?"

"I—I won't," she faltered.

He laughed and, pressing her close again, kissed her still more brutally. Melissa, with a singular sense of relief, surrendered. Her arms crept about Will's neck; her body sought for more complete intimacy. When he half-released her, she continued to lean against him, certain she would fall without his support. He grinned into her blanched face.

"I'm the man for you," he told her hoarsely, "an' you're my maid. That's the truth an' well you know it."

"Guess," she whispered, " 'tis."

He led her to the settle. They sat with her head against his shoulder and her hair falling across him.

"We've wasted a deal of time," he murmured, "an' there's little left. War's a-comin' with the spring. There'll be trouble to Westminster sooner'n that, if court sets. I ride express again tomorrow, and there's much I want you should do."

Melissa marveled at her meekness. The forthright punishment had jostled her mind into a thrilling new pattern. She leaned against Will while his urgent speech wrung agreement from her. At last, he felt her body tighten within his arms' enclosure. She whispered:

"Someone's a-comin'."

His frown imposed silence. A hand beat upon the door.

"Don't answer," he breathed.

The knocking came again. Neither Will nor Melissa stirred until departing footsteps had died away.

21

LAUGHTON and Temple lounged near the hall's entrance. Their low-pitched talk excluded Job, who tried not to think of Melissa and her waxing irritation. He felt more relief than apprehension when, at last, the inner door opened.

Harvey ushered Kathan from the chamber. Freckles stood out on Alex's wan face and the smile he attempted for Job's benefit was little more than a smirk. It vanished entirely when the doctor said:

"The committee has dealt most leniently with you, but I bid you remember that its patience is not endless. You may go now," he added loftily, then turned about.

"Now, sir," Harvey commanded, "be pleased to follow me."

He led the way and Job, quelling protest, followed, with Temple and Laughton treading on his heels. The low-ceiled room harbored the same acrid smells that had depressed him when first he had entered it months before. Now, as then, the physician seated himself behind his table, but today he had company.

Charles Davenport's florid bulk was crammed into the chair on Harvey's right while, from another on his left, Jonathan Knight considered Job with equine solemnity. Laughton closed the door, and he, with Temple, stood vigilantly before it. After a moment's scuffling through papers untidily stacked before him, Harvey looked up and announced curtly:

"You may be seated."

Knight's long leg thrust a chair forward.

"I'll stand," Job said and found such satisfaction in this petty defiance that, for an insurgent instant, he reached further. "Already," he said distinctly, "you've wasted a deal of my time."

Harvey jerked his head so sharply that his spectacles were dislodged. Davenport's fat face turned a brighter hue. Job thought that, for an instant, amusement had softened Knight's mournful expression. It would be pleasant, however, ill advised, to defy his self-appointed judges. He thrust away temptation.

The doctor had recovered balance. He muttered to Davenport, then cleared his throat and stressed his words by successive jerks of his head.

"Job Aldrich, you stand charged before this committee with enemical conduct. What is your answer to that, sir?"

"Might answer better if you told me what you meant," Job returned, and saw Knight's eyelids crinkle. He, among the inquisitors, seemed least an enemy. The physician brandished his pen as though it were a weapon.

"Very well, then. Answer me this: Are you not in secret communication with the Tory vermin of Westminster?"

"I am not."

"Hah! Do you deny that you know the purse-proud scoundrel, Crean Brush, or that he sought you out and privately conferred with you while you were in jail?"

Job's face grew hot and speech, for an instant, evaded him.

"That," he said finally, "was long ago."

"Long ago," the doctor agreed, inviting the others to share his satisfaction. "So long, no doubt, that you have wholly forgotten what the high and mighty Mr. Brush said to you that day."

"He said," Job replied incautiously, "that Dummerston was filled with lawless rascals and invited me to aid in bringing them to justice."

Davenport grunted and the men at the door muttered to each

other. Again, Job thought, fleeting amusement lit Knight's face. Harvey gaped for a voiceless instant then, recovering, sneered:

"And you, of course, refused?"

"I did. I've tried—am still trying, to keep clear of politics."

"Indeed?" Harvey brushed away the profession with a wave of his snuff-stained handkerchief. "Your success, sir, has not been noteworthy."

"Seems," Job agreed.

Further argument would only waste time and imperil his solemnly undertaken resolution. Harvey's spectacles glittered; his head lunged more savagely with each question.

Had not the suspect entered into nefarious compact with Brush? Since then, had he not served as an agent of the court party? Had he not spied persistently on his neighbors? Only recently, had he not communicated with a Tory leader?

The queries stung, but Job met each with stolid denial.

"Now, sir," Harvey demanded, "on the night of Friday, February 25, did you not come to Leonard Spaulding's for the special purpose of spying on a conference held there?"

"I went to Spaulding's with the Houghtons for no other purpose than to dance," Job insisted, thought of his tryst with Melissa returning to torment him.

"You did not leave Houghton's by stealth, the next morning?"

"I did not."

The blunt response pleased the physician. He chose a paper from those before him and, setting his spectacles more firmly, read aloud:

"Saturday, February 26, 1775: Early this day, the suspect, Aldrich, was encountered by Committeemen Laughton and Temple and could give no good reason why he was abroad and so far from home at such an hour."

"I had bedded that night to Houghtons'," Job explained, "and had left betimes because there was work to do. Nat French and I—"

Sweat prickled on his forehead. He saw, belatedly, whither

Harvey was driving him. The doctor was asking with dangerous courtesy:

"And will you tell us, sir, whether you and French worked together that morning?"

He smiled mirthlessly as the silence continued. It had done no good for Job to promise himself that henceforth he would keep aloof from stratagems and conspiracies. He was being dragged into another, deeper mire. He said hoarsely:

"I will answer no more questions," and Harvey nodded as though he had expected the response.

By the door, Laughton muttered to Temple. Knight looked at Job in apparent sorrow and shook his head. Davenport's chair creaked as he whispered behind his hand to the doctor, who nodded and again addressed the suspect:

"Do you refuse to answer this inquiry, sir? I ask you, now, whether you did not send Nathaniel French off on a trumped-up errand when he came to your house. I ask you further," his voice rose spitefully, "whether, after you thus had cleared the way, the pimp of Tory whoredom, William Paterson, did not secretly approach your dwelling and you, with equal stealth, did not receive him? Eh, sir?"

He sat back to look about him in triumph. At length, Knight asked the silent man:

"You still have nothing to say?"

The question was not hostile, yet Job could find no honest way to answer it. Truthful response would betray Spaulding, who had sworn him to secrecy, as well as the lighthearted outlaw and the scheme they both were furthering.

"If I'm charged with all this," Job asked at last, "why isn't my accuser present?"

"Why," Davenport blurted, "are you so tarnal sure he ain't?"

"Because," Job returned, "young Jake Laughton is not here."

He looked toward the door. The foxy man who guarded it flinched and turned crimson. Harvey started as though he had been pricked.

"Eh, sir?" he blustered. "And what is this?"

"Young Jake," Job repeated, pressing the small advantage.

[163]

"Known for weeks that he's been spying on me time and again, but I hadn't been sure till now who'd set him."

Knight glanced sharply from the physician to the flustered elder Laughton, then turned toward Job again and droned:

"Now, lemme get this straight. This day we're talkin' 'bout: you seen young Jake?"

"Not I," the other answered incautiously, "but Leftenant Spaulding did. He—"

Job checked himself and bit his lip. His questioner's mournful eyes did not waver.

"And what," Knight asked, "was Len doin' there?"

Job started to reply, then shook his head.

"Hah!" Harvey snorted. "A likely story. The truth is that Sheriff Paterson did visit him."

"Along of Len?" Knight scoffed. "Who says Paterson was there? Laughton's boy? Then why ain't he here?"

"Fetch him if you say so," Jake's father stammered, but Knight did not heed him. He again was looking closely at Job and, after a thoughtful moment, inquired:

"Aldrich, tell me this: You're pledged to hold your tongue, ain't you?"

Job explored the shrewd question and, half unwillingly, nodded.

"By Spaulding?" the sad voice persisted.

"I'll say no more," Job answered stubbornly, and Knight, turning to his associates, drawled with what might have been relief:

"Hold we should visit with Len 'fore we go further. Great day! Be there so few men amongst us that a child has to do our chores? No use in questionin' Aldrich till we've talked to Spaulding."

Davenport hesitated, then nodded surly agreement. Before Job could speak or stir, Harvey had risen and leveled a quivering forefinger.

"You, sir," he yelped, "will be pleased to heed me. You have escaped—for the moment. I counsel that, before worse befall, you remove yourself from Dummerston town."

Job met the dilated eyes and acknowledged:

"Told me that, first time we met."

The physician, trying to match his composure, nodded and pursued with less violence:

"Yes, that is true. I warned you, then; I do so again. Sell your holding, sir, while still you may, and depart."

"Sell," Job asked, stirred by sudden memory, "to Cap'n Wright, perhaps?"

It was pleasant, however blameworthy, to see the physician's face twitch and grow dark. Surely, it had been he who had prompted Wright's offer.

"Sell," Harvey shrilled, "to him or to Belial. Sell and leave or else be cast out when we cleanse this land of traitors, suspects, trimmers, and dissemblers. Heed me, sir. You will not be warned thrice."

A coughing fit shook him. Job looked from the convulsed figure to the uncertainly scowling Davenport and then at Knight. His eyes moved promptingly toward the door. Laughton and Temple stepped aside and let their late prisoner pass.

Sabbath's silence lay upon the settlement. Since the common and the meetinghouse steps alike were deserted, it was evident that the morning service had not ended. The fragile hope that the offended Melissa would receive him, opposed Job's impulse to go home and hurried him down the road to the Houghtons'.

The house seemed deserted and only echoes answered when he knocked, yet he could not shake off, as he left, the unhappy belief that Melissa was within and vindictively had ignored his summons.

The snow that Nat had foretold came blasting in from the north next morning and for a day and a half kept Job indoors. The carpentry he resumed went forward more easily than his plans for appeasing the last person living he willingly would offend.

He decided finally that confession and submission to whatever penalty Melissa might choose to impose was his only recourse, though it was likely that, before Job saw her again,

[165]

Will would have told her his own version of his rival's appearance before the committee.

While he measured, sawed, and hammered, Job again and again reviewed that ordeal. Harvey's baleful warning distressed him. Trouble that had stirred only torpidly all winter was reviving as the season ended.

Job could not tell whether he was more disappointed or relieved when he floundered down to the Frenches' and learned that Melissa had gone back to Hampshire to see her father, but it was comforting to hear that Will had left that morning, riding with dispatches to Northampton.

22

JOB WAS TO recall, often and bitterly, how merry he and the Frenches had been on their way to meeting that Sabbath. Betty, with Hosea in her arms, rode the horse, and her husband led it. The warmth and misty light of what Nat now conceded might be the veritable coming of spring had turned them all lightheaded so that they laughed and jested more than the pious might have found fitting.

Though the road was an endless strip of mire, the sky was bluebird color, and the network of twigs overhead glittered as though newly polished. Job thought, trudging along beside his neighbor, that this bright serenity after storm might be a favorable sign.

Spaulding, the Houghtons, and perhaps even Melissa, would be to meeting. Before the day was over, Job might learn where he stood with Harvey's committee and an affronted maid. It was easier to face certainty, however dark, than to be washed to and fro by doubt.

When they had reached the meetinghouse and he had helped Betty dismount, he was relieved to find Spaulding standing beside him.

"Hoped," his friend said with a frosty grin, "you'd come. Sabbath meetin'll do your sinful sperrit good, wouldn't wonder, and you've saved me huntin' for you."

He laid a hand on Job's elbow and guided him onto the common, beyond earshot of the unusual number of men who lingered on the meetinghouse steps, before he halted and complained:

"Rather open a beehive barehanded than stand for peace in Cumberland County, these days."

"Trouble?" It was an increasingly ugly word.

"A plenty."

"Harvey and me?" Job asked with difficulty and was heartened yet abashed by Spaulding's snort.

"You're no more'n a drop in Harvey's bucket. Solomon don't like you, an' 'tis mutual, seems. Him an' his tribe are after bigger game. Hull county's likely to blow up in our faces if court sets Tuesday."

"Thought," Job groped, "you were going to appeal to Judge Chandler and—"

"Ehyah," Spaulding interrupted sourly, "and you wa'n't along."

He lunged on, eyes puckered, voice twanging. No less than forty freeholders had ridden to Chester the preceding Friday and had begged the judge not to invite an uprising by holding court. Chandler had received them with apparent sympathy and had served them scandalously weak flip.

"Slick bastard held that by law the court must set but promised he'd adjourn it, once it had. Jest as soon believe I've three legs and a tail."

He sighed, considered Job with worried eyes, and said at last explosively:

"Want you should come with me an' Wyman an' Jonathan

[167]

Knight and whoever else ain't set on ruination, to Westminster tomorrow."

"Westminster?"

Spaulding perked his head and pursued urgently: Harvey's crew planned to invade the courthouse and prevent the court from sitting.

"S'posed to be secret. Solomon thinks 'tis, anyway. Let him have his head an' there'll be an almighty fight, sure's hell's a rod deep."

"Since when," Job blurted, "were you so strong for peace?"

"Peace?" Spaulding repeated, as though the word had a dubious taste. "Wal, mebby I be—right now, anyways. Set peace above startin' a war we ain't ready to fight. Commence one, 'fore the Grants is united, an' first thing we'll see is regulars marchin' into Dummerston."

He grimaced, gulped, and when he spoke again, there was appeal in his voice.

"We'll need men to Westminster that won't fire up like dry pine brush. If you don't hold with riots and sech, you come with us."

The group on the steps had dispersed and was moving into the building. Job wavered. He had sworn henceforth to keep clear of strife, yet apparently this proposal was in the cause of peace.

His heart turned over. Two women and a man were hurrying along the street. Daniel Houghton trudged beside his wife and on her other hand Melissa walked, light and fair as a barren doe. They entered the meetinghouse. Job turned toward Spaulding.

"Yes," he said, almost absently, "I'll go."

Elder Hooker had laid aside his pitch pipe and had declaimed the opening hymn's first line. While strident voices seized and swelled it, Job stole in, to pause beside the door and search the backs of the congregation until he discovered Melissa, standing bonneted and tall, between the Houghtons. While he watched her, he could find no reason to regret his impulsive promise to Spaulding.

Job's presence in Westminster might recommend him to the presumably still-affronted girl. Certainly it would contradict whatever tales of his spinelessness and double-dealing Will might have carried to Melissa.

The antiphonal hymn ended, and the meeting subsided with manifold rustlings. Job, perched on a plank supported by twin kegs that served as the rearmost bench, paid little heed to the rise and fall of Hooker's prayer. He would approach Melissa between morning and afternoon services, explain why he had failed her, implore her pardon, and—he breathed more quickly at the thought—prevail upon her to come with the Houghtons and view his pitch.

Hooker nasally was enlarging his petition. Job, letting fancy run free, saw himself averting riot on the morrow, overcoming Harvey's insurgents, particularly Will French, and returning from Westminster to receive his neighbors' thanks and Melissa's fond admiration.

The congregation stirred and enlarged Hooker's "Amen." The elder did not set the pitch for the succeeding hymn. Instead, he drew a paper from his worn, black coat and unfolded it. Job for an instant lost sight of Melissa and slid along his plank till he found her again.

The time might not be far off, when he and she would sit together during Lord's Day meetings and at their end return to the house that had become a fitting home for her.

Hooker had set his spectacles. He cleared his throat, bent toward the paper, and read:

"In the name of God, Amen: Agreeably to the laws of this province, I, presiding elder of the congregation in Dummerston, Cumberland County, do hereby publish and make known the intention of William French, bachelor, and Melissa Sprague, spinster, both of this parish, to join themselves together in the holy bonds of matrimony. I therefore and hereby publish their banns for the first time."

Job must not stir. Murmurous sound ran like a wind through the meeting, turning all faces toward the bench where the Houghtons sat with Melissa.

Job must be still; he dared not leave. However stealthily he withdrew, alert neighbors would observe his flight and build it into scandal. Already, the more curious were peering about to find him. He could protect himself only by remaining motionless on his plank, hands on knees, face turned toward Hooker, who having dealt disaster, was announcing the hymn.

Rising with the congregation Job knew that searching eyes had found and were probing him for inadvertence that might spice future tattle. He kept his head erect and sang lustily.

The hymn ended, and Hooker endlessly preached.

Others, too, were ignoring the sermon. Spaulding's wife was whispering to her husband. Nat's and Betty's heads were close together. Job watched them indifferently. It was like the time long ago when he had fallen from an apple tree. He had sat, then, dazed and unaware until shock had lessened that his scalp had been laid open and his left arm broken.

He must yield nothing to prying eyes, nor even try to think until he was alone. The sermon ended at last; the meeting rose for the closing hymn. Job stole out into the spring's empty brilliance. He forced himself, fearing he might be watched from apparently empty houses, to walk slowly toward the crossroad.

When, at last, the forest had hidden him from the settlement, the impulse to run beset him, to run blindly and wildly, careless of whence or whither, until he had spent the worthlessness that was Job Aldrich. He trudged on stolidly. Flight could not outdistance the quickening sense of shame or lessen the dull pain.

He had crossed Black Mountain's shoulder and was striding downhill when coherent thought overtook and halted him. Why was he hurrying home? He would find there only further abasement. His land insistently would remind him of Melissa; his house had been emptied of its shining intentions. All he had done and had planned had involved a maid, now lost to him.

If he returned to his pitch, Job would be defenseless against intrusion by the Frenches or less well-meaning visitors. The prospect frightened him, and he felt the imperative need of stricken creatures for solitude. He turned, forced his way through roadside brush, and hurried into the forest.

The silence soothed, the great trees shielded him. Here was the peace the wilderness offered—and then, he amended bitterly, withdrew. He slithered over granular snow, working his way up the mountain's flank until the forest dwindled into scrub and naked ledges rose above it.

He climbed the first gigantic, granite step and, pausing, looked far into the valley. Nat's fields were white patches on the land's rough garment. Dappled hills crowded down to a shining length of river and, beyond them, further ridges lifted an uneven stairway skyward.

Job stared across an empty mile at his pitch. A bright point that was the gable of his house shone among leafless trees. He tried to fix at this distance the outline of Lot Ninety-four and discovered with a dull sense of loss that sight of it no longer quickened the deep, possessive pride.

He had placed his best hopes in his property—and in Melissa. They had blended as the months had passed. She had failed him. Might not his land prove faithless, too?

The east was turning gray beyond Black Mountain's crest and the lately soft wind was taking edge. Job shivered, slid from the ledge, and sought shelter in the woods again, to wander aimlessly along the haphazard aisles.

The rising cloud overtook the sun and darkened the reaches of the forest. The outlandish figure that came toward him might have been born of the thickening dusk. Zurvilla Alvord saw Job, wailed, and turned to flee.

"It's Aldrich," he called. "No cause to fear."

She halted, gaped at him, and, reassured, cried thinly:

"Glory be! Darlin' lad, why are ye skulkin' here?"

She retrieved the basket she had dropped, then capered toward him. Her tow-cloth dress was torn and splotched with wet. There were fresh brier scratches on her fat forearms, and one of her many braids had unraveled to bob like a gray plume above her suety face.

"Dear man," Zurvilla prattled, "what do ye so far from home?"

While Job hesitated, fright returned and shook her piping voice.

"Is it from Them ye be a-hidin'?" she demanded, looking frantically about her. "Be They a-houndin' ye, too, dearie?"

She quaked with dread so plain that Job spoke quickly:

"I've seen no one. I've been—wandering." To distract her, he asked: "And why are you here?"

Zurvilla tittered and displayed her basket. She had been gathering red willow bark, she confided shyly. It was a sovereign cure for ague, if peeled off in early spring with the right words.

Her eyes touched Job's and fled, yet returning met his more boldly. After an instant, she asked:

"In trouble, ain't ye?"

"A—a disappointment," Job returned.

He had no wish to confide in this mad creature and was startled when she shrilled:

"Crossed in love, so ye've been. An' ye've fled with your hurt."

"It's nothing," he insisted, but the woman had halted and, swaying, chanted:

"Zurvilla knows, dearie; Zurvilla sees an' long since she warned ye. Sorrow ye'll know an' bitter pain in a dretful time. 'Tis close now, darlin' man, an' blood'll be spilled by the wicked."

The wild look vanished, and for an instant she squinted at him.

"Tell Zurvilla, sweet lad," she wheedled. "They're a-goin' to Westminster tomorrow, ain't They?"

"So I have heard," Job granted, wondering how to be rid of her. The woman came a step closer and spoke in haste:

"Will ye do as Zurvilla bids ye? Will ye go home, dear man, if she sets you on your way? 'Tis the best place for ye. Rain's a-makin'."

The sky indeed had grown darker still. Job nodded, glad to

[172]

part from her at so small a price. She caught his hand and led him uphill, her shapeless body jouncing at each stride.

"Thar now!" she panted and drew him out upon a familiar trail. "Yonder's your way, dearie."

She seemed as eager to part from him as he from her.

"Zurvilla must haste," she muttered, gave him a toothless smile, and lumbered away.

Job, following the trail toward the distant road, wondered at her agitation and half regretted her departure, for the heavy sense of helplessness enveloped him again and he could find no means to mend what had been shattered. He had gained nothing by his wandering, and he had best go home, though he would find no answer to his problem there.

He had been plodding along, head bent, eyes absently scanning the trail, and now he halted, tardily conscious of a tale stamped on the aging snow. The many misshapen footprints were Two-pound-ten's but, imposed on these, was another single set of tracks, lately made by normally fashioned boots.

A man had walked recently toward the Alvord cabin and had not returned. Job, recalling Zurvilla's nervous haste, grew sure she had expected the visitor. Perhaps he sought one of the raddled old woman's remedies or charms; certainly she could not be involved in Dummerston's tangle of intrigue and enmity.

Job unexpectedly was shaken by angry revulsion. It would have been better if he never had set foot in Cumberland County. He walked on more rapidly, beset by savage disgust that, centering on himself, spread to include an entire region and its people.

He turned downhill where the trail joined the road he had forsaken, hours earlier. The first drops of the storm struck his back like a handful of pebbles as he ran across the clearing. He slammed his door against the downpour and dropped on his bed.

The rain filled the kitchen with throbbing clamor and premature twilight. At least, Job reflected, recovering breath, the storm would keep away those who otherwise might have intruded upon his misery.

His eyes smarted as he matched his blithe expectancy of this morning with the emptiness that would wait on him tomorrow. He shook off self-pity and, rising, bared the fireplace coals and laid wood upon them.

The kindling caught, and flames climbed the logs. Job's mind resumed its futile groping. Immunity that the storm granted would be brief. He should chart his course before this respite ended, but with Melissa he had lost his guiding purpose. Life in Dummerston had been difficult enough. It promised, hereafter, to be intolerable.

Job looked up from the quickening blaze and then, for a long instant, did not stir. Someone had entered the house in his absence—someone who had taken charcoal from the hearth and had printed in uneven, childish characters on the wall beside the fireplace:

"BETTER GOE DAM YOU."

Job stared more respectfully at the admonition. Scripture had recorded a similar warning. He questioned whether the Hand that had written on a palace wall had guided young Jake Laughton's, yet the ways of the Lord were past finding out. Job had been weighed in the balance and found wanting.

"Out of the mouths of babes—" That was Scripture, too.

Once he had brought himself to face it, the divine intention was clear. Azariah Wright wanted Lot Ninety-four. He lived in Westminster, whither Job had promised to go tomorrow. Go, he would—not with Spaulding to avert riot, but secretly and on a personal mission.

When he had sold his property, he might return to Stockbridge; he might make another pitch in deeper wilderness, where men lived too far apart to abuse and deceive each other. Whither he went and whatever became of him, he would quit this valley of humiliation, shaking its dust from his feet forever.

He roused in the night. The storm had ended, and the silence told him that returning cold again had locked the world. Dawn was near when he woke again. He rose and dressed hurriedly, lest Nat appear and cloud clear purpose by protest and persuasion. Job did not pause for breakfast but set out by the trail through the hills that, long ago, he had followed with the sheriff and his posse.

23

IT WAS midafternoon when Job toiled up the final slope into Westminster village, with mud holding back each footstep and windy emptiness within him. He could feel no more than dull relief that, after losing his way and groping through the hills, he at last had reached his goal. Later, he would seek out Wright, but his immediate need was food.

Job, considering the church before him and the wet road it divided, wondered whether he could carry himself to the tavern below the hill at the settlement's far end. He lurched forward, too spent to feel surprise at the serenity of the sun-drenched village. He could find no evidence of the riotous outbreak Spaulding had feared.

Children played before the opposing lines of houses, and their elders viewed the worn traveler calmly. When he had passed the church, Job could see that the courthouse had been occupied, but the handful of loiterers on its steps were strangers and looked inoffensive.

There were more of them than he had thought at first. He heard, as he passed, confused movement within the building and the clash of voices. A man who might be Davenport was staring from an upper window. The road dropped before Job, and he looked down upon buildings he last had viewed from a cell.

The Royal Inn was still more weather-stained, and the cord-wood pile beside it had dwindled and been scattered, but the log schoolhouse and cottage across the way were unaltered.

John Norton, innholder, was plump and pale, with agile eyes and a Scottish rattle in his throat. He welcomed Job fulsomely, ushered him into a dingy taproom, brought him a wedge of cold mutton pie and a leather jack of indifferent ale, then fell to polishing the counter while he measured his guest with sidling glances. As hunger ebbed and vigor returned, Job found perverse pleasure in meeting his host's furtive questions with vague replies and, at length, drove him into forthright inquiry.

"Belike," Norton ventured, dropping his voice, "you're not a Whig, sir."

"No."

The landlord expressed relief with a loud sigh.

"Nor I, sir. Are you acquainted in Westminster?"

Job drained his jack before he answered gravely:

"With the Honorable Mr. Brush."

"The Honorable—" Norton choked for an instant and, recovering, demanded warmly, "Sir, why didn't ye say so earlier? A man of parts, Mr. Brush. A pity he's sitting with the legislature in Albany. Were he here, the rabble would be less bold."

He absently wiped his glistening face with the cloth.

"The courthouse is in the hands of the mob," Norton confided huskily. "Villains from Rockingham, with still worse from Dummerston, have invaded it, swearing that court shall not sit tomorrow. Rebellion, sir; no less."

Excitement drew him from behind the counter. He plumped himself down at Job's table and spoke in a confidential mutter.

Toward noon, today, the rascally Azariah Wright had welcomed to his house across the road rapscallions who had marched down from the north. More men, then, had come up with greater uproar from the south. The crowd had been too large for the cottage, and pre-empting the schoolhouse, it had held a seditious meeting. Thereafter, the ruffians had armed themselves with sticks from the woodpile and, led by Wright, had stormed uphill and taken the courthouse, evicting its sole occupant, the jailer.

The edge of the table pressed a grunt from Norton as he leaned closer.

"But, mark ye," he whispered. "Sheriff Paterson had word yesterday of the mob's intention. He has been gathering a posse in Brattleboro and—"

He grimaced and laid a finger on his lips as the door opened and a muddy young man entered.

"Greetings," he said, pleasantly enough, and to Norton: "A gin sling, Innholder."

Job followed his host to the counter, paid his score, and left, to retrace his way uphill. If the sheriff indeed intended to rout the courthouse garrison, it would be well to see Wright at once. Job had no wish to encounter Paterson again.

He reached the brow of the slope and paused irresolutely. The mud-daubed young man was leaving The Royal Inn. He had not dawdled over his drink. More of the invaders stood before the courthouse now, weighing their makeshift clubs. Will French shouldered his way through the company and, looking aloft, shouted:

"Sign of 'em?"

Daniel Houghton stared down from the courthouse cupola and shook his head.

"Nary. Mebby," he added hopefully, "they ain't a-comin'."

"Wal, keep sharp watch," the other ordered importantly and swaggered back toward the building.

There was new tension in the air, and the presence of his enemy dismayed Job further. He must find Wright, yet he would risk a brawl with Will if he approached the courthouse. Behind him, a hearty voice said:

"Well, Neighbor Aldrich!"

John Hooker smiled and pursued warmly:

"I scarcely hoped to find you here. You've come to join us?"

"I'm looking," Job evaded, "for Cap'n Wright."

Azariah, the elder deplored, had left a half hour earlier with

Spaulding and Wyman to confer with Captain Bellows at Walpole.

"Then," Job said with relief, "I'd best try to find him—"

He looked up and said no more. Will, scowling portentously, was hurrying toward him, followed by a half-dozen club-swinging men. He paused before Job, surveyed him insolently, and turning to his companions, blustered:

"This man is a spy."

"Now gently, gently," Hooker protested, but Will ignored him and demanded:

"Who's payin' you, Aldrich? Billy Paterson?"

His followers muttered and pressed closer. The muddied young man who had been at Norton's was among them. Job said thinly:

"I spy for no one."

"Is it so?" Will jeered. "Jest out for an airin', mebby?"

"Gently," Hooker begged. "He came here to see Wright."

"Ehyah?" Will jeered. "Said so, no doubt, knowin' full well Azariah ain't here."

He cleared his throat with a growling sound.

"Aldrich—" the elder began again, but the gloating voice rode over his:

"Phil Safford, here, trailed Aldrich to the Tory tavern. Found him an' Norton with their heads together. Eh, Phil?"

"Close," the muddied man confirmed, "as two peas in a pod."

"I went—" Job recognized the futility of explanation, shrugged, and said no more. Will announced with heavy satisfaction:

"Come to see Wright, did you? Wal, we'll make sure you're here when he gets back. Take him in, boys."

Job considered the surly faces about him.

"Hadn't you best," he asked, "get still more folks to help you?"

Someone snickered and Will's face turned crimson.

"Now, by God," he blared, "if you—"

Shrill outcry checked him. Houghton, leaning perilously from the cupola, was pointing southward.

[178]

"They're a-comin'," he proclaimed. "They're—" He gulped and announced ruefully, "No, guess they ain't. Yes, they be!" he shouted. "See 'em plain, now."

Houghton reeled, recovered, and added nervously:

"Almighty lot of 'em, too."

Men were stumbling from the courthouse and leaning from its windows to look aloft and bawl unheeded questions. Will jerked his head toward Job, cried, "Bring him along!" and ran toward the building.

Hands on the captive's either arm hustled him across the yard, forced him through the unheeding crowd on the steps and along the courthouse hall. Job was half led, half pushed into the nearer of the twin cells. Its door slammed. He looked about him.

This was where—how long ago?—he had been prisoned with Spaulding. The shattered planks and lock had been replaced, but otherwise nothing had changed. Job felt drearily that he had traveled full circle and was back at the beginning.

Feet pounded overhead. Voices screeched:

"Here they come!"

Someone cackled nervously:

"Hull army of 'em. Got firelocks, too."

The tumult ebbed toward silence. Job peered through the wicket in the cell door. With his face pressed against the grating, he could gain a slanting view of the doorway and the steps beyond. The last who had lingered there were backing into the hall.

Hooker said loudly: "No cause for alarm, neighbors. Be steadfast and let Charles Davenport and me talk with Paterson."

Muttering, which Job had thought might be within his own ears, had swelled and was resolving itself into separate, boding sounds: crunch of boots on gravel, squeak of leather, clink of metal, and gabble of voices.

The sheriff squealed, "Halt." After shuffling and strained laughter, silence came again.

Men, packed in the hall, stared blankly at each other. Job

gained a sidewise sight of Hooker and Davenport. They stood at the head of the steps, stamped flat and dark against the sunlight.

"In the name of the law," Paterson's throaty voice proclaimed, "I call upon ye to vacate His Majesty's property and disperse."

Hooker's level speech ended a still moment.

"Sheriff, we have come, not seeking trouble but to make sure that the court does not sit."

A grumble of approval ran through the hall. Men who had begun to tiptoe toward its rear faced about and rejoined their fellows.

"And I tell ye," Paterson cried stridently, "that it is His Majesty's will that the Honorable Inferior Court of Common Pleas convene here tomorrow, and this is the royal proclamation so ordering it."

Affronting sounds from members of the garrison marred his reading of the document. Job wondered, clammily sweating, what his fate would be if the invaders withdrew, leaving him in the sheriff's hands.

"Now then," Paterson demanded, "do ye submit to the King's will, or must I consider ye all rebels an' deal with ye accordingly?"

Hooker forced his answer through a confusion of voices.

"Judge Chandler has agreed not to hold court. We are here to see to it that he does not—change his mind."

Rage compressed the sheriff's voice into a squall.

"Hear me, ye contumacious bastards, ye treasonable scum: As High Sheriff of Cumberland County, I declare ye in revolt and give ye a quarter hour to disperse."

"Quarter hour!" a posse member yelped. "Clean out the rascals now, I say."

"Hold on a mite," Davenport shouted into the ugly clamor. "Elder Hooker and me, we're willing to parley."

"Parley!" a shrill voice jeered. "We'll hold only firelock parley with rebels and see you all in hell 'fore morning."

"Will ye now?" Davenport pumped out each word. "Then

you'll be with us, Sam Gale, little as we'll enjy your company."

"A quarter hour, no more," Paterson roared, then bade his men, more moderately:

"Move off, boys, to where the air don't stink so strong of treason."

The more valiant who had waited in the hall moved out to the steps and yelled after the retiring posse. Job turned from the door, sat on a cot, and rested his forehead on his hands. He did not stir until, from above, an exulting voice announced:

"They're leavin', all of 'em; they're pullin' foot." It faltered and resumed, less gleefully: "No they ain't neither; they're a-marchin' north."

Job rose and went to the cell window.

Low-flying sunlight cast long shadows across the slope, alternately brightening and dulling the drab column that trudged downhill, led by the sheriff, whose sword of office clanked martially at every step.

The worn company halted before The Royal Inn, and Paterson advanced toward it alone. Norton ran out, wrung his hand, and beckoned to the weary men.

A key ground in the lock, and the cell door opened. Job faced the irate intruder and, after an instant, managed to grin.

"What on earth," Spaulding asked harshly, "is a-goin' on?"

Relief loosened the prisoner's tongue.

"Invited me to Westminster, remember?" he returned glibly. "Maybe you'd better not talk to me. I'm said to be a spy."

Breath hissed from Spaulding, and his angry gesture knocked his hat awry.

"If there's anything," he complained, "that ain't gone crosswise today, I'd like to hear of it. Never seen the like of you for gettin' into trouble because of what you ain't."

Reluctant amusement softened his face as Job told of his errand and Will's intervention.

"Ain't a real good time to dicker over property," Spaulding commented and flung the door wide. "If you're all through visitin' our old homestead, might as well come out."

[181]

The lately crowded hall was empty. Men who had huddled there now stood before the courthouse, talking loudly and flourishing their clubs. Uproar overhead indicated that vehement dispute was being waged in the courtroom. Spaulding snorted and glanced toward the stair. Wright and Wyman were above, trying to drive sense into the skulls of Davenport, French, and other wild men.

"Don't satisfy the God-forsaken dolts," he complained, "that we stood off Paterson's crew with no one kilt. Want we should go after 'em now, cordwood against muskets. Never heered sech nonsense."

He and Job walked the length of the passage and halted at the foot of the stairway. Spaulding listened for a moment to the tumult above, and worry lengthened his face.

"Get through tonight without a fight," he muttered, "an' I'll believe in miracles. Skin me if I wouldn't like to know how Paterson learned we was to march hither."

"Harvey," Job asked, "is he here?"

"Him?" the other answered, frosting each word. "Solomon, seems, had so many sick folks to tend he couldn't get away. Be along, later, when the trouble's over."

He flinched as someone yelled in the courtroom and a chair fell over.

"Guess," Spaulding grinned, "I'll try to calm 'em a mite. Comin'?"

"No," his companion said, "I'll wait for Captain Wright down here."

He stood irresolute after his rescuer had pounded up the stair. Job had no wish to intrude upon a quarrel or to join the men before the building. Most of them must have seen his arrest and imprisonment. He paced the hall in wretched solitude, silently praying that before some new shame was inflicted upon him, Wright would appear. The cell he eagerly had left seemed a refuge now.

Job re-entered and stood by the window. The sun was setting, and smoke rose untroubled from the tavern's chimneys. He marveled that Norton could house the entire posse, then won-

[182]

dered indifferently where he, himself, would spend the night. He would not go back to the pitch, which, after he had talked with Wright, might be his no longer.

Certainly, he thought with an ache in his throat, he could not seek shelter where he had lodged, the night he had footed it back from Westminster. Melissa would welcome him no more warmly now.

Job heard footsteps clack along the hall but did not leave the window till Hooker said quietly:

"I wondered what had become of you."

He entered as he spoke, adding with warm concern:

"And truly regret you were used so rudely."

"And I," Job returned with sudden anger, "have new cause to regret the day I set foot in Cumberland County."

He choked for an instant but when the elder prompted, "Yes?" pursued bitterly:

"I came to Westminster, not to spy, but to sell my lot to Captain Wright and then leave the Grants forever."

Hooker leaned aginst the doorframe and nodded.

"Well," he said and his ruddy face was thoughtful, "that disappoints more than it surprises me."

"Disappoints you," Job challenged, "to find me—a coward?"

The elder shook his head. He still spoke quietly:

"Coward? No. Sometimes, friend, it takes more courage to uphold the wrong than the right. Which," he added, smiling, "likely is heresy, yet I do believe it."

"I come of Quaker stock," Job answered, "and was raised according to the Friends' rule. Still hold fast to it, well as I can, and see no reason to forsake it."

"In God's own time," Hooker assured him, "His purpose is made plain to every man."

24

SPAULDING groaned and sat up. Job came back from the edge of sleep, though Wyman, stretched on the floor beside him, and Knight, sprawled on the other cot, did not rouse. The doorway of the cell where the four had quartered themselves was outlined by dim light in the hall.

Job whispered, "What's wrong?" and Spaulding, pausing above him, confided in a worried voice:

"Keep wonderin' if any of the sentries is still awake."

He strode out into the passage. The lantern, hung from the ceiling, peppered him with specks of brilliance. Job yawned and stretched his sore body. A single, rancid blanket had done little to soften the boards beneath him. It must still be reasonably early, for the revel in The Royal Inn continued.

Spaulding spoke to the men who guarded the courthouse door and Will French's surly voice replied. Job, since his liberation, had tried to avoid Will, who, when they had met, had glared and bristled like a hostile dog. It was strange that Melissa's betrothed should persist in his enmity.

Job told himself grimly that he must expect strangeness henceforth. The purpose that had brought him to Westminster stood unaltered. He wished the night were over, or that earlier he had managed to talk to Wright, and then had left. Sleep would have come more easily anywhere else than here. Wyman's snore sounded as though his throat had been cut; the noise from the tavern was growing louder, and now that Job was fully awake, a swarm of problems and uncertainties were pestering him once more.

Spaulding returned, still grumbling over the sentries' slackness, and, stalking to the window that had been raised a hand's breadth to lessen the prison stench, listened for a long moment to the clamor from The Royal Inn.

"Wish," he muttered at length, "they'd quieten down."

He sighed, stepped over Wyman, and returned to his own cot but not, Job was certain, to sleep. Scarcely more than half the original garrison remained in the courthouse. Men had begun to drift away before nightfall, and after Judge Chandler had come and gone, still more had departed.

Job reviewed with reluctant admiration the prim gentleman's unheralded visit. Chandler's long cloak and silver-buckled shoes, his laced tricorn and carefully tied, powdered hair must have affronted the soiled tenants of the courthouse, yet he had berated them in schoolmasterly fashion and had demanded that he be led at once to their leaders.

The judge had conferred in the courtroom with Spaulding, Hooker, Wyman, and Wright. They were grinning when, at length, they escorted him downstairs. At the door, Chandler paused and shook his cane.

"I have," he announced precisely, "strained legality to avert further disorder. You have no right to occupy this building; you really haven't, you know, but you may remain in possession until morning, when you must yield it to His Majesty's court. I shall convene it in compliance with the law and then adjourn."

He nodded acknowledgment of the gabbled approval. Wright was among those who left with him. Job had considered following the captain to his home, but Spaulding had dissuaded him.

"Azariah lives 'crost the road from the Tory tavern, don't he? Think Billy Paterson wouldn't enjy clappin' eyes an' hands on you? Wait till mornin'."

The noise from the inn was emphasizing the wisdom of that counsel. Boozy singing rose, wavered, and collapsed into wild cheering. Spaulding sighed and turned over.

"Like it real well," he said, "if 'twas mornin'."

[185]

"The judge," Job objected, sharing that wish, "said we could stay here."

"I know," Spaulding granted, "but Billy Paterson didn't. Get more sleep, mebby, if he had."

A reveler opened the tavern door and lifted a shrill voice in the Iroquois scalp yell. A sentry before the courthouse laughed nervously.

Job knew he must have slept, for he discovered that the drunken tumult had ceased and someone was coming quickly along the hall. The man paused, framed in the doorway, and whispered:

"Leftenant?"

"Wal?" Spaulding swung his legs from the cot.

"Will French wanted I should rouse you. He thinks there's somethin' a-goin' on outside."

Spaulding and the messenger clattered down the passage. Job, for the moment, could hear nothing but the pounding of his heart. Only a craven would let the cold and the darkness and a faltered rumor alarm him. He had risen and stood, still shivering, when Spaulding returned in haste and alone.

His toe prodded Wyman until he sat up, swearing. A hand on Knight's collar shook him awake.

"Jonathan," Spaulding bade in a barren voice, "Hooker's upstairs. Find him and tell him to come down. French thinks Paterson's fixin' to drive us out. John, don't jest set there. Come with me."

Knight unfolded himself and stalked from the cell, followed by Spaulding and Wyman. Job, left alone, went to the window.

A half moon hung in the west, silvering fog that covered the lowland and had flowed in about the tavern, now dark, save for a single lighted window. The prospect was so empty of menace that Job was abashed.

He caught his breath. Something was astir beneath the night's surface tranquillity. Sounds of movement came from the depth of the fog: stumbling, a low command, a louder curse, half-stifled laughter, and the shuffle of a moving multitude. The inn's remaining light went out as though to disavow the purpose of the dark column that crawled from the murk and breasted the hill.

Someone ran heavily along the hall and shouted from the foot of the stair:

"They're a-comin'; the hull damned posse. They're a-comin', I say."

Dazed voices answered him, and men stumbled about overhead. From the steps a hopeful voice quavered:

"Mebby they've given up; mebby they're a-goin' home."

"They're turnin' in; they're—" another cried but his warning was lost in the thunder of boots on the stair. The garrison poured along the hall, jostling and cursing, until the foremost, halting at the open door, dammed the rush.

Wyman called:

"Now, stay where you be. If Paterson's seekin' a fight, let him start it."

"Fight," someone objected. "Them with firelocks and us without?"

Knight's response rose clearly:

"Any that's aimin' to run picked a poor time. Hold your tongues, all of you. Let Elder Hooker do the talkin'."

Curiosity and a trace of irrational pride thrust Job from the comparative safety of the cell, to stand in the rear of those who had clogged the doorward end of the hall. The lantern sowed grains of light over irresolute men. They muttered and weighed their cordwood bludgeons, while ominous sounds drifted into the passage: unsteady trampling and bursts of slurred speech.

Wyman, facing the outer blackness, challenged sharply:

"Wal, what now?"

The question set off wild howling that Paterson's repeated commands finally hushed. His uneven voice replied at last:

"We've come to evict ye from His Majesty's prop'ty, ye—"

A hiccup jolted him and he began again:

"The High Sheriff of Cum'land County warns ye for the lash—the last time to yield an' depart."

Hooker stepped forward:

"Now hear me, William Paterson," he bade. "Firstly, most

[187]

of you are drunk and beyond argument; secondly, Judge Chandler has told us we may bide here till morning, and," he added, lifting his voice, "bide we shall."

The posse began a derisive screeching. Paterson shouted:

"For the last time: Stand aside and give over."

Men near Job looked anxiously behind them. By craning his neck, he could see the front rank of the garrison recoil, then surge forward again, to thrust their clubs at the shadowy bulk of the sheriff as he lurched up the steps. He lost footing, reeled, and, recovering, bellowed an order that was lost in uproar.

Paterson drew his sword and returned. Will French's cudgel beat down the blade. He struck again and felled his adversary. The mad yelling ceased abruptly. The hushed instant was ended by the sheriff's furious screech:

"Fire on 'em. Fire, I say."

"Oh, Jesus!" a man near Job moaned and wheeled to flee.

A musket flashed and banged in the darkness, another and then a third. Each report drove higher the shrill tumult in the hall where the foremost defenders charged into those behind them, and they, too, as panic spread, struggled to break out of the press.

Job, lately the rearmost of the crowd, found himself confronting its flight. Blanched faces with mouths agape surged toward him. Men were clawing frantically at those before them. One, with teeth bared and eyes inanely rolling, laid about him with his club.

The posse was swarming up the steps. The sheriff staggered after it, yammering:

"Fire, damn ye; fire! Blast 'em!"

Job looked into the leveled muskets, dove for the cell, and slid across its threshold as the ragged volley seemed to blow the hall apart. The ceiling lantern tore loose and flew through darkness where fugitives yowled, pushing and beating at each other.

The yelping invaders, plying their muskets' butts, drove the

[188]

rout further along the hall. Job crawled inward, thrust the cell door shut behind him and lay shuddering.

The snarling roar of a monstrous dogfight rose and raged at the far end of the passage. Through the beastly tumult, a voice wailed, "No, no, no!" and ended the plea with a shriek. The fleeing garrison stormed up the stair with the posse baying behind it. The courthouse shook to collisions overhead. Through the splintering crash of overturned furniture, men began to cry woefully:

"Quarter! Quarter!"

A window burst outward with a rending noise.

"Quarter! Quarter!"

The appeal was smothered by breathless cheering. It ended abruptly. In the dire quiet, someone wept shamelessly as a child, and men called to each other in tired voices. A light kindled in the hall. Close at hand, Job heard a rhythmic moaning.

The cell door rattled, and he flinched. Cloth rubbed upon wood as someone tried to raise himself. The attempt collapsed in thudding and another moan. Feet trod heavily along the hall and Paterson's spent voice ordered:

"Set guards at the door. Let no one leave or enter."

Those who had moved to obey halted, and one ventured:

"Here's another; hurt, too, seems."

"Jail him," Paterson replied. "Lock 'em all in the cells, till tomorrow."

Job tiptoed to a far corner of his refuge. More men were coming slowly along the hall, and others moved down the stair with the scuffling tread of the burdened. The door, kicked open, let in light that slid down the sword Paterson pointed toward a prostrate figure. Members of his posse bore the limp body to the cell and laid it on a cot.

Prisoners were thrust into the chamber: Hooker, Knight, with others who were strangers to Job. Grunting bearers brought in another wounded man and placed him on the further cot.

For a moment, after the door had been locked upon them, none of the captives spoke. The wicket was a crisscrossed oblong against darkness. Someone uttered thickly bubbling sounds. A hoarse voice asked at last:

"Who's that?"

"Don't know."

"Sore hurt, I'd say."

"Ehyah."

The gurgling paused for an excruciating moment, then laboriously resumed.

"Ain't no one got a tinderbox, for God's sake?" someone asked.

"I'll try to ease him." Job recognized Hooker's calm voice. The elder shuffled toward the ghastly sound.

"Wal?" a taut voice begged, at length.

"This man," Hooker reported gravely, "is past mortal aid. Shot through the head, repeatedly, I think, as well as elsewhere. The other—"

He paused. Darkness magnified the glutinous breathing.

"The other," Hooker began again, "appears—eh, brother?" Job heard only broken mumbling but presently the elder answered:

"Yes, Dan'l; I understand. Rest easy."

He told the others, as he moved toward the door:

"Daniel Houghton of Dummerston lies here, shot through the bowels."

He shouted at the wicket:

"Halloo, there. Send me the sheriff, at once."

The demand was caught up, relayed, and at length brought Paterson pounding along the hall to thrust a purple face close to the wicket and bellow:

"Now, damn ye all; who dared to call me?"

"I," Hooker said. "There is a man here, past succor; another needs a physician. Be pleased to send for Dr. Hill."

"D'ye think," the sheriff jeered, "it matters a fig to me if all rebels perish? His Majesty—"

Hooker's voice cut through the bluster.

"William Paterson, connivance in murder will recommend you neither to your King nor to your God."

The sheriff grunted and turned upon those who had gathered behind him.

"Fetch a light," he bade and pursued, not quite confidently, "Let us view these desperately wounded men."

Three of his posse followed him into the cell. The candle one bore lifted dim figures from the gloom. Jonathan Knight stood mournful and motionless with a wet, red hand pressing his shoulder. Hooker, unbidden, took the light and stepped to the nearer cot.

Daniel Houghton's eyes were closed, and his face was waxen. A blotch on the center breadth of his homespun frock pulsed with his shallow breathing.

"Dare you," the elder challenged, "deny this man medical aid?"

He flinched as the desperate, strangling sound rose, endured, and failed, yet he turned resolutely and held the light above the further cot. Job stole forward. A lowing noise, wordless and aghast, ran through the cell.

"Scarce possible," Knight said hoarsely, "he could still live."

He stepped nearer, still nursing his shoulder.

"Anyone know who 'tis—or was?"

Job could not pull his eyes from the dreadful, garish figure.

Hooker hesitated, then pressed his handkerchief to the shattered face, and, letting it drop soddenly, said:

"William French."

"Mammocked."

The word rose from nowhere and stood alone.

"Butchered most brutally," the elder agreed and swung about to demand of Paterson:

"Is Daniel Houghon, also, to die, untended?"

The sheriff had grown pale. He blustered:

"Watch yer tongue, Hooker. D'ye forget ye're me prisoner? I'll do what seems best to me, me and none else, d'ye hear?"

He turned to go but at the door wheeled and blared:

"What mercy I grant will be ill deserved by—"

He paused with mouth ajar and bulbous eyes fixed on Job.

"Can it be?" Paterson marveled at length and almost gently. "Is it ye, indeed, Aldrich?"

He licked his lips and went on with baleful playfulness:

"Now, had I known of yer presence, me dear sir, I'd have welcomed ye sooner."

He grinned and rubbed his hands together. Fright, piled upon horror, had left Job speechless. His fellow captives stared at him, but Knight and Hooker alone showed concern. The elder ventured:

"Mischance brought Aldrich here. He—"

"Mischance for him," the sheriff agreed heartily, "but a happy stroke for me."

For a relishful moment, he continued to grin at Job, then said sharply to one of his followers:

"Find Gorton and Easton and send them to me in the courtroom."

Paterson took the candle from Hooker, then nodded toward Job and bade his remaining adherents:

"Take him upstairs."

The sheriff had evicted the few members of his posse who had lingered in the courtroom. He had added his candle to several that kept the judges' bench and the space before it a bright island in the dark chamber. By his order, Easton and Gorton, entering with tipsy gravity, had barred the door and then had laid firm hold upon the prisoner's right arm, while the men who had hauled him upstairs gripped his left.

Paterson stripped off his fine, blue coat, folded it with care and laid it across the bench. Job knew the deliberation was prelude to torment, but the last hour had emptied him of dread.

The sheriff rolled back his wristbands and looked down at his hands, clenching and unclenching them tentatively. He nodded approval and, for the first time since they had entered the courtroom, directly addressed his prisoner.

"I'm not a man to leave debts unpaid, Aldrich. Oh, no, indeed. Ye can depend on that."

He stepped nearer. Relish thickened his speech.

" 'Tis a long score, me dear creditor, but 'twill be settled in full, never fear."

He grinned, balanced himself, and proclaimed, as though reading from a list:

"Item: For resisting arrest and assaulting Deputy Gorton."

He struck. Job's head flew back and the candle lights blurred into streaks of fire.

"Item:" the sheriff recited, "for defying the court and breaking jail," and hit him again.

Job sagged against the pinioning hands. Pride pulled him erect. He tried to speak bravely. Paterson laughed at the mumbling sound and blew upon his knuckles.

"And now," he pursued, a lustful grin pushing his eyes into slits, "there's me own debt still to discharge and that, me man, will take longer."

He sidled nearer and bade his men:

"Hold fast."

Job's chin was dripping. Outrage and pain had lit within him a small, stable flame. He collected the thick, salty seepage in his mouth and expelled it upon the swollen figure before him. Paterson looked down at the bright stain on his waistcoat, and his grin grew wider.

"Now, will ye?" he crooned. "Affront me, hey? Defy me, hey? Oppose me, hey?"

He drove a fist into the prisoner's body with each question.

"And there's this, Aldrich—and this—and this."

The brief, impelling fire had burned out. Job, hanging limply on the supporting hands, felt himself hammered to the edge of darkness and beyond.

25

SLEDGE WAS beating on Job's skull, and he tried to cry out. A hand slipped beneath his head and lifted it, increasing the rhythmic pain. The rim of a cup hurt his mouth. He swallowed the bitter draft and slipped back into stupor.

There were intervals when his wandering mind entirely left him. It was day, it was night, in no apparent sequence. He was in constant pain, and someone as constantly served him.

Job had no larger knowledge until, at last, he woke from deep slumber and saw that he lay in a small, bright, unfamiliar room. He touched his mouth and winced. His fingers crept over his sore and bristling face to the bandage above it.

He had thought that he was alone, but now he saw a little boy who sat on a cricket, before a door that parted two narrow windows, and observed him gravely. Job tried to speak, coughed, and tried again.

"Who are you?" His bruised lips framed the words clumsily. The child's eyes did not waver.

"Parmenas," he replied and added informatively, "You been sick."

He was perhaps four years old, lately had been scrubbed, and his dark hair was neatly combed.

"Ma," he announced, "she'll be back soon."

"And who is 'Ma'?"

"My Ma," Parmenas said and smiled shyly.

In the distance men called to each other. The boy listened and offered at length:

"They were goin' to have a hangin', but now Ma says they

won't. Guess," he went on, seeking substitute cause for pride, "there's more folks here than most anywheres—Hey!"

Job sat, wheezing and propped half-upright on his arms, until dizziness passed and the searing anguish in his chest lessened. He discovered he was tightly bound from waist to armpits.

"Ma," Parmenas warned, "wants you should lay still."

More voices were joining in the excited clamor. Job wrapped a blanket about himself and, with hands against his ribs, crept drunkenly to the door. He managed to open it, then leaned, gasping, against its frame.

The courthouse loomed before him and its yard was alive with men who ran toward the swelling crowd that already had blocked the road. Its members muttered to each other and stared southward at something beyond Job's vision.

One watcher suddenly shifted his firelock and began to beat his neighbor's shoulder with the freed hand. His shout was caught up and magnified into shrill, sustained cheering.

A column of drab horsemen pushed through the gathering. Its leader's face was redder than his hair, and his tricorn was rakishly slanted. Behind him, lank riders on mud-plastered nags plodded, two by two, with muskets across saddlebows and sprigs of pine pinned to their hats. Job, half-unbelieving, saw Reynolds pass, sitting his horse crookedly to favor his wounded leg.

Sunlight blazed on the red leader's bared sword as he bawled a command. The column halted and he lifted a brassy voice higher.

"Good people of Cumberland County, Colonel Ethan Allen hath sent me, Captain Robert Cochran, with a detail of the Green Mountain Boys to aid our brethren in striking off the shackles of oppression."

Men were swarming about his followers, patting the weary horses, wringing their riders' hands.

"And it is my purpose," Cochran shouted, standing tall in the saddle, "to defend all who suffer in Liberty's name and smite the heathen who bow the knee to Balaam."

Job shut the door and leaned against it. His bed seemed distant as salvation. He reeled across the suddenly slanting floor

[195]

and collided with a table. While he clung to its edge, knowing he could go no farther, Parmenas came and stood by him unhappily. Job tried to smile.

The door reopened, and a dark, slight woman seemed to be washed inward by the torrent of noise. For an instant she stared at Job, then cried, "Lord ha' mercy!" and ran toward him.

"Ain't it enough," she demanded fiercely, "that others nigh kilt you?"

Step by difficult step, she half bore him to the bed. He submitted without protest to her ministrations. It seemed that he was an ailing child once more and that his mother tended him.

Long afterward, he roused in darkness. He was parched by sullen internal heat, and though he tried to suffer in silence, he must have stirred, for he felt his head gently raised and gulped down the evil-tasting draft.

"Thankee, Ma," he whispered.

It was full daylight when he roused again. The fever had left him, but his body was so spent that he was content to lie, between wakefulness and sleep, while the woman moved lightly about the room. She was younger than he had thought, admirably neat of person, and her bright blue eyes seemed strangers in so dark a face.

Job, at last, was brought fully awake by the arrival of a small, snuffy person, filled with haste and bad temper. Dr. Hill, after subjecting his patient to painful examination, grew additionally indignant, as though his expectations presumptuously had been refuted.

"You, sir," he accused, "have been so close to death that foolery like yesterday's rightfully should have killed you. Permit me to inform you that even a—a human horse with four fractured ribs and his scalp laid open, not to mention lesser contusions and lacerations, will do well to follow my directions, if he wishes to be hale again."

"And when," Job ventured, "will that be?"

"When I so inform you, sir. Good day!"

The crash of musketry set echoes to clattering and wrung a small cry from the woman.

"Now," the physician despaired, "I have missed the obsequies! At this very moment, they are according the mortal remains of William French a military burial."

"He's—dead?" Job faltered.

"And why else, sir," Hill rasped, "would they be burying him?"

He clapped on his hat and left. Job lay still until two more volleys had been fired, then asked slowly:

"How came I here?"

The woman smoothed Parmenas's hair before she answered. The posse's triumph had been short-lived. By daybreak of Tuesday, a swelling host of armed and angry men had surrounded the courthouse, had released the prisoners, the whole and the wounded, and had prepared to hang the sheriff, out of hand.

Cooler heads had dissuaded them, and now Paterson and his lieutenants were in jail and shortly would be marched into Bay Province for safer keeping. Job, at Dr. Hill's direction, had been carried senseless to the nearest house.

She turned away, but his hesitant question stayed her.

"And Dan'l—Dan'l Houghton?"

"Lays to Eleazar Harlow's, with his womenfolks come to nurse him. You've talked too much a'ready."

"I still don't know your name."

"I'm Silence Thayer, a widow-woman."

"I shall always remember you."

She flushed and said firmly:

"Past time you was quiet."

At noon, Silence brought Job a bowl of broth and was openly pleased when he drank it. Her infrequent smile brightened her face, as though sudden light had been cast upon it. She washed the dinner dishes in a small oaken tub while Job admired the intent energy she brought to every task. He considered with new awareness the swept hearth, the shine of pewter and pottery on a shelf, the spotless windows, and the floor bleached and ridged by numberless scrubbings.

He slept again and was awakened by Silence's light touch on his arm. Dummerston folks, the Frenches, she confided in a low

[197]

voice, had come to visit him. They had promised to tarry only a moment, but she would dismiss them, if he wished.

"No," Job said, "I'll see them," yet he half regretted it when they had entered. Betty's eyes, swollen by earlier tears, filled again. She tried to speak and turned away. Nat gripped his friend's hand and struggled with himself before he faltered:

"Glad we ain't lost you, too."

He hurried on, hiding emotion beneath glib speech. They had ridden Cephas hither, with Betty on a pillion, for Will's burial. It had been a real handsome occasion. When Job was well enough to travel, they would fetch him home in Enoch Cook's cart. Meanwhile, Nat would care for his neighbor's pitch as though it were his own.

Job recognized guiltily, after the Frenches had left, that he had offered them no word of sympathy. He lay and scowled at the ceiling, trying to measure how greatly his future had been changed by Will French's death.

"Better," Silence ventured, "if I'd not let 'em in."

She sat nearby and knitted. He never had seen her idle.

"No," he answered, "they were welcome."

"Then leave off worritin' till you're well again."

He turned toward her and grinned sourly.

"Easy to say."

Silence, plying her needles more rapidly, returned in a quiet voice:

"Ezra, he died of lung fever while I was abed with Parmenas. Larned, then, to take each minute when it came and not to reach further."

She turned her head alertly toward sounds outside and already had risen when someone knocked.

"Wal," she challenged, barely opening the door.

"Madam," a faintly hooting voice inquired, "does Job Aldrich lie here? We have business with him."

"Then," Silence replied briskly, "you have come at a poor time. He will see no one else today."

Solomon Harvey's protest rumbled like wind in a chimney.

"We have come, my good woman, to take Aldrich's deposition against the ruffians who assailed him. I am a practitioner of physic and can decide—"

"I am not your good woman, and he has his own physician. I tell you he will see no more folks till tomorrow."

"But this, madam—this is official."

"And this," Silence returned with metal in her voice, "is my house, and mine is the right to judge who may enter it. More argument, and you'll not be let in tomorrow. Bid you good day."

She closed the door and waited vigilantly before it. At length, she moved away but whirled about so fiercely as it opened that Parmenas, entering, blinked at her.

"It's all right," his mother assured him in the gentle voice she reserved solely for her child. She smiled down at him and then looked defiantly toward Job.

"A lone woman with a son to raise," Silence Thayer offered, "forgets sometimes that she's female."

Job woke in the night to find himself free for the first time of acute pain, but he discovered, too, that sleep had not simplified the problems that earlier had troubled him. The firm intention that had brought him to Westminster had been shattered by Will French's death.

Melissa no longer was betrothed. If Job were to return to Dummerston, he might still woo and win her, when her time of mourning had ended, provided the recent courthouse affray did not blaze up into a general war, provided that Job became whole once more, provided—

His indecision exasperated him, yet he could not see clearly beyond his present plight. It was unlikely, even if he entirely recovered, that he would find Dummerston more peaceful, and scarcely more probable that he could replace Will in Melissa's affection. There was something faintly indecent in thinking of her desirously, with her lover only this day buried.

He heard, beyond the closed door of the bedchamber, the whisper of a cornhusk mattress as Silence Thayer stirred. She

[199]

had advised him to take each moment as it came and not to peer beyond it. Holding fast to her counsel, he slept again.

Job and Parmenas, next day, were discussing the art of making willow whistles, when Harvey and his committee returned. While Spaulding, Cochran, and Reynolds, who limped slightly under the weight of the folding desk he carried, trooped in with the physician, Silence retired to the bedchamber with her son.

Spaulding advanced to stand above Job. His voice was grave though his mouth's corners twitched.

"Wal," he propounded, "for a Quaker you don't look real convincin'."

He released the grin and said over his shoulder:

"Rob, this here's our most peace-lovin' settler."

The red captain nodded. Reynolds had opened the desk upon the table. He now came forward, resolutely smiling, but his pale eyes hardened as he observed the battered man.

"I should," he muttered, wringing Job's hand, "have let you kill the rascal."

He went back to the table, seated himself, and picked up a quill. Harvey ignored the chair Cochran thrust toward him and alone remained standing. Job, scanning the grim faces, sensed that the committeemen were not pleased with each other. The doctor addressed him as if he were a larger audience.

He and his associates had been appointed to take depositions against the bloody Paterson and eight lesser felons now jailed in the courthouse.

"Thereby, sir, establishing their guilt beyond peradventure and ensuring that Liberty shall profit to the utmost from our glorious victory."

The last words affronted Cochran, who visibly had been smarting under some earlier grievance. He leaned forward in his chair and rasped:

"'Glorious,' I deny, though 'victory,' I'll grant ye. Truth is, 'twas a wretchedly planned and villainously bungled affair."

The retort Harvey attempted seemed too big for his throat.

[200]

While he gagged and grimaced, Cochran held up spread fingers and ticked off his indictment:

"French, killed; Houghton, with a ball in his belly; Knight, shot in the shoulder; Aldrich, here, beaten nigh to death."

Spaulding broke in, striving to slacken tension:

"There was me, too, knocked down an' tromped across from stern to stem."

Harvey was not diverted.

"No doubt," he hooted at Cochran, "the Green Mountain Boys would have done far better."

"No doubt whatever," the captain returned promptly. "We've cleared all the west Grants of Yorkers with less blood spilled than has been shed in Westminster."

"A pity," the doctor jeered, "that you and your heroes did not arrive until the fight was safely over."

"Wal, now!" Cochran's lips curled like an angry dog's. "We got here no later than Dr. Harvey and had a sight longer way to travel."

His adversary choked again, and his face turned plum color. When he recovered, his voice was shrill with outrage.

"I was necessarily delayed by professional duties and to find someone to ride express, bearing important dispatches to"—he rolled out the names—"the Honorable John Hancock and Dr. Joseph Warren of the Massachusetts Provincial Congress."

"And now," Cochran caught him up quickly, "you talk not of freedom but of swappin' one ruler for another and jinin' Cumberland County to Bay Province."

"I turn to Massachusetts," Harvey said unsteadily, "because she stands foremost in the struggle for Liberty."

He flinched at the bawdy sound Cochran uttered and went on, snatching desperately at composure:

"Furthermore, Captain, the bloodshed you deplore was caused not by bungling but by treachery, sir. Treachery!" he repeated. "Our plans were betrayed to William Paterson, who otherwise could not have assembled his murderous crew in so short a time."

The owlish doctor jabbed his beak at an invisible traitor. Spaulding said sourly:

"Thought we come to get a deposition from Aldrich."

"Yes," Harvey agreed more calmly, "we did; that is true."

He breathed deeply and swung about to face Job.

"Is it not a fact," he asked deliberately, "that you agreed to spy for Paterson and were beaten because you failed him?"

Indignation and the pain that had knifed his ribs when he had stirred left Job gasping:

"It is wholly untrue," he returned breathlessly and Harvey pounced again:

"But it is true that Paterson lately came by stealth to your house and—"

"Now, hold on, Solomon," Spaulding protested. "I know 'bout that."

"Indeed?" Harvey cried. "Were you there during the sheriff's visit?"

Reynolds looked up and ended the instant of silence by saying, almost idly:

"I was. The enterprising sheriff," he went on, openly enjoying Harvey's amazement, "was trailing me, and I took refuge in Aldrich's house."

He paused to consider again the gaping physician and informed him politely:

"Doubtless you now will ask why Paterson hunted me, and my answer is that I would have been worth twenty pounds to him, since I have been proscribed under the Bloody Law."

For a moment, Reynolds observed Job's discomfort with covert amusement, then calmly assured the flustered doctor:

"I was hidden witness to all that passed between Aldrich and Paterson and swear most solemnly that no pledge was asked or given and that the sheriff left, empty-handed."

He averted his face to hide a grin. Harvey peered about him in blank bewilderment and, rallying, demanded of Job in a stifled voice:

"If this be true, how came it that Paterson so maltreated you?"

"Possibly," Reynolds volunteered, "because he had been

cheated out of twenty pounds, head money. Possibly, also, the sheriff best could answer that question."

Spaulding chuckled, and Cochran smiled broadly. Their cryptic amusement exploded the physician's wrath. He turned upon Job and shouted:

"You have claimed you came here to sell your pitch. I advise you to do so, sir, and quit Dummerston forever. If you again ignore my counsel—"

He grew tardily conscious of his associates' amazement and left the threat hanging. Reynolds broke the silence.

"Now," he said, absently regarding the ceiling, "it is my impression, gained I scarce know where, that Aldrich is a difficult man to move against his will."

The tribute did not cheer Job. Violence, truly, replenished itself, as his own damaged state attested. He wickedly had assailed the sheriff and, in due time, had suffered deserved retribution.

Job said in a weary voice:

"I'd sell and go, willing enough, if I knew of any place where folks lived neighborly and peaceful."

He avoided Spaulding's reproachful stare and regretted still further the profession's abject sound when he saw that Silence's bedchamber door stood ajar.

When Reynolds, undistracted by further strife, had taken Job's deposition and the committee had left, the woman returned calmly to her kitchen, sent Parmenas out to play, and again picked up her knitting. She seemed so absorbed by her work that Job was startled when she asked:

"Be you truly a Quaker?"

"My mother was."

"And you set great store by her?" she persisted, dark face bent above her active hands.

"And by what she believed and taught me."

It was so long before she spoke again that he feared his reply had been churlish. Finally, she said in an odd voice:

"Ezra's folks, they live to Castleton. Want I should come and stay with 'em, but I—haven't. Better, most times, to hold fast to what's your own."

"You think," Job challenged, "that I'd be—weak willed to sell my pitch?"

It was strange that he should wait expectantly for the judgment of a woman he scarcely knew.

"I think," Silence replied slowly and clearly, "that God gave rabbits and sech no choice but to flee from trouble. Don't think it's seemly, though, for folks to do likewise.

"Not," she added in haste, her rare smile setting her face aglow, "that you mind me of a rabbit."

"It's certain sure," he told her, only half in jest, "that I haven't outrun trouble."

"I hold," the woman said gravely, "that runnin' from it ain't the best way to be rid of it."

26

ALVAH REYNOLDS, calling next day, found Job in close communion with Parmenas. Silence had suggested with unusual hesitation that she might go over to Hills' for a spell if her patient could spare her. He had asked quickly if she were ill, and she had shaken her head.

"They live handy-by, and I'm weavin' for them, when I can. Parmenas'll fetch me if you need anything."

For days, Job thought contritely, she had neglected gainful work to care for him. He had learned that thanks embarrassed her, and kept his gratitude to himself.

The child, when his mother had left, seated himself nearby with the same patience he maintained under repeated daily scrubbings and combings. Job fell to talking to the sober small person in homespun, bleached by many washings and neatly patched. Parmenas responded, shyly at first, and then with engaging warmth. They were planing to go trouting in the indefinite future, when Reynolds appeared in the open doorway.

"Let it be understood," he proclaimed, before he entered, "that I come as a friend and not as emissary of the assiduous Dr. Harvey."

His laugh and his handclasp, his mock scuffle with the chuckling Parmenas for possession of the bedside chair further endeared him to Job. He accepted, with fondness beyond envy, the gaiety and warm, relaxing ease that accompanied his friend. Reynolds sat down, sighed, and shook his head:

"Faith!" he confessed, "I have been living in a hornets' nest, continually prodded by that pest, Solomon Harvey."

"That patriot, Solomon Harvey," Job corrected dryly, and the other laughed.

"Patriot, pest—it is hard sometimes to tell one from the other. This pestiferously patriotic physician," he pursued, watching Job narrowly, "has questioned me at length concerning your visit from Paterson. I have told him no more than I said here, because I was certain you wished it, though, for the life of me, I don't know why."

"For one thing," Job evaded, "I had promised to keep your presence and mission in Dummerston a secret."

Reynolds's smile faded as he considered the battered man, and mirth had left his voice when he offered:

"Cochran's troop convoys the prisoners to Northampton tomorrow. I should like to deliver a certain parlous brute to the jail there in a worse condition than yours."

"No," Job said. He paused for an instant, then, knowing he could talk without reserve, nodded toward Parmenas, who stood solemnly by the table.

"When I was no older than him, I'd been taught that violence breeds more violence. I have had no reason since then to believe otherwise. Be warned," he added, straining for lightness, "by what has befallen me and leave Paterson alone."

Reynolds gave a despairing gesture.

"Len Spaulding," he smiled, "says you are half Quaker, but he still has great hope of the other half. And yet you settled here!"

"A mistake, seems," Job admitted with a crooked grin, but his voice got away from him, and he asked more harshly than he had intended:

"Is there in all America no place where peaceful men live in peace?"

"None, I think," Reynolds said at length. "Unless," he added slowly and gravely, "you help us build it here in the Grants."

Job found no trace of mirth in the gray eyes.

"A country," Reynolds pursued, "subject to none but its own freemen; a land not ruled by York, whose gentry, Whig or Tory, lord it over their tenantry; nor subservient to Their High Mightinesses, the Wentworths of Hampshire, or the Hancocks, Adamses, and Warrens of Bay Province, before whom Solomon Harvey delights to bow the knee."

He smiled in apology for his earnestness, but his brown face grew grave again, and he leaned forward in his chair, speaking more surely:

"Job, my friend, there is no fairer land than ours. We, who love it, wish to see the Grants, east and west, united and beholden to none—a free country for a free people who obey only those laws that they themselves have made."

Reynolds relaxed and grinned, half sheepishly.

"You need not go beyond Cumberland County to find your New Jerusalem. You can hold fast to your pitch and help us raise it here."

Job said, resisting belief:

"Wouldn't call what has happened in Westminster a real fortunate beginning."

"No," Reynolds agreed, smiling more easily, "yet still a beginning. I'll wager your own birth was attended by commensurate distress."

He dismissed his fervor with a laugh, then turned and addressed the solemnly observant Parmenas.

"If you, sir, are by any chance a spy, suborned by the forces of tyranny—"

The little boy nodded and said:

"Someone's here."

Reynolds sprang up, and Job caught his breath. Melissa stood in the doorway, her face brightened by haste, her hair and crimson habit in faint disorder. For an instant, she looked at Job without recognition; then her eyes widened and a hand crept to her mouth. Recovering, she faltered:

"I hoped Dr. Hill might be here. Dan'l, he's out of his head and talking, wild-like."

"Together we'll find Hill twice as quickly," Reynolds assured her and, turning, muttered to Job: "I'll see you again before we march."

He followed Melissa from the house. Parmenas resumed the emptied chair and hopefully watched a silent man whose mind roamed elsewhere. It was strange that Melissa should have appeared at that moment, a fair and mutely eloquent endorsement of Reynold's argument.

Job spoke of his friend's visit, when Silence returned from her weaving, and for no clear reason found it more difficult to mention the girl's brief appearance. Her sole comment was a wordless, equivocal sound. Later, at his request, she brought him a small, framed mirror from her bedroom.

He stared with alarm at a battered and bewhiskered ruffian in a soiled turban. There was a healing gash on the villain's forehead and, beneath the still-swollen eyes, dark crescents that were the residue of larger bruises.

"I look," Job said, forcing amusement, "like the hind end of a hedgehog. Don't wonder I frighten—folks."

Silence took away the mirror. When he asked her whether she could borrow a razor for him, she promised him her late husband's in the morning.

Job had scraped his face clean, under Parmenas's fascinated scrutiny, when Reynolds reappeared. He greeted Silence, marveled at his friend's transformation, and barely had seated himself at the bedside when she inquired:

"How long'll you be here?'"

He smiled at the brusque query.

"No single second longer, madam, than you deem me welcome."

"Not what I meant," she replied, flushing, and explained in haste that she would like to take her son to Sabbath meeting and leave him there if, meanwhile, Job would not be untended.

"No reason why you shouldn't stay with him," her patient protested, but she shook her head sharply.

"It's better than an hour before we march," Reynolds assured her, "and there's nowhere I'd rather be till then."

"A forbidding female," he offered, when mother and son had left. "Far different from the pretty Sprague maid."

Job's face grew hot.

"It is due to Silence Thayer," he said, "that I am alive and healing."

"Why, then," Reynolds grinned, "I am willing to proclaim her the most admirable of women."

"You found Dr. Hill?" Job asked with an effort.

"We did, and this morning Houghton is improved and in his right mind again."

Reynolds hesitated, then inquired with lurking self-derision: "Have you considered any part of my windy sermon of yesterday?"

"Sufficiently," Job answered, "to return to my pitch when I am able, Harvey or no Harvey."

"Good man!" his friend exclaimed. "And bad news for the furious doctor, who would bend Dummerston to his will."

He hitched his chair closer to the bed and dropped his voice. Spaulding and Wyman and, doubtless, others had been roused by Harvey's domineering conduct. There was talk of abolishing his committee and ousting the doctor from the office of town clerk. Furthermore, the presence of Cochran's command in Westminster—the first public association of the east and west Grants in a common enterprise—had opened the minds of many to the possibility of union.

Reynolds talked enthusiastically of that prospect and the

continuing effort to realize it, until, at last, he checked himself with a rueful grin.

"I am afflicting you with still another preachment. Bear with me," he begged with sudden earnestness, "while I say that, selfishly, I am glad you will be nearby and not roaming hither and yon in search of your earthly paradise.

"For truly," he added, "I have no friend whom I value more highly."

"When you come again to my pitch," Job told him gruffly, "you will be most welcome."

Reynolds lay back in his chair. He asked at length and with uncommon bluntness:

"Is your fancy engaged with the fair Melissa?"

"No," Job said with loud mendacity, then asked more weakly: "Why?"

"No need to shout," the other grinned. "I only—wondered."

"I have never had cause," Job said at length, "to believe that she ever would favor me. Also," he added dryly, "you forget that she was betrothed to William French."

"And you forget," Reynolds grinned, "that, in bereavement, the female heart is most impressionable."

He paused for a moment and then, so evenly balanced between amusement and candor that he baffled his companion, inquired:

"Would it—dismay you if I courted her?"

"I—" Job began, stumbled and resumed valiantly, "You're welcome to try, though I'd never thought of you as—"

"As a rival?" Reynolds supplied to end the other's groping. "Could you ask a better? Consider the odds in your favor, man. I am leaving and you will remain. I am a penniless lawyer; you, a landed proprietor and a wounded hero, to boot."

"You're making game of me," Job protested with an uncertain smile.

"Perhaps," his friend said lightly. "Nevertheless, I warn you to woo and wed the fair Melissa before—"

He stopped and rose as Silence entered.

"So soon?" he asked.

"You said an hour," she reminded him.

Reynolds shrugged and gave his hand to Job.

"Time flies in your company. Good-by, my friend, and take my sermonizing to heart."

He bowed gracefuly to Silence and was gone. She went into her bedchamber without a word to Job. She did not return until voices clashed outside and through them rose the manifold muttering of hoofs, the squeak of leather, and the clink of metal as Cochran's men moved out, convoying the prisoners.

Job fashioned, that afternoon, from a length of green willow a whistle of such ear-piercing shrillness that the enraptured Parmenas immediately was forbidden to blow it on the Sabbath. His mother's admonition was stern, but Job thought she was pleased.

The storm that had burst upon Westminster had spent itself. Many of the more provident insurgents had footed it homeward before Paterson and his fellow prisoners had been marched away. Now the last of the drab militia companies were plodding off to the drums' indifferent beating. They left the village singularly quiet, as though, like Job, it had been spent by violence.

Dr. Hill, appearing Monday morning, removed his patient's head bandage and grudgingly marveled at his improvement. Houghton, he reported, as though it were to Daniel's credit, was recovering more slowly.

"You'll be rid of me in no time," Job told Silence when the physician had left. She did not look up from her mixing bowl.

"Are you in such haste to go?" she asked at length and the question for no clear reason abashed him. He answered awkwardly:

"I already owe you more than I can repay in a lifetime."

"Don't talk nonsense," she advised and plied her spoon the harder.

Melissa and her sister called upon Job the following afternoon. He was grateful, when Silence admitted them, that, lacking other occupation, he had shaved again that morning. There was relief on the girl's face as she and Beulah approached

[210]

his bed. He grinned and told them, fearing lest his heart's violence shake his voice:

"In time, I'll look 'most human again."

Melissa remained drooping and sorrowful. No doubt, Job thought resignedly, she willingly would have had him dead in Will's stead. While he groped for fitting words of sympathy, Beulah rescued him by taking both his hands in hers and saying, moistly:

"Been thinkin' a deal of you while I've tended Dan'l."

Her husband was better, she pursued in response to Job's quick inquiry, but improvement had been slow.

"A thousand times I've reproached myself for lettin' him go. If he'd only stayed to home—"

Her eyes filled, and she turned away. Melissa still stood beside the bed and smiled wanly down at Job. He faltered:

"The worst part of lying here has been the knowledge that, otherwise, I might have been of help to your sister—and you."

"You're—kind," she murmured and added sadly, "Dan'l would get well faster, I think, if he was home."

Again he sought for words that might cheer the desolate girl, and managed to say with shallow confidence:

"Nat'll be coming with a cart when I can travel. Maybe we'll all go back together."

Melissa raised her eyebrows and said in a brighter voice:

"I heard you were quittin' Dummerston."

Beulah and Silence were talking with the glib heartiness of women who found little of interest in each other. Job told the girl fervently:

"I'll never leave, unless you wish it."

Melissa smiled down at him, lightly pressed her hand against his cheek, and then rejoined her sister. They both declined the refreshment that Silence dutifully offered, but before they left, Beulah returned to the bedside.

"Heartens me," she confided huskily, "to see you doin' so good. Wish—" she paused, gulped, and urged tightly:

"Pray a mite for Dan'l, now an' then."

When the visitors had gone, Job lay motionless, fancying he

still could feel the warmth of Melissa's palm upon his cheek. He glanced at length toward Silence. She was moving briskly about the room with her face so barren of expression that he felt her disapproval. A vague sense of guilt impelled him to say:

"If Dan'l had you to care for him, likely he'd get well as fast as me."

"Two," Silence retorted, "should be enough to nurse anyone, if—"

The way she pressed her lips together made him still more uncomfortable. At last he prompted:

"If?"

She bent over the fire an inordinate time, then, straightening herself, said as though the words were wrenched from her:

"He'll improve a sight faster from now on, wouldn't wonder."

Job had never seen this mood upon her. Discretion whispered it would be best to let her alone, yet he persisted:

"I still don't understand."

Silence hesitated, then, facing him, said levelly:

"I mean that, with your friend gone, there's no reason why a forward wench should tarry here."

She colored under his stare and, wheeling about, seized the broom and began unnecessarily to sweep the floor, while Job's amazement curdled into resentment.

"You're unfair," he said hotly. "Melissa—"

"Has been oglin' an' bridlin' with Alvah Reynolds," Silence completed for him, stressing her words with violent broom strokes, "while William French is scarce cold in his grave."

"That," Job stumbled, more nearly angry with her than he had imagined he could be, "is not true. Alvah—"

He recalled how Reynolds had rallied him about Melissa and went no further.

"Ain't it?" Silence inquired coldly. "Wait and see whether Dan'l Houghton don't improve real fast now that all the spare menfolks has left."

She resumed her sweeping. Job lay still, oppressed by the

very sense of clumsy inadequacy that had constantly attended his disputes with Amos's widow. It greatly distressed him, too, that the woman who had befriended him beyond measure should be rancorously unjust toward a girl she barely knew.

He closed his eyes and pretended to doze. Though neither he nor Silence referred again to her outburst, they addressed each other with stilted courtesy for the remainder of the day.

Job woke on the morrow with a sense of well-being that made him more than willing to overlook the recent discord. Silence, who had been abroad early, returned as he roused. She bade him good morning, in a voice so odd that he wondered whether she still was resentful, and flung herself upon the tasks that waited her.

He admired her brisk dexterity while she scrubbed Parmenas, helped him into his clothes, and set breakfast upon the table. At length, he offered appeasingly:

"Seems there's nothing you don't do well."

It was a long moment before she replied harshly:

"Except curb my wicked tongue."

She looked toward him in what might have been appeal and while he fumbled for reply, added bitterly:

"Lackin' a man to rule me, I don't get put down when I deserve it. Pity there ain't a ducking stool in Westminster."

"Well, now," Job stammered, "don't take it to heart. No call to be so hard on yourself."

"Yes there be," Silence returned, as though each word scored her throat. "Dan'l Houghton, he—died this mornin'."

27

IT COULD have been no worse, Job thought drearily, if the day of his departure from Silence Thayer's home had been raw and darkened by the promise of storm. Sunlight that distilled heady fragrances from the quickening earth, turned the bloodroot blossoms of the dooryard into fiery stars, and daubed the hills with the red of opening maple buds had not visibly cheered his hostess or her son.

Job paused in the doorway, his hand still upon Nat's shoulder, to recover breath and rummage once more for words he knew he could not find. He looked from Silence's severely set face to the wet and woeful countenance of her child and felt responsive tears sting his own eyelids.

Ever since Dr. Hill grudgingly had admitted that his patient had become hale enough to travel, Job repeatedly had tried to express to Silence the depth and permanence of his gratitude, and each time she had managed to avert his thanks. He knew with despair how impossible it would be to voice it adequately now while villagers were mutely gathering about the cart to watch the last victim of what men already had begun to call "The Westminster Massacre" take his leave.

Job said hoarsely to Silence: "I'm beholden to you beyond any measure. In time—"

She shook her head almost angrily, and he abandoned the vain attempt. Instead, he smiled down at the disconsolate child and found it easier to say to him in comradely fashion:

"Let's not forget all we've planned to do sometime. I'll be back to take you trouting almost before you know it."

Parmenas gave him a watery smile. Silence said curtly:

"You'll always be welcome."

Job nodded to Nat and, with his support, walked to the cart. Men from the silently observant group helped lift him onto the blankets spread over the vehicle's floor. Nat climbed in over a wheel and spoke to his horse. They rumbled out to the Great Road and rolled slowly southward. Parmenas, from the doorstep, looked wistfully after them, but his mother had gone hurriedly into the house. She must not, she told herself sternly, let the son she constantly exhorted to greater fortitude and reticence see her with tears in her eyes.

Silence lifted the pillow from the chair where Job lately had sat, started to put it away, then paused, and after looking warily about her, laid her dark face for an instant against the hollow his head had made.

"Sure we ain't," Nat asked in unmerited tribute to Cephas, "goin' too fast for you?"

"No," Job told him and added firmly, "I can't get home too soon."

It would, his friend informed him, be quite a spell before a still-ailing man could return to his own clearing. Until he was wholly well, he would bide with the Frenches.

"No call," Nat went on hastily, "to worry about your pitch. Wheat's a handbreadth high, burnin's done, and the ash house filled."

The mild voice wove in and out through the car's rattling. There had been little more trouble in Dummerston than was usual. A recent town meeting had removed Alex Kathan and Enoch Cook from their posts as assessors for failure to buy ammunition for public use. It had been a real lively meeting. Harvey had wanted the dismissed men punished further, but Spaulding and others had blocked him.

The freeholders, Nat pursued proudly, had been unanimous on one measure. All had joined in voting elegant resolutions of sympathy for Will's folks and for Daniel Houghton's. Job asked with forced indifference:

"Beulah, she's to home?"

"Ehyah; Melissa, too. Hear, though, they're fixin' to visit their father in Keene, for a spell."

Nat babbled on concerning rumors that had come north of more critical trouble in Bay Province, but Job no longer heeded. He had seen neither bereaved woman since their call at the Thayer house and his subsequent difficulty with Silence. She, and the rest of Westminster village, had attended Daniel's burial, but thereafter she had never mentioned either Beulah or Melissa.

Job had been grateful for that omission, yet her unjust accusation had continued to rankle. He was fervently certain that Melissa was in no wise inclined to folly, and the belief that Silence had misjudged her had tempered his estimate of an otherwise admirable woman. That reservation, during the weeks of convalescence, had turned Job more warmly toward Parmenas, who had repaid him with a disconcerting reverence and affection.

There had been times when he had wondered whether his odd, close comradeship with a little boy might not rouse his mother's jealousy, yet it had always seemed to gratify her.

The rhythm of hoofs, the cart's deliberate motion were loosing and blurring Job's thoughts. He was drenched by sunlight and deliciously at ease. Nat glanced over his shoulder and smiled to see that his friend's eyes had closed.

The end of movement and the sound of the very voice that had run through his slumber wakened Job.

"Beulah," Melissa was saying, "'tis Job Aldrich he's a-bringin' home."

Nat spoke with a proprietary air:

"Sent for me to fetch him. He's asleep now an' still far from hale."

Job lifted himself on an elbow. The cart had halted before the Houghton pitch. Yonder was the house of cherished, and the barn of unhallowed, memory. Close at hand, Melissa and her sister stood together and looked up at Nat. Job told them:

"He's at least half mistaken; I'm not asleep."

He managed to smile into the startled faces and then was

[216]

forced to lie back again. The women came closer to the cart and looked down at him with expressions more befitting mourners at a coffin's side. Tears welled into Beulah's eyes, and Melissa turned her head away sharply.

"My—my sympathy," he stumbled. "I only wish—"

Beulah valiantly bridged the wretched silence. She was thankful Job was mending. They both had thought often of him. They would ask him in now, but the house was all at sixes and sevens while they were packing to set out for Keene.

Melissa had faced Job again. She was dearer to him with her fairness wilted by sorrow than ever she had been at her loveliest. He asked hoarsely:

"You'll be gone for long?"

They would be back, Beulah promised, but she couldn't say when.

"Know Pa'll want us to stay, but—but Dan'l—I'll feel— nigher to him here. We—"

Speech left her, and she looked in dumb appeal at Job. A warm, releasing surge of pity made him heedless of Nat; let him see only the dully wretched faces of his love and her sister. He said to them earnestly:

"I beg you to remember, when you do return, that I always shall be ready to serve you, whenever, however, you may have need for me for purpose small or great. This I do truly mean," he pursued, keeping his voice firm by extreme effort, "and I ask you never to forget it."

He looked for an instant from Melissa, whose fingers were pressed against her mouth, to her sister's damp and tremulous face, then wearily lay back.

The cart moved on while the women silently watched it out of sight. Beulah, as she turned toward the house, wiped her eyes on her sleeve, yet when she spoke, her voice was startlingly severe:

"Might take to heart, Melissa Sprague, 'tain't every vixen gets a second chance. Was I you, I'd think on that an' be thankful."

The girl tossed her head, and the impenitent gesture drove her sister further:

"Heered what Job Aldrich said. He meant it, too, every word. You'll never find a better man, however far you hunt."

"Never, far's I recall," Melissa smiled, "had to hunt at all."

"Warnin' you, m'lady," Beulah promised ominously, "you'll mebby hunt a plenty someday, and come back empty-handed."

"If," the girl retorted, "you're harpin' again on Mr. Reynolds, I saw him only once."

"No," her sister corrected in a bleak voice. "Once when you knowed I saw you with him and twice more when you thought I didn't."

The belated revelation left Melissa speechless and uneasy. She wondered whether her sister stored away further detrimental, still-unspoken knowledge, and said in hasty penitence:

"I meant no harm. If you—disapproved, why didn't you say so?"

"Because," Beulah answered dully, "a woman whose man is dyin' can think of little else."

Melissa pressed her sister's arm.

"I know," she murmured with sympathy. "You forget I suffered loss, too."

"I don't," Beulah told her, unappeased, "but seems you do. Mebby, when I come home again, I'd best leave you to Keene and tell Pa why."

"No!" Melissa cried in genuine alarm. Her parent was a conservative person who still believed daughters were best corrected by sound birchings. Besides, she thought, consternation spreading, exile to Keene would make it unlikely that she again would meet Job Aldrich's friend whose grace and wit, no less than his merry daring, had profoundly stirred her.

Reynolds had said before he had ridden away, leaving a singular emptiness within the girl, that he was likely to be often in Dummerston hereafter.

"Beulah," Melissa said fondly, "we'd be lonesome without each other. I'll truly try to please you henceforth, And," she added artlessly, "if I stay to Keene, I'll not see Job Aldrich—ever."

"Ain't sure," her sister said darkly, "if that wouldn't be fort'nit for him."

"And I ain't sure," Melissa giggled, aware that the crisis was over, "but what you're a mite tetched by him, yourself."

The rumble of the cart rose through Job's agreeable drowsiness, faded, and swelled again. He considered dreamily the impulsive pledge he had made to the forlorn sisters, and prayed that hereafter he might be granted opportunity to fulfill it. It had been a happy portent that Melissa and Beulah had been the first to greet him on his return. It might be that, out of great travail, a new, bright beginning had been born.

Job watched the slow brush strokes of branches across the sky until, all at once, they vanished and he was roused by voices calling his name and a tentative cheer. He knew, after a puzzled moment, that they were passing through the settlement. Nat twisted about to grin down at him.

"Seems," he offered, "folks is glad to have you back."

Job's throat tightened. It was greatly comforting to have won, however accidentally, the approval of a onetime hostile town. The cart jolted uphill and began, at last, a long, deliberate descent. Its passenger tried to judge its progress by the passing treetops and the slant of the road. At length, he strove to sit up, hoping to see the trail leading upward to his house and land.

The effort was too great, and he lay back with only mild disappointment. In time, he would rejoin contritely his angrily deserted pitch; in time, too, Melissa would return. A calm sense of home-coming possessed him.

Job could tell by the road's rise and fall that they were nearing the French farm. The cart wheeled into the yard and voices cried gaily, "Welcome home, neighbor!"

Betty, smiling through her tears, was fumbling with the tailboard and, beyond her, Spaulding, Wyman, and Hooker grinned sheepishly at Job.

[219]

"Thankee," he stammered, "I—well, thankee."

Hands, reaching in, lifted him gently and bore him into the house.

Job lay at ease in the bed Nat had brought down from above and had set up in the far end of the kitchen. The friends who had welcomed him had left. The draft Nat had administered, the broth Betty had brought spread warm contentment within him. The neighbors, the Frenches had informed him, had sent in enough provender to last a week: cider brandy from Negus, a cob-smoked ham from the Spauldings, pudding from the Cooks, fresh-baked loaves from the Kathans, and other and lesser tributes. Nat, numbering them, held up a battered crock.

"Two-pound-ten," he reported dryly, "fetched this. 'Tis one of Zurvilla's brews an' guaranteed to heal you forthwith, crazy old critter."

"Beholden to her—to all of you," Job murmured, too tired to reach for some memory the woman's gift had stirred.

He woke in the night with the lately evasive recollection so clear and sharp that he lay, wide-eyed and breathless. He could almost see the strange seizure that, long ago, had stricken Zurvilla, could almost hear the thick voice predicting violence, bloodshed, death, and sore anguish for Job.

All this, he thought with unwilling awe, had come to pass. Why, then, should he not believe and be fortified by the remainder of her prophecy? The woman had promised that, after great suffering, he would acquire what all men sought and few attained.

Presently he fell asleep again, and Melissa moved sweetly through his dreams.

Job was sitting up with a blanket across his knees, next day, when Nat came in, scowling and muttering to himself. Two-pound-ten, he said in response to Betty's question, was abroad and zestfully spreading calamity.

"Says there's been fightin' to Bay Province an' the milishy's whopped the regulars. Likely tale!"

"Likely or not," Job offered quickly, "it's no concern of yours or mine. We're Grants, not Massachusetts, folks."

"Ehyah," Nat granted. "Way I feel, too."

28

INFREQUENT northbound travelers on the Great Road, during the last week of that bright April, moved against the flow of a human river. They met in Massachusetts unkempt battalions, armed but unmartial in their stumbling haste, and these, further upstream, dwindled into shabby companies, platoons, and unorganized smaller groups of farmers, more familiar with ax and scythe than with the ancient firelocks they bore.

The failing current, when the highway had entered the Grants, was fed by men who ran from roadside houses and by others who hurried out of divergent byways through the forest. They composed the rear guard of a dust-colored host, rolling southward toward Cambridge and the raw entrenchments that were rising about beleaguered Boston.

To all appearances, the newly kindled war had not spread but instead was draining out of the north country, leaving the unmolested spring to stipple the quickening hills with green and bring shad-blow and cherry into foamy flowering.

Job, agreeably drugged by sunlight, sprawled in the chair Nat brought out for him each fair morning or crept about the dooryard on still-uncertain legs. He could not believe that beyond the rim of his small, serene world, men were marshaling to kill each other or that certain of his neighbors already had set out to join them. The trouble surely would have ended before they had footed it clear to Boston town.

So he had told Spaulding when his friend had called to announce, with an odd mingling of sheepishness and bravado, that he, Wyman, and Jacob Laughton would be off to the war in the morning.

"There's cheaper ways to wear out sole leather," Job said bleakly, "than to walk more than two hundred miles, there and back, on an empty errand."

"Wal—mebby," Spaulding shrugged, peering toward the future through puckered eyelids. "Still an' all, might take quite a spell to get Tommy Gage an' the knothead who hires him to listen to common sense. S'prise me little if it lasted all summer."

"I thought," Job returned with malice, "that you were a Grants' man, not a Bay Province cat's-paw."

The other jerked his head, acknowledging the thrust.

"Ehyah, I know. John an' me, we've soldiered, an' we've agreed that, lackin' a better fight, closer to hand, we'd best jine in.

"Gravels me," he added placatingly, "more'n it does you, to take up any cause Solomon Harvey favors."

"And of course," Job assumed, "Harvey'll be going, too."

"Wal, now," Spaulding replied with equal irony, "seems not. Solomon, he'd like real well to expose himself to carnage an' sech, but he's discovered he can serve Liberty best, right where he is."

There was, he pursued, still solemnly, no loss without some small gain, since Laughton, Harvey's right hand, also had volunteered. Young Jake had insisted that he was going, too, but had been dissuaded by a major whaling.

Spaulding paused, looked from Betty to Nat and back at Job again before he said in an altered, more earnest voice:

"Harvey's been a mite abated, since Westminster. Don't let him get his tail over the lines again. Like to find the town still here when I get back."

It had been more than a fortnight now, Job calculated, since Spaulding and his companions had left. No word had come from them or further news of fighting in Massachusetts. The trouble, likely, would burn itself out, as the courthouse fight had flared up, died, and left no aftermath.

Young May seemed twin sister to June. Already, the hillsides were tapestried with infinite shades of green, and Nat's spring plowing, finished uncommonly early, lay like a brown rug across his clearing. Job's host had spent a day in turning over soil on his guest's pitch and had planted Indian corn for him.

Each morning, the convalescent could mark the further growth of lucent young leaves on the dooryard maples and daily felt that a new, potent quality in the fragrant air was cleansing and mending him. Reynolds had compared the Westminster affray to the travail that precedes birth. Job was acquiring the tranquilly confident belief that the old, distressing pattern of his life here had been destroyed and was being replaced, through divine grace, by a fairer and more rewarding one.

Holding fast to this conviction, he could endure without impatience the gradual restoration of his damaged body. He was strong enough now to help his hostess with the dishes: a practice that he suspected Nat silently decried. Job also tried to amuse Hosea, a child less than half the age of Parmenas and with little of his senior's grave charm.

Otherwise, he was content to bask in the dooryard and let his mind run free. He thought of Silence Thayer and never without a stir of unreasonable homesickness. Often he imagined lavish and entirely impossible ways of discharging his debt to her. He thought, too, of Reynolds and wondered when he would see his friend again, but most frequently he recalled Melissa Sprague as last he had seen her, muted and woebegone. With the aid of Providence, it would be Job's privilege to restore to the girl the blithe loveliness that first had drawn him to her. All things, he was certain, worked together for good.

That belief was fortified when, in mid-May, Two-pound-ten Alvord came stumping to the French pitch, bringing, contrary to his custom, stupendous good tidings. Men of the west

Grants, led by Ethan Allen, had taken Ticonderoga. The great fortress had fallen without loss of life to attackers or defenders.

This triumph, following the Lexington victory, surely would end the war. The tonic belief and the bright future it disclosed inspired Job, on the day following Two-pound-ten's call, to visit his pitch. He rode the French horse, and Nat, still nervously protesting, carefully led the animal up the familiar way. The trees stood back at last, and they entered the clearing. For a long moment, Job did not trust himself to speak. He had feared, lately, that importunate longing for sight of his own land might have led him to picture it too brilliantly. That had been needless worry. His property, lying all about him, was even fairer and dearer than he had imagined.

There were larger, more costly houses but none better built or in aspect more seemly than his, with its fine tall roof, noble chimneys, and solid, attendant log barn. Surely no other precinct on earth was so filled with warm promise as this clearing where May's sunlight had spread a glory and turned the newly leafed surrounding trees to torches of green fire.

"Don't look too bad," Job said to Nat.

He dismounted and, companioned by his still-anxious friend, walked slowly about, numbering his blessings. The wheat, standing nigh a foot high, was smothering what weeds had invaded it. The apple seedlings were handsomely leafed, and blades of the lately planted corn already were saluting the sun.

A barren dark oval near the clearing's center marked where Nat had burned the timber he and his neighbor had felled and piled. The stone ash house had been filled. Job sifted a handful of its contents through his fingers with approval. The kitchen's air was dank and chill, but the chamber's orderliness warmed the heart. Nat had scrubbed young Jake Laughton's warning from the wall. That, too, was a good omen. Job, emerging, looked about him and drew a deep breath.

"Unlikely," he told Nat gruffly, "that a man ever had better neighbors than you and Betty."

His friend scuffled his feet and mumbled.

"Twice, since I came here," Job went on in a grave voice,

"I've been minded to quit and go—I don't know where. There'll be no third time. We'll stay together, henceforth, me and my pitch. That is," he amended, smiling, "when I'm a mite stronger; say, in another week."

Ten days after that first inspection, and then over the Frenches' protests, he returned to his own place. He dreamed that night, so vividly that it woke him, that Melissa came to his bedside and smiled down at him while, in the gloom behind her, a dim figure he knew for Silence Thayer's stood with face hidden and wrung its hands.

Job puzzled next morning over the vision and then straightway forgot it while he doled out his scant strength to the immeasurable work at hand. At first, he was obliged to limit himself to the comparatively light labor of transforming the stored ashes into a crop of salts.

He had throned the kettle supplied by Nat on a makeshift stone fireplace in the clearing, and there, early and late, he boiled ash leachings until the syrupy drip from the wooden stirring paddle told him the brew would harden and crumble when it had cooled. In the beginning, he was compelled to rest while the potash crystallized. Later, he devoted the hitherto idle intervals to hoeing his corn.

He was more than pleased by the quality of the salts. Their light-brown clarity indicated the presence of far less dirt than field ashes usually contained. Such potash should bring at least ten shillings a hundredweight. Nat had gathered with extreme care. It would take many a day's work on his neighbor's behalf before Job had paid off his debt to him. Nat himself involuntarily reminded his friend of an earlier, neglected obligation.

French appeared in the clearing one morning, wearing a singular expression compounded of pride and embarrassment. He had been chosen, he stammered, at the last town meeting, delegate to the impending county congress, along with Jonathan Knight and Solomon Harvey. The congress was to convene June 6, and that was his and Betty's wedding day. It would pleasure her if Nat took her and Hosea along to the meeting.

"That is, if 'twouldn't put you out to do the chores while we're gone. 'Twill be only three days."

"Certain sure," Job agreed and added as an afterthought: "Where's the congress to set?"

"To Westminster," Nat replied and, after a moment, demanded, "What ails you?"

"Only," his friend said bitterly at length, "my cussed ungrateful nature."

More than a month had passed since Job had been lifted into the cart at Silence Thayer's door. Since then, he thought while guilt pressed down upon him more heavily, he had sent her who had nursed him no word, no token payment on a score he never could discharge in full.

He tried to lessen self-reproach by recalling Silence's cruel misjudgment of Melissa and then impatiently thrust the pretense aside. Whatever she thought of him and his callous neglect was wholly deserved. There also was the deceived Parmenas, the gravely admiring small boy, to whom Job recklessly had made many promises and had fulfilled none. He saw that Nat was regarding him anxiously and said in haste:

"You've reminded me that I've done nothing to requite the Thayers for their great kindness to me. Will you take a gift for them to Westminster with you?"

Betty on Cephas, with Hosea perched before her and her husband leading the horse, set out for the county congress two mornings later. Job accompanied them as far as the trail to his pitch and bade them farewell there. He had done what he could to amend his neglect. The bundle, lashed to the cantle of the French saddle, contained, beside the travelers' effects, some fifty pounds of ash salts wrapped, for want of better covering, in the donor's oldest shirt. Nat carried, in his appearing-out coat, a willow whistle of surpassing range and volume.

Its maker grinned, picturing Parmenas's delight and his mother's suppressed consternation. He turned uphill lest, by watching the Frenches out of sight, he bring them bad luck, and was startled by the sudden wish that he was accompanying them to Westminster.

Job, three days thereafter, approaching his neighbors' house at evening chore time, saw chimney smoke and, entering the barn, found Nat already at his milking. Yes, he granted, they had had a real good time, Betty, specially, but it would take something less muddled up and quarrelsome than a county convention to lure them so far from home again.

"Never," Nat complained mildly, "heered folks talk so much an' do so little. Voted the county should raise a milishy but can't recall anything else we agreed on."

He shook his head and sighed.

"Some hollered that we should stay part of York; others wanted we should jine with Hampshire. Harvey, he was for givin' Cumberland County to Bay Province, and there was some favored makin' the hull Grants a separate district. Uncertain of mind, seemed, but real strong of lung. Glad I'm back where it's quiet."

"You—you delivered what I sent by you?" Job stumbled. Nat nodded and rose with the pail.

"Ehyah. Mis' Thayer, she sent you somethin' in return. 'Tis in the house."

His neighbor followed him into the kitchen, greeted Betty, and accepted with some confusion the articles her husband brought from the bedroom: a heavy package, a folded paper, and Job's own shirt, washed, ironed, and carefully darned.

"Dear sir," Silence had written in a firm hand, "thank you for yr thought but it is twicet to much for all my outlay so am sending back the rest. Parmenas says to give you his respect & friendship. Obediently, S. Thayer."

Job was touched, yet also inwardly amused by the thought of Silence being obedient to any but her own stark standards.

"Kind of her," he said vaguely.

Betty offered with apparent carelessness, though she watched him closely:

"Real agreeable woman. Hope Hosea turns out as good a boy as hers."

"Visited with them?" Job asked.

"Stayed with 'em," she corrected. "Settlement was so full she took us in. Promised us," she added with satisfaction, "to bide with us for a spell, come fall."

29

E MIGHT, Job thought without regret, get back his entire strength more swiftly if he did not spend each new, small increment as he acquired it. He woke each morning, certain that today his vigor would be limitless and, by nightfall, discovered again that he had dealt out his whole store.

Thrice, when he had banked his fire and had knelt, before slumber, to thank the Giver for His continuing, great mercies, Job had fallen asleep at his prayers and, waking cramped and shivering, had crawled stiffly into bed.

During this green and golden time, while spring ripened into summer, he felt that he had gained, at last, what he had come north to find. Peace lay upon his clearing. The smoldering war was far away, and the demands that the advancing season had imposed upon a farming folk seemed to have smothered local strife.

He had finished rendering the contents of his ash house. The brown, dry crystals, stored in an attic bin, were the equivalent of cash that later he would spend prudently upon his farm. He had planted what he had deemed sufficient beans and squash to carry him through the winter, but their amazing growth promised him a surplus that he could barter for other necessities. The corn, too, was flourishing past expectation. It would yield all the seed he possibly could plant next year and a respectable amount of meal, besides. The wheat had turned blue-green and stood waist high. There was miraculous fertility in the black forest soil.

During this serene time it seemed to Job that he hardly knew where he himself ended and his land began. So might he feel toward Melissa when, in a bright, still undetermined future, she came to share his home.

Job often wondered when she and her sister would return to Dummerston and how, meanwhile, they fared. He spent the infrequent days of rain in completing the attic stair, cleansing his dwelling of dust and litter that had gathered in his absence, and even devoted one fair afternoon to washing and polishing the small-paned windows. Surely, the excellences of his house and land would make amends for what lacks Melissa discerned in their owner.

Job's calm contentment was marred, at length, by Nat, who, toward the end of June, came hurrying into the clearing. Two-pound-ten, he panted, was abroad with bad news. There had been another almighty fight, Boston-way.

"Seems we—that is, Bay Province folks—tried to take an' hold a hill to Charlestown, but the regulars they beat 'em offen it; killed a mort of 'em, too. Sounds bad, don't it?"

"It may not be true," Job objected, but his friend shook his head.

"Any ill tidings Alvord brings is likely to be right," he said with faint bitterness and looked more closely at his neighbor.

"Be you," Nat demanded, "ailin' an' ain't told us?"

"Me? No. Better every day. Who said so?"

"Wal," the other said, flushing, "I wondered, else, why you was goin' to Zurvilla."

"Zurvilla?"

"Ehyah," Nat pursued in haste. "Two-pound-ten says twice he's seen a man leaving his cabin when he came home an' each time his sister's said 'twas you."

"I haven't," Job said slowly, "stepped off my pitch but for the few evenings I've spent with you."

"Wal," his friend surrendered, "the wild old thing's crazier'n ever, seems."

He returned to his original concern:

"Still an' all, you don't look real rugged. Workin' yourself clear down to the rind, I'd say. Why'n't you lay off for a day— go fishing, mebby? Trout are bitin' good."

The suggestion woke penitent recollection in Job.

"Well—" he hesitated and, increasingly pleased by the thought, proposed briskly, "might go tomorrow, if you could spare me Cephas."

"An' welcome," Nat said, puzzled. "Ain't troutin' on horseback somethin' new?"

"I was just minded," Job told him, "that, long ago, I promised to take Parmenas Thayer fishing."

Parmenas came from the house as Job tethered his mount in the dooryard. The little boy chuckled with delight when he was caught beneath his arms and swung high.

"We been wonderin'," he began happily as Job released him, then checked himself to say more sedately: "Ma, she won't be home till dinnertime. She's weavin' to Hills'."

"Then how would it be," Job inquired, "if you and I caught her a mess of trout?"

Parmenas drew a long breath.

"Glory be!" he said devoutly.

"There's a likely brook down the road a piece," the other suggested. "Would you just as soon fish that?"

"I can't think of anything else I'd just as soon," Parmenas assured him earnestly.

"Good. Then run and tell your Ma, while I dig worms."

Job regretted, during the following hours while he watched the child's rapture, that he had so long delayed fulfilling his promise. It would be pride and happiness to have a son like this small, intent person who stole, barefooted, along the brook's edge and faithfully used the ash-sapling rod as his tutor bade him.

Parmenas's laughter when he jerked a trout from a pool, his calm philosophy when the largest he had hooked shook free, would have amply rewarded Job for a longer journey. They had a lordly string of fish when they returned to the road where Cephas was tied. The little boy, straddling the pommel in front of his companion, twisted about and looked up as they halted before the Thayer house.

"Thankee," Parmenas said.

Job thought well of Silence for the way she was rearing her child and more kindly still when she welcomed him. Her handclasp was warm; her smile transformingly bright. She would be a truly comely woman if she had not disciplined herself into forbidding rigidity.

"Grateful to you," she said, scanned him with care, and granted, "You look good, considerin'."

"Thanks to you."

"Nonsense."

Silence reddened, bade rather than asked Job to stay to dinner, and fell to washing her still enraptured child with uncommon vigor.

Job had an unexpected feeling of reunion when they sat together at the table. His hostess's crisply voiced liking for Nat and Betty had half atoned for her long-ago slander of Melissa, and the admiration in the eyes of the damply sleek Parmenas was heartening. Silence talked more than usual. Westminster had been so quiet since the county congress that it didn't seem possible there was a war anywhere, though many folks said darkly that the trouble would spread, and neighbors who could be better employed spent a deal of time watching each other.

Mr. Brush's wife and stepdaughter had left the great house to join him in Albany, but John Norton, his agent, still remained, and Pollard Whipple was often absent on mysterious errands. There were young milkweed greens with the fried trout and afterward vinegar pie of exquisite flavor. Silence

[231]

blushed again when Job told her, truthfully, that he had eaten no such food elsewhere. While she cleared away dinner, he went out to the tethered Cephas, untied the parcel from his saddle, and, returning, asked Silence:

"Would you do me and a friend of mine a favor?"

He held the package behind him while she looked at him warily.

"There is a gentleman of my acquaintance," Job pursued elaborately lest Parmenas guess his meaning, "who stands high in my esteem. I should like you to devote whatever this will bring to his special requirements."

He held out, still in its original covering, the potash Silence had returned to him by Nat's hand. She stepped backward, shaking her head.

"No. I've been paid, already."

"I beg you to take it."

"No," she repeated. Her obstinacy irked him.

"Would you deprive—my friend," he asked only half in jest, "to gratify your stiff-necked pride? It is not for you; it's for him."

He set the package on the table. For an instant, she turned her face away, yet it was expressionless when she met his eyes again.

"Obleeged," Silence said at length, took up the present, and bore it away.

She returned from the bedroom with a quilt over her arm and began to stitch a loosened hem. Job recognized the design spread across her knees and said:

"Blazing Star."

"Menfolks," Silence returned, pleased, "mostly don't heed such things."

"It was my mother's favorite," he told her. "I'm not likely to forget."

Job glanced from the window and rose.

"It's past time I started home."

Silence looked up from her sewing.

[232]

"It'll pleasure Parmenas—and me," she said quietly, "whenever you visit us."

Silence wondered, when Job had left, if her invitation had been overbold. She had had to watch her tongue since the first words he and she had exchanged. The unhallowed longings Satan had thrust into her mind when she and Dr. Hill had undressed the senseless man still dwelt there, however rigorously she curbed them.

Job Aldrich was kind and thoughtful and amazing gentle, and yet the most dangerous man, she warned herself again while a weakening heat suffused her, she ever had known. Ezra, her own husband, had never quickened the perilous, desirous confusion that Job's eyes, or his handclasp, or even his voice could rouse.

Perhaps, Silence thought once again, she was by nature truly evil. Or it might be that the lawless carnality that beset her in one man's presence was retribution sent by the Almighty because, since Ezra's death, she had been proud that she and Parmenas had been sufficient to each other. Job had called her "stiff-necked." She must take exceeding care that he never suspect how easily and eagerly she would yield to his will.

"I wish," Parmenas said resignedly, "that Mr. Aldrich lived right here to Westminster."

"Wouldn't wonder," his mother returned, ignoring her recent self-admonishment, "if you saw him again, when we go a-visitin' to the Frenches in the fall."

Shadows were long and thrushes were chiming in the forest when Job turned off the highway and took the road toward Dummerston settlement. He forgot the late hour and his own weariness when he reached the Houghton pitch. A figure in its dooryard raised a hand in hesitant greeting that sent his heart into his throat.

Job rode toward Melissa, dismounted, and instead of the graceful compliments he strove to utter, said clumsily:

"Welcome home. Didn't expect you'd be back so soon."

"Neither," she told him, "did I."

[233]

She was no longer the wan mourner of weeks before. He never had seen her look quite so fair.

"Beulah," Melissa began, "found she was—" She paused, grew red, and resumed, "—well, homesick, I guess. She—" Again she stumbled. "—she ain't too well. The journey tired her and she's sleeping now."

Job asked to end the awkward silence:

"You're here to stay?"

"Guess so," she answered with a trace of resentment, "providing she don't change her mind again."

"I beg you," he urged hoarsely, "not to forget what I told you when I saw you last."

"I shan't," she promised with a smile that took his breath away. Job blurted, implicitly offering this glowing creature all his substance:

"I'd be honored, when your sister has recovered, if you and she would let me show you what I've done on my pitch."

"Be pleased to," she returned politely. "That is, when Beulah's better."

The anxious look she cast toward the house made it clear that she was dismissing him. Job rode away, happily exploring the luminous future. The sun was setting when, having returned the horse and declined the Frenches' invitation to supper, he came a-foot to his own pitch.

As he approached the house, the door was flung open, a gay voice hailed him, and Alvah Reynolds, hurrying forth, caught him by the shoulders and shook him fondly.

"Faith," he complained, "you're a sorry host. I had begun to think my horse and I must spend the night here alone."

He was leaner and more worn, yet his eyes were still merry, and his laughter came readily.

"Alvah," Job said with difficulty, "I'm glad to see you. It's been a long time."

Already he felt the ease and quiet pleasure his friend always brought, yet he apologized as he led Reynolds back toward the house:

"If you had warned me that you were coming, I'd have had something better to offer you. I—"

Job paused on the threshold to stare at the replenished fire, the spider on the hearth, and the kettle, bubbling thickly on the crane.

"I've made free with your supplies," Reynolds confessed, "and if, my friend, you are so high-stomached that you consider mush and fried pork poor provender, you should sample the rations issued at Ti to the raggle-taggle mob assembling there."

"There is also," Job amended, thrusting his guest into the kitchen, "a drop or two of cider brandy."

"Now that," Reynolds laughed, "you keep so thriftily hidden I couldn't find it."

Job returned from the cellar, jug in hand, and filled two horn cups.

"Health," he said and forced a question. "How long can you stay?"

His friend drank and blinked.

"Till daybreak; no longer. It is only by accident that I'm here at all."

He sat on the bed's edge, long legs a-sprawl, and sipped his liquor while Job busied himself at the fire. Reynolds had become, he announced with comic solemnity, a lieutenant in Warner's Grants regiment. This was part of the army, if such it could be called, that was assembling at Fort Ticonderoga to invade Canada.

Job's guest had ridden into Hampshire with dispatches from General Schuyler to Colonel Stark and had no more than reached Dummerston, on his return, when his horse had cast a shoe. When the smith, Haven, had replaced it, it had been too late for further travel, and Reynolds had sought lodging here.

He paused and looked thoughtfully at his friend's bent back before he went on in a careless voice:

"I already had spent more time than I should in escorting the Widow Houghton and her fair sister from Keene. I'll

[235]

wager you're too laggard a suitor to have learned they have returned to Dummerston."

"Then you will lose," Job retorted, lifting the kettle from the crane, "for I have just come from the Houghton pitch."

He had tried to match the other's ease, yet he wondered with a twinge of discomfort why Melissa had not mentioned Reynolds.

"Faith," the man grinned, "you have taken my counsel to heart, then. My envious felicitations, sir. Shall we drink to the nuptial day?"

He laughed and did not mention Melissa again. When supper had been cleared away, host and guest sat late before the fire, talking without restraint of the odd peace that seemed to have come upon Cumberland County, now that men were fighting elsewhere. Reynolds did not share his friend's belief that the war soon would end or that the struggle for liberty would incline the embattled provinces to favor the Grants' desire for union and independence.

"Schuyler, himself, is a grasping Yorker who gobbles up all the men we send him and cries for more, yet promises nothing in return. I'm beginning to believe that what freedom we gain, we must get for ourselves."

"By starting," Job asked, "a war of our own?"

"That," Reynolds replied soberly, ignoring the sarcasm, "I still do not know."

By the stars, it was well past nine when they went to bed. The sun had not yet risen when they had breakfasted and Job's guest was ready to leave. He finished buckling his saddlebags to the cantle, then said with singular gravity:

"Good-by, my dear friend. I shall think of you often."

"And I of you, daily."

Reynolds swung himself into the saddle and by the swift movement shook off his solemn mood.

"In a year I'll return," he promised with a grin, "when my enlistment is over—always providing I manage to remain in this wicked world.

"A year hence," he emphasized. "You had best be wed by then and a father, as well."

He rode jauntily away. Job stumbled back into the house.

A week after Reynolds's departure, Melissa and her sister arrived, unheralded, to view Job's pitch. They could not have come at a worse time, he reflected with despair as Nat brought them into the clearing, with Beulah sitting sidewise on Cephas and the girl walking stiffly beside him.

Job was unshaven, barefoot, and the dust stirred by his hoeing plastered his sweating person. The greeting he stammered did not visibly cheer his visitors.

Melissa's response was so stately that he knew she had been compelled to come. Beulah, smiling down feebly from her perch, explained in a breathless voice that she hadn't been too well, that it had been a longer walk than she had bargained for, and that if Nat, by good fortune, had not met them, she likely would have fainted.

"Want, though," she insisted, with a reproachful glance at her sister, "that you show 'Lissa how real good you've settled. Great day! Ain't you done a deal since—since Dan'l and me was here!"

Her eyes filled, and she looked away. Job, not heartened by Nat's grimace of sympathy, guided the girl about the clearing, intuitively viewing it through her unimpressed eyes. Suddenly, the lush corn seemed wilted, the wheat sparse, and the lately flourishing beans, squash, and apple seedlings woefully undernourished. He tried not to think of his own appearance, but at length it wrung apology from him.

"Oh," Melissa replied, brightly, "it's always better to see things as they really are than prettied up for visitors."

The house, itself, more nearly pleased her. Job, encouraged by her comments on its size and convenience, tried to tell her how often he had pictured her, gracing and brightening his home, but the impulse failed when she said:

"It's a real handsome place, but, goodness, it's far from everything. You must be lonely here, specially winter times."

"Never," he insisted, and Melissa gave a small laugh of disbelief.

"Well," she granted, "I suppose a body can get used to anything; not that I don't think," she added contritely, "that you've worked a lot to better your pitch."

Job's aspect must have betrayed his misery when he and the girl returned to where Beulah still sat disconsolately a-horse, for Nat, standing beside Cephas, said quickly that he was taking the visitors home to dinner and hoped his neighbor would join them.

"No," Job replied, purpose emerging from chaos, "but if you'll lend me Cephas after, I'll see them back to their own place."

Determination hardened while he washed, shaved, and put on clean attire. He would not meekly suffer the hurt that Melissa, designedly or otherwise, had dealt him. Submission would blast his hope of winning the spitefully perverse girl and tarnish his pride in the property whose betterment he had dedicated to her. Job set out in haste for his neighbors' but at the edge of his clearing paused and looked back. Whether Melissa liked it or not, there was no better pitch in all the Grants.

In the Frenches' dooryard Cephas drooped, tethered to a tree with his saddle still in place and the pad of a pillion now affixed behind it. Nat beckoned to Job from the barn, and when his friend had entered, closed the door and muttered his tidings.

Betty had just told him why Beulah had returned to Dummerston.

"Come back to have her baby here an' that's God's truth. With child by Dan'l and is set on bearin' it in her an' his home. Wal, better late than never, I s'pose. Anyway, that's why she's hard to get along with."

"Melissa," Job asked dryly, "she's not with child too, is she?" and Nat chuckled.

"Wouldn't jedge her too hard. Women in a family way can be a real affliction."

Job halted Cephas before the Houghtons' doorstep and carefully helped Beulah to alight. She thanked him sadly and hurried into the house. Melissa had slipped down, unaided, and was about to follow.

"No," he told her. "I've something to say to you."

She lifted her eyebrows but halted, and the shock he always felt when their eyes met weakened his determination for an instant.

"You must know," Job said, rallying, "my prime reason for bettering my pitch. I've hoped since the day I first saw you that you might come to favor it and me enough to live there."

Color came into her face, heightening her loveliness and compelling him to add more gently:

"Whatever you don't like about my home—and me—I'll do my best to mend."

"I never have said," Melissa told him with unwonted meekness, "that I disliked either."

Job asked huskily:

"Then have I leave to court you?"

Her eyes reproached him; her bright mouth trembled.

"How can I tell," she faltered, "when I still am so lately bereaved?"

"Will you let me serve you, then, in any way I'm able? Will you give me hope?"

"Job," she began at length and thrilled him, for she never before had addressed him by his given name. "Job," she said again and more imploringly, "how can I tell now, with Will so lately dead? Can't you wait till I've done with mourning for him?"

"Wait," he persisted, though he felt it cruel to press her, "for how long?"

"Till a year from now," Melissa murmured. "Only a single year. Would that be too long if, at its end—"

The sorrowful voice died away. She drew her eyes from Job's and stood waiting, desolate and fair.

"Let it be a year, then, if you wish it," he agreed slowly and added, summoning hollow cheer, "After all, Jacob waited seven years for Rachel."

Melissa looked up with new interest.

"Jacob who?" she asked.

Job rode homeward in unexpected tranquillity. He had salvaged more than had seemed possible from the morning's disaster. He had anticipated, even would have welcomed, a destructive quarrel with Melissa. Instead, by dealing with her firmly, he had become her acknowledged suitor. He would devote every minute he could spare in the year before him to helping the girl and her sister. If ardor and fidelity could accomplish it, the time of waiting Melissa had set would be happily shortened.

He had crossed Black Mountain's shoulder when his mind was jerked away from contemplation of the brightened future by sudden encounter. Ahead of him, Pollard Whipple stole out into the road, looked sharply to left and right, and seeing a horseman's approach, scuttled back into the trail that led to the Alvord cabin.

Job curbed the impulse to pursue. He had no wish to tangle himself again in whatever intrigue might be reviving in a lately placid town. His thought swung back serenely to Melissa. Beyond the manifold virtues he already had discovered in her, she now was proving herself to be a loyally devoted sister.

Beulah lay on her bed in a suffering posture yet she told Melissa with vigorous severity:

"Might at least have acted polite an' praised his pitch."

"Your idea, traipsing over there," her sister answered sullenly. " 'Twas none of mine."

"Job Aldrich," Beulah persisted, ignoring the accusation, "will have the best farm in town, one of these days. You could go a deal further an' fare worse, young lady."

"I'm in no haste to wed," Melissa said airily.

Her sister propped herself on an elbow to launch her warning:

"Time's a-comin', if you don't mend your ways, when no man'll want you. I—"

"Just so happens," Melissa replied with irksome complacency, "Job Aldrich asked leave, not a quarter hour ago, to court me."

"And," Beulah supplied, taking the darkest possible view, "you were brainless enough to tell him no."

"Gave him leave," Melissa corrected, smiling, "but said he'd have to wait till I was certain sure. Needn't worry about me, sister. Already found out more about men than you're ever likely to learn."

Beulah, bested, lay back wearily and half-whispered:

"Haven't strength to argue, 'Lissa. Sickens me an' I don't want harm to come to Dan'l's child. I must rest a spell."

Until her sister's delivery, Melissa thought bitterly, she would be outnumbered in all disputes: two against one.

30

SCRIPTURE MAINTAINED that a man could not serve two masters, yet Job, in all earnestness and piety, did his utmost to confute the Gospel. Six days he labored on his pitch with new, protective zeal, born of Melissa's indifference to its excellences. The Sabbath he dedicated equitably to worship of the deity and to the girl and her sister.

When morning meeting was over, Job hurried to the Houghton farm and there devoted the remaining daylight hours to tasks two forlorn women were unable to perform. These, as Beulah's pregnancy advanced, multiplied in number and variety, for she relished her role of expectant mother and dwelt at length upon each anxiety and discomfort. Though her half-doleful, half-complacent recitals were tedious, Job heard them patiently, for Beulah plainly favored him and was always his ally in whatever disagreements he had with Melissa.

The girl's lot was ever more trying, and he did his best to ease it. He joined with other men of the neighborhood in cutting and piling wood enough to last through the winter and in making hay for the cow that Beulah had purchased in case she herself should be unable to supply milk for the baby. Margaret Kathan, Abigail Haven, and women from other nearby pitches often came a-visiting, and once Solomon Harvey was leaving as Job arrived. The physician greeted him with level courtesy, more disconcerting than his usual enmity.

This half day's weekly service, Job felt ardently, was little enough to pay for the limited intimacy Melissa granted him. She was friendly, politely grateful, yet so promptly rebuffed his attempts to court her that he became convinced it was better to wait. He would practice fidelity and diligence on her behalf until, in time, she recognized that he was essential to her.

It was a bleak sort of wooing, but Job could contrive no better. He was troubled by the impression that the Frenches covertly disapproved of his weekly visits to the Houghton pitch. Perhaps they resented his attendance upon the girl Will had been about to wed. Certainly there was no reason for Nat and Betty to believe that Job was neglecting his own property. None in Dummerston or, likely enough, all of Cumberland County, had returned as rich a harvest from an equally small investment.

Job had threshed out more than fifteen bushels of wheat. His corn had yielded equally well. He turned his surplus beans and squashes over to Nat in exchange for a red heifer calf, the first permanent resident in the new barn. By the time approaching autumn had set fire to the ridges, the winter's wood had been stored and enough tree stumps had been grubbed out to add another quarter acre of tillage to his holding.

Job was unable to rouse Melissa to more than passing interest in his accomplishments, yet he still was sure that in time she would come to share his pride. The latter half of the year was compensating him richly for the woes of the former, and he was too intensely occupied to weigh the tidings, good or ill, that tardily reached his clearing.

The war that had flared up in the spring seemed to be dying for lack of fuel. The inert host camped about Boston town was dwindling as winter approached, and the army that had gone north from Ticonderoga probably would fall apart, too. A handful of Job's neighbors, styling themselves "the Dummerston Cadets" were drilling twice weekly on the common, but he had too many claims upon his every waking hour to permit him to attend, even had he been so inclined.

In early November, Nat brought a letter, soiled and creased by passage through unnumbered hands since Reynolds had penned it, more than two months earlier.

"My friend," he had written, "this bedlam embarks tomorrow to conquer Canada, which, if our regiments display toward the foe a tithe of their enmity toward each other, will be ours in a fortnight. Schuyler is ailing, and the command, it is rumored, may devolve upon one Montgomery, another damned Yorker for whom our colonel already cherishes the liveliest detestation. So wish me glory, my dear Job, though I suspect this will be less available than frostbite, mutiny, and attendant ills. Should I survive these, I shall see you again eleven months hence. I trust you employ the year of my absence as I have prescribed. Hail and farewell, my most valued friend. Alvah Reynolds, Cap't (no less!) in Warner's Reg't."

"Bad news?" Nat ventured.

"No," Job said, rousing, and handed him the letter.

"Don't sound—wal, real promisin'," his friend commented at length.

"Not too," the other agreed absently. The fact that Reynolds was to be absent for a year and that Melissa had resolved to mourn over Will for a like period could be no more than coincidence.

December was well begun and Beulah's time was drawing near when a borrowed horse and chaise brought Silence Thayer and Parmenas to visit the Frenches. To Job, supping that night with his neighbors and their guests, she seemed almost a stranger. Excitement had lent her face color and vitality that

[243]

made it downright comely, and he was aware for the first time how gracefully she moved.

After the meal, Parmenas approached the men who sat before the fire and, hauling himself up onto the settle beside Job, regarded him with quiet reverence. Job ran his hand over the small, sleek head in unconscious imitation of Silence's customary caress and asked:

"Done any more trouting?"

"Just once," Parmenas answered. "I like it better with you. Guess," he went on thoughtfully, "I like everything better with you."

Nat chuckled.

"Mebby," he told the small boy, "you'd enjy helpin' him grub stumps."

Parmenas looked up hopefully at Job.

"Could I?" he breathed. "Could I, truly?"

Betty and Silence returned from the bedroom where they had gossiped maternally over the slumbering Hosea. Job rose to leave and, looking down into the child's still hopefully upturned face, said on impulse to his mother:

"I'd like it real well if he stayed with me while you're here. That is, if he'd like it, too."

"Oh," Parmenas gasped and could go no further, but waited, hopefully watching Silence. She said at last with her rare, transforming smile:

"No reason why he shouldn't, if he won't be in the way."

"I won't; honest and true, I won't," the boy insisted.

"Well, then," Silence said. "I'll get his things. It'll be for just a little while," she warned her son. "We're goin' home, day after tomorrow."

Job moved about his pitch next day, accompanied by a second, smaller and more substantial shadow than his own. He had resigned himself to neglecting his work while he took care of his impulsively bidden guest. Now, he was surprised and touched to find how earnestly the child tried to please. He stood well out of harm's way while Job hacked at a stump, learned quickly to bring his host the tools he required, was diligently helpful and profoundly contented.

They sat together before the fire, after supper, talking as though they were of an age, until the child collapsed against Job and barely woke when he was borne to bed. While they breakfasted, next morning, Parmenas said soberly:

"I wish today was yesterday or we weren't goin' home till tomorrow."

"Yes," Job answered honestly, "I wish that, too. Maybe—"

He checked himself, knowing it would be better to say no more until he had talked with Silence.

She came uphill in midmorning, accompanied by Nat, to be welcomed politely by Job and with an unlikely mixture of affection and regret by her son. Thereafter, Silence looked about her intently.

"It's a real good pitch," she said finally. "Don't mind ever seeing a better. Early, too, by the way it lays, and I like a house that sets so it gets the most sun."

She and the men walked about the clearing, Parmenas trudging ahead with a proprietary air. Job felt it was not lip service but genuine interest that made his visitor marvel at the size of the corn stubble. Silence tested the soil knowingly, rubbing it between her palms, touching it with her tongue, and at last nodding approval. She said little while he showed her through the house, but when they had returned to the doorstep, she told him quietly:

"You're fixed real fort'nit. No wonder Parmenas don't want to go home."

Job flushed with pleasure. He looked toward the little boy, who waited beside Nat, and spoke what had been in his mind all morning:

"Let him stay with me till Saturday. I'll take real good care of him and fetch him home to you, then."

"It would please him greatly, I know," Silence said, "but 'twould spile a whole day for you."

"Now it's in my mind," Job told her, "that I spoiled a number of days for you."

[245]

"Repaid me for that," she said almost angrily. "And more, too."

"Then," he urged, "even the score by letting Parmenas stay, unless he wouldn't want to."

"No fear of that," Silence said and dazzled him with her smile.

Friday noon, while host and guest were finishing dinner, Nat knocked and entered with Jonathan Knight and Enoch Cook clumping behind him. Job, sensing an urgency beneath their overhearty greetings, suggested that Parmenas go out and play for a spell, then considered the visitors, stiffly seated at the table, and prompted:

"Well?"

Nat twisted his hands, and Cook rumpled his straw-colored hair. Both of them looked at Knight, who droned:

"Come to talk to ye 'bout Harvey an' his dinged committee."

"What have they done?" Job asked uneasily.

"Taken to detectin' conspiracies again," Knight returned in a dry voice. "Whar ye been, for Gossakes?"

"Busy," Job retorted and, smarting under the implied reproof, added, "Thought you and Harvey were hand in glove."

"Ehyah," Knight agreed nodding acknowledgment of the thrust. "So'd I, for a spell. Ain't ready, though, to be ruled by any one man; Solomon, specially."

It had been folly, Job reflected, tasting again the bitter flavor of the old distress, to presume that peace could endure in Dummerston. It was flattering, nevertheless, that, in a still-obscure crisis, neighbors should turn to him.

"Best," he suggested, with more sympathy than he had intended, "if you tell me what this is about."

Knight roused. His words buzzed like a bluebottle on a windowpane, and he absently rubbed the shoulder that had been wounded at Westminster. Solomon, he reported, had acted real subdued for quite a spell after the courthouse fight. With war enough elsewhere to suit anyone, he had appeared willing to leave peace undisturbed in Dummerston.

Harvey had tried to buy for the town the gunpowder Cook

and Kathan had refused to purchase, but the armies seemed to have taken it all. At length the doctor had found a man in Greenfield with half a keg to sell, had bought it on his own responsibility, and had stored it in his barn.

"Wal," Knight pursued stridently, "someone stole it—someone favorin' peace, I'd say, for he poured the keg down Solomon's well, ruinin' the water for quite a spell an' the powder, permanent. That's when Harvey went off the handle again. Him an' Temple an' Davenport hold the town's rotten with treason, an' they've got together a passel of young rascals to purge it."

"An'," Cook supplied, "Alex an' me, we're the chief suspects."

Knight nodded.

"Temple and his bullies," he told Job, "forced their way into Enoch's house, skeered his wife an' children into conniption fits, an' tuck his firelock."

"Me," Cook elaborated with an attempt at a grin, "that, along with Kathan, got dismissed as assessor, because we was against war."

"What town meetin' did to you," Knight informed him severely, "was lawful an' proper. Way Harvey an' his committee's carryin' on ain't one or t'other. Served Alex worse than they did Enoch," he went on, turning to Job again. "Claimed he's a royalist spy and shet him up on his pitch, promisin' to shoot him if he as much as steps offen it."

"John Hooker," Cook said antiphonally, "he preached against folks who set neighbors against each other. Next mornin', there was a picture of a coffin pinned to his door."

Job broke the sudden, tight silence.

"Well?" he challenged.

"Wal," Knight echoed, "decent folks are gettin' more'n a mite tired of Solomon. Hold it's time we got rid of him."

"Aiming," Job asked acidly, "to raid his house, or shoot him if he leaves his property?"

"No, by God," Knight retorted. "It's got to be done fair an' aboveboard. Call a town meetin', I say, an' throw him out of office.

[247]

"That," he continued, more calmly, "is what we come for. Takes a petition by ten freeholders to summon a meetin'. Want Job Aldrich to be the fust to sign. We," he added, taking a paper from his coat and laying it on the table, "will set down our names after yours."

Job looked from one still face to another.

"Why," he asked at length, "should I be first?"

"Because," Cook told him, "folks think high of you."

"Damn nigh kilt to Westminster, wa'n't ye?" Knight inquired. "Makes you a hero, in a manner of speakin'. Your name fust on the petition'll carry weight. Ain't no time for the law-abidin' to set on their hunkers, while Solomon Harvey persecutes the unoffendin'."

"No," said Job, at length and slowly. "Guess it isn't."

He rose and took inkhorn and quill from the cupboard.

There was a bite to the air, and Cephas's hoofs rang on the frozen highway as Job rode back from Westminster. He had been wise on a lowering day to begin his homeward journey at once, though he had fancied Silence had been disappointed that he had not tarried. Perhaps he mistakenly had alloted her a share in her son's open desolation. He, standing in the doorway while Job remounted, had looked so woebegone that the man had assured him:

"It'll be spring before you know it, and then I'll be back to take you home with me for a longer visit."

"Not," Parmenas gulped, "till spring?"

"Don't," his mother warned him quickly, "be presumin'."

"Real friends," Job grinned down at the small boy, "can't ever be presuming with each other. Maybe I'll be back before spring, if the winter stays open."

"You'll be welcome," Silence said calmly and led her son into the house.

It would be lonelier on his pitch without his small comrade, Job admitted, as the Great Road led him uphill and down toward Putney. It was just as well, though, that Parmenas had gone home before the forming opposition collided with Harvey and his committee. A spasm of anger tightened Job's belly as he thought of Cook's house invaded and of Kathan as lawlessly kept on his pitch. He was glad his name stood first on the petition for a town meeting, proud that he had signed it.

He examined this strange new fervor closely. It was contrary to all he most earnestly had believed, yet he could not honestly deplore it. He had joined in lawful resistance to unrighteousness, and the pride he had half decried stemmed from the simple, estimable fact that his like-minded neighbors, in emergency, had turned to him.

Job rode down a long hill and then past Putney's houses, each encircled by dead leaves and evergreen boughs piled about the foundation for winter protection. The raw settlement had a new, still eloquence. Passionate desire for self-ownership and peace that was kin to Job's own had inspired plain people to invade a wilderness and build with unmeasured travail and trust their hopeful little settlements.

Liberty, he reflected with sudden, odd assurance, was neither a war cry nor the watchword that distinguished the elect. Liberty was land of your own to use as you found best; it was friendliness and helpfulness; wheat, standing tall and golden in a clearing; cattle, housed in a new log barn; ash salts, brown and wet in a kettle bottom; belief in the goodness of God and your neighbors and the black, responsive Grants' earth. All these comprised the liberty that true men did well to uphold.

Job was bewildered by his sense of rededication. Perhaps this was what Hooker had meant when he had said, long ago, that the Almighty made known His purposes in His own good time to every being.

Putney now lay far behind. In little more than another hour, Job would be home. He grunted and sat more erectly in the saddle. Ahead, where the track to Kathan's pitch forked off from the main road, a dwarfish figure, lugging an oversize firelock, had scuttled across the highway to drop into the roadside brush.

Young Jake Laughton had been clearly visible, his purpose entirely evident, yet for an instant Job's mind stuck and would go no further. It was one thing to be told that Kathan had been limited to his farm, with his life forfeit if he moved off it; it was another, infinitely more shocking, to see that sentence implemented and a boy eagerly set himself in murderous ambush.

God's will, it was apparent, had revealed itself starkly to Job.

Cephas halted willingly. The rider slid from the saddle, pulled off his boots, and stole forward, eyes fixed on the spot where Jake had disappeared. Now, he could see the depression about the aspiring assassin's body and, advancing with exquisite care, looked down at last across the intervening bushes at the boy himself.

Jake lay prone behind the cocked musket that rested across a boulder and bore upon the downhill way to Kathan's home. Rage, chill and ruthless, impelled Job. Brush rattled, twigs rasped across his clothing as he strode into the ambush and stood above the boy, who had twisted about convulsively. His mouth gaped witlessly. Fright had set eyes to flickering in a thin, colorless face.

"Hunting for something?" Job asked bleakly.

Jake gave a gagging sound. His grimed claws tightened on the musket's stock, and he answered at last in a stifled squeal:

"No consarn of yours, you—you stinkin' traitor."

He shifted the weapon slightly as he spoke.

"Drop the firelock," Job bade, "and get up. Get up," he repeated when the boy failed to stir, "else I'll kick you apart."

He leaned forward, dragged Jake to his feet, thrust him aside, and picking up the musket, lowered its hammer. The initials "E.C." were burned into the maple butt. Job turned upon the boy, who was shaking so violently with rage or dread that he could barely stand.

"Wait," Jake quavered, "till the committee larns what you've done. Wait till I—"

He gulped. Tears of helpless fury spilled down his cheeks, unheeded. He flinched when Job gripped a thin shoulder and bade levelly:

"I want you should tell your friends this: Whoever tries to bushwack Kathan'll suffer worse than Alex. Understand?"

He loosed his anger for an instant and shook the frail figure until its teeth clicked. Jake sobbed, as Job released him:

"You wait, that's all. Doctor'll deal with you."

"One thing more," his adversary told him, with a mirthless grin. "Don't let me catch you playin' Injun again. Stay far away from me, hereafter, or I'll—I'll unbreech you at mid-day on the settlement street and whale you till you can't set."

He pushed the boy aside and stepped out into the road, then paused.

"As for Harvey," Job said, "I've quite a lot to tell him myself. Afterward I'll take this firelock back to Enoch Cook."

31

HARVEY'S BESPECTACLED gaze went up and down the man who stood on the doorstep with a musket under his arm.

"You wished," the physician asked at length as though there had been some mistake, "to see me?"

The lofty query fortified Job.

"Ehyah," he replied. "Special."

"You may come in," Harvey granted at length, "leaving your firelock here."

Job shook his head.

"That," he said cheerfully, "I will not do. This is Enoch's property," he pursued, turning the piece over to display the initials burned into its stock. "He lost it when your crew forced their way into his house. Then, young Jake Laughton, he lost it this afternoon. Don't want to chance it's getting lost again."

He was pleasantly aware that he was speaking with new decision. Harvey's eyes grew wider still.

"You will leave your weapon here," he insisted with a trace of bluster, "or I will not admit you. I am alone and unarmed."

"Ehyah," Job retorted, "as Alex Kathan would have been if Jake had done your will and murdered him."

The doctor jerked his head.

"What is this, sir?" he cried. " 'Murdered'?"

"Attempting to, anyway," Job amended. "Caught the young weasel trying to bushwhack him with Enoch's musket. Alex is my good neighbor and—"

"And," Harvey broke in viciously, "a bird of your own sinister feather. Kathan's case," he went on more augustly, "was duly considered by the committee, and he was informed of the sentence passed upon him. He knows what the consequences will be if he ventures off his pitch. I take no responsibility for what Jacob Laughton has done or has not done."

" 'Tis your habit, seems," Job returned, "to be elsewhere when bloodshed is in prospect." He was gratified to hear breath hiss from his adversary, and deliberately added, "You and your committee aren't what I'd consider proper tutors for a growing boy."

A remote portion of his mind decried the satisfaction he was finding in open defiance of his long-time enemy. He ignored the protest and pressed on:

"Warned Jake to leave Alex be. I'm warning you and your committee now."

" 'Warning'!" the other hooted. "I, sir, am warning you that we are not to be swayed by the threats of an armed bravo who, likely enough, is drunk in the bargain. The Committee for Detecting Conspiracies in its own good time will have something to say to you."

"Granting," Job answered recklessly, "that the freeholders don't say different."

The comment left Harvey gravely thoughtful.

"Yes," he acknowledged at length, drawing his snuffbox from a pocket and absently tapping its lid. "I have received, as town clerk, a petition for a special meeting, signed by all the mar-plots and dissidents in Dummerston, with their dupes. Your name is deservedly foremost.

"I marvel," he continued with more vigor, "at your temerity, effrontery, and barefaced duplicity. I welcome such a meeting, though I scarcely dare hope you'll be present."

"I shall be," Job promised, "if I'm not shot from ambush before then."

The taunt darkened Harvey's face and unbalanced his voice.

"I earnestly hope you do attend so that hair-splitting legal-ists may have no reason to complain that you were tried, sen-tenced, and punished in your absence. Whom the gods destroy, sir, they first make mad."

"Ehyah," Job agreed. "Wouldn't wonder."

The physician favored him with a final stare, then strode into the house, slamming the door behind him.

Cook, summoned to his dooryard by a horseman's shouting, looked in bewilderment from Job to the proffered weapon.

"Gossakes!" he stumbled. "How came you by that?"

He listened, wide-eyed, to the other's curt explanation and sighed when it ended.

"Goes from bad to worse, don't it?" he deplored.

"It'll go no further." Job bit off each word. "Solomon Harvey will be without his clerkship or his damned committee when town meeting's over."

"Great day!" Cook said mildly and stared. "Never heered you talk like that. What's come over you?"

The visitor laughed and gathered up his rein.

"Seems," he said cryptically as he moved away, "that the road from Westminster and the road to Damascus have more in common than you'd think."

Nat, when Job led Cephas into the barn, expressed extrava-gant relief at his friend's return.

"Begun to wonder," he added, "whether you hadn't jined up with the Widder Thayer."

His mock concern became genuine.

"There's one woman after you, anyway. Zurvilla Alvord's been here, all het up to find you."

"Zurvilla?" Job repeated vacantly.

"Ehyah," Nat answered and, curiosity overwhelming him, inquired, "What you and her contrivin'?"

"I haven't even laid eyes on her for months."

"Wal," French surrendered, "she's all of a swivet. Madder every day, if you ask me."

"Had a mite of trouble on the way home," Job volunteered and told of his encounter with Jake and interview with Harvey. When he had ended, Nat shrugged and said with a forced grin:

"Promises to be quite a town meetin', don't it?"

Daniel Houghton's widow bore a girl child that Sabbath morning. Job, arriving unwarned, found the house filled with women. Their babble was pierced by a thin voice that seemed determined to perpetuate Beulah's earlier complaints.

The intruder was entirely willing to withdraw, particularly since the tight-lipped Melissa seemed to place him foremost in a newly acquired grievance against his sex, but before he could get free, Abigail Haven firmly led him into the chamber where mother and baby lay.

"Wanted," Beulah said weakly, "you should see Dan'l's datter. Namin' her Frances Elizabeth after his mother. Ain't she sweet?"

To Job, the small creature seemed to be singularly lacking in charm, but he lied valiantly. He would have followed Abigail from the room, but Beulah's gesture delayed him.

"Don't," she muttered, "pay no mind to 'Lissa. Upset, she is, over what she's—we've jest been through. Persevere, an' I'll help you all I can."

Job was halfway home when he met Two-pound-ten Alvord stumping along the road. He looked grimier and hairier than usual, but his greeting was fervent and obscurely relieved. While cane and shuffling feet beat out a rhythm, he explained that he was abroad to warn all freeholders of the meeting that would be held at Davenports', midmorning of Wednesday.

[254]

Alvord hesitated, stubbled face twitching, then went on so hastily that his words jostled each other.

"Sister, she's a-cravin' to see ye. Comfort her—me, too—if ye'd visit with her a mite."

He ceased jigging and dropped his voice into a husky mutter.

"Been beside herself, sister has, since Dr. Harvey, he come to see her."

Two-pound-ten pattered away on his mission while Job reluctantly took the trail to the Alvord pitch. Its littered yard was empty, and the door of the sway-backed cabin barred. There was no response when he knocked. He had called Zurvilla's name thrice before he heard faint stirring within.

"It's Job Aldrich," he announced loudly. "Moses bade me come."

Zurvilla's face was gray; her eyelids redly swollen. The smile she attempted failed utterly.

"Come in," she breathed. "Quick, for They may be followin' ye."

She opened the door barely enough for Job to squeeze through and quickly barred it behind him.

"Ye're—ye're real welcome," the woman faltered and then stood, plucking at her mouth, while her flabby body shook. Her terror was unreasonably contagious. Job fancied he could smell the very scent of fear in the rancid air. Pity for the addled creature and anger toward the man who had frightened her sharpened his voice.

"What's been done to you?"

Zurvilla flinched, tried to reply, then shook her head helplessly.

"No need for haste," he told her more gently.

The woman struggled as though dread had laid actual hands upon her. She begged at last and piteously:

"Sweet man, ye won't let Them—let Them hang Zurvilla?" Her voice slid up into an anguished squeak. "Promise ye won't, dearie."

"What nonsense is this?" Job demanded. "Who's talked to you of hanging?"

[255]

" 'Twas—" she piped, gulped, and tried again: " 'Twas Solomon. Told her They hang traitors."

The vestige of self-possession left her. Zurvilla plumped down on the unmade bed and wailed as openly as a wretched child. Job caught her damp hands and pulled them away from her face. It was more difficult to capture the frantic eyes, but at length they met and clung to his in mute appeal.

"I'm your friend," he soothed. "I'll let no one harm you. Tell me quietly, now: Why did Harvey come here? Why did he threaten you?"

"Wanted," she wheezed at length, "that Zurvilla should lie 'bout ye; wanted she should say ye an' her'd been a-spyin', together."

"And you wouldn't?" Job asked, almost absently. His mind had begun to follow a trail of recollection that might lead him out of this wilderness if he could quiet and question his terrified companion.

"Zurvilla," the woman was whimpering, "wouldn't tell him anything; not even when he said—said They'd hang her."

Her hands tightened on Job's. He prompted her gently:

"We haven't seen each other since spring. That's the truth, isn't it?"

She nodded, drearily.

"But," he pursued, "you did tell your brother that I had come to see you when, truly, it was Pollard Whipple and—"

Job stopped short, for amazingly the lately ravaged creature had tossed her head and simpered.

"An' Benjy Gorton," she supplied. "Kin to me, Benjy is. They brought Zurvilla pretties an' she—"

Her bridling complacency was swamped by resurgent fright. She clung desperately to Job's hands.

"Ye won't," the woman implored, "ever tell Brother Moses. Madden him dretful to larn that Zurvilla—"

Her voice died away.

"That Zurvilla," Job completed for her, "told Gorton and Whipple what she had learned from Brother Moses."

The sound of her indrawn breath was like tearing cloth.

"Who told ye so?" she cried, shuddering. "Not Zurvilla. She promised Benjy faithful she wouldn't—an' now They'll hang her."

She wept so wildly that Job, all else failing, gripped her fat shoulders and shook her into silence. The shabby intrigue was plain to him now. What Harvey had magnified into widespread conspiracy had been nothing more than a mad crone's tattling.

In all likelihood, Zurvilla had been remotely responsible for the Westminster riot and the more recent destruction of the town's powder.

The woman's lamentation had dwindled into convulsive sniveling. She was less responsible than a child for what she had done, and besides, Job thought with a stir of sympathy, she had little cause to be loyal to neighbors who ignored, mocked, or openly abused her. He asked:

"You trust me?"

She gave him a wet half smile.

"Aye," she muttered. "Allus befriended Zurvilla, bless ye."

"And you, me," Job returned. "Will you do as I bid, if I swear no harm'll befall you?"

"Aye," she said again, but so uncertainly that his intention faltered. He recalled Harvey's vindictiveness, Alex Kathan's plight, and pressed on:

"Then listen to me carefully and heed what I say. You are to speak to no one, not even your brother, of what passed between us, until I give you leave."

"Zurvilla won't," she promised eagerly. "Not ever. If she did, They—"

"Until I give you leave," he repeated loudly. "Come Wednesday, I may bring certain men to visit with you. If I do, you must tell them all you have told me."

"No," she shrilled with vehemence that startled him. "They'd hang Zurvilla. Solomon said so. They'd—"

"Solomon Harvey," Job shouted, to beat down her frenzy, "will lay no finger on you. Will you believe me and do as I bid?"

[257]

The woman's eyes, finding no security elsewhere, returned at last to her counselor's face.

"Zurvilla'll try, sweet lad," she whispered, "but she's dretful skeered. She'd hang herself rather'n let Them take her."

"No one," Job insisted, "is going to hang anyone. Believe me and obey me."

He looked back as he unbarred the door. The woman had cast herself, face downward on the bed, in a shapeless, shaking heap.

The clean outdoor air was like a draft of cold water to the parched. God, Job thought soberly as he strode away, had placed a potent weapon in his hand. It would be better to keep it secret for use at need against Solomon Harvey.

Job and Nat, bound for town meeting, were climbing the mountain road when a breathless voice called them and Two-pound-ten came along the trail from the Alvord cabin, as though a tempest drove him. His frantic strides threatened each moment to upset him; his cane stabbed wildly at the frozen earth. He had lost his fur cap, and his unbound hair flapped on either side of his gaping face like vestigial wings. Though he advanced with headlong speed, alarm outran him and chilled the watchers.

Alvord stumbled and would have gone down if Job, leaping forward, had not caught and held him. While they reeled for an instant, grappling each other, Nat cried:

"Lord above! Two-pound-ten, what ails you?"

The man pulled himself free. His body shook to the whip-saw sound of his panting.

" 'Tis sister," he wheezed at last. " 'Tis Zurvilla. Can't—"

He coughed thinly and looked at his companions in dumb appeal.

"Can't," he gasped with extreme effort, "can't get her down."

"What on earth—?" Nat began, but Job already was running along the trail. Dread, formless yet sickening, impelled him. The wind of his passage blew coldly on his face and, entering his body, froze his heart.

The cabin door stood open. Job collided with its frame, re-covered balance, and entering, stood for a long moment, looking toward Zurvilla. He and the woman were equally still.

A log fell apart in the fireplace, and Nat stumbled across the yard. Zurvilla's head was cocked, almost roguishly, by a leather thong. One end had been noosed around her neck; the other, lashed about a rung of the ladder to the chamber under the cabin's eaves. Her bare feet, barely visible beneath the hem of her gown, dangled a yard above the puncheon floor.

Nat had halted, breathing hoarsely, behind Job, who said without turning:

"Small wonder he couldn't get her down."

His voice sounded profanely loud in the hushed chamber. His friend gabbled, resisting belief:

"Can't be she's dead; can't be she—she hanged herself."

"In a manner of speaking," Job answered dully. "I thrust her toward it, and Solomon Harvey, more than me."

He roused and said to the pallid Nat:

"Maybe we can free her before Two-pound-ten gets back."

When Alvord reappeared, they had laid the unwieldy body on the bed where three days before, Zurvilla had sat and wailed and Job had wrung a pledge from her. That enforced promise, he thought bleakly, had helped her toward this end.

Two-pound-ten leaned on his cane and babbled tearfully. Zurvilla had been poorly, neither relishing her victuals nor sleeping well. She had made breakfast for him this morning and had gone aloft again to her bedchamber.

"After a spell, she asked me to fetch water from the spring. When I come back, she was a-hangin'."

He choked and wiped his eyes. Job told him quietly:

"We're due at town meeting, but we'll tell the neighbors and return."

"I'll stay," Nat volunteered. Job shook his head.

"No," he insisted. "You're more needed where we're going."

Horses were tethered on the common where children played, but in all the settlement no man was visible. The meeting already had commenced, and as Job and Nat approached Davenport's house, they could hear from within a familiar, hooting voice rise and fall.

It dinned in their ears as they stole in. The kitchen was filled with solemn men whom Harvey, standing behind the table he shared with the moderator, vehemently exhorted. The doctor faltered for an instant while the late-comers found places on the rearmost bench.

Job felt tension in the air and shrank cravenly from the course he had resolved that he must follow. Harvey cleared his throat and resumed what evidently was a defense.

"Now, what," he demanded with a lunge of his head, "is this 'tyranny' that Jonathan Knight claims we are exercising? I was empowered by the freeholders to form a committee that would protect Dummerston from its enemies within; from certain serpents, I might say," he added, glancing briefly toward Job, "whom we have warmed in our bosoms."

The doctor's challenging eyes searched his audience before he resumed:

"Enoch Cook has been punished deservedly. The royalist spy, Alexander Kathan, has been placed where he will do no more harm. There are more dangerous and subtle seditionists still at large."

Again, the bespectacled glare raked Job, and now the hollow voice assailed him more directly:

"There is one subversive in particular who has done the town much harm; one man who has dabbled, unchastized, in treason until he has grown bold; so bold that he came armed to my house lately and warned me to desist in my efforts to uphold liberty; so brazen that he was first of the petitioners who demanded this meeting; so barefaced in his iniquity that he has dared to come here today."

He wiped his face with a snuffy handkerchief while the room filled with muttering that might be either approval or dissent.

"I invite the freeholders," Harvey cried, shaking a long forefinger, "to make their own choice. Will they turn their town over to our enemies or purge it of this villain?"

[260]

The savagely plied voice lashed Job to his feet.

"Well," he began, but then his mind and voice dried up as massed, inquiring faces turned toward his. He groped wretchedly for words and lost the remnant of his courage when he saw Harvey and Davenport exchange maliciously amused smiles. Job was about to sit down, defeated, when recollection stayed him.

A childish old woman who had befriended him was dead, slain by terror that the vindictive doctor and his committee were nurturing industriously in Dummerston. Job thought of the flabby weight in his arms, after he and Nat had cut Zurvilla down, and could almost see the poor body lying on the bed like a heap of dirty clothing.

"Something," the moderator was inquiring with covert derision, "that you want to say?"

Job nodded, drawing a long, relieved breath. All at once, he was sure of himself, and lately slippery words were forming in his mind, ready for utterance. In a crooked fashion, what he was about to speak was a tribute to Zurvilla Alvord, the moonstruck creature whom Solomon Harvey had frightened to death.

"Ehyah," Job replied. "There's a deal I want to say. When the town clerk speaks of a 'villain,' I suppose he means me. So he's considered me since first I set foot in Dummerston."

"And with due cause," Harvey cried.

"Maybe," Job pursued, "maybe not." The apostles must have felt like this when pentecostal fires had loosed their tongues. "If so be I'm a villain, what enemies of the town am I accused of serving? Can't be Britain or York, since I've suffered a-plenty at the hands of their minions. Am I a villain because I've come to believe that Grants land belongs to Grants folks, whatever the King or York's governor or the Continental Congress says?"

He could not tell the meaning of the wordless sound that ran through the kitchen, but he saw Knight nod approval and was greatly heartened. Harvey was leveling a forefinger at Job as though it were a cocked weapon.

"I accuse you," he proclaimed, stretching each word to its

utmost, "of being the spy who has carried what he had learned by sniffing and prying to the foes of Liberty in Westminster."

"Well, now," Job replied, amazed to find himself able to grin, "I've been paid for spying in strange coin, if you consider what was done to me at Westminster.

"You must remember that," he added politely, "even though you did get there a mite late."

Someone chuckled, and the doctor's face turned purple. Job was finding harsh delight in open conflict, however much a peaceful man should decry it. Thought of the shapeless figure, dangling with head askew, rid him of compunction.

"I ask you," he told his wrath-inflated adversary, "to explain to the meeting just what traffic I've held with the enemy, whoever that is. To my mind," he drove on before the other could reply, "the worst enemy to the law-abiding in Dummerston is Solomon Harvey, who preaches violence he won't undertake himself, and seeks to turn freemen and their land over to Bay Province."

"Hear, hear!" It was Hooker's voice, and Job grinned again. Davenport, leaning forward in his chair, was speaking urgently to the fuming town clerk. Harvey shook his head and lifted a shrill voice.

"I would remind the meeting," he cried, for the moment ignoring Job, "that the committee I head was duly established on the recommendation of the Continental Congress."

"Same Congress, ain't it," Knight inquired, "that claims the Grants belong to York?"

The question roused again that equivocal, windy sound. Job lifted his voice above it to demand:

"And I would ask the meeting whether it wants to keep a committee that urges youngsters to go gunning for men like Alex Kathan and frightens old women out of their wits."

Harvey turned toward him again and spoke bitterly, yet more warily:

"Kathan is an acknowledged royalist and, we believe, a traitor to boot, a foe to liberty. That we intend to prove in due time. Meanwhile—"

[262]

"Meanwhile," Cook broke in, astoundingly, "you let that limb, Jake Laughton, hunt him with the firelock you stole offen me. Peculiar sort of liberty, I call it."

The physician polished his spectacles with trembling hands. He replaced them and began uncertainly but acquired confidence as he went on.

"We maintain that Dummerston is riddled with treason. A traitor warned Paterson of our march to Westminster. It was by treachery that the town's store of powder was destroyed. Treachery, neighbors, and this man Aldrich has been party to it!"

"Now it is possible," Job said steadily, "that I know more of this so-called 'treachery' than you and all your committee."

"What I maintained," Harvey cried and smirked. "That I do not doubt. D'ye deny that you are well acquainted with Zurvilla Alvord?"

"I—have been."

"Then I charge," the physician shrilled, viciously mouthing each word, "that this raddled old hag wheedled information from her brother and passed it on to you."

It was strange that the meeting's scrutiny no longer troubled Job. He stood erect and calm, waiting until tumult subsided before he replied clearly:

"And I charge that you, Solomon Harvey, lately visited a weak-minded creature and, by your promise to hang her, frightened her beyond endurance."

"Aha!" Harvey pounced. "You have seen her recently then?"

"No later than this morning," Job said deliberately.

He ignored the gloating physician and, instead, addressed the men before him.

"This 'treason', neighbors, that has been blown up so big; this widespread treachery that is said to riddle Dummerston has been used as a goad to drive men whither Solomon Harvey wished them to go. Zurvilla Alvord has confessed to me that, for the sake of trinkets and dainties Tory agents brought her, she gave them information."

Job paused for a moment and stared at the confused town clerk before he went on:

"The babblings of a witless old thing who knew not right from wrong is the sum and substance of a 'conspiracy' that Solomon Harvey has tricked out for his own ends."

Hooker ended the heavy silence.

"Nevertheless," he said gravely, "the woman must be warned; perhaps even punished."

"She has been already," Job returned, "most violently warned by the town clerk. I promise you she will not repeat her offense."

Harvey, reassembling his shattered truculence, jeered:

"And how comes it, sir, that you are so certain of her reform and contrition? Can it be that you are protecting her for your own ends?"

"I promise the meeting," Job returned solemnly, "that henceforth she will be blameless in all things. A simple creature," he went on, voice tolling in the stillness, "was frightened beyond endurance by Dr. Harvey's threats and hanged herself this morning."

He looked at the gaping moderator, the suddenly bleached town clerk, and from them to aghast faces turned toward his.

"Must Alex Kathan," he asked at length, "be murdered also in liberty's name?"

Harvey's backward reaching hand at last had found his chair. He lowered himself into it carefully. Laughter of children on the common entered the hushed chamber where men looked sidewise and whispered to each other. Hooker, at length, deliberately proposed:

"I hold that the town clerk's committee has—outlived its usefulness, neighbors. Mr. Moderator, I move that it be discharged."

Only Temple's voice feebly opposed the measure. Knight hauled his gaunt body upright.

"Like also to move—" he had begun mournfully when Harvey's abrupt gesture halted him.

Vitality had left the physician. His brown clothing seemed

to hang loosely upon a suddenly lesser person. Though he had risen, he still held fast to his chair for support and his voice was strangely muted:

"I am fully aware of the nature of the motion Jonathan is about to propose. I submit that I already have been humbled sufficiently to satisfy even the most vengeful."

Faint revival of an earlier animosity shone in his eyes as they encountered Job's. An echo of his former wrathful hooting crept into the doctor's voice as he pursued:

"The inhabitants of this town in due time will become sensible of the artful insinuations of my inveterate enemies. They, notwithstanding my fidelity to my country's cause, have rendered it necessary that I should resign all my public offices, including that of town clerk. Neighbors, I bid you a long farewell."

He bowed jerkily, crushed by defeat yet clinging so firmly to a remnant of dignity that Job unreasonably pitied him. Harvey, looking neither to right nor left, marched to the door, opened it, and vanished. After a still instant, Knight offered dryly:

"Move the meetin' accepts all Solomon's resignations."

32

NO THAW had relieved the stubborn January cold, and that, Nat had predicted, meant a severe winter but an early spring. Half his prophecy already had been justified. Brooks had been tightly frozen since late December, and the river ran silently beneath unbroken ice. Days of blinding whiteness, laced by shadows of tender blue, nights when the stars hung barely treetop-high, consistently were followed by still another storm that erased roads again and increased the monstrous drifts. Life in Cumberland County had resolved itself into continuously thwarted attempts to resist complete imprisonment by the snow.

Left to himself, Job might have been entirely happy. He had the companionship of his stock: Abigail, the heifer calf, and Buck and Ben, young black steers, already half broken to the yoke, that the emancipated Kathan had pressed upon him as a thank offering. He was felling trees in fair weather for a larger spring burning and, in foul, worked with chisel and borrowed gouge on a mantelpiece for what someday might be his and Melissa's bedchamber.

Nightly, Job knelt to praise his Maker for undeserved, continuing favors. Peace, more profound than the winter usually imposed, now lay upon Dummerston, with Harvey's committee dissolved, its organizer resident in Chesterfield across the Great River, and John Hooker serving as town clerk in his stead.

The war, too, seemed to have moved further from the Grants. There was a stalemate at Boston town, and reports of fighting in Canada were confused and likely enough false. For all its severity, this might have been the best winter Job had known, if it had not been for Melissa.

As the weeks crept numbly past, Job was beset by the insurgent conviction that there were more rewarding ways of wooing a maid than by the faithful performance of chores she was unable, or unwilling, to do herself. His devotion to Melissa did not blind him entirely to her deficiencies as a housekeeper, but he never referred to them until one fell Sabbath afternoon toward the winter's end.

Job had plodded on snowshoes to the Houghton pitch through still another storm to find small Frances Elizabeth screeching lustily, her mother distracted, and Melissa pale and almost dowdy in a bedraggled short gown and wet-blotched petticoat. She had slipped, she explained wearily, while bringing in wood and had fallen, full length.

[266]

Her distress inclined Job to ignore the unswept kitchen, the ash-strewn hearth, and the remains of dinner that had not yet been cleared away. He gave the barn a sorely needed cleaning, fed the cow, and returning to the house with an armful of logs, was cheered to find that Beulah had retired to her bedchamber, where by the unusual silence he judged she must be nursing her child.

Melissa's disconsolate look and his own long deprivation moved Job, when he had set down his burden beside the fireplace and, turning, found the girl standing beside him, to reach out and take her hands. She tore one free, as he tried to draw her closer, and slapped him smartly.

"You've no right," she cried in a tight voice, "to force me. I said a year."

He stared at the white, quivering face and said stiffly, at last: "I ask your pardon."

"If you must tousle someone," she drove on, ignoring his apology, "you had best go elsewhere."

"As you please," Job told her and added deliberately, as chill anger laid hold on him, "though this place will be even worse kept without me."

He picked up his hat and, looking toward Melissa again, saw her face contort before her spread hands hid it from him.

"Oh, please!" she wept. "I didn't mean it, truly, I didn't. I'm cold and lonely and—and hopeless. I can't do everything."

The desolate appeal quenched his wrath. She stumbled toward him, still softly sobbing, and submitted while he held her in a straitly brotherly embrace. For an instant, her head lay against his shoulder. She faltered as she drew away:

"You—you won't hold it against me?"

His face still smarted, but he felt her smile would have been recompense for greater indignity. He left early, for the storm was thickening.

Immediately Job had departed, Beulah, who had beamed on him fondly and had been extreme in her protestations of gratitude, assumed a foreboding air.

"Wal, my fine lady," she began, "if you're set on—"

Melissa lightly interrupted her:

"I know by rote what you're goin' to say. If I lose him, 'twill be my own fault, and so it will, sister dear. I can have him or lose him as best pleases me."

She knew her boast would be maddening and was pleased to see Beulah's face redden.

"'Pride,'" the woman warned hollowly, "'goeth before destruction.'"

Melissa shrugged and laughed.

"Must I tell you, once more," she asked indulgently, "that—"

"That you know how to deal with men far better'n me," her sister completed for her. "I've heered that often enough. You'll get your comeuppance someday, 'Lissa."

"I've heard that often enough, too," the girl retorted.

In Beulah's bedroom, the baby began again to wail. Her mother sighed and padded in to tend her. Melissa was half sorry to see her sister go. Quarrels had become the chief respite of this endless winter. Barring them, each day was like its unnumbered forerunners. The baby cried, Beulah complained, the cold persisted, and no word came from Alvah Reynolds.

March was still young when, in accord with Nat's foretelling, the weather grew unseasonably warm and monumental drifts began to settle. Snow became saturated slush and each road a torrent. Thereafter, the awakening earth thrust off its sodden covering, and mud, glutinous and fathomless, forbade all travel.

Job was compelled to forgo a Sabbath meeting and the subsequent visit to the Houghton pitch. While mire-bound, he finished and installed the mantelpiece in the bedchamber-to-be. He was pleased with his handiwork. It granted the still empty room a severe grace that Melissa's presence would warm and immeasurably increase, provided—

He was irked by the new, recurrent doubt. The recent quarrel had meant nothing. The girl had been overworked and nerved up, though, in truth, the house she and her sister kept showed little evidence of industry. The worst part of the year and of Job's wooing surely was over. If Melissa were not still considering marriage with him, she would have dismissed him long since.

He would bring her here again when his clearing was at its best. Already the enlarged wheat field was an oblong of heart-stirring green. No female in her senses could be indifferent to the fairness and the promise of the Aldrich pitch.

Before another week had ended, Job and Nat, working together with Cephas and the still-uncertain young oxen, had assembled enormous piles of timber for the spring burning.

The meetinghouse had been brutally chill, as though retreating winter had sought refuge there, but, here in the open, sunlight drove into the marrow of a man's bones and routed the last trace of cold. The windy world was all a-glitter. Sky and puddles were of an identical bright hue. Job, skirting the drying mudholes that still pocked the road, reflected that young spring, like any maid, had put on her best appearing-out raiment to greet the Sabbath.

He rapped at the Houghton door, and Melissa, responding, looked at him for an unsmiling instant and then said tartly:

"Thought maybe you'd left town."

Her irritation, Job told himself complacently, was flattering since it indicated that she had missed him. He had no chance to reply for the girl had stepped aside and a red-faced man, wearing an old-fashioned bag wig, blue clothing, and mud-dappled riding boots, was advancing with a plump hand outstretched.

"Eliphalet Sprague, sir," he intoned, "father to these headstrong baggages and, by what Beulah has told me, your grateful debtor."

His warm, moist clasp drew Job into the kitchen where the woman, seated with the uncustomarily quiet baby in her arms, smiled and would have spoken but her parent, thrusting forward a chair, pursued:

"Set ye, sir; you're more than welcome."

He had ridden from Keene to see how his daughters fared and had been greatly relieved to find they had wintered so well.

"Thanks, I have been informed, Mr. Aldrich, largely to you."

While Job mumbled disavowal, Sprague resumed his own chair, clasped hands upon his well-filled waistcoat, and proclaimed:

"A fortunate meeting, sir, and a glorious time for all who value liberty."

He observed Job's puzzled look and leaned forward eagerly.

"Then, you haven't heard? Word came to Keene this morning that our army has won a great victory. Howe and his bloody host have fled to their ships, sir, and Boston town is ours."

He leaned back, relishing the other's amazement. Melissa, clearing the table where the family lately had dined, gave a small, disparaging sound. Job, recovering his voice, said slowly:

"Then, the war is over."

"If," Sprague amended, "news equally good reaches us from Canada. I fear for our forces there. Winter, in the north, sir, has caused great suffering and many deaths among them."

He flinched at the crash of breaking crockery.

"My best platter!" Beulah mourned. "'Lissa, what on earth ails you?"

"Nothing," she answered in a muffled voice, but Job, bending to help her recover the scattered fragments, saw that tears stood in her eyes.

"It's been," her sister was deploring, "a cruel, hard time for me. If it hadn't been for Job here—"

Melissa rose, to stand straight and quivering with her hands full of the platter's shards.

"And what kind of a winter," she cried in a strange voice, "d'you think it has been for me, slavin' an' seein' no one but His High Mightiness when he is pleased to visit us?"

"'Lissa," her father bade. "Hold your tongue."

The girl swallowed loudly, yet could not quell her wild revulsion.

"I know," she quavered. "It ain't polite to tell the truth, though I'm sick of Beulah's complainin' an' contrivin' an' Job Aldrich's Quaker piety."

[270]

"Quiet, my girl," Sprague warned, his face still redder, "or else I'll have something more to say to you."

"Yes," Melissa cried, her face twitching, "you're against me, too. I wish— If only—"

She gave a choking sound, groped for the latch, and flung herself from the kitchen. Beulah looked appealingly at her parent.

"Ehyah." he nodded. "I'll deal with her," and lumbered after the girl.

"What—what happened?" Job asked stupidly.

The woman answered in urgent haste:

"She—she ain't herself today. Maids go wildlike sometimes when they don't know their own minds."

"I don't see," he said slowly, "why she should be—against me."

"She ain't," Beulah insisted with a trace of desperation. "You've spiled her; that's the truth. Done too much for her. Wish Pa'd give her a sound hidin', ungrateful vixen."

"I've tried—to deserve her."

"As 'tis," the woman began earnestly, "you deserve a sight more than—"

Frances Elizabeth's tentative whimpering rose suddenly into outcry that smothered the rest of her mother's comment. When the child had been quieted, Beulah asked earnestly:

"Will you be guided by me?" and when he had nodded, pursued: "Needs a firm hand, 'Lissa does. Don't s'pose you feel inclined to slap her silly?"

"Not—exactly," Job confessed.

"Then go," the woman urged, " 'fore her an' Pa come back. Visit us no more, but make her come to you. I'll tell her you've vowed to keep away from her until she asks your pardon. Will you?"

"Why," he hesitated, "if you think that—"

"I know my sister," Beulah interrupted in a conspiratorial murmur. "Always wants most what it's hardest for her to get. Leave her alone an' she'll recognize how much you've been to her."

"Since you say so," he agreed with an unexpected touch of relief.

Neither Melissa nor her father had reappeared when he took his leave.

There was always Job's pitch, divinely ordained to be his refuge and his strength.

The yield from the burning had overflowed the ash house, and he plowed the surplus into the soil. He was acquiring an unexpected fondness for Buck and Ben and Abigail, the lanky heifer—the first creatures in his life to be wholly his.

It still was, in large measure, for Melissa's sake that Job worked with a quiet, persistent passion, but he was wryly amused to find how easy it was to follow Beulah's counsel. The end of each day's unremitting toil found him too spent to walk as far as the Frenches', let alone the Houghton pitch.

"Great day!" Nat protested, viewing the expanse his neighbor had plowed. "Ain't farmin' for a hull fam'ly, be you? Kill yourself, if you don't ease up."

"No, I won't," Job insisted. "I'm enjoying myself real well."

He had spoken, he considered with mild surprise after Nat had left, no less than the truth. The separation Beulah had recommended was less of a trial than Job had feared. When his desire for Melissa grew distractingly intense, he could moderate it by recalling her undeserved abuse of him.

It was well for men and maids to discover each other's frailties before, rather than after, they had wed. The recent months had taught Job much concerning Melissa's. Let her learn, by her suitor's continued absence, that he was something more than her docile servitor. He would give the girl, as her sister had advised, ample opportunity to repent.

Job had planted all his crop by early June and had begun his potash-making when one afternoon he looked up from the bubbling kettle and saw a man whom he thought a stranger come toward him.

"Hi, thar!" the intruder hailed.

"Well, now!" Job returned. He added, after a moment, "You look a mite—pulled down."

Spaulding grinned.

"You, too. Deal has happened, seems, since we last met."

He was sharper of feature, hollow-eyed, and his frock and breeches were too large for him.

"Welcome home," Job said belatedly and lifted the kettle from the fire. "This calls for a dram, wouldn't wonder. Maybe two or three."

They sat on the doorstep with a jug between them.

"To you," Job pledged, lifting his cup. "Back for long?"

"Back to stay," Spaulding corrected, a shade grimly.

He tilted his head and tossed in the liquor with a practiced hand.

"Still ain't real sure," he confessed, omitting the usual polite protest as his host refilled the emptied cup, "whether I was a-fightin'—if you can call it that—on the right side or the wrong."

He sipped his second drink and went on, eyes puckered, voice twanging. His friend's presence and the cider brandy spread a comforting warmth in Job that the acid recital failed to dispel.

Spaulding had mostly forgotten, since 'fifty-nine, how dirty, pest-ridden, and almighty tedious war could be.

"Stuck to it, though, till m'enlistment run out—more fool me, mebby—an' then, when we tuck Boston an' the hull army traipsed off to defend New York, I come home. Didn't object, special, to savin' Bay Province, but damn' if I'll risk my hide for Yorkers of whatever stripe."

He spat and looked sadly into the empty cup that Job hastily replenished. The fiddlestring voice grew tauter as Spaulding elaborated his grievance. If any part of America was misruled and misused, it was the Grants, which everyone wanted to milk dry and gave nothing in return.

"'Tain't no war of ours," he insisted, gimlet eyes boring into his companion, "that they expect us to fight. You done more for your country—yours an' mine an' our neighbors' country—

[273]

by runnin' Solomon out of Cumberland County than all us knotheads that jined the army."

Job flushed and drank hastily to hide his pleasure. York, his friend was complaining, hung onto the Grants like Pharaoh to the Jews, and there was no Moses in sight to free an abused people. There was talk that the colonies soon would declare for independence.

"Independence, that is, for everybody but us Grants folks. God-dam Congress says we still belong to York. Wal, push us a mite further an' we'll take our own freedom, spite of all the rest of Ameriky—an' Britain, to boot."

For an instant, indignation choked him. He coughed and, recovering, added bleakly:

"John Wyman, he thinks different, now. John's a captain in the Rhode Island line an' real military. Wait, sez he, an' we'll get justice. In the pig's eye!"

"Have you heard aught of Reynolds?" Job asked suddenly.

"Jest," Spaulding returned, "what I was goin' to ask you."

Job answered, slowly, "I've had no word of him in nigh eight months," and was chilled when the other said gravely:

"Then he's a prisoner—or worse. Warner pulled his regiment back out of Canady, long since. Got tired, wouldn't wonder, givin' everything for a cause that would gain the Grants nothin', an' marched his folks home again."

Spaulding shook his head.

"We're takin'—I mean," he amended sourly, "the United Colonies is takin' an almighty whopping to Canady."

Heaviness that another draft could not lighten oppressed Job as he thought of the possible fate of his dearest friend. Spaulding might have sensed his distress, for he looked about the clearing and said briskly:

"Done a deal since last year, ain't you? Take out a few more trees yonder, and you'll have a sightly view down the valley."

Long ago, Silence Thayer had said the same thing. Job was startled when his companion asked:

"Ain't minded to go to Westminster with me tomorrow, be you?"

Since his return, he explained, he had learned that Grants leaders were planning further resistance to York authority. Spaulding wanted to talk with Wright, Bellows, and others, and would be glad to have his friend's company.

"Still got two weeks' salts-making ahead of me," Job replied.

The vague thought that had distracted him was taking shape. He could see clearly now Parmenas's woebegone face and recalled the promise he, himself, had made the child.

"Beholden, though," Job ventured, "if you'd bear a message from me to the Widow Thayer."

"Wal, now!" Spaulding jeered. "Never heered your fancy lay there."

"It doesn't." Job felt his face grow hot. "Tell her that, if it pleases her, I'll come to fetch her little boy, a fortnight from tomorrow."

33

"MY RESPECTS," Nat said, "to Mis' Thayer."

"Tell her," Betty added, "we want she should visit with us again real soon."

Job mounted Cephas and began his journey to Westminster in a soberly happy mood. He deserved a holiday. All his crop was flourishing beyond belief. He had rendered double the ash salts he had made last year.

" 'He will be merciful to His land and to His people,' " Job recited reverently. He laughed when Cephas, lurching uphill, grunted what sounded like an equine "Amen," yet the grateful belief remained. Cumberland County seemed a serene, green island in a sea of conflict, though anxiety for Reynolds still lay like a weight within his friend's midriff.

Job's contentment failed as he rode through the settlement and realized belatedly that he must pass the Houghton pitch. It would be childishly petty to go by without pausing to see how the women and the baby fared, yet faithfully following Beulah's counsel, he had remained away so long that his sudden reappearance might be unwelcome. He had no wish to rouse Melissa to another fury.

It was Beulah, herself, who decided for him. She had been hanging out a washing and, seeing him approach, dropped a wet napkin back into the basket and hurried forward. They met midway between house and road.

"Morning," Job said awkwardly. "It's been quite a spell."

The woman's look was reproachful; her voice, heavy with accusation:

"'Tis weeks an' weeks, Job Aldrich, since we laid eyes on you and now, when you do choose to come a-visitin', 'Lissa's gone to Brattleboro with the Havens."

She plainly considered this, too, his fault. He reminded her indignantly:

"It was you who bade me stay away."

"Only for a spell," she insisted. "Land of goodness! Didn't mean forever."

Beulah shook her head in despair. She would ask him in, she explained, but she had just got Frances Elizabeth to sleep. If he would tarry till she wakened, it would pleasure Job to see her.

"Like it real well," he said, stretching the truth, "but I'm going—further."

The woman's black eyes bored into him and he added, as indifferently as he could:

"Riding to Westminster to bring back Parmenas Thayer for a visit."

"Wal," Beulah surrendered, after a heavy interval, "mebby someday you'll find time for your other friends."

"I had no cause," Job pointed out, "when last I was here, to think your sister wished me to return, and you yourself said—"

"I know," she intervened impatiently. "Keep tellin' you I didn't think you'd take it to heart."

[276]

Argument with her was like trying to catch a trout bare-handed. She, whom Job had thought his ally, was berating him for following her counsel. Melissa, Beulah was saying, had been wore down by the winter but was more like herself again, now that summer was here.

She looked at Job with an odd intensity and asked:

"More tidings from Canady?"

"Little enough and mostly bad." The familiar pang of concern impelled him to add, "I still have had no word of Alvah Reynolds. I fear," he forced the admission through a tightening throat, "that my friend is dead."

Twice, Beulah seemed about to speak before she said in haste, lest otherwise her intention might fail:

"Wouldn't mourn over him too much, providin' you still favor 'Lissa. Mean," she went on, urged by Job's bewildered stare, "the rascal cast a spell-like over her. He stood between you."

"Stood between us! That is not true. I know it is not."

She flinched from the sharpness in his voice, yet persisted doggedly:

"An' I know his elegant airs well nigh twisted the poor girl's head offen her shoulders."

Job tried to speak quietly.

"I tell you you are mistaken—or worse. It is easy to smirch the repute of the absent—and the dead. I'll listen to no more slander of Alvah Reynolds. Bid you good—"

"No!" Beulah wailed, caught his rein, and looked up at him imploringly. "Never meant to anger you. You've been Dan'l's an' my good friend. I'm a lone widder with a fatherless datter an' only want to see you an' 'Lissa wedded. Maybe I shouldn't have said what I did."

"That," he agreed coldly, "I would not dispute."

"Then you mustn't leave with a grudge betwixt us," she begged so piteously that his indignation wilted. "You promised I allus could turn to you at need."

"And so you can." Job forced himself to smile down into the beseeching face. "I promise you that again, most solemnly."

Beulah gave a gusty sigh of relief.

"An' you'll visit us soon?"

"As soon as may be," he evaded and rode away.

Job found the encounter had dulled the morning and replaced late gaiety with fuming resentment. It had been at Beulah's express bidding that he had left Melissa severely alone, and his obedience had only served to exasperate the widowed woman and led her to defame his cherished friend, who, Job thought with a painful tightening of his throat, might now be lying in a Canadian grave. The charge against Reynolds had been malice, nothing more, and difficult to forgive.

Men called greetings, as he rode through Putney, and he responded absently. He wondered, while Cephas breasted the hill beyond the settlement, whether a grain of truth could be hidden in Beulah's accusation. Reynolds, before he had ridden off to war, had advised Job, with chaffing solemnity, to make a wife and mother of Melissa within the year. Could it be that Alvah had resigned his own desire for the girl because he believed, with some warrant, that he owed his life to his rival?

Twelve months had passed since Reynolds had left. Then, the year of mourning Melissa had set for herself, the year of probation she had fixed for Job, must have expired, too. It was strange he had not considered that till now.

Perhaps she had put him off in the hope that the blithe young man would return and claim her. It was easy, though humbling, to believe that she was secretly in love with Alvah. Maybe Beulah had been more truthful than Job had been willing to believe. Women, he decided, and took satisfaction in the discovery, were difficult for men to understand.

Resentment was clearing away confusion and doubt. This much was certain: he had proved that he could do without Melissa. Indeed, it had been a relief to work his farm, undistracted by her constant and thankless demands upon him. His pitch, at least, was not subject to whims, vapors, and perversities. If the wench he patiently had courted thought she could hold him in reserve until she discovered whether she might have Reynolds or no, why then, Job decided with a twinge of anger, she would find in due time that she was less thrifty than doubtless she imagined herself.

The highway slowly unwound through blazing sunlight and fragrant shade, continually fashioning new beauty from lush foliage, shining lengths of the Great River, and the green benignity of hills. Dark thoughts rode with Job through the summer's splendor and did not forsake him until he dismounted in the Thayer yard and, turning, saw Silence in the doorway.

"Your love is here," a wild and frightening inner voice clamored in Silence and would not be hushed. "He is fairer and lordlier than you have pictured him, with shoulders formed for your weary head. His body was planned to meet and quicken yours; his hands, for sweet adventuring. He is a tower on Zion's wall and his mouth is sweeter than wine. Honey and milk are under his tongue."

"You're welcome," Silence told Job briskly. "Wintered real well by the look of you."

He followed her into the kitchen. It was unfair to compare it with Beulah's, or even Betty's, for no other woman kept her house so well.

"But where," Job demanded, "is Parmenas?"

"A-bed."

"Not—sick."

"No," Silence assured him and picked up the garment she lately had laid aside. "He's there," she pursued, seating herself and plying her needle, "till I mend his other breeches."

She nodded toward the bedchamber. The boy, lying blanketed on the trundle bed, ruefully confessed:

"I fell into the brook."

"Wanted," Silence reported tartly from the other room, "to catch trout for your dinner and nigh drowned himself. Have to eat leavin's this noon, and wait after that till his clothes dry."

"Leavings here are better than beginnings elsewhere," Job told her, and she bent her face over her sewing.

They dined on savory odds and ends, fortified by freshly baked rye-and-Injun bread, though the resurrected Parmenas, in patched breeches and his spare frock, was too solemnly excited to eat. Job found it seemly and pleasant to discuss with his hostess what he already had done on his pitch and what he planned. Silence agreed that, in these times, it was better to have potash than cash. She approved of his larger plantings of corn and wheat. He could not fail to sell both at a profit, if armies remained in the field.

Job felt discomfort only when the talk strayed, beyond Cumberland County, into the war-ridden outer world, and he spoke incautiously of Reynolds's continued absence.

"Easy-appearin' young man," Silence commented with a trace of bleakness and added: "Mis' Houghton and her baby: they keep well?"

"Well enough," Job replied, reddening for no clear cause, "now 'tis summer. Had a poor time during the winter. Beulah's sister, she stayed and cared for them."

"Real nice, for all concerned, wouldn't wonder," Silence said and an awkward stillness fell.

"Figure," her guest told the patient child, who had been sitting with his bundled belongings on his knees, "it's past time we were starting back."

It was absurd, he was sure, to fancy that Silence was relieved to see him go.

"Be a good boy," she told Parmenas and ran a hand over his head, before she turned to Job and directed: "Leave him to Hills' when you fetch him back."

"Hills'?"

She explained quietly: It had been long since she had visited Ezra's folks, and now Daniel Jewett, who was hauling flour to Ti, had offered to carry her to Castleton. It would have been a rugged journey for so small a boy, and she was glad to leave Parmenas behind. Dr. Hill had offered to board him until she returned.

"He can stay with me," Job insisted.

Silence ignored the appeal on the small upturned face.

"Don't want," she answered firmly, "he should wear out his welcome. May be most two months, goin', visitin', an' returnin'."

"I'll keep him till I'm tired of him," Job promised, grinning down at the enraptured child. "I need an extra hand on my pitch this year."

Silence watched him mount and, leaning down, swing Parmenas up before him. She whirled about, then, and vanished into the house. It had been, Job thought, as though she were on the verge of tears, though he could not imagine Silence Thayer indulging in such weakness. It was too bad she kept herself stoppered so tightly. She would be a real sightly woman otherwise.

He wished he had not marred, by his mention of Melissa, an otherwise harmonious visit. It might have been better for all concerned, he thought with insurgent bitterness, if he had never come to know and court the girl.

Beulah turned from the window.

"Rode right by as though we was strangers," she repeated. "Makes no difference to you, s'pose, if the Widder Thayer does get him."

Melissa flushed and bit her lip. Her sister had deftly pricked the girl's already injured pride.

"An' it's high time," Beulah pursued with acid relish, "you stopped lookin' for that Reynolds to come back. He's havin' his fun elsewhere, or he's been kilt. Job Aldrich's mournin' him for dead anyway. You've fallen down 'twixt two stools, m'lady."

"That's what you say," Melissa retorted.

"'Tis what everybody'll be sayin'," her sister corrected maliciously. "Neighbors are prob'ly already tellin' that Aldrich give you the go-by."

The taunt rankled. Melissa had rehearsed carefully how she would deal with Job when her period of mourning ended. She had intended to be appealingly uncertain, neither rejecting her hapless suitor nor openly accepting him. The stipulated year and another fortnight had passed and still Job had not come near her. His indifference and Beulah's disparagement were not to be borne meekly.

Melissa still was certain that she could do as it pleased her with any man—save Alvah Reynolds, and he, she thought desolately, must indeed be dead. Whether or no, she would go to morning meeting next Sabbath, clad in her best, and trust that Job would be there.

"Wait," she bade her sister haughtily, "and you'll see how wrong you are."

"So far," Beulah returned, "I've done a deal of waitin' but precious little seein'."

Elder Hooker wrestled mightily in prayer while Job, seated with the Frenches and his own small guest, ignored the striving figure in the pulpit and watched Melissa. The dark blue habit and bonnet greatly became her. Long ago, at another morning meeting, he had looked upon her ardently and had met with what then had seemed absolute disaster. The world and he had changed greatly since that far-off time.

Hooker's singsong voice was calling the Almighty's attention to the needs of the broken fragments of the army that had crept back from Canada to Ticonderoga. Job thought of his missing friend and was obscurely irked by Melissa's demure composure. The elder implored that divine grace be lavished upon the Continental Congress and suggested that the independence its members sought be not withheld from dwellers in the Grants.

Job pulled his eyes away from the girl and looked down at his neighbor. Parmenas brought to Sabbath meeting an admirable sobriety. Hooker's prayer ended at last.

"Let us sing unto the Lord a new song," the elder intoned.

Perhaps it was not exactly a hymn, he pursued in his everyday voice, but Leftenant Spaulding had fetched it back from Boston town and it befitted troublous times. It was called "Chester," no one seemed to know why, and Len had consented to fiddle the air for the meeting's instruction.

The tune, even when sung by the violin's thin voice, had a martial rhythm, and when Hooker read out the song and the congregation chanted it, line by line, the meetinghouse seemed to fill with the tramp of armed men. Job could not recall, when morning meeting ended, the exact words, which had to do with tyrants' rods and slavery's chains, but the valiant melody marched so sturdily through his memory that, for a moment, as he moved out of the building with Parmenas, he was unaware that Melissa walked beside him.

"Well, now!" he hailed her awkwardly.

She smiled and told him in hushed haste:

" 'Tis—forward to ask it, I know, but—would you squire me home?"

He stared at her with astonishment and a trace of suspicion.

"Oh, please!" she murmured. "I must talk with you."

"I'm honored," he told her dryly and, glancing down at his companion: "This is Parmenas Thayer; he's helping me this summer."

"I'm honored," the child echoed faithfully.

Job hurriedly committed his guest to the Frenches' care and rejoined the girl. Betty, opening the snack basket, said to Nat:

"Right, wasn't I?"

"Looks so," he conceded unwillingly.

Parmenas, concerned eyes following his idol and the girl, asked at length:

"Is he—is he goin' to—marry her?"

"Seems," Nat said with faint bitterness.

"She's pretty," Parmenas said.

Job and Melissa walked the length of the village street in silence. She had wanted to talk with him. Let her, then, be the first to speak. They had passed Harvey's late dwelling before the girl said sadly:

"Still angered with me, ain't you?"

Her face glowed within the shadowing bonnet. Job, resisting its appeal, asked in turn, "Should I not be?" and was staggered when she answered promptly:

"Indeed you should, but I've hoped it wouldn't be for long. Already," she went on with a wan smile, "it has seemed like forever."

"It has been your doing," he reminded her gruffly, "not mine."

His surly response did not lessen Melissa's confidence.

"Don't," she begged, "let us quarrel again."

She stole a sidewise glance at his composed face and pursued plaintively:

"I only seek to beg you for pardon."

Job could find in her voice and aspect none of the sorrow he felt for his lost friend. Beulah, for her own purpose, must have stretched the truth. Melissa could not be in love with Reynolds and still appear so wholly unaffected.

"Once," she was saying wistfully, "you told me you could forgive me anything."

The bright, parted lips, the wide, gray eyes invited him.

What Job had thought firm determination was beginning to crumble. He assured her:

"That is still true."

"You ever have been," the girl said softly, "a generous friend."

"But never," he returned with failing resolution, "more than that."

Melissa secretly felt the glee of an angler with a fish firmly hooked.

"I have feared of late," she sighed, "that you were no longer even my friend."

"You are still," Job told her hoarsely, "the fairest creature I have known."

Scruples easily were abandoned when he faced this prospect of long-delayed fulfillment, yet still he hesitated. Melissa had held out her hands to him. Their yielding warmth made him excruciatingly aware of all her body's hidden loveliness. A still, small voice cried warning. Job made no attempt to draw the girl closer. Instead, he tried to hold her eyes and informed her, almost savagely:

"I'll be hoodwinked and trifled with no longer. Before I tell you more, you must answer one question."

She had kindled, Melissa realized, wavering between triumph

[284]

and alarm, more of a fire than she had bargained for. Job's
harshness was thrilling her against her will. She had enticed
him deftly, but now he was driving her. She pretended to
misunderstand.

"Oh Job," she pleaded archly. "Wait; not here where anyone might see us."

He had held her eloquent hands before, had believed he was
about to win her, and straightway she had betrothed herself to
Will French. He had taken great pains to serve her, and she
had flouted him.

"You will answer me, here and now," he bade. "Do you
still favor me when I tell you that Alvah Reynolds is alive
and well?"

Suddenly the fingers within his grasp were chill and damp,
and her face had gone white. Melissa repeated:

"Alive and well?"

"Does that concern you so greatly?"

"But—but," the girl groped, "you told Beulah you believed
him dead."

"I did."

The eyes that met his no longer were softly beguiling.
Melissa's color was returning; her voice had taken edge.

"You admit," she cried, "that you told her so to torment,
to trick me?"

"No," Job said. "Not that."

She was deaf to denial.

"You lied to Beulah," she raged and wrenched her hands
away. "You took great pride, no doubt, in the falsehood that
gulled a defenseless maid. You—you whited sepulcher!"

The tirade granted Job sobriety and a singular sense of relief.

" 'Defenseless,' " he told Melissa, "I never should deem
you."

He considered his companion's lurid face, her taut pose, and
having stretched the moment to the utmost, said in a level
voice:

"I admit I lied, but 'twas not to Beulah. For all I know, my friend indeed is dead. I lied to you, Melissa, who by voice and deed repeatedly have deceived me."

He met her incredulous stare with a barren smile.

"I am surfeited myself," Job said lightly, "with being 'tricked' and 'gulled.' I bid you good-day."

34

THE WAR LAY all that summer beyond the Grants' horizon and drew no nearer. In Dummerston, rye and wheat grew amazing tall; the corn was heavily eared, and men worked their pitches, only momentarily disturbed by tidings that Moses Alvord, no less industrious since his sister's death, bore through the town.

Congress had declared the thirteen colonies independent; Britain was pouring troops into Canada; the Continental army was in trouble on Long Island. Such news was of smaller importance to settlers than their ripening crops and the still-covert efforts of Grants' leaders to pry the land entirely away from York.

In mid-September, Hooker, back from a visit to Westminster, sent word by Two-pound-ten to the Aldrich pitch that the Widow Thayer had returned and would be pleased to receive her son at Job's convenience. The summons both relieved and disappointed him. He had begun to worry over her continued absence, yet he had hoped that she would come for her child, so that she might see and admire what one man and a small boy had accomplished in a single summer.

Parmenas, when he and his host set out on Cephas for Westminster, said dolefully:

"Wish that we lived here."

"And I," Job returned. "We've had a real good time."

"Guess," the child agreed, "I never had so good a time."

Silence, the man reflected, would be pleased by her son's appearance. He was brown and hard as a walnut and outgrowing all his clothes. His mother never would know how comforting and sustaining Parmenas had been. His companionship, obedient and unfailingly cheerful, had kept Job from brooding over his break with Melissa or from any mad attempt at reconciliation. He had learned with little regret that Beulah, with her child and sister, lately had gone back to Keene.

The unhappy episode was over and done with, yet, as he rode past the Houghton house, standing drearily empty in the gay autumnal morning, momentary sadness oppressed him. The forsaken dwelling was a reminder that part of his own life irrevocably had ended.

He was wondering sourly what scandalmongers had made of the rupture when he was startled by Parmenas's inquiry:

"You'll have to go to Keene to marry her, won't you?"

The gossip evidently had been lush and widespread. Job considered the earnest, upturned face and answered dryly:

"It won't be this year."

"I wish—" Parmenas began, caught breath, and said no more.

Whatever melancholy had beset the child vanished completely when they turned into the Thayer dooryard and he saw his mother waiting there. He gave a stifled sound, slid unaided from Cephas, and ran to her. She bent and, catching him up, stood for a long, still moment, her cheek against his, while Job, with a knot in his own throat, more slowly dismounted and spent an inordinate time in loosening Cephas's girth. When he looked toward them again, Silence stood with Parmenas's hands fast upon one of hers.

She tried to speak, whirled about, and led her son toward the house. On its doorstep, she turned and said with valiant clarity:

"There's pork an' milk gravy for dinner. Hope you still fancy 'em."

She was composed and brisk, once more, when Job entered the kitchen, but he never had seen her so nearly pretty. She had filled out a mite. Likely enough, he thought with a throb of sympathy, she had eaten heartier while away than she could afford to at home, with a growing child to feed. It was her nature, though, that seemed to have changed most. Job jested with Parmenas during dinner, for the pleasure it gave him to see Silence's hitherto infrequent smile transform her face.

He learned that Ezra's parents were well and had persuaded her to stay with them longer than she had intended. She had had a real good time but was glad to be home again.

The journey had not wearied her or slackened her industry. When the meal was over and dishes washed, she promptly drew her spinning wheel from its corner and seated herself before it. She had undertaken, she explained in half apology, to make linen for the Jewetts in payment for her trip to and from Castleton.

Job watched the lithe body, rocking in concert with the treadle and the fluent movements of the hands that engaged the flax and drew out the thread. He offered at last:

"You're a prime spinner."

Silence shook her head.

"Not with this," she said firmly. "Coarse flax makes poor spinnin'."

A reminiscent smile parted her lips, and she went on more gently:

"Had the best flax my folks could lay hands on for my weddin' gown. Swingled, hatcheled, an' carded it myself an' it spun out so fine, I could draw a fourteen-knot skein through jined thumb an' forefinger. Like silk, it was."

She turned to her work again. The wheel hummed serenely. It was a pity, Job thought, that Ezra had died young. A man couldn't ask for a more useful helpmeet. He wondered whether she had read his thought, for she glanced toward him and spoke hastily of anxiety, Castleton-way, lest the British come up the lake and invade the Grants.

"Best thing, maybe," Job returned, "not to resist 'em, if so be they come. They've done less to harm us than the Continental Congress that says we must be ruled by York. That," he added with a wry smile, "no doubt sounds Quakerish to you."

"I ain't sure," Silence said and looked at him carefully. "Anyway, I don't think you mean it."

"No?" he asked. "Suit you better if I was for war?"

"Whether you are or no," she told him, "I'm certain sure that if anyone threatened your pitch, you wouldn't—jest set there."

"Well—maybe," he granted.

"No 'maybe' about it," Silence insisted crisply. "You know you wouldn't."

"Yes, ma'am," he submitted with overstressed meekness that, surprisingly, roused her mirth. He had never heard her laugh before. It was a pleasant sound. She sobered quickly and, as though her gaiety had been indiscreet, spoke of a meeting Grants folks had been holding at Dorset when lately she had passed through the town.

Job nodded. It had been the first time, he explained, that delegates from the east and west Grants had met in joint convention. Leftenant Spaulding had attended as Dummerston's representative.

"Time," he pursued, "that, with everyone else against them, Grants folks should turn to each other."

"Seems," Silence deplored, "that each month is fuller of trouble than the last."

"It'll ease off soon," Job assured her. "Winter's always a peaceful time."

"Must be," she said slowly, "real cozy on your pitch when snow's deep—jest in your own house with everything troublesome shut out."

He wondered how she could voice exactly his own belief.

"Frenches," he answered, "hope you'll visit them before winter."

The spinning wheel sang softly while Silence mutely debated with herself and, reaching decision, shook her head.

"No, not this fall. Done all the visitin' I can afford for a spell. I'll have to bide where I be, till I pay what I owe folks. Trip cost me more than I figgered it would."

When Job at last rose regretfully to leave, Silence bade him farewell serenely, but Parmenas's composure failed him.

"Don't want you to go," he quavered, ignoring his mother's frown. "Maybe," he continued hopefully, "you'll find you can't get along real good without me."

Tears ran unheeded down his face. Job told him gravely:

"Tell you what we'll do, Parmenas: If I find I need you, I'll come after you. If you need me, you set right out and fetch me. Is that all right? Then, don't forget."

He mounted, kicked Cephas promptly, and called back to the desolated small boy, standing with his mother in the doorway:

"Remember what I said. Let me know if you need me."

Parmenas nodded. He followed his mother back into the kitchen where for a long moment she stood motionless.

It was silly and, doubtless, wicked in the bargain, for a grown woman to let herself be so deeply stirred by any man. Maybe it was folly to think there had been a change in Job Aldrich, yet surely there was a new unsettling quality in his voice, and the way he had looked at her, now and then, had turned her heart completely over.

Perhaps what Silence never had dared hope truly was coming to pass. It might be that the man's fondness for her son was an indirect wooing of her.

"Wish," Parmenas said so appositely that it frightened her, "that 'twas you he's gonna marry."

"Don't," Silence advised and felt her cheeks flame, "talk sech nonsense."

"I do wish it," he maintained. "Mebby he would, too, if he wa'n't goin' to marry that Sprague maid."

"Who said he was?"

The child flinched at the sharpness of the question, and she instantly was contrite.

"There now," she soothed. "I shouldn't have hollered. You,"

she pursued, resisting belief, "have no cause to think he's going to wed her."

"Have, too," Parmenas insisted. "Mr. French, he said so."

"Folks," his mother forced herself to scoff, "say a deal besides their prayers."

"But he is, too, going to marry her," her son persisted in shrill distress. "I ast him today when he would, and he said not till next year."

"Wal," Silence said at length and calmly, "that'll be real agreeable for both of 'em, I'm sure."

She sat down at the wheel and resumed her spinning with steady hands. Her instinct had been right from the beginning. The moment she had laid eyes on the flighty wench she had known Melissa was setting her cap for Job.

Silence engaged the flax and carefully drew out the thread. Maybe the Lord was punishing her with lawless thoughts and unhallowed longings because she never had harbored them righteously for her husband, faithfully though she had tried. If this were so, she could only submit to the penance. On the other hand, if Satan were tempting her, if he were polluting her with soul-imperiling desires, she welcomed the combat. She did not fear the Evil One. There were ways of thwarting him.

Silence continued spinning. At length she said to her son:

"'Twas real nice to Grandpa's. He and Grandma want we should come an' live with 'em."

"It's nicer to Aldrich's," Parmenas returned.

"You don't remember Castleton," Silence reminded him. "It's real sightly. You'd like it there."

"Guess," Parmenas resisted, "I wouldn't like it very much. S'pose I was there an' Mr. Aldrich needed me here."

"Needed you?" his mother said without expression. "Yes, that would make a difference, wouldn't it?"

Job rode homeward in new tranquillity. He had enjoyed beyond expectation his visit with Silence Thayer. Travel, unaccountably, had mellowed her. He would miss Parmenas in the coming months and, he was surprised to find, would miss his small comrade's mother, too. Job wished they lived handy-by. He wished also that he could lighten the indebtedness of a resolute woman. A widow, with a son to raise, singlehanded, had a stony row to hoe, and Job, who had been greatly favored by the Almighty, could spare enough from his ample harvest to lessen her load and scarcely miss it.

Momentarily, he could think of no way to accomplish such a project. She was as proud as Lucifer, the Widow Thayer, yet an understanding and even a comforting person when she chose to be. Job might contrive some errand that would enable him to see her again—and Parmenas, of course—before winter barricaded the road. Otherwise, he looked forward to the time when snows would wall him in and impose their truce on the distant, senseless war.

He turned off the highway at length and rode in low sunlight, past the empty Houghton house. Job looked at it and smiled. Freedom from hapless servitude to Melissa, he appreciated all at once, was not the least of the blessings the summer had brought him.

The squeal of a fife and a drum's rattling ran to meet him as he rode up into the settlement. Women and children ringed the common where the Dummerston Cadets were drilling while young Jake Laughton beat out and Two-pound-ten shrilled the measures of "The White Cockade."

A score of men—sheepish striplings and more earnest elders —were marching in sketchy compliance with the commands Jonathan Knight shouted. Their weapons were as diverse as their clothing. Fowling pieces, ancient Queen's arms, blunderbusses sprouted unevenly above the wavering column. Davenport's sweating bulk dwarfed the French fusil he shouldered. Cook bore the musket Job had returned.

"Rear half files to the right," Knight yelped. "Double your front. No! Goddlemighty, no!"

The formation had buckled and now fell apart. Job drew rein to admire the drillmaster's reproof. A dry voice inquired:

"Why ain't you in the host of righteousness?" and Leonard Spaulding grinned up at him.

"Don't have to tell me," the man pursued. "Fust place, you've got no firelock; second, you're all for peace—in a manner of speakin'."

"Why aren't you drilling?" Job retorted, and Spaulding shrugged.

"Done all the soldierin' I crave. Statesman, now; jest back from Dorset."

"Now, then!" Knight was proclaiming in a martyred voice. "We'll leave off marchin' for a spell an' exercise in loadin' an' firin'—nigh as we can, that is, without powder or ball. Billy Negus, you get 'em into line, any way you can."

He wiped his face with a despairing gesture. Spaulding bade Job:

"Light for a spell. Want to talk with you."

The other obeyed and, with his arm through the reins, followed his friend toward the meetinghouse steps.

"Recover firelocks," Knight chanted. "Half cock firelocks. Handle primers— No. Not like that!"

Spaulding seated himself with a groan.

"Heered," he asked, "what we done to Dorset?"

He kept his voice resolutely indifferent, but his little eyes glittered.

"Wal, we voted the Grants free of York, voted that we be henceforth a separate district, voted ourselves," he twanged, repression failing, "clear out of the Union—if them poops to Philadelphy don't give us our rights."

His steel-bright gaze for a moment held Job speechless.

"And then what?" he managed at length.

"Allow Congress," Spaulding answered promptly, "ample time to make up their minds—if sech they have. Then, by God, if they won't give us statehood, we'll make the Grants a free and separate nation."

The audacity of the intention took Job's breath yet quickened unexpected pride.

"Now we'll try again," Knight was announcing with shallow

optimism. "Handle primers. Prime. Close pans. Cast about to charge. No, no, no!"

"We'll make this a free land," Spaulding said reverently, "with no man above another, a just land, where freemen vote as it pleases 'em and all are alike before the law."

Job recovered his voice.

"Opposing," he asked, thrilled, despite himself, "Britain with one hand and America with t'other? David fought only one Goliath."

"Might consider," Spaulding chuckled, "he'd likely have had an easier time if there'd been two of 'em, already a-fightin' each other."

He paused, then went on, in a lower voice:

"Grants is petitionin' Congress again. If again they refuse us—wal, there'll be a new nation born in Westminster come January, wouldn't wonder."

"Cast off firelocks," Knight commanded hoarsely. "Poise firelocks. Sweet an' sufferin' saints, Nat French! Your ramrod's still in the barrel."

"S'prise me none," Spaulding drawled, surveying Dummerston's armed might, "if they drill a deal poorer'n they'd fight."

"Nor me," Job agreed. His companion peered at him.

"S'prise me even less, if the Grants need defendin', to find you in the forefront of the battle."

"That," Job acknowledged, recalling Silence's prediction, "might be, too."

It was Spaulding who, returning from a journey through Cumberland County on behalf of the Dorset resolutions, brought Job a letter and a package from the Widow Thayer.

"That good fortune ever may attend you," she had written, "is the constant wish of Parmenas and S. Thayer."

Job, unfolding the Blazing Star quilt he had admired, found that his eyes smarted. He presumed that the gift was a proud woman's attempt to requite him for his care of her son, but there was a trace of finality in the accompanying note that momentarily troubled him.

[294]

35

THE NOVEMBER night had laid down so heavy a frost that the sledload of lumber Kathan brought early in the morning for the corncrib Job intended to build slid smoothly across the clearing. Alex lingered to talk with cautious satisfaction of the recent battle on Champlain that had destroyed the Continental fleet. He appeared unexpectedly reconciled to the prospect of Grants' independence.

It was better, in his opinion, for the land to become a separate nation than to remain an appendage of rebellious New York. Kathan was still a firm, if muted, royalist. Job retained only a vague memory of their amicable discussion. The happenings that succeeded it were stamped forever on his mind.

He worked happily until, an hour after Alex had left, Nat rode hurriedly into the clearing. Job had been thinking again, while he sawed and hammered, of Silence Thayer and wishing, once more, that he might ease her burden. He half disbelieved his eyes when he saw that his neighbor carried before him a wilted and tear-stained Parmenas.

Fright twisted Job's bowels and weakened his knees. He gaped witlessly at Nat, who, in a tone of extreme exasperation, announced that he had ridden over to Havens' for a set of hinges and, returning, had overtaken the small boy, midway between the Great Road and the settlement.

"Seems he stowed away in a wagon, far as Dummerston. Says he has to see you. If you can get more out of him, you're a better man than I be."

Parmenas looked beseechingly at Job.

"Told me—" he quavered, swallowed loudly, and tried

again. "Told me if I needed you I was to come after you. Ma—"

His face puckered and he choked.

"Is she ill? Is she—?"

Job's throat closed. The child shook his head.

"She's real well, only—"

He wept in quiet wretchedness. Nat volunteered:

"Mistrust you won't be, once she lays hands on you."

A thin wail escaped Parmenas. Job lifted him from the saddle and said to his neighbor:

"Better maybe if he and I talk this over privately. Wait," he begged, still ridden by anxiety, "till I find out what's happened."

He bore the boy into the kitchen, set him on the bed, closed the door, and withstanding the impulse to shake information from the small, quaking figure, asked as calmly as he could:

"What's the trouble, Parmenas?"

"We're goin—" the child gulped, "we're goin to Castleton."

"Now," Job said impatiently, "that can't be. Your mother's just back from there."

He laid a hand on the boy's shoulder. The friendly pressure was more than Parmenas could bear.

"We are too goin'," he wept openly. "She wrote Grampa an' had a letter back from him. We're goin' next time Cap'n Jewett hauls to Ti, an' I won't see Abigail, nor Buck an' Ben, nor you, ever again."

His lamentation gradually subsided into convulsive snufflings. Job said at last with a gathering sense of outrage:

"She has no right—no cause. Why should she?"

He felt as though suddenly he had stepped from solid ground onto emptiness. Silence had withdrawn, without warning, stabilities he had come to prize: courage and understanding and tart common sense. He had not known until this moment how greatly he valued these.

Parmenas was finding reproach in the continued stillness.

"Mebby," he faltered, "I shouldn't have run away—only you said—"

"I know, I know," Job admitted absently and, smitten by a new alarming thought, asked:

"Where's your mother today?"

She was weaving to Jewetts', the boy reported with waxing uneasiness. She had sent him off to school with a basket of lunch. He guessed—tears welled again—that he must have left it in Bartlett's wagon.

"When she comes home she'll be worried," Job said and found himself confronting fell possibilities.

Silence would be more than merely worried when she could not find her son. If he knew her, she would turn Westminster inside out and, failing to recover him, would rouse the entire countryside. Job, if he moved quickly, still might save her untold terror.

"Parmenas," he said, "you must do as I bid you. Nat French will take you home with him. You're to stay there till your mother comes for you. I'll ride Cephas to Westminster as fast as may be. No," he responded to the unuttered appeal, "we'd go too slowly if I took you along."

"Will I—will I have to go to Castleton?" the boy ventured.

"Not," the man promised at length, "if I can possibly prevent it," and went out to consult with Nat.

It was going to require more patience than endurance, Job appreciated as Cephas plodded uphill, to reach Westminster in time. Reckless haste would break down the elderly horse. He must be moved along with all reasonable rapidity yet with due consideration for age.

A new unwelcome idea added itself to the rider's distress. Silence during her sojourn in Castleton might have found a man to her liking. It could be that she was going back to wed him. Certainly she had changed, had become warmer, more beguiling, when last Job had seen her. The dire thought kept pace with him, all the tormenting miles to Westminster.

Silence came to the door as he dismounted from the wheezing horse.

"Scarce expected you again," she said crisply. "Parmenas should be home any minute now."

[297]

The impersonal greeting half confirmed Job's suspicion.

"Parmenas," he corrected, following her into the kitchen, "won't be home till you fetch him. He ran away, and the Frenches are caring for him. I came as fast as I was able, lest you be alarmed."

"Ran away?" Silence repeated blankly. "Whatever for?" The words came with difficulty through Job's stiff throat.

"He didn't want you to live in Castleton. No more," he added hoarsely, "do I."

The blue eyes were dazzling in the still, dark face.

"Ran away!" she said again. "He—"

Her voice died. Job tried to control his own.

"I told him to come to me if he was in trouble—and he did. I told him today," he pursued, finding fresh courage, "that I'd do all in my power to dissuade you."

Silence looked at him calmly. Her voice was level:

"Seems best to go. Ezra's folks want us, and we'll live easier. There's nothing to hold us here."

A strong wind blew through Job's mind, sweeping away the rubbish of uncertainty, disclosing an underlying sure purpose he had blindly ignored till now. He said, shaken by the violence of his heart:

"If nothing else holds you here, I greatly need you."

Silence drew a sharp breath. Color drained from her face. She stood quite still while Job asked, more unsteadily:

"Is there someone in Castleton you favor more?"

Her face was hidden. He heard his pulses' wild drumming, the tick of the clock. Silence said as though the words were torn from her:

"You are to wed Melissa Sprague."

"I shall wed," Job told her loudly, "no woman on earth, unless it be you."

He felt, as he spoke, that, despite his own persistent error, God's hand had guided him whither, from the first, it had been intended he should go.

Silence was trembling. She insisted obstinately:

"You are plighted to her."

"Never," he cried. "Neither now, nor hitherto, nor here-after, whether you will have me or no. I—"

He could say no more for she had turned. He saw the pale radiance of her face and her eyes' soft brilliance. The taut, defensive severity had vanished, baring her as wholly as though her clothing had been stripped away, and the look she gave him was beseeching and a little frightened.

"Then," she began and tried to smile, but the valiant effort failed. Silence shook her head helplessly and held out her hands.

Her pliant body was in his arms, and he as tightly clasped by hers. Her questing flesh clove to his; her mouth was warm and assuaging. Their long kiss left him breathless. Through the din in his ears, he heard her tender voice imploring:

"Hold me close; oh, closer, closer still, my love, my lord and master. Keep me yours; never let me go."

The room whirled as her lips found Job's again. He told her at last and hoarsely:

"You are mine, to have and to hold, henceforth and forever. My woman. Do you understand?"

She laughed and clung to him.

"Yours," she whispered, "to use as it pleases you. Teach me how best I may serve you. Beat me, if I merit it."

She was crying against his shoulder. He spoke to her gently, and Silence said at length, midway between mirth and tears:

"I have been weeping for two blind people and their mis-spent distress."

She caught his arms and, thrusting him from her, lifted her wet face to search his.

"Is it true," she begged, "that I shall ever be your woman? Will what I am and what you teach me to be suffice you? How can I believe that when, only lately, you still were courting Melissa Sprague?"

She caught and clung to him in an agony of doubt. Job told her gently:

"You said we had been blind. Sweetheart, I have regained

[299]

my sight. Melissa means nothing to me. You are my whole desire."

Silence smiled up at him. He marveled that he ever could have considered this tremulous, glowing face forbidding.

"I shall try to believe it," she whispered. "I—I wish she did not frighten me."

"We are naught to each other," Job insisted. "I shall never willingly see her again. Wed me soon, beloved, and cast away fear."

Silence's hands, locked behind his head, pressed his mouth down upon hers. She said at length and breathlessly:

"Will you wait a little while, only a few months? There is much I must do before I come to you."

"If—if you are indebted," Job ventured, "I am well off and all that I have now is yours."

Silence shook her head.

"It isn't that. Sale of this house and its fixings will pay all I owe, but I will not come to you empty-handed. I must spin and weave and sew, filling my hope chest before you take me."

"I already have a quilt of your making," he reminded her, and she shuddered.

"I shall pray early and late," she murmured, "that never again may I know such despair. It is strange that any maid should have the power to terrify me."

She looked at Job so appealingly that he bent and kissed her again. When he released her, Silence hesitated, then begged:

"Will you wait till next summer, till July?"

"Why should I complain of a few more months," Job surrendered and drew her to him, "when I have waited all my life for you?"

They sat, at last, beside the hearth, considering the immediate and more distant future. Silence would borrow the Sabins' horse and chaise on the morrow and retrieve her runaway son. It was well, she and Job agreed, that winter was near. The imprisonment it would impose would afford them both undistracted time to prepare for their life together.

Silence, complying with custom, must fashion for herself

an entire wedding costume and make fabrics for her new home, as well. Job would build what additional furniture a household of three persons required. His newly betrothed finally compelled him to leave, for he had ignored the promptings of the westering sun.

It was black night when Cephas and he reached the French pitch. Nat came out to the barn with a lantern and watched while the horse was unsaddled and rubbed down. Parmenas was in bed and asleep. Betty had saved a bite of supper for her neighbor. The lilt in the other's responses ill befitted a tired and hungry man. Nat looked at him narrowly but held his peace.

Job waited until he had entered the kitchen, then, as gravely as he could, announced:

"Come next July, Parmenas'll have little cause to run away. He and his mother—well, they'll be moving in with me."

Betty squealed, flung herself at Job, kissed him, and then, overcome by her daring, fled into the bedchamber.

"Glory be!" Nat exclaimed, wringing his friend's hands. "Mistrusted all the while 'twould be—someone else. Never was so pleased to be mistaken."

Silence, next morning, was forced to decline the Frenches' invitation to stay for a night or a week. She had promised to return the borrowed horse and chaise at once, but before she bore away the solemnly gratified Parmenas, who was willing to assume entire credit for her betrothal, she spent an hour alone with Job in the house that would be hers. She left a comforting memory of herself in the chambers he would spend the winter furnishing.

Silence clung to Job before they left the dwelling.

"I know," she wept, while he was brought close to tears, himself, by the new dependence of a lately redoubtable woman, "that we're right to wait, but it's bitter to find you and then let you go."

"July," he told her, "is not so far away, and I may see you oftener, this winter, than you think."

"Don't see how you can," she resisted, wiping her eyes, and added, smiling, "See what a ninny you've already made of me."

Job had learned from Nat that Haven, the smith, had taken a likely young mare in trade and was willing to let her go for one pound, cash or equivalent, rather than carry her over the winter.

"That ain't too much," Silence agreed, "providin' she's sound."

"Nothing," he replied gravely, "is too much that brings us nearer to each other."

Job bought Nancy, after much argument, for seventeen shillings worth of ash salts. The bright bay Narragansett mare proved handy as a pocketknife, and he rode her twice to Westminster before the snows became too heavy for travel. He was returning from his second visit when, on the long hill down to Putney, he saw in the distance a horseman, toiling toward him.

Job idly watched the other's approach and then sat straighter. It was no more than a trick of eyesight, he told himself impatiently, or some accidental resemblance that had set his heart to pounding. Despite resolute incredulity, he drew rein at last and stared at the advancing traveler. He wore a faded uniform and had come a long way, for his horse moved wearily and the rider was bent forward with his face half hidden. As he drew nearer, Job said, with the wild feeling that he hailed a specter:

"Well, Alvah!"

The other jerked up his head. He grimaced, gagged, and at last cried shrilly:

"Job Aldrich! Man, I thought you dead."

"I've been certain sure you were," Job retorted, blinking.

Reynolds ranged his mount alongside his friend's and beat Job on the back.

"I wrote you twice," he protested, "from Canada, where I was stricken with camp fever, then captured and imprisoned."

"I've heard nothing of you," the other returned, "in nigh two years."

"Oh God!" Reynolds said prayerfully. "Is there naught that doesn't go askew in a mad world? I rode into Westminster only this morning and then on to Putney, yonder, to confer with certain worthies there. Will you turn back with me, my friend?"

He was plainly bone-tired and the long body in the too-large uniform of bilious green, turned with rusty red, sagged as he spoke.

"It's nearer to my pitch," Job urged. "Come home with me."

Reynolds paused an instant, then nodded.

"Lead on," he bade, with a wan remnant of his once jaunty smile, "and I'll follow—if my fiery charger doesn't fall down."

"You know the way," Job said quickly. "Come on as slowly as you please. I'll ride ahead and make ready for you."

Reynolds thrust himself back from the table, sighed with satisfaction, then refilled his cup from the bowl of flip upon the hearth.

"After sober, or nearly sober, reflection," he reported, "I think I shall live. And now," he begged with his engaging grin, "that I've talked of myself to a revolting extent, I beg you to tell me in return how you have fared."

Job had learned that his stricken friend had been left behind when the army before Quebec had begun its retreat. He had spent many months in Canadian hospitals and prisons and only lately had been exchanged. Leaders in the west had sent him to Westminster to make preliminary preparations for the convention of the united Grants, soon to be held there.

"I need no assurance, since my eyes, at least, still are sound," Reynolds was saying, "that you are in health and that you prosper. It is time you did the talking. What else has befallen you?"

Job said bluntly, "I am to wed in July."

For an instant, his friend sat motionless, then raised the horn cup, drank, and carefully set it down.

"Faith," he said lightly, "I often have thought of the counsel I gave you concerning a certain maid. And now—"

"I am plighted," Job interrupted with a trace of defiance, "to Silence Thayer."

"Oh!"

A wide grin dispelled Reynolds's momentary amazement. He sprang up and wrung Job's hand.

"The Widow Thayer! My dear, dear friend, I wish you all the happiness a wretched world affords."

He bent quickly, filling his host's cup and his own, and his lately haggard face seemed hale and youthful again, as he cried:

"A toast to the fortunate lady!"

"Who has made me," Job supplied, still defensively, "the most fortunate of men."

"It shall be my privilege," Reynolds ran on, "to wait upon your betrothed at Westminster and present my felicitations in person. I now drink to you jointly."

He drained his cup and, turning, stared long at the fire, eyes sparkling, a reflective smile softening his mouth, before he asked idly:

"And what of the fair Melissa?"

Reynolds left early next morning, for there was a hint of snow in the air, his mission was uncompleted, and he soon must report to his regiment at Fort Ticonderoga.

"I shall return in July," he promised, as he led his horse from the barn, "for I intend to dance at your wedding. Always providing," he amended more gravely, "that our friends to the north do not pipe another more compelling tune."

A week after Reynolds's departure, the grimly elated Spaulding rode up to the Aldrich pitch through the heaviest snow waning January had let fall.

" 'Fore you're closed in for the winter," he explained, while Job began the rites of hospitality, "wanted you should know whar you be. This ain't the Grants no longer, boy. 'Tis a new an' sovereign nation, declared independent by the convention to Westminster."

Spaulding's little eyes glittered, and his crest of gray hair flared truculently.

"We did," he admitted with a trace of regret, "endorse the principles of the revolution, whatever they be. Still an' all," he drove on, voice twanging, "this continent ain't seen the like of what else we've done: Set up a free state, beholden to none, with every man—every least one, mind you—entitled to vote an' slavery shet out of the land forever.

"Let the damn' Congress," he snorted, accepting the bowl from his host, "an' the God-damn Yorkers stomach that, if they kin. Let's drink, boy, to the nation of New Connecticut. That," he added less exaltedly, "is what we're a-callin' her, till we get a better name."

He gulped valiantly and thrust the bowl at Job, who, accepting it, asked:

"Did you see Alvah Reynolds at Westminster?"

"Wal now," Spaulding returned. "He was there for a spell, but seems I heered from someone that the rascal had gone over to Keene."

36

A SURF OF snow rolled across Vermont, the newborn, now newly renamed, and independent state. Little news came from beyond its borders to winter-bound settlers, and all of this was bad. The Continental army had holed up in the Jerseys and might not see another spring. Philadelphia was threatened. Regulars and mercenaries were pouring into Canada.

Winds, shrill with ill omen, ranged the land. Their keening increased Job's unwonted distress. Storms that hitherto had locked him contentedly away from the world kept him a lonely captive now. The house that Silence had visited only fleetingly was dismally empty without her. Work, however industriously he pursued it, could not lessen his yearning for his betrothed.

For eight weeks on end, while drifts grew and the cold endured, Silence could have been no further beyond her lover's reach if she had died. He berated himself for not having over-ridden her plea for delay. He should have wed her out of hand, since the remainder of his life, at best, would be too short a space to spend in her companionship.

Job was worried, too, by a malevolent, insistent voice. It whispered to him, sleeping and waking, that his days were misspent, that he was squandering precious time. He tried once, as winter waned, to force his way over smothered roads to Westminster but was forced to turn back.

Both mare and rider were mud-plastered and exhausted when, in mid-March, Job reached his goal, yet he had thrust open the door before Silence could reach it. He felt, as his arms received her, healed and whole once more.

They stood, locked and brokenly murmuring, until at last he released her and said reproachfully: "You have been work-ing too hard," while at the same instant, she told him, "You look half starved."

"So," he assured her, "I shall be till July."

They laughed, but worry clung to Job during their too brief hours together. He described the furniture he was building, and Silence, in turn, led him to a hinged box and, opening it, dis-played the blankets she had woven and a bolt of fine homespun she purposed to make, when they had wed, into a new appear-ing-out suit for him.

"No," she said quickly, when he would have delved further, "below is my wedding raiment. It would be bad luck to let you see it beforetimes."

She closed the lid, smiled, and said:

"On our marriage night, you may inspect it at your leisure."

"On our marriage night," he corrected, holding her close, "leisure is one thing I shall entirely lack."

The formless, nagging anxiety beset him again. July 6, which Silence had set for their wedding day, was bright and distant as a star and, perhaps, he thought with a twinge of fright, as

[306]

unattainable. Job held his betrothed at arms' length and protested again:

"You are thin; you're doing too much."

Silence shook her head confidently. The weaving stint she had undertaken for the Jewetts was almost done. Thereafter, she intended to fill her hope chest to overflowing.

"It is a woman I want to wife," Job said, only half in jest, "not a bale of goods. I desire more, not less of you."

"You're not real portly, yourself," she retorted and pursued, smiling, though her voice grew strained, "If you wish a more buxom bride, there's always Melissa Sprague."

He ignored the jibe and begged in sudden urgency:

"Marry me soon. Let the banns be published next Lord's Day and wed me three weeks thence."

"Must I?" she asked so meekly that it shamed him. "Dear one, my plans all are made for July."

The Jewetts, she went on briskly, were setting out for Rutland the first of that month. Parmenas's grandparents could meet him there, and he would visit them for a spell.

"I—I greatly wish," she added with uncommon shyness, "to be alone with you in our house for a little while. I hoped it would—please you, too."

"Sweetheart," Job surrendered, "do as seems best to you. I only—"

He left explanation incomplete. It was impossible to describe, even to her, this recurrent sense of looming danger, and Parmenas, returning from school, averted further argument. Silence, nevertheless, reviewed the dispute when Job had left and wondered whether she was glad or sorry that she had prevailed. If he had forced her, she would have yielded.

April dried the mud of March; shad-blow and cherry dappled the quickening hillsides, and Job's pitch, lately his servant, became an implacable tyrant. He admitted ruefully that it had been wise to set the wedding day so far ahead. It would be July before he had all his crop planted, his salts-making completed, his house painted with ocher he already had purchased. Tasks crowded in, jostling, hurrying him, so completely occupying his days that Reynolds, appearing unheralded in early May, seemed a visitor from another world.

Job was planting corn when his friend rode into the clearing and, flinging himself from the saddle, embraced him heartily.

"Faith!" Reynolds cried. "We have changed roles, you and I! Last winter, I was the semi-invalid. This summer, by appearances, it is you."

"Been working a mite," Job admitted, "but nothing ails me that an evening with you won't cure."

The other grimaced and shook his head. He had been recruiting for a month in Vermont and nearby Hampshire to fill Warner's regiment and must hurry on to overtake the few ragamuffins who had enlisted and the sergeant, left in charge of them.

"I came only to bid you hail and farewell and to ask a favor of you," he continued, brushing dust from his patched and shabby uniform with undue attention. "That is," he grinned, "unless you are ready to turn your back on Hymen and follow Mars."

"Hardly."

"And who could blame you?" Reynolds asked. "Not I. Yet it does seem," he went on more aggrievedly, "that all the good people of this region are stubbornly indifferent to the war."

"And who could blame them?" Job retorted quickly and his friend nodded.

"I know. Vermont has been scurvily used by York and the Congress. My friend, this land and your lives are in danger now."

A chill ran along Job's spine. This might be the substance of the vague dread that had haunted him all year. The conviction grew as Reynolds went on with singular sobriety. A great army was coming out of Canada against Ticonderoga. If that decrepit fortress fell, it would leave Vermont's settlements exposed to invasion.

"Burgoyne, my friend, has enlisted a horde of Indians. You know what that will mean if he uses them."

"Ehyah," Job acknowledged, dry-mouthed.

"So must most settlers," Reynolds scowled, "yet in all of Dummerston, I have found only a single volunteer and he, too puny to accept—one Jacob Laughton, and overvindictive for his size. His father has been killed with Washington in the Jerseys."

"I hadn't heard," Job said slowly.

"Nor had young Jake and his mother until yesterday. If I had five hundred like him in animosity and twice his size, I should fear neither Indians nor fiends of hell—if there be a difference."

"Folks will fight either," Job predicted, "if this land be threatened."

"Faith, I hope you are right," Reynolds shrugged. He looked at the sun, said he must be going, declined his host's offer of a stirrup cup, yet lingered and blurted at last:

"This is the favor I came to ask of you. The Widow Houghton and her sister have returned to Dummerston."

"Oh?"

"It was my privilege to escort them hither from Keene. The estimable Beulah," Reynolds went on more easily, "believes that existence in a tavern will pollute her child, though I, myself, can think of no more agreeable place to be reared."

His grin faded and he said with uncommon awkwardness:

"If it should be that Melissa Sprague—or her sister, naturally —needs aid in any way, will you, my dear and trusted comrade, make every effort to inform me at once?"

"I will," Job answered gravely and marveled at his friend's relief.

"Good lad!" he cried. "I leave, then, with a lighter heart."

Reynolds had ridden away before Job recalled, with a qualm, that he already had made a contrary promise to Silence. Nothing, he thought confidently, as the weeks passed, would come of either pledge. Summer was near, and he believed he could feel a new tranquillity in the air. There were no further tidings of the invasion Reynolds had predicted. Job finished painting his house, mowed and stacked his hay, and, twice, in the last fortnight of his bachelorhood, rode to Westminster.

Each time, he galloped his mare past the Houghton pitch, but no one hailed him and he caught no glimpse of Beulah or Melissa. He was able to assure Silence, when she learned of the sisters' return, that he had seen or spoken with neither.

Job's betrothed had sold her house with most of its furnishings and already had hired the chaise that would bring her more cherished belongings to her future home on the first day of July. She then would return to Westminster, see Parmenas launched on the journey to his grandparents' home, and thereafter stay with the Frenches until Elder Hooker married her to Job.

The month drifted serenely toward its close. Nat, on its final day, asked Job when Silence would arrive, and when his neighbor confessed ignorance, said:

"Betty'll care for her, whenever she comes. Why'n't you an' me 'tend the Laughton vendoo for a spell in the morning?"

The elder Jacob's widow, he explained, had been left straitened and was auctioning off certain of her late husband's possessions, including his farm gear. It was possible that Nat or his neighbor might pick up a bargain.

Job, dismounting next morning in the stony hillside clearing, was sorry he had come. The implements, tools, and apparel, ranked before the gaunt house, were piteous reminders of their dead owner, and the assembled bidders maintained a funereal air. Young Jake's presence was disturbing, too. His angular face was set in a precocious look of enmity that he visited impartially upon all present. Job wished more fervently still that he had stayed at home when Ebenezer Haven drove a cart into the yard with Beulah Houghton seated beside him, her child in her arms, and Melissa sharing a makeshift seat with the smith's wife.

Betty ran out as the chaise halted before the French house. She hailed Silence and her son with pleased surprise. Yes, the visitor admitted, she had planned to come later, but Parmenas had been anxious to see Job.

"Gone with Nat to the Laughton sale," Betty said and, marking the small boy's disappointment, proposed eagerly, "Let's you an' Parmenas an' Hosea an' me ride over an' surprise 'em."

Job's hope that the assembled bidders still were shielding him from Beulah and her sister was blasted when a plaintive voice inquired:

"Are you set on neglecting all your old friends?"

Melissa looked pale and strangely fragile.

"No," he replied fatuously, "Oh, no indeed."

He rejected the ridiculous impulse to flee, headlong. Silence, a most sensible woman, would understand and sympathize.

"And you're about to wed," Melissa said breathlessly. "You have my best wishes."

"Thank you," he said and then asked quickly, "You're unwell?"

"No," she gasped. "It's just—"

She no longer stood beside him but lay with mouth agape in a colorless, upturned face.

Job knelt in the center of waxing commotion and fumbled with the clammy wrist. He found the pulse at last and, reassured, looked vainly among those crowding in above him for the stricken girl's sister. Someone advised, "Best take her to the house." He raised the limp body and the crowd gave way as he bore Melissa across the yard. Beulah, suddenly appearing, waddled beside him. She complained:

"Been poorly but she would come today."

Job was unaware that he carried his burden past the nose of the horse that Silence had halted.

An hour later, he and his betrothed sat stiffly together in the chaise, before his house, while Parmenas strayed among the crops with an expert's air.

"'Tis time," Silence said, "we was gettin' back."

She spoke precisely and her dark face had no expression. Job told her in desperation:

"You're being tarnal unreasonable."

"Maybe I am," she admitted. "Only—"

She swallowed with a clicking sound and said no more. He

was unwilling to plod again through the dreary circle of dispute. Other women, even his own mother, had bewildered him, but never before had he lost contact with his betrothed. Tears and reproaches would have been easier to handle than this injured reticence. Silence still believed, or pretended to, that he had purposely broken his word to her. She called to Parmenas now. He came trudging obediently toward the chaise.

"Haven't you," Job asked, "punished me enough?"

"Maybe," she answered, eyes on her approaching son, "it'll be best not to talk any more now. Maybe you'll understand if we wait till I come back, day after tomorrow. That'll give you more time—"

"To chase after Melissa?" he asked bitterly and Silence flinched.

"That was cruel," she said and he told her:

"You haven't been real merciful, yourself."

He caught her chill hands and begged:

"Sweetheart, please—"

"Later," she insisted.

Parmenas stood beside the chaise and smiled up at Job. He alighted and set the child beside his mother. She said, "Goodby," and clucked to the horse. Her lover watched them cross the clearing.

He should not have let her go while nonsense still wedged them apart. She perversely had magnified accident into a breach of faith. Silence still was jealous of Melissa, yet that, he reminded himself contritely, was only because she loved him.

Job got his hoe and went into the corn, but misery accompanied him. He would not pull free of it until he had talked again to Silence. Two days must elapse before he would see her—two days of wretchedness.

That was not so, he thought with sharp relief. He could end the ordeal this very afternoon, by riding after his betrothed and, when they had reached Westminster, wringing forgiveness from her.

Job hurried to the barn and saddled Nancy but with each deliberate mile, the pursuit became more questionable. It might be wiser, it certainly would be more dignified, if he did not abjectly follow his beloved but let her return to him, rightfully chastened by two days' suffering. He told himself that she deserved it and, looking up, saw with dismay that he was passing the Houghton pitch and that Beulah, arms waving in frantic appeal, was lumbering mutely toward him.

Near Putney, Silence drew rein, turned the unwilling horse around and drove back toward Dummerston.

"Forgot something," she told her puzzled son, "that I'll have to tend to 'fore we go home."

She had been wickedly vindictive, causelessly jealous, and she could not suffer for another hour, let alone two days, the memory of her lover's desperate face and his pleading voice.

"Sweetheart, please!" Job had said, and she had ignored him. He should, Silence thought with a regretful thrill, have beaten her instead of pleading. There was no need for violence now. She would penitently beseech his pardon, confess her cruel misuse of him.

Her humility increased as she turned off the Great Road. Job had told her the simple, entire truth, yet she, in blind anger, had refused to believe—she who, in the depth of her repentant heart, was certain Melissa meant nothing to him.

The chaise halted so abruptly that Parmenas was almost unseated. His mother did not heed his protest. She was looking toward the Houghton house. Job's mare was tethered in its yard.

"Ma—" her son began.

"Be still," she bade. It seemed to her and her patient child that they had waited a full half hour before she carefully backed the chaise around.

"Ain't we—?" Parmenas ventured.

"You hush," she said so harshly that he drew away.

"Don't," Silence begged in haste. "I'm sorry I hollered. Set real close to me, Parmenas."

He was all that remained to her in an overturned world.

Job stood in the Houghton barn, whither Beulah had led him with whispered persuasion, and looked dazedly at his conductress. She had collapsed upon a milking stool's inadequate support and was dabbing her apron against her eyes.

"What," he demanded, uncertain whether to be alarmed or angry, "is this? Where is Melissa?"

"A-bed," Beulah gulped. "Sleepin', I hope, poor, strayed lamb."

She wept quietly.

"I'm in haste," Job told her. "Why have you brought me here?"

The woman's swollen eyes besought him.

"'Twasn't jest me. 'Twas God, I do believe, that guided you. Promised once you'd give me help if ever I needed it," she pursued disjointedly, her fat person shaken again by half-suppressed sobbing. "Got no one else now. Pa'd kill her, if he knowed."

"I still," Job said, resisting ghastly suspicion, "don't understand," and his stupidity feebly enraged her.

"'Tis 'Lissa," the woman wailed. "With child by your fine-mannered friend. Can you understand that?"

She rocked on the stool. Job lifted a hoarse voice through the muffled lamentation:

"How do you know? When did you learn?"

"Not," Beulah wheezed, "till I got her home from Laughtons' today, though lately I've suspicioned. My little sister!"

In another moment, Job told himself inanely, this nightmare would fade and he would find himself in his own bed. The woman was quavering:

"You're Cap'n Reynolds close friend; must know where he is. Tell him to come back an' wed 'Lissa."

"I can't," Job gasped. "The banns have been published and within another week, I'm—"

He checked himself, unwilling, even by mention, to involve Silence in this ghastly revelation.

Beulah seemed to have spent her store of tears. She spoke with a humble earnestness that almost achieved dignity:

"Dan'l, he's—left me, an' there's no one else to help but you. You said you'd always be ready if we was in trouble. Will you find Alvah Reynolds an' tell him—what he's done?"

"I'll do all I can," Job evaded.

The woman did not respond to his hurried farewell. As he tiptoed from the barn, she still perched on the milk stool, a fat, crushed figure, her head upon her hands.

Job had mounted and had ridden a furlong homeward before he recalled why he had been abroad and then he did not halt. He had been too shattered by the girl's plight to risk discussing her with Silence. It would abolish her suspicion, were he to tell her the whole sorry tale, but the thought revolted him. He once had wooed Melissa, and Reynolds was his friend.

Leaden cloud, rolling up in the west, had cast gloom over the land. Job returned to his pitch with his mind equally darkened. It was still raining when he rose, next morning, no more resolute than when he had gone to bed. He spent the day in sweeping the house and polishing the furniture he had made for his betrothed—the black cherry table and stools, the cupboard, chairs, and lordly bedstead of hard maple. Industry failed to drive away wretched uncertainty.

When the skies cleared that afternoon, he had reached only negative decision. Melissa's plight was no concern of his. He would not imperil further his future by trying to solve it.

That determination fell apart during his wakeful night. One reproachful voice insistently reminded him of his promise to Reynolds. A second, more spiteful, recited Job's long-ago pledge to the girl and her sister, and his recent half-assurance to a desperate woman.

He rose wearily at daybreak, still rocked by indecision. A new, more acute anxiety beset him when noon had passed and Silence had not arrived. The sun was two hours beyond midday when he rode in haste toward Westminster.

Before he had dismounted in the empty dooryard, his eyes had perceived what his mind still refused to accept. The doorstep was strewn with litter Silence never would have tolerated.

The small, leering windowpanes no longer were crystal-bright.

The door was latched. Job beat upon it and roused only a hollow sound that sickened him. A sharp voice confirmed his worst suspicion.

"Ain't a bit of use. Her an' Parmenas set out early yesterday with the Jewetts."

A gaunt woman stared at him. Her eyes were avidly bright.

"Thankee," Job said and groped for a stirrup.

"Didn't ye know?" his informant demanded. "Ain't you weddin' her?"

He did not answer but rode slowly back toward Dummerston.

Job had smothered at once the wild impulse to follow his betrothed—his lately betrothed, he amended carefully. She was almost two days' journey away; he had with him neither provisions nor scrip to undertake pursuit. And since she had gone willingly, leaving no word, who was he to oppose her decision? He was Job Aldrich, whose life, to all intents, had ended. "Out of the depths I cry to thee, O God."

Further prayer was beyond him. Later, there would be self-reproach, anger, and increasing pain. Job felt no more than numbness now and a dull amazement. His mare stepped out briskly. He sat her, with head bowed. His mind could not reach beyond the single, monstrous fact.

The far end of the settlement's street was filled with a crowd, unusually large and attentive to watch what appeared to be only another militia drill. Nancy, her further progress blocked, halted. Job looked over his neighbors' heads to where Davenport, Cook, Temple, Negus, and the tall, young Reuben Spaulding stood on the common behind Knight. He flourished a paper and harangued the gathering in an auctioneer's chant:

"Six we got; make it seven. Six of us are willin'; who'll be the seventh, lucky volunteer?"

Men in his audience muttered and looked sidewise at each other.

"Folks," said Knight reproachfully, "you've heered Gen'l St. Clair's writin'. Needs more troops to Ti, else she'll go over an', like as not, the Continental cause with her."

Job turned at the patter of bare feet. His mare snorted as young Jake Laughton brushed past and wriggled into the crowd.

"Continental cause," a sour voice called, "ain't none of mine long as Congress don't reck'nize Vermont."

"Wal now, Newton," Knight advised, "you be certain sure to tell the Injuns so, when the man-burnin', woman-killin' devils come a-visitin'. Who else'll march with us to Ti? Got full milishy equipment for another man. Len Spaulding, he's to the convention to Windsor, so Reuben, here, he brought his pa's gear along."

Jake had burrowed through the press. He shot out of it now and almost fell.

"I'll go," he shrilled, recovering. "British bastards, they killed my pa."

"Jake," Knight advised severely, "you watch your talk."

He looked down more kindly at the scrawny figure and cleared his throat.

"Son," he said, "best go home an' age a mite 'fore you take to soldierin'."

Someone tittered and the boy's pinched face flamed.

"I'm past sixteen," he squalled and glared about him, inviting denial, before he turned to Knight again.

"Got no gear," Jake confessed, "but lemme have Leftenant's. They—they killed my pa, I tell you."

"Son," Knight asked, "what d'you weigh? Oh, no; not nigh to seventy pound! Give you the benefit, an' call it sixty. Wal, now! Firelock; that's twelve pound; hatchet, mebby four more; pound of powder, four of ball, makes twenty-one, don't it? Then, there's gun worm, priming wire, powderhorn, flints, an' mebby ca'tridge box; say twenty-three pound, so far.

"Five days to Ti," he droned on, "means we'll set out with five pound of pork an' ten of meal. Forty-eight, or fifty pound in all. Jake, you'd be carryin' close to your own weight. You couldn't march two miles."

"I could," the boy insisted. "Know I could. They killed—"

"No. Can't take you."

Jake plunged back blindly into the crowd.

[317]

"Anyone," Knight asked dryly, "moved to take young Laughton's place?"

"I will," Job said.

"Fed my stock," Job told French in a level tone, "and left all to rights, far as I remember. Abigail won't freshen for another month."

He leaned on his musket and met the wretched eyes of his friend.

"If Betty wa'n't due in three," Nat faltered, "I'd go with you. As 'tis, we'll care for your belongin's, best we know how. Is there aught else we can do?"

"Beholden," Job told him after hesitation, "if you'd let me spend the night here. I'd—I'd rather not go up to my pitch again."

37

THEY HAD BEEN marching, time out of mind. Each morning Knight shook his followers from sodden slumber. They built a fire and cooked the first of their identical daily meals. The mush and fried pork frequently were scorched and always smoke-tainted. Thereafter, they resumed their journey, before the sun had cast enough warmth to loosen knotted muscles in backs and legs, and plodded in waxing heat along an interminable wooded valley between the hills' green ramparts, to camp wherever nightfall found them.

Today, Job thought wearily, would match its forerunners. He and his companions would follow the trail through the forest. They would skirt clearings where children would flee, squealing, and their elders would demand the strangers' identities and intentions and always would ask affrightedly if they had found signs of Indians.

Likely, the travelers would pass through further infant settlements whose inhabitants would regard them with more suspicion than welcome. There was excuse, Job admitted, scanning his companions, for such wariness. Grimed, bearded, and haggard, they were a ruffianly crew.

Nine marched today where—was it only yesterday?—there had been eleven. The man from Wells, whose name Job could not recall, had journeyed with them a few hours and then had dropped out, smitten, he had said, by cramps. Cooper, who had joined them in some other town, had boasted all day of his valor—and had vanished during the night.

The company had progressed like a snowball, gaining here, losing there, but the Dummerston seven had held together, and the Kent brothers, grim, quiet men from Dorset, had not faltered.

Job looked up from the trail they were following through baking forest. Davenport, whose clothing each day had grown more ample, trudged before him and, ahead of Davenport, Knight stalked with his firelock slung from his uninjured shoulder. They and the others were enviable men.

They would reach the fort, serve their time, and soon, with God's permission, would return to the comfortable niches they had vacated. Job would find Reynolds at Ticonderoga, give him Beulah's summons, and then—? He had no answer, no purpose or expectation beyond that moment.

They had marched another sweltering hour when Knight halted them. A lake, if he remembered rightly, lay off to the west. Spent as they were, they could not possibly reach the fort before tomorrow and they were more likely to be well received if they looked and smelled a mite better. They could profitably clean themselves before they went further.

The company stripped on a sandy beach, where the breeze off the long, blue water was almost cool. They bathed themselves, scrubbed their shirts, and all save young Reuben Spaulding, who was infatuated with his yellow, new beard, shaved.

Laughter rose for the first time in days, and at length they returned to the trail, but they had traveled no more than an hour when they met a herald of calamity. A squirrely man, wild-eyed and perched high on a reeking horse, reined in to block the way.

"Who be ye," he cried, "an' whar d'ye think ye're a-goin'?"

"To Ti," Knight answered curtly. "And who be you?'

"Ti!" the rider shrilled and rocked in the saddle. "Ti's been taken; Ti's been sold out. Treachery done it."

His white-rimmed eyes glared down expectantly at the silent men.

"Now ain't that too bad?" Knight drawled at last. "An you're a-going to rouse the country, most likely?"

The horseman gave a throaty wordless sound, spurred, and went bucketing down the trail. Job and his companions watched him out of sight, then looked at each other.

"Wal?" Davenport asked.

"Wal!" Knight returned and led them on.

The man was a deserter and a manifest liar to boot. So they told each other loudly, making a strained jest of his tidings, yet unwilling apprehension oppressed them all and lay most heavily on Job. If by any chance the tale were true, then he already confronted that emptiness he had felt must lie beyond his journey's end. If the fort had been taken, Reynolds was dead or a prisoner, and Job had come through great travail upon an empty errand.

Cook had begun to hum softly, and out of the tentative sounds, a tune took form. Job recalled how, filled with vainglory at their journey's beginning, they had chanted it as they had come down off the mountains into Manchester. He found that his own voice had joined with Cook's:

"Let tyrants shake their iron rod
    And Slavery clank her galling chains,"

Others were singing the valiant words.

[320]

"We fear them not; we trust in God
New England's God forever reigns."
Job's step was lighter, though his eyes were moist.
"Lift her higher," Knight called back, grinning.
"What grateful off'ring shall we bring;
What shall we render to this Lord?
Loud Hallelujahs let us sing
And praise his name in every chord."
They sang themselves out of the forest and tramped along
a proper road in half-sheepish silence, yet their feet still beat
out "Chester's" rhythm.

A throbbing murmur that scarcely, at first, had reached their
ears was swelling into a floodlike roar. Beyond a hill, the road
ran straight between houses of a settlement.

"Great Goddlemighty!" Temple bleated.

The way before them was choked by a dust-colored, restless
host. Muskets bristled above it. Furled standards lurched like
masts of storm-driven craft. The multitude surged forward,
eddied, withdrew. It parted before yelping officers and closed
behind them. The drab horde, no more martial than the Dummerston Cadets, extended beyond the settlement, and along
the distant road, further human driblets were flowing to join it.

It was not an army; it was a wounded, vast creature that
thrashed blindly with an injured roaring and exuded a rank,
wild animal stench.

The throng was split by an advancing column. Men in fustian, homespun, leather, fulcher cloth marched wearily, yet
with slanted muskets in approximate alignment. A begrimed
drummer beat out a measure, and an officer whose sweat-soaked
uniform was so heavily plastered with dust that its original hue
was dubious led the way. He bawled a command and, stepping
aside, watched his ragamuffins wheel into a field, then turned
to glare at Job and his companions.

"You there!" he called in a parched voice. "Why are you
straggling? What is your regiment?"

"Ain't got one—yet," Knight replied. "We're Vermont milishy, a-headin' for Ti."

"Are you, by God!" the officer marveled. "Now, I may safely claim that I've seen everything."

The smile that had spread over his dirty face vanished quickly.

"Ticonderoga, sir, was evacuated last night and before you is what remains of its garrison. I am Colonel Scammell, and the third New Hampshire will gladly welcome recruits."

He waved toward the field where his command was stacking muskets. Job's companions moved eagerly forward, but he lingered.

"Sir," he said, "it is needful that I find Colonel Warner's regiment."

"Then," Scammell rasped, "you will have further to march, sir, for the Vermonters are with the rear guard. Follow that road two miles. They should be camped no further."

Job at length got free of the mobbed settlement and breathed clean air again. He had been jostled, stepped on, cursed, and had barely escaped injury when sentries, posted before the door of a building whose sign proclaimed it "Zadok Remington's Tavern," plied musket butts to drive back the thirsting who tried to enter.

Most clearly, he remembered a horseman in dusty blue and buff who had forced his way into the crowd and how his long, sad face had lit up when a sweating colonel with a broken plume in his hat had approached and cried:

"General St. Clair, the third Virginia is all present or accounted for."

Stragglers, hobbling to rejoin Ticonderoga's retreating garrison, looked curiously at Job, but none halted him. Presently, the way was empty, and he lengthened his stride. It would be easier, alone, to find Reynolds. And after that? He was too weary to consider the future. It was in God's hands.

Job tried to recall Scriptural reassurance, but a perverse quirk in his mind brought him instead poor Zurvilla Alvord's long-ago prediction. After great distress, she had promised, he would find what all men desired. The addled creature might have been a better prophetess than he had thought. Maybe death was the greatest benison life could bring a man.

He climbed a hill and came upon troops bivouacked in an open field.

"Naw," one of them answered Job's question. "We ain't Warner's. We're Bellows' Hampshire Milishy. Guess the Vermonters are still to Hubbardton, three, four mile further."

The road ran through forest, but after a mile or so, it led Job past a spacious, well-tilled clearing with the shine of water beyond it. The red house painfully reminded him of his own newly painted, deserted dwelling, and he hurried on.

A wilted man sat on a stump, his firelock beside him, and paused in rewinding a bloody bandage about his bared foot to ask Job:

"How far to Castleton?"

"Castleton?"

"Castleton, Castleton," the other repeated irritably. "Come through it, didn't ye?"

"I came," Job said slowly, "through a settlement, maybe five miles back, but I didn't ask its name."

"Wal," the other said with scorn, "that's Castleton. Might brighten ye a mite, was ye to ask questions, now an' then."

Job went on without response, crushed by Fortune's new malevolence. He had been close to Silence, yet had not felt her nearness. Wherever she dwelt with Parmenas and his grandparents, each step put further distance between her and her rejected lover.

The road, still littered by the cast offs of the fleeing army, led uphill and came out of the forest. Sunlight illumined the ledges of a brown bluff, far to Job's right, but the smoke of twinkling campfires already had spread premature dusk in the little valley below him, where trees had been felled and a log house half built, and like aroused ants men were swarming.

Job approached, unchallenged, the nearest who were washing beside a small, mild stream. He asked for Captain Reynolds of Warner's regiment and learned that this was Colonel Hale's 2nd New Hampshire. If he followed the brook through Colonel

Francis's 11th Massachusetts, he would find the Vermonters far to the right.

Job said, "Alvah!" and Reynolds who had been conferring with a hulking giant, ventured, at last, still only half believing:

"Good God! Is it you? Why—how—?"

His grin dispelled the palsy of amazement and the alarm that had flickered for an instant in his pale eyes. He gripped his friend's shoulders and said to the burly man in a green and red uniform no better than his own:

"Colonel Warner, I ask the privilege of presenting Job Aldrich who has come, a volunteer, to join us."

The smile that wrinkled Seth Warner's beefy face did not quite reach his obstinate, blue eyes.

"You're most welcome, sir," he said and added to Reynolds, as though concluding an argument:

"We will move out, Captain at seven tomorrow morning; no second sooner."

He walked heavily away. Reynolds shrugged and muttered to Job:

"St. Clair ordered the rear to camp not more than two miles behind the main, and we are nearer six, yet nothing will sway Seth when he turns bullheaded. If Burgoyne presses pursuit—"

Again he raised his shoulders. While he had spoken, he had led Job away from the line of now brighter fires that were strung along the brook. The men found a fallen tree and sat together in awkward silence that Reynolds ended by asking quietly:

"What has brought you, my friend?"

"A number of things," Job said, trying to match his composure. "Among them, my promise to get word to you if Melissa Sprague was in need."

"A need," Reynolds inquired gravely, after a moment, "that only marriage will requite?"

"Ehyah."

"So I suspected, the moment I saw you."

Job's friend was silent again. He said at length:

"If we all are not in Tophet, or a more blessed abode, by this time tomorrow, I'll return to her as soon as may be—

not," he stressed, "perforce, but because I know no maid I would as willingly wed.

"You see," Reynolds pursued gravely, "you, my dear lad, have untangled a grievous snarl for me. While you, to whom I owe so much, favored Melissa, I could not offer her marriage. Thereafter, if the melancholy Widow Houghton had not opposed me, this might not have happened. I don't know. I can only say truthfully that I am glad that it has. I shall do my earnest best to stay alive until, at least, I have given our child a father."

He laid a fond hand on Job's shoulder and said in a new, unsteady voice:

"I wonder whether, since the world began, another man has been as fortunately befriended as I. Have you no reproaches? No pious indignations?"

"I scarce," Job said with difficulty, "could preach to you, considering the ruin I have made of my own life."

Reynolds' grip tightened on his companion's shoulder.

"Tell me," he bade.

It was vast relief to bare the sorry story. The thickening twilight had blurred Alvah's face, yet Job could sense that sympathy and contrition dwelt there.

"Oh, God!" Reynolds said, when the other had ended. "It seems I was designed to cause you naught but ill. And yet," he went on, reviving swiftly, "I may have done well to bring you here. Dear lad, if it were not so late, you might visit your errant betrothed this very night. You passed the Thayer pitch on your way hither—well maintained fields with a red house among them."

"I seem," Job confessed in a resigned voice, "to have lived lately in ignorance of everything. I didn't know I had been in Castleton until I had left it behind. I don't even know how far into July we have gone."

"This is the sixth."

Job said in a barren voice: "It was to have been my wedding day."

"A wedding," Reynolds insisted after a pause, "that has not

been canceled, but postponed, for, if I know you, you will re-capture your runaway tomorrow and bend her stiff neck till she cries for mercy.

"Always providing," he amended, worry returning, "that Gentleman Johnny Burgoyne is a still more slothful soldier than that ox, Seth Warner."

If dawn had not come so soon, Job would have sworn that he had lain awake all night, his mind struggling with plans for the impending meeting with Silence, his ears constantly assailed by the stir, the mutter, the spasmodic coughing of a thousand restless men.

A moment ago, it seemed, there had been unrelieved dark-ness, yet now the east was bright, the stars gone, and the little valley below him was filling with tumult. The early-risen were splashing on the edge of Sucker Brook, and the crowding trees on the further hillside were taking individual shape.

Job rose stiffly from the hollow that had served him for bed, laid most of his garments beside his firelock and equipment, and clad only in his breeches, went down to bathe. If he were to see Silence this day—his heart turned over at the thought—he must appear before her as well groomed as might be.

He was picking his way among the stumps of an abandoned clearing when the slope beyond the brook exploded. The rend-ing crash was followed by a burst of cheering. Smoke billowed through the foliage, and the men at the brookside turned and ran, save one who lay quietly in the water and another who crept a little way on hands and knees and then pitched forward.

Faces, starched by terror, swept uphill toward Job. As he fled with them, another volley tore the world apart. Somewhere a drum awoke and rattled frantically, while along the line where Warner's regiment had lain, officers bellowed commands.

Relief lessened Job's fright when he regained the hollow where he had left his belongings. He had been additionally tormented, during his flight, by dread that he might be slain in nothing more decent than his stained and snagged breeches. Smoke was drifting across the distant slope. On his either hand, muskets began to speak singly, by twos and threes, and then in ragged volleys.

Job muttered as he got into his clothes and gear:

"Don't fumble; one thing at a time; keep your head."

The sun had risen. Once more, the still-hidden enemy poured gunfire from the hillside, and young light turned the spouting smoke crimson, as though the forest bled. Far to the left, a giant was popping monstrous corn and had roused a wild howling. Closer, a voice roared:

"Keep covered, Vermont! Be thrifty with your powder!"

A gust tore through the trees, sprinkling Job with bark and shorn twigs. He lowered himself into the hollow and peered over its edge, musket in hand. The panicky yelling to the left was fading into the distance. Behind him someone said petulantly:

"Hey, shift over a mite."

He obeyed and a hatless man in grease-blackened leather jerkin and breeches dropped beside him and, thrusting his firelock forward, cuddled a bristling jowl against it.

"Jeeze," he breathed, "they're a-comin'."

On the slope beyond the brook, the enemy had begun to fire at will, with the sound of a dozen carpets madly beaten. Red coats, like flames of a forest fire, were flickering through the woods.

"They're a-formin'," Job's companion blurted. "Goin' to try the bayonet, damn 'em. There's the grenadiers' fur hats, an' see them brass-bound caps? Them's light infantry."

The scarlet host now was only half concealed by intervening trees. Job's finger, unconsciously tightening on the trigger, set off his firelock aimlessly. His neighbor looked at him in silent scorn, then grunted and pointed across the valley.

Tarnished sunlight spun from the buttons, gorget, and epaulet of the brilliant figure that strolled from the woods, mounted a stump, and looked carefuly about him. The officer cried a command; his sword flashed, and the red line moved into the open toward the opposite hillside. It sparkled, smoked, and thundered. The line wavered, dropped bits of itself, yet lurched

[327]

on. Above the jagged roar of musketry, Warner's bull-like voice bellowed:

"Pour it in, Vermont! Blast the God-damn Yorkers!"

The firing died away, smothered by powder fog that the morning breeze languidly blew down the valley. Bright fragments of the broken assault were strewn in the clearing, many of them twisting and groping. The officer who had launched the charge lay behind the stump, one gaitered leg across it. A piteous wailing assailed Job's ears.

His companion bit the end from a paper cylinder, stoppered it with his thumb, primed his gun, and rammed the cartridge down its barrel.

"Swear to God," he exulted, " 'twas me knocked over that popinjay offi— Whup!"

Invisible violence had struck with a thwacking sound. The man lay silent and unnaturally flat. His unclosing hands fell limply from his firelock. Job glanced at the matted, wet scalp, gulped, and looked hastily away.

For an instant, he struggled with nausea and the blind impulse to flee from this fuming precinct of hell where muskets banged unevenly, death flailed the hillside, and the wounded cried like souls in torment. He half rose from the hollow, wavered, then slowly settled himself into it once more.

That murky slope yonder, stabbed by gunfire, was enemy country that lately had been Vermont and, only a little way behind where Job lay, Silence and Parmenas, in a red house, listened anxiously to the distant sound of battle. Beyond them were an imperiled, newborn state and its threatened people. If Job had run, he would have left the best of himself forever at Hubbardton. He still was faintly sick, and his hands shook as he reloaded his firelock. Behind him, Reynolds said quietly:

"Wise man, to take cover."

He smiled down at Job, who, wondering how long his friend had watched him, retorted thinly:

"You don't follow your own counsel, seems."

"Oh," Reynolds grinned. "Officers are expected to expose

themselves. It heartens their men with the pious hope they'll be shot."

The lamenting voices were loud in a momentary silence. Job, trying to ignore them, asked:

"Is it over?"

It might well have been over, before now, Reynolds answered sourly, if the 2nd New Hampshire, led by its colonel, had not broken and run at the fight's beginning. As it was, Warner's Vermonters and Francis's Massachusetts men were standing off the best of Burgoyne's army.

He paused to listen to the reviving bicker of musketry far to the right where the brown-ledged bluff stood up against the sky.

"Apparently," he offered at length, "it's commencing again, yet it soon may be over—if only the British aren't re-enforced."

The distant gunfire was swelling into a throaty roar. Warner lumbered toward them.

"Alvah," he panted, "the rascals have got over Zion Hill and are on our flank. Take your company and extend our line. I'll see what Francis can do on the left."

Reynolds smiled at his friend and turned away.

"Hold on," Job bade. "Guess I belong to your company," and followed the other toward the mounting sound of battle.

Job was to remember, all his days, the noise, the powder stench, and the wilting heat; the Vermonters, firing from cover; the advancing red ranks that faltered, reformed, then broke apart and fled. Suddenly, it was over, and he stood, dazed and breathless.

He had shot at men who, when the jetting smoke had thinned, had become no more than heaps of gay clothing on the ground. He had felt no compunction. Each of the fallen had lessened the danger to Silence and to her and his land.

And then, while Reynolds's company was reassembling and its captain was merrily calling Job a renegade Quaker, sounds came from across the valley, unbefitting a beaten enemy: hoarse roar of drums and squeal of fifes; bugles' brazen chant and a great burst of cheering. Reynolds looked blankly at Job and said:

"They've been re-enforced." He listened a moment and added with quiet despair: " 'Tis the damned German hirelings."

The muskets were speaking again. Volleys were beating against the Massachusetts regiment and, through the measured explosions, new and sharper sounds rose, as though enormous hands were clapping.

"Rifles!" Reynolds said. "The jägers, too!"

Shrill outcry to the left was overwhelmed by triumphant bellowing. Men stared into each other's pinched and twitching faces.

"Had a plenty!" one gasped, and ran. Another and a third fled after him. All at once, the woods were filled with fugitive, shadowy figures.

Warner came plunging like a moose toward where a handful of the stouthearted lingered. The colonel's face was purple; he bawled blasphemy.

"The hell-deserving, Christ-forsaken Dutchmen have broken our left. Francis is dead, and the God-damn fight lost."

He collapsed in rage upon a rotting log and beat bark from it with his great fists. Downhill, a rifle smacked and one of the hesitant few who had tarried with their captain cried out and dropped. The slope below Job was alive with men in green-cockaded black hats and green uniforms turned with scarlet.

"Best get started," Reynolds advised his friend grimly. "We're all that's left of the rear guard."

Warner already was fleeing with vast, lumbering strides. He cried to his fellow fugitives, "We'll rally to Manchester!" and vanished. Reynolds called:

"I know this country; follow me."

A sledge smote Job's shoulder, as he turned, and drove him against a tree. He had been hit, yet miraculously, he was running after his friend. Warm moisture flowed down his arm, though for the moment he felt no pain.

Still trailing Reynolds, he half-circled the hill, crossed a clearing, and burst through brush onto the road. For a moment, he tried to match strides with his guide, then stumbled. Reynolds glanced back, halted, and, returning, cried:

"You've been hit. Why didn't you tell me?"

"Better wounded and free," Job grinned wanly, "than unharmed and a prisoner."

He sat at the roadside and rested his swimming head upon his knees. Surely God would not bring him so close to Silence and then withhold His mercy.

Reynolds had flung his coat aside and was tearing his shirt into strips. Pain, that had begun to lance Job's shoulder, increased while his friend bound the wound, improvised a sling, and then asked:

"Can you travel?"

"Miles."

"It'll be less than one, I promise you."

Reynolds held the uninjured arm and stepped out carefully. The sun was hot, yet Job was shivering and, with each stride, the anguish in his shoulder increased.

"Better than halfway there," his friend said at length.

"Don't think—" Job began thickly.

"Yes, you will, by God, if I have to drag you. One, two, three, four. One— Steady now!"

An invisible fist was beating on the wound. Job was shod with lead. Reynolds finally put an arm around his reeling friend.

"Almost there. March it out."

The lately bright morning had darkened. Job stumbled and would have fallen, but for the supporting arm.

" 'Let tyrants shake their iron rod,' " Reynolds sang slowly, " 'and Slavery clank her galling chains. We fear—' and here we are. It's over, my dear friend."

Job could see only dim movement. Voices spoke about him, but whatever they said was broken into nonsense by the pounding of his heart. Hands that he knew were Silence's and others, unfamiliar, laid hold upon him. . . .

Job lay in a darkened room. He heard hoofs trample outside and a man speak angrily. The pain had subsided into a dull ache, and his free hand discovered that his wounded shoulder had been newly, more firmly bandaged. The room spun as he strove to rise. He tried again and was sitting, swaying and breathless on the bed's edge, when Silence entered.

Her face had been no more firmly set when first he had looked upon it, but her blue eyes were filled with strange humility.

"No," she begged, rather than commanded. "Lay down. Want to kill yourself?"

She pressed her lips together to still their trembling.

"Yesterday," Job answered, "it seemed that—I'd just as soon."

Silence looked at him in mute appeal; then, with a small, wordless sound, she fell to her knees before him. Her face was pressed against Job's chest, her arms went gently around him.

"Will you take me back?" she wept. "Will you have me to love and obey and serve you all my life? I cannot blame you, if you won't. Your friend has taught me how blind and wrong and evil I have been."

"Silence," Job said. She had lifted her tremulous face, and he kissed her.

He was dizzy when, at last, she drew her mouth away. He heard the rattle of a backing cart and, in another room, voices and hurried movement. Job asked:

"Where is Alvah?"

He had left, Silence said, in haste for Manchester and thence would go to Dummerston. Half of Castleton, fearing the British, was fleeing toward Manchester, too. The Thayers were taking Parmenas with them.

"And you?" Job asked in alarm.

"You and I," Silence told him, "are staying here."

"No."

"Yes," she insisted. "It would be murder to take you."

"We would be in danger here."

"I have no fear," Silence said confidently. "If the British come, I shall hide you."

[332]

She rose as though the matter were settled. He met her determined eyes and informed her gravely:

"We are going to Manchester."

"Job, it would—"

"We are going to Manchester," he repeated. "Did you not, just now, promise to obey and serve me?"

For an instant, she withstood him, and then said quietly: "Yes, Job."

They lay for a fortnight in Manchester. Silence, Parmenas, and his grandparents found lodging with their Thayer kin, and Job in the home of Gideon Ormsby, nearby. It was not a tranquil sojourn. The little village was filling with the reassembling fragments of Warner's regiment and refugees from the north who caught up and inflated each dire rumor.

German mercenaries had occupied Castleton and Rutland but came no farther. The true purpose of the invasion still was hidden. In Job's presence, Silence tried to hide her anxiety, yet she grew more haggard as the days crept by. At last, when he had become hale enough to sit with her before the Ormsbys' small dwelling, she released her anguish in a passionate outburst:

"Will we never be home again?" she cried. "Will we never return to Dummerston and wed and—and forget all this? What have we done to merit this punishment?"

"Sweetheart," Job soothed, startled by her vehemence, "I beg you again to wed me now."

"Not now," she returned obstinately. "Not until we can go from our marriage to our own house."

"And so we shall," he insisted, "if—"

"If Burgoyne's Indians do not destroy our home and us," she completed for him, bitterly and, in contrition, tried to smile.

"I'm a cowardly female," she confessed. "I wonder you tolerate me. It's just that—"

She did not complete the explanation, yet he knew what she meant. The Ormsby house faced east, toward the steep, green wall of the mountains, and Job, basking in the dooryard, traced, till his eyes were tired and he ached with longing, the thread of road that twisted to the summit. Beyond that barrier, no more than a long day's journey, lay his pitch and his friends, his crops, his stock, and all the dear importances he had forsaken and, it seemed in his homesickness, he would never regain.

Deliverance came when he least expected it. Silence and he were sitting before his lodgings, late one afternoon, and Job was railing against his continuing weakness, when he broke off to stare at two dusty riders who approached, each leading a spare horse.

Reynolds and Spaulding drew rein and hailed their friend with joyous relief. Still only half believing, he watched them dismount, tether their animals, and stride toward him. Reynolds bowed gracefully to Silence, then wrung Job's hand, tried to speak, choked, shrugged helplessly, and turned away.

"Wal, now!" Spaulding twanged to cover his companion's distress. "We been a-searchin' for you all over hell an' half of York State. I've come to take you home, boy. They's a wedding we can't rightly hold till you folks get there."

"A wedding," Reynolds added unsteadily, smiling down at Job, "that my wife must attend in my stead, since my leave is spent and Colonel Warner refuses to extend it."

German outposts, he explained briskly to atone for his momentary collapse, were pulling back, and it was evident that Burgoyne would thrust, not into New England but New York.

"God speed him, s'I," Spaulding acclaimed and, turning to Job, demanded:

"Fit to travel, be you?"

Silence stirred and was about to speak, but her betrothed forestalled her.

"I am," he answered stoutly, "or will be, tomorrow."

"Good man!" Spaulding applauded. "We'll set out real early, then."

"I—" Silence began but Job's look stilled her. She sat, stiff and mute, while the others talked of the constitution framed at Windsor that had confirmed Vermont's independence, of

Reynolds's marriage, of Nat French's unremitting care of Job's possessions, but, when the others had left, she spoke with hushed violence:

"It's forty mile to Dummerston, if it's an inch. You aren't well enough to attempt it."

"Each homeward mile," he told her confidently, "will heal me further."

"And nigh kill me with worry," she added, her face set in the old, determined look. "I won't let you."

"Forty miles," Job persisted, "will be an easy journey when, beyond them, we shall have forty years—maybe more—together."

"No."

"Yes."

"Not yet, not till you're stronger."

"You and Parmenas," Job bade firmly, "will be ready at daybreak tomorrow."

He met her blue eyes steadily and at length saw them waver and soften.

"As you will," Silence submitted and laid a hard, warm hand upon his. Job smiled at her. The long travail was almost over. By this time tomorrow, they would be nearly home and the next day would be wed.

He and his wife would take lifelong joy in each other—in their work, in their love, in their many children. He was sure of the future now. He had learned how best to deal with Silence. He trusted, still smiling at her, that severe measures seldom would be necessary. Job Aldrich was still, in essence, a well-disposed and peace-loving man.